Books by Kristie Cook

— SOUL SAVERS SERIES —
www.SoulSaversSeries.com

Promise
Purpose
Devotion (February 2012)

Genesis: A Soul Savers Novella (October 2011)

Find the author at www.KristieCook.com

Promise

HER LIFE IS FULL OF PROMISE...
BUT NOT ALL PROMISES CAN BE KEPT.

KRISTIE COOK

Soul Savers

BOOK ONE

Ang'dora Productions, LLC
Naples, Florida

Published by
Ang'dora Productions, LLC
15275 Collier Blvd
#201-300
Naples, FL 34119

Ang'dora Productions and associated logos are trademarks and/or
registered trademarks of Ang'dora Productions, LLC

Cover design by Brenda Pandos

ISBN 978-0-9845621-2-1

First Edition July 2010
Second Edition August 2011

Printed in the United States of America

Dear Reader,

When *Promise* was first released in 2010, I was thrilled and ecstatic and couldn't wait for readers to enjoy it. But something kept nagging at me. Well, some*one*. You can call her Alexis, the main character of the series, who kept bopping me upside the brain, muttering, "But that's not what really happened and you know it." She was right—she usually *is* right when it comes to her story. I should have known better.

You see, *Promise* had gone through extensive editing, with many sharp eyes and brilliant minds providing assistance and input to make it the best it could be. Unfortunately, the best intentions led to scenes being changed or deleted when they probably shouldn't have been. Even the order of the events in the first third of the book was altered.

For over a year, I've had this fantasy that I could put the story back to how it should be. When my publisher and I decided to re-do the covers and add in excerpts of the next book at the end of the existing books, it provided an opportunity to make my fantasy real.

This book you hold in your hands is the re-release of *Promise*, containing revisions, new material and an entire, never-before-published scene. This is the story as the author intended.

Sort of. You see, what I really intended was for *Promise* and *Purpose* to be read as one book. I originally wrote them as one and for a variety of reasons, I had to split it. I still think they should be read together, as if they were one book. I think of *Promise* as the prologue to the series or, even more so, as *Purpose Part I*.

If you only read *Promise*, you're getting only half the story—just the romantic beginning. You miss the second half and the true ending, which is the springboard for the rest of the series, where the love story evolves beyond the love between husband and wife to love of family to love of all humanity . . . and beyond.

So my hope is that you pick up *Purpose* as soon as you can and read the two together, as I truly intended. But I thank you for starting here, with *Promise*, and for giving me, and Alexis, a chance.

Happy reading!

Kristie Cook

For Shawn, Zakary, Austin and Nathan Cook

And Chrissi Jackson

Acknowledgements

A ginormous thank you to all of you who helped make this a reality, either through direct involvement or much appreciated moral support.

My parents, Valerie Templeton and Danny & Keena Perguson, and all of my "boys," Shawn, Zakary, Austin & Nathan Cook, for your patience, understanding and support.

My biggest cheerleader, supporter and the best business partner, Chrissi Jackson; and Terry Frank and Lisa Adams. Without your encouragement, this would still be a fun little indulgence never seen by anyone else.

My first readers, the girls: Alys Roark, Heather Call, Lesley Turnpaugh and Charlotte Waldon, for giving me your time and support when this was still just a mess of words.

And thank you, reader, for giving me this opportunity to touch your life, if only for a few hours. I hope you enjoy this story and come back for more.

Chapter 1

9 Years Ago

The sensation of being watched clung to me like a spider web, invisible threads bristling the back of my neck and down my spine. I brushed my fingers across my shoulders, as if I could drag the feeling off and flick it away.

It was ridiculous, of course. Not just ridiculous to think I could pull it off so easily, as if it really was strands of a web, but it was even more absurd to feel it in the first place. Nobody ever held that much interest in me. Occasionally, people stared with curiosity when they picked me up on their "weird radars," but usually they just ignored me. No one ever watched so intensely.

Yet the hairs on the back of my neck stood on end at the feeling as I visited my favorite Washington, D.C., monument for likely the last time. I sat on the stone steps with the stately Thomas Jefferson behind me and gazed over the Potomac River tidal basin, enjoying the peace just before sunset. Well, trying to enjoy it anyway.

I blamed the ominous feeling on my unruly imagination, with it being twilight and the sky looking so foreboding. It was the perfect backdrop for one of my stories. The sun hung low— an eerie, orange ball glowing behind a shroud of haze, a column of steel-blue cloud rising around it, threatening to snuff it out. I envisioned something not-quite-human watching it from the shadows, waiting to begin its hunt under the cover of darkness.

That's all it is, just my fascination with mythical creatures, I told myself. *Uh-huh. Right.*

Surrendering hope for a peaceful moment, I hurried to the closest Metro station. The feeling of being followed stuck with me on the train ride home, but at my stop in Arlington, I forgot the sinister sensation. Some kids from school stood near the top of the escalator as I stepped off. I'd witnessed before their favorite summer activity: dressing in all black and hassling people exiting the Metro station. So mature, but what can you expect? They were younger—they hadn't graduated with me over a month ago—and apparently, still stuck in the rebellious phase that I'd never been through myself.

I usually took the elevator to circumvent them, but had been too distracted tonight.

"Hey, there's the weird girl who heals," one of them said loudly to the others. "It's s'posed to be really freaky to watch."

"Hey, freak, got any tricks to show us?" another called.

I pretended not to hear and crossed the street to avoid them. My eyes stung, but no tears came. I wouldn't allow them. It was my own fault—I'd been a klutz with the Bunsen burner in Chemistry and my lab partner saw my skin heal the burn almost instantly. People harassed me about it every day the last two months of school. If I didn't let them get to me, they were usually just annoying. Usually.

Night had crept its way in during my ride home. I walked quickly through the bright commercial district and turned down the darker residential street for home, still four blocks away. Footsteps behind me echoed my own. I quickened my pace. *Two more days. That's all. Just two more days and we're out of here.*

"C'mon, dude, we just wanna know if it's true," a boy's voice said.

"Yeah, just show us. It doesn't hurt, right?"

I glanced over my shoulder. Three teens followed me and I caught the glint of a blade in one of their hands. I realized their plan to satisfy their curiosity—slice me open and watch the wound heal. *What is* wrong *with people? Of course, it hurts!* Bungalow-style homes lined the street, each with an empty front porch. Not a single person sat outside on this summer's evening. No one to witness their fun and my agony. My heartbeat notched up with anxiety.

Pop! Crack! The streetlights along the entire block blacked out at the sounds. I inhaled sharply and halted mid-stride. The footsteps behind me ceased, too.

"What the *hell?*" Surprise and fear filled the boy's question.

A couple appeared from nowhere, three houses down, standing in the middle of the street. It was too dark to see their features and I could only tell their genders by their shapes. The woman's high-heeled shoes clicked on the pavement as they walked toward me. The man, big and burly, pulled his shirt over his head and handed it to the woman. Without breaking stride, he took off one shoe and then the other, leaving him with only pants. *What the . . . ?*

I considered my options. The woman and her half-naked companion blocked my way home, but I wouldn't just raise my chin and walk brusquely by them, pretending they meant no harm. Because I just knew they did. I stood trapped between the boys with the knife and the bizarre couple. Somehow, I knew the knife was less threatening.

"Boo!" The woman cackled as the boys took off running. As she and the man closed in on me, the alarms screamed in my head.

Evil! Bad! Run! Go!

My sixth sense had never been so frightened. I couldn't move, though. Fear paralyzed my body. My heart hammered painfully against my ribs.

The couple stopped several yards away. The woman studied me as if assessing a rare animal, while the man lifted his face to the sky, his whole body trembling. I followed his gaze to see the thin, gauzy clouds sliding across a full moon. The woman cackled again. Panic sucked the air from my lungs.

"Alexis, at last," the woman said, her voice raspy, like a long-time smoker's. "We'll get such a nice reward for you."

My eyes widened and my voice trembled. "D-do I know you?"

She grinned, a wicked glint in her eyes. "Not yet."

Or ever, if I can help it.

I turned and ran. My pulse throbbed in my head. Breaths tore through my chest. My mind couldn't focus, couldn't make sense of this absurd couple and what they wanted with me, but my body kept moving. The bright lights of the commercial area I'd just left beaconed me to their safety.

The woman abruptly appeared in front of me before I was half-way down the street. The shock sent me hurling to the ground and my head smacked hard against the pavement. Stars shot across my eyes. My hands burned from asphalt scrapes. Fighting the blackness trying to swallow my vision, I rolled onto my side, gasping for breath. A sticky wetness pooled under my temple.

My eyes rolled up to the woman, who now pointed what looked like a stick at me. Her lips moved silently as she waved a pattern in the air. I felt pinned to the ground, though nothing physically restrained me. Panic flailed uselessly below the surface of my paralyzed body, making my breaths quick and shallow. I was done for. They could do anything they wanted with me. There was no escape now.

My vision faltered. Now two women stood over me, two sticks pointed at me. Two moons wavered behind them. I didn't know if it was fear or the head injury that caused everything to slide apart and together again. I squeezed my eyes shut.

But I couldn't close my ears, couldn't block out the gnarl. My eyes popped open with terror, expecting to see a wild beast, but the feral sound came from the man. His eyes rolled back, showing only whites. His hands clenched into fists. His muscles strained, the veins protruding like ropes along the bulges. His body shook violently until the edges of his shape became a blur.

"I can't hold it," he growled.

"Then don't," the woman said. "Don't fight it. It's time!"

A ripping sound tore through the night as the man lurched forward, his skin shredding. A gelatinous liquid spurt out of him like an exploding jar of jelly. His pants tore into ribbons as his body lengthened and grew. The shape of his limbs transformed. His face elongated, his nose and mouth becoming a . . . *Holy crap! A snout?!* I gasped, a scream stuck in my throat. By the time his front . . . *legs* . . . hit the ground, fur covered his body. He was no longer man. He was— *A freakin' wolf?!*

The beast moved closer, a low growl in its throat. Its stench of decaying corpses and rotting leaves overwhelmed my sensitive nose, the disgustingly sweet odor gagging me and forcing me to breathe through my mouth.

Pop! Another woman appeared, again out of nowhere.

Her pale skin glowed and her white hair shimmered in the moonlight.

"I smell blood," she said, her voice a flutter of wind chimes. "Mmm . . . delicious blood."

The scrapes on my hands had already healed, but not the cut on my head. It must have been deep enough for a normal person to need stitches. For me, it could take ten minutes to heal. So my blood was still fresh.

I could only smell the wolf's rancid odor as it hovered over me.

"Back off, *mutt*," the white-blonde snarled as she stepped closer. "This is too important for the likes of you."

"How dare you!" Stick-woman gasped. "We had her first!"

"Alexis is mine. Always *mine*!"

What the hell is happening?! What do they want with me? Whoever they were, they wanted to do more than just terrorize me. I could hear it in the way the blonde said I was *hers*. She wanted me to hurt . . . or worse. Cold fear slid down my spine and hot tears burned my eyes.

Pop! My heart jumped into my throat as another man materialized in the darkness and strode toward me. *Not more!* The wolf growled. Both women hissed. Goose bumps crawled along my skin.

The man stepped in front of me, placing himself between me and the others.

Good! Very good! Safe! My sense slightly calmed me.

"You're alone?" the blonde asked. "Ha! You haven't a chance."

The wolf lunged at my protector. He raised his hands and thrust them out toward the beast and it flew back as if blasted by something unseen. I heard a thud and a whimper as it hit the pavement. I blinked several times, disbelieving what I just saw.

The women hissed again. The first one raised her stick, pointing it at my protector. The blonde took a step toward me.

Pop! Another person appeared, between the two women and my human shield. The women responded immediately—their teeth gleamed in the moonlight as their lips spread into grins.

No way could my protector stand up against this second man. The new one was taller, wider in the shoulders, thicker in the torso and arms than my protector, who was now out-numbered and out-muscled. The second man took a single step toward us. I didn't dare look up at him, afraid of what I might see. But I felt his eyes rake over me. My trembling turned to quakes.

My sixth sense continued shouting conflicting alarms, everyone's intentions so strong. *Good* and *Evil* both screamed in my head and I couldn't tell which this new person was.

But then he turned to face the women and their expressions darkened. And I knew. He was on our side. I swatted down a leap of hope, though. The attackers still out-numbered my protectors.

The wolf, now back on all fours, stalked toward us. The fur on the back of its neck rose. Hunger shone in its eyes as its lips curled back in a snarl. Its pace quickened, my heart galloping with it. It lunged once more. I tried to scream. My constricted throat only allowed a whimper.

Then the wolf flew backwards again and fell to the ground a second time. The bigger man's hand hung in the air, palm straight out facing the wolf, as if he'd hit it, but I never saw the contact.

Both women eyed me with obvious greed. Then their eyes shifted back to my brawny protector and confusion and even fear flickered across their faces. He turned his hand toward them. Their eyes widened, looking as terrified as I felt.

They disappeared with two *pops*.

"I've got Alexis! Take care of that one!" The lankier man easily lifted me into his arms and sprinted toward my house.

The beast's stench continued to fill my head, a persistent odor that wouldn't leave even as distance separated us.

A wolfish howl behind us diminished into a human cry of pain. I shuddered in the arms of the stranger.

ↂ

"Alexis, honey." Mom's voice, soft and distant, pulled me out of unconsciousness. "Honey, it's time to get up."

"Huh?" I mumbled, disoriented.

"We need to go."

I forced my eyes open and squinted at her against the brightness of daylight. She knelt on the floor next to me, where I was wrapped in a blanket, a pillow under my head. *How did I get here?* The last thing I remembered was the stranger running with me in his arms.

Renewed fear gripped me and I sat up with a gasp. Pain shot from the base of my skull to the backs of my eyelids. I pressed my fingers to my temples. *Was it real?* I examined my hands. No scrapes. I touched my head. No bump or cut. It meant little, though. They would have been healed by now anyway.

"What happened last night?" I asked, my voice husky.

"Hmm?"

I started to tell her about my night. Her brows pressed together as I told her about the boys with the knife.

"I can't believe how mean kids can be," she interrupted. "You should have let me move you after the burn."

I shook my head, just once. It hurt too much to move it more than that. She misinterpreted it, though, thinking I still protested her offer to move to avoid my humiliation. I hadn't wanted to leave so close to graduation. But that happened months ago. It didn't matter anymore.

"I know," she said. "We're moving now and you can have a fresh start."

"No, that's not it. There was this couple in the street, too. And the man . . . he changed into a . . . a *werewolf.* And the woman—I think she was a *witch.*"

Mom's eyebrows arched. "Honey, do you realize what you're saying?"

I did. And it sounded ludicrous. In fact, in the morning light, I knew it was more than ludicrous—it was absolutely impossible. But it had felt so real . . . .

Confused, I studied her inhumanly beautiful face. She always said we had similar features—chestnut hair, almond-shaped, mahogany eyes, smooth, light-olive skin—her words, not mine. It described her in an understated way and was overkill for me. I resembled her, but she looked like an angel and I looked like her very human daughter.

She also looked, impossibly, twenty-six years old. Mom didn't age. One of her quirks. By the time I was fifteen, we had to tell people we were sisters because she looked too young to be my mother. I called her Sophia in public, but Mom in private.

"You have the wildest dreams," she said with a small smile. She nodded and patted my arm.

"But—" I pulled my arm from her, knowing what she was doing.

"It was a dream, Alexis. We don't have time to discuss it," she said, an edge to her voice now.

Right. A dream. That makes more sense. Something deep inside, past the throbbing in my head, denied that theory, but there was really no other explanation. Witches and werewolves . . . people appearing and disappearing . . . . *How can that be real?* Logic told me it couldn't but . . . my intuition knew *something* happened.

I broke my eyes from hers to hide my denial, not in the

mood to challenge her now. My head hurt too much to argue, feeling like someone jabbed around in my brain while I slept. Also, I'd seen the stony look on Mom's face before: *Drop it*, the look said.

I glanced around the living room and noticed the emptiness for the first time—no furniture, no boxes stacked against the walls, nothing. "Where is everything?"

"Packed in the moving truck." She sounded nonchalant, as if it made perfect sense.

"*What?*"

It didn't make sense at all. That wasn't the plan. Mom was supposed to end it with her boyfriend last night and we would pack the truck today and leave for Florida tomorrow. *Why the sudden rush?* She didn't believe my story, so that couldn't be it. It had to be the boyfriend. It was almost always the boyfriends.

"We need to get out of here," she said. "*Now.*"

I knew the tone and moved as quickly as my aching head allowed. Our moves always felt like forced escapes. Sometimes it was because of an accident, but most often because of the boyfriends. Though this move had actually been planned, it now had the familiar feeling we were once again making an escape. At least this time I knew where we were going and why.

I still felt sluggish as we traveled south on I-95. Images of the werewolf and the witch flashed through my mind. I fell asleep and dreamt about them, but they were good in this dream. Not monsters. And they fell in love. I spent a good portion of the trip outlining a book about their supernatural romance, my first full-length novel that I felt compelled to write immediately.

As the drugged feeling lifted and I could think clearly, I analyzed those strange events. People tried to hurt me and possibly wanted to kill me. I thought. Maybe the werewolf and the witch and the other bizarre parts weren't real. Maybe I hit my head harder than I realized and imagined those parts. Or maybe the real events mashed up with an actual dream and I had everything confused. But I was certain I was attacked. Fairly certain, anyway. And the way the white-blonde said I was "hers" told me it wasn't the last time I'd see her. If she was even real.

My memory felt like a ripped-up photo taped back together but missing vital pieces. Some details, like the wolf's terrifying eyes, were so clear, while others, like my protectors' faces, were blank. This made me question the reality of it all, but I couldn't dismiss the fear. It was too deeply embedded into my memory.

If someone had attacked me, though, Mom would know. She wouldn't have dismissed it so easily. She was too protective of me. Even going off to college on my own was never an option. She gave up her job in corporate sales because, she said, she was ready for a change. She'd been in sales for as long as I could remember and was quite successful at it. One of her quirks was her power of persuasion—she could sell a truckload of beef to a vegan. But she had always wanted to own a bookstore and there happened to be one for sale just ten miles from the college I'd chosen. I was actually glad she was coming with me. She was my best friend, after all. My only friend for years. I had to wonder now, though, if she was really coming to protect me.

Hundreds of miles passed under the truck's wheels before I built the courage to ask and braced myself for her reaction.

"Mom . . . are there people who want to hurt us? I mean, because of who we are?"

She gave me a sideways glance. "Alexis, I would not let anything happen to you."

"I know, but if there are people out there . . . shouldn't I know? Don't you think it's time I knew things about us?"

She opened her mouth, then closed it again. The corner of her lips turned down in a frown. "I can't tell you, honey. I just can't. Not until the *Ang'dora*."

Right. The *Ang'dora*. The enigmatic "change" that was somehow connected with our quirks and everything that made us weird. I knew little about it. I knew little about us.

"Are you asking because of your dream last night?" she asked. "Because you know it's–"

I cut her off with a sigh. "Yeah, I know. Not real."

I *wanted* to believe her. That was the easy and safe explanation, but I just couldn't.

Mom held our secrets tightly, even from me, and I'd given up pleading for information years ago. She had told me many times she was bound to a promise made when I was an infant: I couldn't know our secrets until I went through the *Ang'dora* and became more like her. When other families' skeletons included domestic violence, sexual abuse or various addictions, ours seemed rather innocuous. After all, they were just weird quirks. Of course, it was annoying and frustrating that I couldn't know why we had them, but when I let myself feel normal, I often forgot to be annoyed and frustrated. So most of the time, I pretended I didn't care and allowed myself to live behind a façade of normalcy. Because all I really wanted was to have a normal life—a career as an author, true love, a family.

But now I did care. Whether I was really attacked or not, it was time I knew who we were and why we had strange quirks. I hated snooping behind her back, but her refusal to explain left no other options.

The move presented an easy opportunity for poking around. I volunteered to unpack the house while Mom prepared to open the bookstore. When she took me up on the offer to do her room, I didn't expect to discover anything she didn't want me to. And I didn't. I found false identification for both of us—drivers' licenses, birth certificates, passports and the like—giving us different last names, but they weren't helpful. I grew up with several surnames, a different one each time we moved, though most often we went by "Ames," as we did now. I was pretty sure that was the real one.

I couldn't even research Ames and our other surnames, though. Besides Sophia and Alexis, I had no first names to go on. We had extended family somewhere, but I'd never met them and Mom rarely discussed them. Without knowing their names, I could have searched genealogical records for years and never known if I was even in the right family. By the time the first day of classes came around, I knew nothing more, but I had a new plan and the college library would be perfect for its execution.

That was the day the dreams stopped. Until then, I repeatedly dreamt of that strange night, particularly of one of my heroes. Not the one who carried me away, but the other one, the bigger one. I still never saw his face, just a shadowy figure, but it was him. *Who are you?* My dream-self asked every time. I never received an answer and he stopped visiting my dreams the first day of classes. Perhaps because a very real guy entered my dreams . . . and my life.

Chapter 2

I dropped two classes before school even started. It was actually Mom's idea. I had a novel to write. When she read the outline I developed during our move, she said school could wait, the book couldn't. An unexpected statement from her, but she had her own sixth sense. Mine told me if people were unusually good or bad, as if I picked up on a brainwave revealing their overall intentions. Mom could feel truths—and she was never wrong. She felt the truth my book would be published. She even said, mysteriously, it *needed* to be written.

On the first day of college, with several hours between my morning classes and my one night class, I took the opportunity to do some research and planted my butt in a hard plastic chair at a library computer station. I wasn't researching for my book, though, and not for class either. This time was for me. I finally concluded that all I really could research were our quirks—I knew nothing else about us. I found a somewhat promising trail on the Internet and spent the entire afternoon researching telepaths.

When I was done, I stared at my notes and felt like an idiot. *Telepaths?! I seriously wasted hours on* telepaths? I shook my head at the absurdity. Mom and I had peculiarities, but we certainly couldn't read minds. Besides, telepaths, well, *didn't exist*. Did they?

I sighed and glanced at the clock, then bolted out of my seat, grabbing my bag and papers. Communications started in seven minutes. I rushed through the library, dodging tables and students, and practically ran down the stairs and into the lobby. **Evil? Good! (evil?) No, very good!** My sense screamed loudly, surprising me.

I stopped dead in my tracks and my eyes scanned the area. *Did they find me again?* No. Everyone here looked perfectly normal, going about their business of checking out books at the nearby front desk. No one paid me any attention. But that wasn't the only reason the alarms surprised me. My sense had never questioned itself before, never sounded so confused. *What's going on? Who is it?* I inhaled a deep breath. My sense had settled on good. That's all that mattered. And I didn't have time to worry about anything else. I had to go or I'd be late.

I rounded the corner to the door and slammed right into a large, hard body. *Sweet and tangy. Mmm . . . .* Having a powerful sense of smell was often unpleasant, but it was worth suffering through bad body odor and nasty garbage for this. He smelled delicious. But he sounded annoyed or angry as a low growl rumbled in his chest.

"Sorry," I muttered.

I looked up to see the face belonging to such yumminess. *Whoa! Talk about yummy!* He was absolutely gorgeous. Too gorgeous. I looked away immediately, embarrassed by my behavior. I bent down to gather the papers I dropped—and so did he. To complete my humiliation, I shocked him with static electricity when our fingers touched. I blushed. He chuckled quietly.

"Alexis Ames," he murmured under his breath. If it hadn't been my own name, I wouldn't have even understood—he said it so quietly. His thumb underlined my name on the class schedule he handed back to me. I took it, mumbled "thank-you" and bolted.

I hurried across campus, slipped inside the classroom with a minute to spare and took the closest open seat, where a syllabus already waited on the desk. The instructor stood at the head of the room, carefully watching the clock above the door. He started his introductions at six o'clock sharp and rudely rebuked a couple of students who arrived late, commenting that tardiness was a sign of disrespect. As if his tone was not. *Note to self: Be on time for this one.*

I'd felt the burn of eyes on me when I walked in the door and took my seat. Normally I would have disregarded it. I was used to it, especially the last couple months of high school, when everyone was curious about my burn. But as I sat there, trying to listen to the professor as he monotonously listed his credentials, I could feel the eyes again, making the back of my neck tingle. It wasn't a threatening feeling, but an uncomfortable sensation of curious eyes. I glanced over my shoulder, pretending to check out the classroom. *Oops.* I was caught. But I couldn't tear my eyes away.

Wow. Beautiful. That was all I could think through the haze filling my brain, obscuring any other thoughts. I never understood how a guy could be considered beautiful until now. He was stunningly attractive like Mom was—beyond what should be allowed for any human.

His eyes held mine until I finally came to my senses and pulled away. He smiled as I slid my eyes to the front of the room. And then it hit me. *Oh, no! Why me?!* I had barely glanced at him the first time, but I knew without a doubt: he was the same guy I'd run into like an idiot less than five minutes ago. Apparently, he recognized me, too, and found it funny. I wished one of my quirks was the ability to disappear. And I wondered how he'd beat me to class.

"Most of your projects will be done as teams," the professor droned. "You'll be with the same team throughout the semester. I won't make any changes, so I suggest you learn to work out any differences. Your team number is in the upper-right corner of the first page of your syllabus. Your first project is due next week, so get into your groups now to make introductions and get started."

The professor was the type high-school students fretted about when they thought of college—demanding, commanding, condescending, anal-retentive. He was nothing like my other instructors. My calculus teacher would make the subject bearable because at night he was a stand-up comedian and his one-liners were laugh-out-loud funny. A funny mathematician—not an oxymoron. Who knew? My women's studies instructor was the eccentric cat-woman. Not the superhero, but the crazy, old maid who lived with a bunch of cats.

Based on Mr. Anal's instructions of where teams should gather, I didn't have to move. Two girls—one a cute, girl-next-door blonde and the other a scowling, black-haired Goth—and two guys joined me in our designated section of the room.

Including Mr. Beautiful.

Of course. Just my luck.

He was the last to join us, after switching his syllabus with one on an empty desk—he wanted to be in our group and I figured he knew somebody. When he headed our way, his athletic build straining against his shirt, even Ms. Grumpy Goth straightened up and smiled slightly. But then I caught a quick, but odd reaction from the other three and I knew immediately he hadn't chosen our group because he knew anyone.

Mr. Beautiful nodded at each of us as he took a seat and the others shrunk back slightly. A look of fear, or maybe just astonishment, flickered in their eyes. A slight smile played on his lips when he looked at me last. I couldn't figure out what the others saw because I didn't notice anything. Well, I did notice *something*, but nothing warranting *that* kind of reaction. My sense remained quiet.

Then I realized there *was* something—a strange nudge in the back of my mind. There was something different but unidentifiable about him. I could barely introduce myself before I zoned out through the other introductions and tried unsuccessfully to determine the nudge's meaning.

During a break halfway through class, I bought a soda and wandered outside. The hot, heavy air wasn't exactly refreshing, but it was a nice break from the closed up, conditioned air inside. The sun had officially set and the sky was still a pinkish-purple in the west, the tops of two palm trees silhouetted against it. A couple of people sat on the top step, talking. I walked down the stairs and leaned against a lamppost, sipping my drink.

"Alexis, right?" a silky, sexy voice asked behind me, making me jump and slosh soda over my hand.

I turned to see Mr. Beautiful. Of course he would sound lovely. I already knew he smelled good, too. *Yep.* He strode over to me and I could really take in the scents. *Hmmm…sweet, like mangos and papayas, citrusy like lime, and spicy like…hmmm…I think sage…and just a hint of man.* My quirky sense of smell was not only stronger than normal, but also allowed me to pick out the individual layers of a complex scent. His was natural—it didn't have the chemical undertone like cologne or soaps did—a fresh fragrance, making me think of sitting in the sun on a warm day.

"Uh, yeah," I muttered. The lamp over us cast its light directly on his spellbinding face, making my mind foggy and unable to form coherent words.

It wasn't right for a guy to be so incredibly attractive. Besides how tall he stood—towering at least a foot over my five-two—I noticed his hazel eyes first. They pulled me into their staggering beauty, with a wide ring of emerald green on the outside of the irises and brown around the pupils with gold specks that seemed to . . . *sparkle*. They were fringed with such long, dark lashes that it was unfair they were on a guy. His facial features were flawless—a square jaw, full lips and a golden suntan— better than any movie star or model. Sandy brown hair, longer on top and streaked by the sun, topped off his perfection. And then he smiled magnificently and the gold flecks in his eyes sparkled brighter, like when the sun hits gold flakes in a mining pan. My brain slid out the exit door and my insides melted like chocolate. *Get a grip!*

I tried to remember his name. He had to have introduced himself to the team. I must have been really focused on that mind nudge, because I drew a blank.

"I'm Tristan . . . in case you didn't catch it."

I nodded as if I knew. "Yeah, nice to meet you, Tristan. Um, sorry about running into you earlier."

"I'm not," he murmured so quietly, I probably wasn't supposed to have heard.

We both stood there awkwardly . . . well, *I* felt awkward, anyway. I expected him to leave, but, strangely, he didn't.

"So . . . how was your first day of classes?" he finally asked.

I looked up at him in surprise. *Why are you talking to me? No one talks to me.*

"Uh, fine, I guess. You?"

"This is my only class today and, so far, it's perfect." He

chuckled, as if there were some underlying meaning to his answer.

"Lucky. This is my third."

"Busy day." Another moment of awkward silence passed before he continued, probably thinking it rude to walk off now. "This is my only class this semester, actually. Too much other stuff going on to take a full load right now."

I told him I could relate and, for some reason, babbled through my entire schedule, my hand flitting anxiously between twirling the tab of my soda can and tugging at my hair.

"Women's studies, huh?" He lifted an eyebrow, a gleam in his eyes. "Maybe I should look into that one. Sounds . . . interesting."

I laughed. It sounded unusually high, anxious. "It's almost all girls . . . but I'm sure they wouldn't kick *you* out."

Did I really just say that aloud? I blushed. He laughed, the pleasurable sound making my heart flip.

I struggled to concentrate through the rest of class, mentally replaying the five-minute conversation with Tristan and chastising myself for acting like a schoolgirl with her first crush.

"Which dorm are you in?" the blond girl-next-door asked me after class. I thought someone called her Carlie.

"Oh, I live off campus, with my . . ." Oops, almost said Mom. I was out of practice. ". . . with my sister."

"Oh, too bad." She sounded genuinely disappointed. "I thought we could walk back together, maybe hang out. I'll see you Wednesday afternoon for our team meeting."

"Yeah, see you then." I thought maybe college was different than high school. People were actually friendly.

As soon as she left, though, prickles of fear trailed down my spine. I'd have to walk to my car alone, in the dark, and that scared the hell out of me. I was probably just extra jumpy from my sense's false alarm earlier, but it felt like the opportune time and place for an attack. My attackers probably didn't even know where I lived now, but I had no guarantees. They'd found me once. They could find me again. If they even existed.

I stuffed my books in my bag and retrieved my keys. I gripped them with their points jutting between my fingers to use as a weapon, clutched the bag's strap in my other hand and inhaled a deep breath.

"I'll walk you out to the parking lot," Tristan offered, slinging his own backpack over his shoulder. He glanced at my fist full of keys. "You shouldn't be alone on campus at night."

I exhaled with relief. "That'd be great."

Though I'd just met him, I felt safe with Tristan. Not that I wanted him or anyone else involved, but I hoped those strangers wouldn't try to attack with other people around—real people, not boys with little pocket knives.

As we walked in silence, I wondered what was wrong with him. There had to be something because he paid attention to me. Of course, I was usually the one avoiding everyone else, only because I knew there would be a negative reaction at some point. But Tristan . . . I didn't *want* to avoid him. Something inside me seemed to settle—to click into place—with him already.

I knew I was making a mistake, setting myself up for disappointment . . . or worse. Guys who even had a fraction of his looks could pick any girl, throw her a bone and she'd do anything for him—like his homework. That was the only reason they talked to freaks like me . . . unless they thought we were an easy score.

I didn't want to think that way about Tristan, though. It wasn't fair. But if either were true, he'd be the one disappointed. For now, I'd give him the benefit of the doubt and pretend like it was perfectly normal for him to be talking to me. Again.

"So you live close by?" he asked.

"Yeah. Cape Heron, with my sister, Sophia. She bought a bookstore."

"The Book Nook? The one on Fifth?"

"Yeah, you know it?"

He lifted his chin in a nod. "I live in the Cape, too. I noticed it was re-opening soon."

"In a few weeks. It's been closed for over a year, so it's needed a lot of work."

"Let me know if she needs any help. I'm good with my hands." He waved his hands in emphasis.

I tried not to think about what his hands may be good at. It made me giddy.

I was glad she'd already hired someone. *Mr. Beautiful around Mom?* They might meet at some point, considering we had several team projects over the semester and he lived near the bookstore. I thought I would kill her, though, if she ever hooked up with him. Although he couldn't possibly be interested in me, I didn't think I could stand for him to date her . . . *to be my mother's* boyfriend. *Ugh!*

"I'm taking a gamble here, but I'd say that's your ride?"

Besides a motorcycle, my 15-year-old, white VW convertible was the only vehicle in the parking lot. The other classes must have let out early for the first night. He walked me to my car.

"Guess I'll see you Wednesday?" he asked as I opened the door and dropped my bag on the back seat.

"Yeah, I guess so."

"Be careful." He paused, then added, "Driving home, I mean."

"Um, you, too." I eyed the shiny motorcycle. I didn't know what kind it was, but it definitely wasn't a Harley-Davidson, the only kind I really knew. It looked more like a racing bike, the kind seen screaming down the highway at ninety miles an hour, the rider hunched over the handlebars, dangerously weaving around traffic. He had a risky side. Maybe that's what the mind-nudge detected.

"You don't like bikes?"

"I like Harleys." I hoped that didn't offend him, if it was a Chevy-versus-Ford kind of thing.

He chuckled. "My other one is a Harley."

My eyebrows shot up. "Your *other* one?"

"I like toys." He shrugged with a grin. "See you Wednesday."

I sat in my car and watched him walk away in my rearview mirror. About halfway across the parking lot, his whole body seemed to shift, to relax. I hadn't even noticed he was tense—he'd seemed so cool and casual. I wondered what made him anxious. Surely someone like him couldn't be nervous talking to someone like me. As he fired up the bike, he glanced over at my car and I started my own engine so he wouldn't think something was wrong. *Don't mind me. Just ogling.*

Before I left, I put the top down. The balmy air hung with humidity, but I hoped the wind on the highway would equate to a cold shower and douse my internal heat.

$$\text{\reflectbox{C}\kern-0.3em S}$$

Wednesday morning I rushed again, this time to my women's studies class. It was the last place I wanted to be, so I took my time getting to campus and now I was running late. *Why did I take this stupid class anyway?* Tuesday had been a productive day for writing. Going to this pointless class now seemed like a waste of a valuable hour. It would be a long day on campus, too, with the team meeting in the afternoon. Of course, that meant seeing Tristan again, but after a delicious dream the other night and waking up to the disappointment that it could never come true, I'd told myself to stop thinking about him.

I walked into class right at 9:30, but it hadn't started yet. A low thrum of chatter among the students filled the room. Not all were female; there were three guys. *No . . . four today.* My mouth nearly dropped open. Tristan sat at the back of the room, talking to a couple of scantily clad girls. He stretched his arm across the desk next to him and shook his head, saving the seat for someone. I wondered who the lucky girl was as I headed to an open desk.

I retrieved my books from my bag when he caught my eye and grinned. He nodded at the desk next to him and winked. I stared at him, a dense fog filling my brain. When I shook my head to clear it, he pushed his bottom lip out and gave me sad eyes. A small giggle burst through my lips and before my brain registered that I moved, I was already back there. So much for not thinking about him.

"*What* are you doing here?" I whispered.

"I told you, it sounded interesting, so I picked up the class. Maybe I'll learn something." The smile he flashed caused my heart to flip. He was good at making my heart do gymnastics.

"I'm sure it's not what you're thinking," I said, waving my syllabus as I took my seat.

He held up his own copy. "Do you really think I enrolled in a class without knowing what it was? Give me a little credit, please."

My face flushed. "Sorry. It just doesn't seem like the type of thing you'd be interested in. I feel like it's a waste of time and *I'm* a woman."

"Hmm . . . maybe I can make it interesting for you."

I lifted my eyebrows. *What does that mean?* He smiled and nodded at the front of the room. I tried to focus on the instructor's lecture, but my eyes wanted to pull to my right. Sitting next to Tristan in class was like driving down a highway parallel to a breathtaking landscape—I knew I should keep my eyes straight forward, but they kept drifting to the side to enjoy the view.

Unable to control myself, I snuck a glance at him out of the corner of my eye. I was shocked to see his face full of pain or anger. I wondered what he was thinking. Was this feminine junk too much for his manly ego? The next time I peeked, though, he seemed perfectly fine. He peered back at me, the gold flecks sparkling. He pushed his notebook to the side of his desk, toward me, with a note written in the margin.

How many cats do you think she has?

I suppressed a giggle. I'd wondered the same thing about the teacher on the first day of class. I wrote on my own notebook: *12?*

He flipped over to a blank sheet and his pen dashed across the page. I started to think he was just taking notes when he pushed the notebook toward me again. He'd drawn a cartoon picture of the teacher with twelve cats surrounding her. I had to cover my mouth with my hand to keep from laughing aloud. We exchanged written jokes about her and the cats, adding things to the cartoon drawing, throughout the remainder of class.

"What are you up to between now and that team meeting we have later?" he asked after class.

I wrinkled my nose. "I have calculus in ten minutes. Then I'll probably torture myself some more and try to get homework done before our meeting."

"Not a math geek, huh?"

"Not even close." It was the only freshman core class I hadn't tested out of. But that was more than he needed to know.

"Well, you have fun with that. See you later. And thanks for making class interesting."

I cocked an eyebrow. I should have been thanking him. I had practically fallen out of my seat with silent giggles.

"Seriously. It's no fun writing notes to myself. I don't play along nearly as well as you do." He grinned. Then he did it again: he winked at me. My insides softened as I gawked at him. *I'm such a fool.*

"I'll see you later," I finally muttered when my head cleared. I made a beeline for the door before I made a bigger idiot of myself.

After calculus, I grabbed a soda and a bag of trail mix at the student union and headed for the seating area where our team would be meeting. I had just spread out my calculus text and notebook on the table when the familiar voice murmured close behind me, sending a tingle up my spine.

"I've been waiting for you for a very long time."

It's like he keeps finding me . . . but why would he want to? Not that it bothered me. It should have, but it didn't. He made me feel . . . good. Despite the mind-nudge.

"If that's the case, then I should turn you in for stalking me," I replied drily as Tristan dropped his bag on the table and took the seat next to me.

"Hmm, let's consider this. You show up in *my* communications class, then in *my* women's studies class that I decide to pick up and have no idea which one you're taking, and now you're right here where I need to be in thirty minutes. *I* could turn *you* in for stalking."

Of course, he was just teasing, but my face reddened anyway.

"I wouldn't, though, turn you in, I mean. You can stalk me anytime." He grinned. I blushed harder. *Mr. Beautiful is* flirting *with me.*

"Yeah, well, I don't have time right now. First, I need to get this homework done."

"Ah, right, your own personal torture. Need some help? I *am* a math geek."

I laughed. "Geek" was the last word anyone would use to describe Tristan.

That's how it all started. With two classes together and team projects to work on, I saw him every other day during the week. He helped me with my calculus, I helped him perfect his essays and we kept each other company between classes. Each time we were together, I felt another click in my heart and that was probably not good.

I honestly couldn't explain my behavior. I should have pulled away, if I knew what was good for me. Instead, I was drawn *toward* him. He brought something out in me I never knew was there. I couldn't pinpoint what it was, but it felt good. *Emotionally* good. Well, physically good, too. But also emotionally. Really.

Even more than my own behavior, I certainly didn't understand his—he could easily take his pick of girls. I didn't complain, of course. For weeks, our conversations centered on homework, college and the weather—pretty boring, yet safe topics. The more time we spent together, the better I felt around him. The mind-nudge had all but disappeared. Even when he'd flirt with me or get this certain look in his eyes or shift his body closer to mine, I didn't mind. Well, my body didn't. It would zing with anticipation of his touch. But my mind still protested, worried he'd be like . . . others. Then he'd pull back, as if there was a line I didn't want drawn but was there nonetheless—one neither of us could bring ourselves to cross. Yet.

Spending time with Tristan on campus left little time for my research. But there wasn't much to do, anyway. The deeper I sunk into it, the more outlandish it became. All I found were myths—telepaths, witches, werewolves, vampires—and even then, each had only one or two of our characteristics. Nothing matched, not even fantasy. I came to a dead-end with no idea where to go next.

But I was okay with that. With nowhere to go and Tristan consuming my thoughts, I easily drifted back to my comfort zone—hiding behind a mask of normalcy. I wanted nothing more than to be normal, just to have a chance with him. Such foolish desires, on so many levels.

I just didn't know *how* foolish.

Chapter 3

I used to think Mondays were nothing but a rude awakening from the lovely dream of the weekend. Now I looked forward to them. Tristan and I spent little time together on Fridays and I didn't see him at all on the weekends, so when each Monday finally came around, I was ridiculously giddy as I entered our women's studies class. Except for the fifty minutes of calculus, we spent from nine-thirty in the morning to ten at night together. Of course, we were in class and team meetings the majority of the time, but sometimes it was just us.

One such Monday in late September, we sat outside on the quad's lawn. The air was still warm, but we didn't drown from the humidity. I kicked off my flip-flops and sat on the grass, absorbing the sunshine. I closed my eyes and tilted my face to the sun for a few minutes, but I felt Tristan watching me, making me self-conscious. I surrendered and reluctantly pulled my books out of my bag.

Tristan had a notebook on his lap and pencil in hand,

already working on something. I left my calculus for later, not wanting to bother him, and pulled out the communications text instead. I still had three chapters to read before I could even start on the paper he was probably already writing. He was always several steps ahead of me in our assignments, but, for some reason, still had me review his nearly perfect essays.

I stole a glance at him one more time before delving into the text. He caught my eye, smiled and winked, bringing that fog into my brain. *Why does he* do *that to me?* Apparently pleased with my dazed reaction, he grinned wider and bent over his notebook. The way his pencil flew over the page, I could tell he wasn't writing. He was drawing. But when I leaned over to get a look, he pulled the book up so I couldn't see and shook his head. I blew out an annoyed breath and, lifting my chin with petulance, I turned to my book. He chuckled under his breath.

"Hey, Tristan," a vaguely familiar female voice called from behind me a little later.

He glanced over my head and his body went rigid.

"Hey," he muttered.

"We're going to the Phi Kaps' house for a pool party. Wanna come?" a different female asked as they came closer.

He shot them a strange look, almost like he was angry.

"On a Monday?" he asked, his voice full of skepticism. I could hear something else underneath—a steely hardness.

"It's the Phi Kaps. Any day is good enough for them," the first girl said. "So, you coming?"

The girls stood by his side now, towering over him as he remained seated. If he looked up, he'd have an eyeful of long legs in short shorts and big boobs in tight tops, but, for some unfathomable reason, he looked at me instead. I recognized the girls from our women's studies class and they were exactly who I'd picture Tristan with—a much better match than me, no doubt. Apparently, they felt the same. They didn't give me so much as a glance.

I wondered if Tristan was the college party type. There was definitely something edgy about him. And what warm-blooded male would pass up a pool party with college girls—especially *these* girls?

"No, thanks," he replied, holding my eyes, the steely undertone still there.

I blinked in surprise. Both girls' mouths fell open. They obviously weren't accustomed to rejection. They glanced down at the notebook in his lap, shot their eyes at me and then back at him.

"What*ever*," they both huffed and stomped off.

Tristan relaxed as he took a deep breath and let it out slowly. I didn't understand his rejection until it occurred to me he was just being polite.

"You can go, if you want," I said. "You don't have to stay here with me."

He smiled. "Not interested. In going, I mean."

"Seriously. I'm used to hanging by myself."

His smile faded and his eyes flickered. "Do you *want* me to go?"

Yeah, right. I definitely didn't want him to go. It made me sad and lonely to just think about it. But he didn't need to know that. *How did I get here, where being alone was a bad thing?*

"Does it matter what I want?" I asked, a slight edge to my tone.

"It matters very much to me," he murmured.

My heart skipped. I stared at the ground, my face hot, and picked at a blade of grass.

"No, I don't want you to go," I whispered. "I just don't know why you'd want to stay. Most people don't hang around this long."

"I'm not most people."

He definitely was *not* like most people, but I knew he wasn't thinking along the same lines I was. I didn't know how to respond, so I just returned to reading my textbook, hoping he would forget the conversation.

"Can I ask you a question?" he asked later as we walked to one of the on-campus cafés before communications class.

I shrugged and looked up at him. "You can always *ask*."

He lifted an eyebrow. "Ah. So, then . . . will you *answer* a question for me?"

"Depends . . ."

"I guess I'll try my luck." He peered down at me as he opened the door to the café and stepped back for me to enter. Holding doors open for me seemed to be second nature to him, just like walking me to my car every day and other gentlemanly behavior. No, he wasn't like other people. "What did you mean earlier when you said most people don't hang around this long?"

Crap. Crap, crap, crap. I should have known he wouldn't forget it. Why had I even said it? I quickly ordered a salad and used the time as he ordered his own food to come up with a non-answer.

"So . . . you're not going to answer?" Tristan asked after we sat at a table by the window.

I shrugged. "I just meant most guys wouldn't pass up a pool party with hot college girls to do homework."

He leaned toward me, looking into my eyes. The gold sparkles in his were bright and enrapturing. My breath caught. "That's not what you meant."

I forced myself to breathe, my head swimming from the intensity of his gaze.

"It's pretty close," I finally said. He continued staring at me expectantly. I sighed. Then I tried to switch directions with my own question. "Do you know those girls well?"

He shook his head. "Only from class. Girls like that, though. . . they seem to think I *want* to know them."

"And you don't?" I scoffed.

"No."

I didn't understand him. "Is that why you passed it up?"

His eyes narrowed and the corners of his lips twitched as if fighting a smile. "I see what you're doing. You answer mine first."

I pursed my lips together as his eyes held mine, challenging me. I finally pulled my gaze from his and stared at my uninspiring salad. "Seriously . . . that pool party was an example. Most people wouldn't hang out for hours just doing homework and discussing trivial things."

I didn't add "with me," although that was the original meaning. It would point out something was wrong with me. I expected him to lose interest before he ever knew those things.

"I haven't found any of our conversations trivial," he replied. I looked back up at him and tilted my head, an eyebrow cocked. "You have?"

I snorted. "It's not exactly exciting stuff."

His eyes flickered. "So . . . you're bored?"

"No!" I sighed again, getting frustrated. "That's not what I meant."

"Are you going to tell me what you mean, then? Or are we just going to continue in circles?" He sat back in his chair and took a bite of his apple. A drop of juice glistened on his bottom lip and the image of licking it clean for him flashed in my mind. I blinked it away. He still sat there, waiting for my answer.

I sighed yet again; it was nearly a groan. *How could he do this to me?* He was too irresistible for my own good.

"Fine." I took a deep breath and spewed out the words.

"I really don't get why you choose to hang out with me, doing nothing special, when there are so many other things you could be doing with so many other people. Most people would be long gone by now."

"I told you, I'm not like most people." He leaned forward, over the table, his eyes intense again. My insides quivered and warmed under his relentless gaze. "I'd rather hang out, doing nothing special with you because you *are* . . . special."

My eyes widened. He moved his hand toward mine, as if to take it. I had to will my own hand to remain still before it jumped out to his and beat him to the first move. My skin tingled and my heart beat erratically. Before he even touched me, though, a quiet groan rumbled in his throat and his hand was suddenly in his lap. His eyes broke from mine and he looked away for the first time since we sat down. I exhaled slowly and quietly, allowing a moment of silence to pass as I recovered.

"You obviously don't know me very well," I finally muttered.

He sat back again and his gaze came back to me, looking as calm as always, as if nothing had just happened. "Hmm . . . I know you and I are very much alike."

"In what alternate reality? We seem to be complete opposites."

He was perfect. I was ordinary . . . except for the weird things. He was a math whiz and I was an English major. He was athletic; I was far from it. He was beautiful. I was . . . me.

He nodded, a thoughtful look on his face. "Hmm . . . yes, in many ways we are opposites, you're right. But, we're much more alike than you realize. You're not like most people either."

So he *did* notice. Yet here he was.

"And that's why I passed it up. College parties are no good for me. Trust me. You, on the other hand, are *very* good for me." He lifted his eyebrows, as if asking if I understood. I just stared at him for a long moment.

"I don't get it," I finally whispered.

He shrugged. "You don't have to. It's just the way it is."

That was about as deep as it ever went for the next few weeks. We never came back to that strange conversation, when I had let my guard down more than I ever had before. We both seemed to notice there was some kind of connection between us and neither of us could break it. Perhaps he was right. Maybe we were more alike than I realized. I felt another click in my heart as another piece settled into place.

ℤ

October brought mid-terms and, of course, Halloween. Mom buzzed excitedly about her first real store event since the Grand Opening—a Halloween party for the kids. I had put off serious studying for exams because I was spending so much time writing. The first few chapters poured themselves out of my head and I was falling in love with my main characters. I preferred spending time with them than with the overzealous feminists or derivatives and functions. With mid-terms looming, I had to switch gears.

First, though, I promised to help Mom decorate the store for Halloween before it opened one morning. Mom had hired her first employee, Owen, even before the Grand Opening, insisting that I spend my time writing, not working. But I wanted to do something for her since she did so much for me. And, admittedly, it was also for selfish reasons. I hoped it would assuage my guilt for sneaking around so much, even if I hadn't learned a thing about our background.

"Good morning, little dudette," Owen greeted when I entered the bookstore bright and early that Thursday morning.

He looked like he should still be in college, but wasn't. I didn't ask, but I guessed he'd dropped out to enjoy the Florida lifestyle of sun and fun, although I thought he was on the wrong coast. He seemed to belong in California, hanging out with the surfers.

I grunted. I'd stayed up until one in the morning reading about women playwrights and their portrayal of female characters.

"Hmm . . . not a good morning?" Owen asked.

"It's eight a.m., I don't have classes and I'm not in bed. What could be good about it?" I muttered.

He nodded and laughed. "Yeah, know what ya mean."

I watched as he enthusiastically cleaned the counter, contradicting his words.

"You look like a morning person to me."

He threw me a disgusted look, though his sapphire-blue eyes gleamed with humor. "I take that as an insult."

"So you're not always like this?"

He scrubbed his hand through his blond hair as he seemed to think about it. "I have no idea. Don't see this time of day whenever I can help it."

He winked at me. It was cute, but it didn't have that mind-fogging effect Tristan's wink did. He wasn't ugly or even unattractive, but . . . well, not Mr. Beautiful. In fact, in the looks department, Owen compared to Tristan like I compared to Mom—pleasant, but not striking. She thought Owen looked like a sweet James Dean, one of her favorite actors from the old movies she loved so much.

"Honey, you look exhausted," Mom said as she stepped out from a row of bookcases. "Maybe you're trying to do too much. Owen and I can take care of this."

"I'm fine. I just need some caffeine. I think I'll go get some coffee across the street before we do this."

"Why don't you two go get some for all of us?" she said.

"Take a five out of the drawer."

Mom didn't excite easily, but the way she gushed about Owen—how great he was, such a good worker, funny, yada, yada—you'd think he'd stepped right out of the pages of a book about Mr. Right. When I asked her why she didn't go out with him, she said she needed a man-break. Besides, she'd said, he was closer to my age than hers. Yep, she was trying to set us up. Hence, sending us both to do a one-person job.

"That's okay, Owen," I said. "I think I can manage."

I tried to hurry across Fifth, the main business street of Cape Heron, but my body just wouldn't cooperate. It still longed for my warm, comfy bed. I'd been surprised to find the late October mornings so cool. There was a bigger difference in seasons down here than I expected, although they were subtle changes—the mornings were cooler, the highs hit the low eighties instead of the nineties and it didn't rain every afternoon like it did throughout the summer. As I headed to the coffee shop, I enjoyed the salty breeze off the nearby Gulf of Mexico, letting it awaken my senses.

The Cape was a sleepy little resort town—at least it had been when we moved here in the middle of summer—among many dotting the Gulf Coast between Sarasota and Fort Myers. The region had been growing busier recently as the first snowbirds left their summer homes in the north and came south for the winter, so I wasn't surprised to find the coffee shop busy.

It was actually an old-style diner with wood and vinyl booths and a row of peg-like stools pinned in front of the counter. The smells of smoky bacon, sweet pancakes and pungent coffee mixed in the air, reminiscent of the many diners we stopped at during our moves. I also smelled the residue of last night's old-lady night cream and Ben-Gay on the elderly couple in front of me.

While I waited in line, I observed people, a habit I learned years ago when I started writing fiction. People-watching was fun, something I could do with all of my alone time, and I learned a lot to use in my characters. I was lost in thought while watching an older man with gray caterpillar eyebrows and a matching mustache sip his coffee and read a newspaper at the counter. His mustache crawled as he silently moved his lips while reading. He'd make a great werewolf, perhaps a pack leader.

"Hello, sexy Lexi," a lovely voice murmured in my ear, raising the hair on the back of my neck.

I spun around to find Tristan just behind me, leaning over, very close. *Mmm . . . he smells so good.*

"Sorry, you don't like Lexi, do you?"

Actually, I love the way it sounds from you. Did he really call me sexy?

"It wasn't the Lexi part," I said pointedly.

His eyes sparkled brighter. "So, I *can* call you Lexi?"

"Not in public." I never went by Lexi specifically because of that nickname.

"But in private is okay," he said. It wasn't a question. And he followed it with his devastating smile, making certain parts of my body tighten. My turn was up and the cashier had to ask me three times for my order before I even realized she was talking to me.

"Make that four coffees," Tristan said to the cashier as he pulled his wallet out of his back pocket. "I got it."

"Business expense," I said, holding up Mom's money folded between my index and middle finger.

"Save it. You can have the receipt and she still gets the expense." He paid while saying this, so I reluctantly stuffed the bill and the receipt in my jeans pocket with a scowl. I didn't like owing him.

I grabbed little cups of cream and packets of sweetener as

I waited for the order. When the four cups were placed on the counter, I tried to figure out how I would carry three of them.

"Let me help," Tristan said.

He grabbed one of the Styrofoam cups just as I did. An electric pulse flew through my hand and up my arm as our fingers touched. I flinched and looked up at him. He smiled and a gleam sparked in his eyes. He felt it, too, it seemed, but hadn't pulled back. It was, admittedly, a pleasurable sensation. It was the first time we'd actually touched—except when I collided with him that first night. When there had also been a shock. *Weird . . .* I took the other two cups and walked out without a word.

My stomach tightened as we crossed the street—Mr. Beautiful and my goddess-like mother were about to meet. The cowbell on the front door jangled when we walked in and Mom came from the back room, her arms loaded with glossy hardcover books. She looked up at me, then behind me at Tristan. She stopped dead and the books crashed to the floor. Her mouth fell open, as did mine. Mom never dropped things—she had excellent reflexes. She just stood there stiffly, still staring at him. *Please,* please *don't let them . . .*

"Um, Sophia?" I said, puzzled by her reaction. It wasn't exactly what I expected.

She continued glaring at Tristan and I realized I should make introductions, but my voice trailed off in the middle of them. Mom paid absolutely no attention to me and I suddenly felt like the outsider. Her eyes narrowed tightly at Tristan as she lifted her chin. Out of the corner of my eye, I saw Tristan just barely nod. Mom, almost imperceptibly, tilted her head in response. And then, to my complete embarrassment, she turned on her heel and marched to the back room. She barked something to Owen and he rushed out, stiffened when he saw Tristan, then nodded and hurriedly picked up the books.

"Sorry about that," I said.

"Sure, no problem." Tristan still watched the doorway to the backroom, as if expecting her to come back out . . . or wanting to follow her.

I moaned internally.

"Thanks for the coffee." I made my voice light so it wouldn't betray my feelings of defeat and disappointment.

He pulled his eyes away from the backroom and turned to me.

"My pleasure. I'll see you later." He leaned closer and whispered, "Bye, sexy Lexi."

Stunned, I looked up at him. He flashed a smile, then strode out of the store, leaving me in a daze. *Could he possibly . . . ?* Not *him and Mom? Maybe . . . just maybe?* My heart sped with hope.

But then I remembered Mom.

Chapter 4

I trudged to the back room where she paced around a stack of boxes.

"What was that all about?" I demanded.

"What?" She stopped pacing and widened her eyes with false innocence.

"Um, your warm welcome to Tristan?"

"Oh, that. Sorry. I just thought . . . oh, never mind. It's not important." She smiled weakly. I didn't buy it.

"Mom," I whispered through clenched teeth, hoping Owen didn't overhear us. "You were really kind of rude. That was so embarrassing. I think I really like this guy."

Mom's eyes grew wide with surprise. "You really *like* him?"

I nodded and a sheepish smile played at my mouth. It was the first time I'd admitted it aloud. I was still trying to be annoyed, though, so I fought the smile.

"How do you even *know* him?" She sounded angry, startling me into forgetting *I* was upset with *her*.

"He's in a couple of my classes and on my communications team."

Mom's face looked furious as she glared at me. "I can't believe you haven't told me about him!"

I moaned with guilt, avoiding her glare by looking at the floor as I pulled at my hair. I tried to avoid the full truth. "Well, it's not like there's anything to it."

"That could change. So what's the rest?" She knew me too well.

I continued to stare at the floor, yanking and twisting my hair. "Well, I was afraid that . . . you and Tristan . . . well, you know how you are . . . ."

My insides squirmed uncomfortably. Mom surprised me with a loud, "Ha!" My head snapped up to see her smug expression.

"That, my dear, is one thing you don't need to worry about," she said harshly. "I have absolutely no interest in him and I strongly wish you wouldn't, either."

"*What?*"

"He's trouble, Alexis. Trust me."

"Mom!" I nearly shouted, forgetting about Owen. I quickly lowered my voice. "That's not fair! You don't even know him."

She was silent for a moment. She had to know I had a good point. Then she said through clenched teeth, "I don't need to. I can tell he's not good for you."

"Well, I think he is and I'm an adult. I'll make my own decisions."

Her eyes widened with shock. Her mouth pressed into an angry line. Then she stormed away, back to the front of the store.

I stood there, livid, trying to figure out what she wouldn't like about Tristan. He hadn't been here ten seconds or even said a word. *How could she be so judgmental?* That wasn't like her at all.

I eventually dragged myself out to the front of the store and drank my coffee in silence. The heavy tension nearly suffocated me as we hung orange and black streamers, cut-outs of bats and black cats and fake spider webs around the store with as little conversation as necessary. I bailed out as soon as I possibly could and went home to study. But I couldn't concentrate so I escaped to my writing.

❦

"So, you really like him?" Mom had suddenly appeared in my doorway, startling me back to the real world. Wondering why she was home so soon, I glanced at the clock by my bed. It was already eight o'clock. *Ugh.* I had lost another day of studying. I got up from my desk, stretched, and then plopped down on my bed.

"Yeah, I do. Who wouldn't? He's absolutely gorgeous!"

"Yes, well, looks aren't everything." Her tone was curt, almost cold.

"Of course, they aren't! You know me better than that."

She sighed. "You're right. So, what else?"

"He's kind, he makes me laugh and he's a real gentleman. And I *think* he likes me."

"You don't need to like someone just because they like you, Alexis. What about Owen? He's funny and kind."

"Mother, will you stop it? You're being condescending." I glared at her.

She crossed her arms. Her voice hardened. "I'm just looking out for your best interests, Alexis."

"And you think *Owen* is in my best interest?" It came out as almost a sneer.

"Owen or just about anyone other than this Tristan!"

I sprang to my feet. "So, you want me to date, but I can only like the guy as long as it's someone *you* pick."

"I just don't want you to get hurt!"

"And how do you know Owen or whoever *you* choose wouldn't hurt me?"

"And how do *you* know Tristan isn't just like James?"

Ouch. That hurt and she knew it. She probably figured likening Tristan to James would be all it took to change my mind. It only made me angrier.

"And I guess it's *impossible* for Owen to be anything like James, since you know him soooo well."

She narrowed her eyes and kept her voice low but hard. "Owen is *nothing* like James. You can trust me on that one."

"But you can't trust me with Tristan?"

"*No! I can't!*"

I flinched. She dropped her head, pinching the bridge of her nose. After a long moment, she finally looked at me, concern filling her eyes.

"It's not you whom I don't trust," she said, her voice now soft. She took a few steps closer to me. "How well do you even know Tristan?"

"Better than you do," I spat. I groaned in frustration, though, because she had a point—after all this time, I really didn't know Tristan at all.

"I'm just worried about you." The concern in her voice wiped my anger away.

I sighed. "Do you want me to date or not?"

"I think it'd be good for you to date. You need to come out of your shell. But I want you to date someone *nice*. Tristan . . ." She hesitated.

"What?"

She didn't answer, but her meaning was obvious.

"I just don't want you to get hurt," she said again. She wrapped her arms around my shoulders. I laid my head against her for a minute and then looked at her face, into her warm, brown eyes.

"I'm willing to take the chance with Tristan," I admitted and she frowned. "Mom, you know me. I don't make friends easily because I don't trust people—for very good reasons. James, for one. But I'm trusting my sense with Tristan and I *feel* that he's different. I want to spend time with him . . . as long as he wants to spend time with me. I want to get to know him better."

"He'll want to get to know you, too, honey. It's not a one-way street."

"I will control who knows what about me . . . and you. It's not like we're going to get *married* or anything." I chuckled at the thought of it ever getting that far.

She didn't find it funny. She stared at me for a long moment, pressing her lips into a hard line. Then she abruptly spun around and marched out of my room.

"Even if he's not like James, he *will* hurt you," she said over her shoulder. Just before she ducked into her room, she added, "Just remember who you are, Alexis."

What the hell was that supposed to mean?

"Why don't you tell me who I am?" I yelled. I stared down the empty hallway, I guess expecting her to come back and explain. Or for the answer to magically appear. Of course, neither happened.

I spun around and kicked my bag in frustration. A notebook slid out and several loose papers scattered across the floor, including my research notes. I picked them up and glared at them for a long moment, blaming them for everything—not them specifically, but the mystery of who I was. It seemed to be at the heart of everything wrong with my life.

I finally balled up the stupid papers and stuffed them in my desk drawer. I didn't need them anymore. The ideas were absurd and a waste of time. The research was only useful for my writing.

I couldn't sleep. Mom and I didn't argue frequently and I hated it when we did. She was my best friend, the only person in the world I could trust. I stopped trying to make friends in middle school, when everyone turned on everyone else so easily. I was an easy target—the perennial new kid who just wasn't quite normal. Even if they didn't know my quirks yet, they knew there was something different and were quick to poke fun and spread rumors. But Mom was always there for me, with a comforting hug and a shoulder to cry on when the kids were especially hurtful. I could talk to her about anything. Well, almost anything. Our history was the only taboo subject. Until now.

And I really wanted, no, *needed*, to talk to her about Tristan. It didn't look likely that would happen any time soon, though. Especially after she'd brought up James—and compared Tristan to him! Not that I hadn't thought about it before.

James . . . I shivered under my comforter. Not with chills, but with renewed anger.

It was the last time I'd shared anything with anyone besides Mom. I should have known better, but I was fifteen and naïve. I'd experienced enough kids taunting me, but James was different . . . so I thought. He didn't give any particular bad vibes, but I became more attuned to my sixth sense later . . . after him . . . *because* of him.

He seemed genuinely interested and unusually friendly and somehow finagled out of me nearly all of my secrets. Although all the girls talked about him and would do anything for him, I wasn't ready for anything more than friendship. But that's not what he had in mind. On the last day of school, I let him take me to a party and learned that he only saw me as an insecure girl who would respond to the first guy who paid her any attention. His mood—his whole demeanor—changed as if, by pushing his hand away when he made his first move, I had hit some kind of switch.

"You're really rejecting me, Alexis?" he seethed. "After I accepted you, you're rejecting *me?*"

I felt like I'd been slapped. I had misunderstood every single kind gesture from the very first smile. He just wanted in my pants. Blood rushed to my face with a mix of embarrassment and anger. I stormed through the house, looking for an escape.

"You thought I'd sleep with *you?*" he shouted as he followed me out of the house, dozens of people following him to witness my shame. "Did you think I'd feel sorry for you because you're such a damn *freak?*"

I'd heard that one before. I could even get over whatever damage his twisted words had done to my insignificant reputation. But he continued and I spun around in disbelief as he aired everything I'd confided. My body trembled. My hands balled into fists. I could barely breathe. He ranted, sauntering closer to me as he did.

"Your own dad didn't want you! Ditched you before you were even born. Probably knew you'd be a freak. And your mom . . . well, she's hot, but she must have been thirteen when she had you. And with all the boyfriends . . . she's just a fucking *whore!*"

The next thing I knew, my right arm pulled back and, like a slingshot, flew forward. My fist jammed into James's nose with a crunch.

We moved the next day. Not because we ran away from my humiliation or a potential lawsuit or battery charge, but because when I hit James, he sort of flew about fifteen feet backwards, bowling over a group of witnesses—I had more power in my punch than was normal for a fifteen-year-old girl. Actually, more power than a grown man. I wasn't usually so strong, not like Mom. But I had never been so raging mad either.

That last betrayed trust set the final layer of blocks in the emotional wall I built around myself. There had been others like James, but I'd learned my lesson and shut them down without ever giving them a chance. I just couldn't take the risk of that humiliation again. But now here I was, with another interested guy. There was a difference, though: the feeling was mutual. I just didn't know how smart that was.

❧

I awoke at 8:04. *Crap!* Class started in less than an hour.

Thank God it was Friday. I had the whole weekend to study for mid-terms, get them over with on Monday and then, since I had no Tuesday classes, I had the rest of the week off for fall break. That meant lots of time to write.

I rushed around the house, relieved Mom had already left. I had nothing to say to her and no time to say it. I rushed to school and to women's studies. I finally relaxed when I saw Tristan and his warm smile waiting for me. All of my worries and hurriedness washed away into peace as soon as I sat down next to him. With the mind-nudge gone, he now had some kind of calming effect on me. So I was surprised at what Carlie had to say that afternoon. We ran into each other in the bathroom, right before our team was meeting to prepare for Monday's mid-term.

"Tell me if it's none of my business, but are you and Tristan going out or something?" she asked while I washed my hands and she primped.

"Um . . . no." I watched her reflection in the mirror, trying to understand where she was going with it. *Does she like him?*

"Okay, good." Her deep-blue eyes showed relief.

So that was a yes. A tinge of jealousy pricked my heart. But then she shocked me.

"Because he's kind of creepy, don't you think?"

"*What?*" I suppressed a surprised chuckle. *Tristan* creepy?!

"I don't know what it is. I mean, yeah, he's really hot. Drop-dead gorgeous, actually. But he's just . . . I don't know . . . *different*, somehow."

I wanted to laugh. I was so concerned about how unusual I was and she thought *he* was *different*.

"Something just bothers me about him," she continued. "I think it's something about his eyes, *in* his eyes."

Like the sparkle? *I like that sparkle!*

"He's always been really nice," I said in a lame attempt to defend him.

"So you *do* like him?" She peered at me, and then made a face. I didn't know what to make of it.

"Just as a friend," I lied.

"Oh, okay. Personally, I would stay away. He just seems a little . . . dangerous. And you seem so nice." She smiled at my reflection, then fluffed her short, blond curls with her hands.

"Thanks for the, uh . . . heads up." I didn't know what else to say, so I left for the group.

I had a hard time focusing on our studies because I paid more attention to the interactions among our team members. Everyone's body language seemed cool toward Tristan. They didn't sit too close to him and held their bodies turned slightly away. They talked to him and laughed at his jokes, but not quite as warmly as they did with each other. *Do the others feel the same way Carlie does?*

I studied Tristan, trying to look at him with a fresh perspective, trying to see what they might see. But I saw and felt nothing . . . except his beauty, his laughter, the lovely sound of his voice, the kind tone it held when he spoke to any of us, the intelligent remarks he made when we actually discussed the exam, the sparkle in his eyes when he smiled . . . . He caught me looking at him and winked. And, yeah, there's that—the way my brain went pleasantly woozy when he winked.

I barely remembered leaving the study group and driving home, still pondering Carlie's remarks and everyone's behavior toward Tristan. Carlie thought there was something dangerous about him and she hardly knew him. Mom took one look at him and didn't like him. *Am I missing something?*

Knowing I couldn't concentrate on studying or writing when I arrived home, I went for a walk. I meandered along the streets without paying attention to where I went, wondering why I just couldn't sense what everyone else seemed to notice. *Are my alarms broken? Or is everyone else just wrong about him? And if they're right, why do I feel pulled to him, like a magnet to its opposite?*

A familiar voice brought me out of my internal wanderings. I looked up and, with mild shock, found myself at the city park, bordering the north end of the Cape's beach. It was a small park, with a playground to my left and the beach just a few yards beyond it, a parking lot that could hold about twenty cars to my right and basketball and tennis courts straight ahead. An old banyan tree, pines and palms shaded the area where I stood, sunlight filtering through their leaves. A group of guys played basketball, talking smack to each other, and Tristan was in the group.

I snorted. I thought I'd been walking aimlessly. So how, of all places I could wind up in Cape Heron—Fifth Street, my usual beach, the library, the ice cream shop, all within four blocks of our cottage—did I end up here, nearly a mile away from home? Right where Tristan was? Talk about a magnet being pulled . . . .

I told myself I was being ridiculous. I told myself to turn around and go home. To listen to my mother. To trust her sense of truth. But how could our senses be at such odds? Of course, she never said she felt the *truth* about Tristan hurting me. Not so specifically, as she usually did when she was relying on her sixth sense. And I *did* know what my sense told me: his intentions were good.

With that thought, I did what any sensible young woman would do. I hid behind the banyan tree and watched the basketball game.

I quickly realized there was only one other person on Tristan's team and, to my surprise, it was Owen. I shouldn't have been too surprised—this was a retirement town and half of the Cape's young set was probably on that court. Although the teams weren't even, two against five, it was obvious Tristan and Owen were winning. They were good. *Really* good.

I watched for about five minutes and the game ended. When no one on the other team wanted to play another game, Tristan and Owen decided to play each other. Before they started, Tristan took off his shirt and tossed it to the side of the court. *Oh. My!* Naturally, I continued watching.

It said a lot about Tristan's playing ability that it drew my attention away from his chiseled chest and six-pack abs. Now that no one else was around—or so they thought, they still hadn't noticed me—Tristan and Owen really got into the game. They seemed to be trying to one-up each other as they sped up and down the court, now talking smack to each other, and they were even better than they let on while playing the other team. And Tristan was noticeably better than Owen. It was unreal watching him. He was always at the other end of the court faster than seemed possible. His shots often made the ball a blur. And when he jumped . . . how could anyone jump so high or so far? Sometimes Owen did something nearly as incredible.

Owen made a three-pointer and Tristan grabbed the ball

and shot it from under Owen's basket, the one closest to me. I watched with amazement as the ball sailed across the court and swished into the opposite net.

Then they both froze with their backs to me.

The ball bounced toward the side of the court. They ignored it as they turned in my direction, both in a guarded stance. *Oops.* I hadn't realized I'd been creeping closer, watching them in awe, and now I was caught. When they saw me, they both looked like *they'd* been caught doing something wrong.

Tristan was the first to relax. A warm grin lit his face.

"Alexis," he said, walking over to the chain-link fence surrounding the court.

I felt myself relax, too. I had frozen when they had. Since they knew I was there now, I took a few steps closer.

"Hey," I said stupidly.

"What's up?" Owen asked, now at the fence, too.

"Um, nothing. I was just taking a walk and saw you guys playing." I felt like an idiot now, like I'd been caught spying or stalking. *Why had I stayed?*

"Been watching long?" Owen asked. He glanced sideways at Tristan. Something in his tone made me feel even guiltier.

"No, not really."

"Oh, too bad. 'Cause I was just smokin' Tristan here," he said with a laugh, his tone suddenly lighter now.

"Ha! In your dreams, ya scrawny scarecrow," Tristan teased. I couldn't help my smile. Although his sleeveless shirt proved Owen wasn't exactly scrawny, his blond hair stuck out everywhere, so he did look somewhat like a scarecrow.

"C'mon, moose!" Owen ran for the ball and dribbled it between his legs. "We got a game to finish."

"You'll stay?" Tristan asked me.

"I should be heading home. It's a long way back . . . ."

"Please?" He smiled. "You can watch me make hay of the scarecrow."

I laughed. "All right, for a while, I guess."

I sat on a small stand of bleachers and watched as they finished their game. It wasn't nearly as fascinating as it had been earlier; they seemed to be holding back now. By the time Tristan hit forty points, their cut-off, I'd convinced myself of what a fool I'd been, thinking there was even a chance to be more than just friends with him. So I hopped off the bleachers, waved at them and headed for the beach, the quicker way home. As I stepped onto the sand, I glanced over my shoulder. They both walked in the opposite direction, toward the parking lot, confirming my doubts. After all, if he had any interest, wouldn't he have called me back over? *Yep, I'm such a fool.*

"You filthy slut!" a gruff voice snarled, catching my attention.

A man dressed in grease-stained jeans and a t-shirt, a younger woman in a bikini and a small girl, also in a swimsuit, were coming off the beach. His hand gripped the woman's upper arm as he dragged her toward the parking lot. Loaded with a bag and beach chair, she obviously had a hard time keeping his pace. The girl, maybe six or seven, ran after them, stopping frequently to pick up the plastic sand toys she kept dropping.

"Please, honey," the woman begged, "you're hurting me."

"Good! You deserve it. You need to get some damn clothes on."

"But we're at the *beach*."

"Doesn't mean you need to be flauntin' all ya got! You're a married woman!"

I watched the ground as they crossed my path. Though they were in public, I felt like an intruder. I pretended not to notice the squabble as it heated up behind me and picked up my pace to distance myself, but the voices only became louder.

"Shut the hell up, bitch!" the man yelled.

"Daddy, *no!*"

I automatically turned at the girl's scream. The woman lay on the ground, staring wide-eyed at the man, who held his fist in the air as she held her hand over her jaw. The little girl dropped her toys and ran at the man. And as soon as she was within arm's reach of her dad, the woman was suddenly between them, taking another blow.

The anger built inside me as I watched with horror.

"Daddy, stop it!" The little girl tried to grab her dad's thick arm.

"Don't hurt her, Phil," the woman begged from the ground. "Please don't hurt her."

Phil raised his hand again. I don't know who he meant it for, but his intentions didn't matter. As he swung, his daughter threw herself at him, taking the smack in the shoulder. She crumpled to the ground next to her mother.

The anger within me surged to rage. I was madder than I'd even been with James, who'd insulted my mother but hadn't physically hurt an innocent child. Blood pounded in my ears, drowning the rest of the world out except for the girl's sobs. My vision tunneled and everything around us blurred except this man's face. With narrowed eyes and flaring nostrils, he showed no signs of surprise at his own actions or even regret. He looked like he would do it again if either his daughter or wife rose from the ground. And the only thought I had was, *This human debris needs a dose of his own medicine.*

Not even realizing I had moved, I was suddenly in front of him, pulling my fist back. I threw the punch straight at his jaw.

Chapter 5

His black eyes widened with shock. He wasn't a skinny teenage boy, though, and he didn't soar backward as James had done. But he did stagger back several steps with the force. His hand flew to his jaw, cupping it—a mirror image of his wife. Then his eyes darkened even more with his own rage.

I just stood there, frozen in shock at what I'd just done. My chest heaved with panted breaths and my arms hung at my side, my hands still balled into fists. A dull ache throbbed in my knuckles.

"You need a little lesson, young lady," he threatened. The mother and daughter both whimpered.

Oh, crap! Crap, crap, crap! My heart raced. *What the hell was I thinking?!* If I'd been thinking clearly, I would have remembered Mom's self-defense lessons and done something to incapacitate him, like kick him in the groin. But, no, I had been stupid, thinking he would have taken my punch like James had. Or, actually, I hadn't been thinking at all. Fear replaced my anger and any extra strength I had dissipated.

He rolled his head on his neck, as fighters do when they're warming up. Then he stepped toward me. My stomach dropped to the ground. My heart gave up its race and just stopped beating altogether. I took a few clumsy steps backward, tripped over my own feet and fell. Phil advanced again. I instinctively raised my hands. They trembled over my face. *At least it's me now and not them.* I squeezed my eyes shut and waited for it.

I heard a thud, but felt nothing. I peaked between my fingers. Phil was gone. He lay flat on his back on the ground ten yards away, staring up at . . . *Tristan.* A whoosh of air expelled from my lungs.

"I suggest you get out of here *now,*" Owen, now next to Tristan, said to the wife-beater. His words were polite, but his tone was menacing. I never expected Owen to be so threatening.

"You need to mind your own damn business!" the man barked as he sat up.

"*Go!*" Tristan bellowed, his fist in the air, his arms bulging with obvious power.

Phil winced and his face paled under his dark tan. He scrambled to his feet and moved toward his wife. Tristan stepped between them.

"*NOW!*" he roared.

Phil bolted for the parking lot. Tristan followed, his fists clenched. I sat there, shaking uncontrollably, wondering what he would do. I didn't want to watch, but I couldn't make myself turn away yet. The mom and daughter watched Tristan, too, their tear-filled eyes wide with fear.

"Tristan, let him go!" Owen called after him. Tristan took a couple more steps, then stopped. Phil jumped into an orange, older model Camaro and peeled out. Owen rushed to me first. "You okay?"

I blew out the breath I'd been holding.

"I'm fine." I nodded at Tristan. "Is he?"

"I don't know." Owen walked toward Tristan as he headed back to us and they both stopped within a few feet of each other.

"Did he hurt her?" Tristan demanded.

"Alexis is fine. Are you?"

Tristan nodded. "What about the other two?"

They started back toward us. I crawled over to the little girl.

"Are you okay?" I asked.

She sobbed as she held her shoulder. The mother shook her head, dark strands sticking in the tears flowing down her bruising cheek.

"We need to go home," she whispered.

"You can't go home!" I gasped. "Won't he be there?"

"Not yet. He'll come later. But the longer we're gone, the worse it'll be," she explained.

"Then don't go!"

"You don't understand . . . ."

She was right. I had no clue why she would want to go home to the bastard.

"Is there anywhere else you can go? We can take you somewhere."

The woman didn't answer me, but stood up and brushed herself off. She pulled a pair of cut-off shorts and a t-shirt out of her beach bag and put them on. She held out a sundress to her daughter, who slowly rose to her feet, wincing as she put weight on her left foot. The mother then pulled keys out of her bag and shook them.

"We'll go to my sister's," she said. She tried a smile. It looked forced. "I drove us here. I can get us to her house."

"Isn't there something we can do for you?" Tristan asked.

She bit her lip and blinked rapidly, holding back more tears. She answered quietly, "I think you've done enough."

She turned and headed toward her car. Her daughter tried to follow, limping and still holding her shoulder. Tristan gently scooped her up and he and Owen followed her mom to a blue Ford coupe as I just stood there, watching. Disbelieving what just happened.

This was so not good. I'd let my rage get the better of me again. Last time, that meant an immediate move. And I wasn't ready to move again. I liked it here.

But this time was different. I may have looked stupid, trying to take on a full-grown, stout man, but at least he hadn't flown back from my punch. At least I hadn't looked freakishly strong. The coward he was, Phil would never admit that a small, young woman had nearly taken him down. But his wife . . . would she tell anyone? Probably not, but only, sadly, because she feared her own husband.

So that left Owen and Tristan. What had they seen? They'd been worried about me, more than the others. Did all they see was Phil threatening me? Did they not witness what I'd done to him? Could I be so lucky?

Tristan set the little girl down in the passenger seat of her mom's car, then he and Owen watched as they left, Tristan taking a few steps forward, as if he wanted to follow them. I thought about sneaking off, down the beach, but Owen turned to me right then and waved me over. I needed to find out exactly what they saw anyway. Because if it was anything worth mentioning—even if he just thought it stupid or brave—Owen would probably tell Mom everything.

"She'll go back to him," Tristan muttered as I walked up.

"Seriously?" I asked.

"Probably," Owen said. "But we've done all we can."

"No, we haven't," Tristan grumbled, that steely undertone in his voice.

"Tristan . . . leave it alone," Owen warned, eyeing him carefully. "Maybe you should go. I'll take Alexis home."

Tristan spun around. "I'll take her."

Owen shook his head. "That's not a good idea. Sophia—"

"Sophia can deal with it!" Tristan barked, apparently not over his anger. I cringed and his eyes flew to me.

It was very fast and I could have imagined it, but for half a second I thought I saw what Carlie might have been talking about. The sparkles of gold in his eyes looked different, more like sparks of fire. His eyes looked . . . *frightening*. Maybe everyone else had been right. I waited for the nudge to return. Or even for the alarms. But nothing happened.

He must have seen something in my own eyes, though. His face immediately softened and his body relaxed. What anger he might have had just a second earlier—whether at the wife-beater or at my mom, I wasn't sure—didn't show in his eyes as he studied my face.

"Are you sure you're okay?" he asked, his voice returning to its smooth and silky self. Again, he was worried about me, as if I'd been the one punched.

I forced a small smile and went with it. "Yeah, I'm fine. Just a little scared. Are you sure *you* are?"

The gold flecks sparkled now as he smiled slowly. He nodded. "If you are, I am."

I turned to Owen and wished I could read his mind, hear his thoughts. If he saw what I'd done and took me home, he might make a big deal of it with Mom. Of course, if I let Tristan take me home, Owen could always call her and I wouldn't know until I faced her. It didn't matter. He worked for her. If he had anything to tell her, he'd have plenty of opportunity to do it any time. And if I had to choose who to take me home . . .

"Thanks for the offer, Owen," I said, "but Tristan can take me. I'll handle Sophia."

Owen narrowed his eyes as they bounced between Tristan and me.

"I'm gonna lose my job," he said with a sigh.

"No, you won't," I promised. "It's not exactly in your job description to be worried about how I get home."

He muttered something under his breath. Tristan smiled slightly, as if he'd heard.

"You're sure?" Owen asked me as he turned for his car.

"I'm positive. Sophia will get over it. Besides . . . it's not like she's my *mother*." So, that wasn't exactly true, but they didn't know.

Owen snorted, jogged to his car and left.

I looked up at Tristan. "You really don't mind?"

The corners of his mouth twitched. "A little late to be asking, don't you think?"

"So . . . you do mind? You need to be somewhere else? I can walk . . . ."

After all that happened, I really didn't want to walk all the way home by myself now. But I would if I had to.

He chuckled. "I said I'd take you home."

He put his thumb under my chin and tilted my face up toward his. That strange current pulsed through my jaw and up to my temples. He gazed into my eyes, creating a slow burn in my belly.

"There's nowhere I'd rather be," he murmured. The burn bloomed into a fire within. He smiled before letting go. "Ever been on a bike before?"

I followed him to the motorcycle, pleased it wasn't the crotch-rocket he usually rode to campus. The Harley came to life with its distinctive rumble. I climbed on and looked around for something to hold onto and found chrome handholds on each side of the seat. He looked over his shoulder at me and glanced down at my hands. He probably expected me to hold onto him. Part of me wanted to, but that was a closeness I wasn't quite ready for.

"Ready?" he asked.

I nodded.

It would have been a lot less tense if I *had* held onto him, because it couldn't have been more unnerving with that small space between us. As the bike rumbled under us through the streets of the Cape, arcs of electricity jumped between us. I felt woozy by the time we pulled in front of the cottage and not from the vibration of the motorcycle.

"That was . . . different," he muttered after shutting off the engine.

Mom's car was already in the driveway. I hoped she would stay inside and mind her own business.

"Thank you," I said as Tristan and I stood in the driveway. "For everything, I mean."

He smiled, but it didn't reach his eyes. "Did I scare you?"

"Um, no," I lied.

"I'm sorry. I was a little pissed off."

Yeah, me, too. I smiled to show him it was okay.

"What were you thinking anyway?" he asked.

Son of a witch. He *had* seen it all. And now he'd want an explanation. At least he wasn't staring at me like some kind of mutant. At least he was even here, in my driveway—he hadn't left me at the park, so he couldn't be too freaked out.

"You looked like you wanted to *hit* him or something," he added.

I blew out a breath, fighting the urge to whoop with relief. *Okay, he didn't see everything.* He and Owen must have turned just in time to see Phil advancing on me, maybe just before I fell, when my hand was still fisted.

"I don't know." I cleared my throat and, again, went with

it. "It made me so mad to see him hurt them. I just wanted to stop him and it worked, I guess. For now, anyway." I sighed at the thought that I'd probably made things even worse for the woman and her daughter. I'd been so stupid. "I'm just glad you got there when you did."

"Me, too." He looked into my eyes and I saw something unreadable in his. *Concern?* It was still there when he changed the subject. "So, what was with you today? I tried to catch up with you when the team was done, but you took off like you were escaping. You seemed lost in thought all afternoon."

The team meeting felt so long ago now, it took me a moment to realize what he meant. Of course, he'd noticed. He usually walked me to my car and I hadn't even thought about it. "Yeah, I guess I was . . . lost in thought. Sorry if I was rude."

When I looked up at him, he seemed to search my eyes for an explanation. I didn't give one. I couldn't tell him about Mom or Carlie's opinions.

He held my eyes as he lifted his hand to my face and stroked a current across my cheek. A shudder tried to work its way down my spine, but I fought it back.

"You'll make it up to me," he said with a smile.

"I can do that," I promised with my own smile.

And with perfect timing, the cottage's front door opened.

"Alexis!" Mom said sharply.

I didn't take my eyes off Tristan to look at her. I *couldn't* take my eyes off him. He held them, trapped within his gaze.

"Get in the house," Mom demanded. "I need to talk to you."

Of course you want to talk now.

I sighed and finally pulled my eyes away from the beautiful hazel ones.

"I better go," I muttered.

"See you later, *ma lykita*," he said quietly.

I raised an eyebrow. He smiled and shook his head. Mom cleared her throat from the door. I sighed with frustration.

I gave Tristan an apologetic smile and then marched into the house. I spun on her, ready to tell her how much her timing sucked when I noticed the suitcase by the door. My eyes stung with the reality. Owen must have called her. This was what she had to talk to me about.

"We have to *move?*" I said. "But I—"

Her brows furrowed and then her face softened, as did her voice. "Oh, no, honey. I'm sorry. I'm just going out of town for a couple days."

Whew. So Owen hadn't said anything and, unless she became aware of something, she had no reason to feel for the truth.

"I . . . have a book sellers' convention to go to. You know, my first holiday season coming up, I need to make sure I know everything I should be doing." She spoke a little too quickly and wouldn't look directly at me. She was lying but I didn't know why. "Owen said he can come in at one tomorrow and close up, if you can open the store and stay until then. Of course, we're closed Sunday and I'll be back Sunday night."

"No problem," I muttered.

She searched my face for a long moment. "Do me a favor, please? Keep your distance from Tristan at least until I get back? We can talk about it then, okay?"

I shrugged. I hadn't really planned on seeing him anyway. I never saw him on the weekends.

"Please? Promise?" She nodded her head, part of her persuasion technique. Next, she would reach out to touch my hand or arm.

I glowered at her, refusing to let her get to me. "No, Mom, I won't promise. It probably won't matter, but I won't make any promises I don't *want* to keep."

Her eyes hardened as she studied my face. She didn't even try her next move.

"Fine," she snapped. "I'll see you Sunday night."

She grabbed her suitcase and I headed for the kitchen. I heard the front door open and, almost in a whisper, she said, "I love you."

I sighed. "I love you, too."

I turned around, but the door was already closed. I didn't know if she heard me.

I walked over to the front window in the living room to watch her through the blinds, guilt filling my heart because she'd left on such a sour note. To my astonishment, Tristan was still there, leaning against Mom's car as she dropped her suitcase in the trunk. *Why hadn't he left? Is* he *going to bust me?* Perhaps Owen wasn't the one I should have been worried about. I sat on the floor, my back to the wall next to the open window so they couldn't see me, but it meant I couldn't watch them. I could only listen. And my worries were way off base.

"Stay away from her, Tristan," Mom ordered. "She's not ready yet."

"You mean *you're* not ready yet."

"That, too."

"It's out of your hands, Sophia."

"We'll see about that." A second of silence.

"You're going to see them, aren't you?"

Mom answered with her own question. "When was the last time you saw *your* . . . kin?"

"I've never gone back and I never will." Complete sureness in his voice.

"And you expect me to trust *you?*"

Tristan sighed. "You have to, don't you?"

"Why should I? She's my *daughter,* for heaven's sake." *Oh!*

She just blew our cover! My breath caught and my hand flew to my mouth, afraid they'd heard.

"It's time to let go, Sophia. I think she'll be okay."

"You *think*? I need more than that, Tristan. I need one-hundred-percent surety!"

More silence. When Tristan spoke, his voice was low and grim. "You know I can't give you that."

"*Exactly.*" Her icy tone sent a chill up my spine. Her car door slammed and the engine started. She peeled out of the driveway and a minute later the motorcycle fired up and rumbled away.

I threw myself across the couch and stared at the ceiling. *What the hell just happened?* I'd been so worried about the incident in the park and this was even crazier. Mom and Tristan apparently knew each other. Well enough that Tristan knew where Mom was really going and Mom believed she couldn't trust him with me. *What is going on with them?*

I mentally played back the conversation several times, trying to figure it out. Then realization dawned on me. Mom had mentioned his kin—she must have dated his father or brother or other relative.

She'd had many boyfriends over the years and it always ended badly. She never explained what happened with most of them, whom she seemed to love one day and couldn't get away from fast enough the next. We moved immediately after every break-up. I could only figure she was unable to love a man and let him love her, because they were usually good men, according to my sense. *Except for Lenny . . . .*

My mind flashed the memory of Mom throwing Lenny across the room, his body hitting the wall with a thud, blood smears on the white paint as his limp form slid to the floor. Two minutes before, he'd tried to kiss me. I was twelve. "Don't worry, he's not dead," she had said once we were in the car, driving to a new city. I shuddered at the memory. He was seedy and vile and, if they were related, it would explain her reaction to seeing Tristan. It would also explain his non-reaction when Mom said I was her daughter.

But why did they hide this from me? Why all the secrets?

The phone's ringing startled me out of my thoughts and I blinked in the near darkness that filled the room—I'd lain there long enough for the sun to move to the west side of the house. I searched blindly for the phone on the end table.

"Hello?" My voice sounded rough, thick from the big lump in my throat.

"Is it safe?" Tristan's lovely voice. "From Sophia, I mean."

I didn't know what to say at first and briefly considered lying, but there was no point. After all, I hid just as much as he did, probably more. Besides, if my theory was correct, it wasn't fair for us to hold Lenny or anyone else against him. And whatever Mom was so concerned about, it couldn't be too bad—she'd made it clear to him she was leaving me home alone.

"Yeah. Actually, she's gone for the weekend."

"Ah." The line fell silent for a moment, then, "Would you like to go to the beach with me? The sun will be setting soon."

Such a banal question. He wasn't asking me to go clubbing or jump in bed with him. He asked me to go to the beach and watch the sun set. So insipid it was almost cliché.

But, for me, it was the question of my life. At least to this point of it. Tristan had asked me out. *Asked me out!* Well, sort of. Close enough. It was certainly a step in a new direction from hanging out on campus and running into each other around town.

My answer could literally be life-changing. Mom had just asked me not to see him until she returned and we could discuss it. Going out with Tristan, even just to the beach, meant once again disobeying her. This was beyond some teenaged rebellious stage, though. Just like my fruitless research project, this was about growing up. Making my own decisions for *me* and *my* life. Being an adult. My answer had to be *mine*, not my mother's.

Saying "yes," however, could be my biggest mistake ever. Perhaps he was dangerous, as Carlie had said. Perhaps he would hurt me, as Mom had warned. Taking this next step with him was opening my heart up—just a tiny bit, but more than I had since James had caused me to seal it shut. And if he did hurt me, I'd have no one to blame but myself.

But rejecting him likely meant losing any chance with him whatsoever. Missing out on something that could be truly amazing. Always wondering what might have happened. And going back to living in solitude and having to watch him from a distance as he moved on to the next girl. That thought bothered me, more than it should.

I could either walk through this door that he'd opened or I could shut it forever. Either way was a risk. But taking such risks, making such decisions was part of being an adult. Sometimes being an adult sucks.

Chapter 6

"Alexis?" Tristan asked, still waiting for my answer.

I swallowed, my throat dry and sticky. Then I made my decision—I followed my heart and gut, hoping I wasn't about to do irreversible harm to my relationship with Mom. Or about to destroy myself.

"Um, yeah. That'd be great."

"I'll be there in five minutes." I could hear the smile in his voice.

Not able to sit still, I waited outside, pacing the driveway. I heard the Harley from more than a block away and butterflies fluttered in my stomach by the time Tristan arrived.

"Ride or walk?" he asked over the rumble after pulling into the driveway.

"Let's walk."

Our cottage was less than two blocks to the beach, the street covered with the broad canopies of the many-legged banyan trees that were larger than the Old Florida-style cottages they guarded. It was a gorgeous evening, the warmth of the afternoon still hanging in the air. We walked in silence the entire way.

I tried to ignore all the questions soaring through my mind, because they all had to do with a conversation I probably wasn't supposed to hear. I wished I had the chutzpah to just flat out ask him who he was and what happened between him and my mother. But I didn't. Besides, I'd realized this afternoon, there were two problems with seeking the answers to my questions.

One, it would likely lead to me being on the other end—the one answering questions instead of asking. If I wanted to know more about Tristan, then I had to be prepared for him to know more about me. And I wasn't ready for that yet. At least, not the deep stuff. He already knew too much—one of my biggest secrets—Sophia was my mother. Surely he had to have his own questions about how that could be, which leads to the second problem. Two, getting into the deeper conversation about all of our secrets meant giving up any kind of normalcy to our relationship—or whatever it became. And I wasn't ready for that, either.

I was probably lying to myself, trying to make it all more than it could ever be. But, for now, I wanted to at least pretend this was a normal girl-meets-boy situation.

"Penny for your thoughts?" Tristan asked, breaking the silence as we crossed the boardwalk accessing the beach.

"Hmph. They're worth more than that," I teased.

He chuckled. "Okay, a Benji for your thoughts?"

"Huh?"

He pulled a one-hundred-dollar bill from his pocket. I raised my eyebrows and he put it away, laughing. "You're right. *Your* thoughts are priceless."

We walked to the edge of the water, kicked off our shoes, and then turned and meandered along the wet sand. It gave me a chance to edit my thoughts before sharing them.

"I wouldn't go *that* far," I finally said, "but . . . I was just thinking that we've been hanging out for a couple months now, and I hardly know anything about you."

"Ah. What do you want to know?" He peered down at me from the corner of his eye, seemingly hesitant—like I felt when someone asked about me.

"Um, well, where are you from?" That was an easy one, especially in Florida. Hardly anyone was *from* here.

He was silent for a moment, as if it was difficult to answer, and then said cryptically, "Lots of places . . . nowhere in particular."

I could relate to that. It could be my own answer.

"So . . . you moved around a lot?"

He shrugged. "You could put it that way."

"What do your parents do?"

"They don't do anything. They died a long time ago."

"Oh." *Oops.* I didn't know I was headed into heavy stuff. "I'm sorry."

He looked down at me and smiled gently. "You didn't know. I hardly remember them anyway. It was a long time ago. I was raised by . . . distant relatives, I guess you could say."

"Did they bring you here?"

"Oh, no, I came here alone." There was that steely undertone again. "I've been on my own for quite a while."

More silence as I thought for a minute. I remembered what he'd told Mom . . . he'd never gone back and he never will. How awful it must be to lose his parents and then to have to live with what must have been dreadful relatives, people like Lenny. My theory must have been true. I decided to leave that subject alone.

"So where were these 'lots of places' you grew up?"

"Pretty much everywhere, but mostly Europe."

"*Really?*" That one surprised me. "But you don't have any kind of accent."

He chuckled.

"I've been in the U.S. for a few years and I adapt easily and pick up the local accent quickly." He changed his tone and spoke with a perfect English cadence, "Would you *rahther* I *hahd* an *ahccent?*" Then he switched to French, rolling the R's, "Or, pear'aps Francais eez better, *ma lykita?*"

I laughed. Although I couldn't understand it all, the French accent was especially delightful with his lovely voice.

"Do you speak other languages, then?"

"Seven altogether."

"Wow," I breathed with awe. I tried to imagine growing up in Europe, living as transient a life as we had, but in places such as London, Rome and Paris. I probably glamorized it, but it seemed much more exciting than my life.

"If you came here by yourself, what brought you here?"

He didn't answer at first and kicked at a wave. Then he shrugged and said, "Just needed a change."

"Oh." That was a non-answer.

He looked down at me. "Actually, I want to be honest with you. I came here for a job . . . or an assignment is more like it . . . and stayed because I like the people."

"Oh, okay." I hadn't realized he had a job. I started wondering what he did besides a couple college classes. He had mentioned once he had lots of other things going on in his life, but he never talked about anything.

"But if I told you any more, I'd have to kill you." His tone was serious and I looked up in surprise. He laughed.

"Oh, I see. CIA or FBI?" I played along, remembering the old secret-agent movies Mom liked to watch. "Oh, wait, probably Scotland Yard. Or maybe the KGB?" I widened my eyes in mock horror.

He laughed again. "You're way off."

"I'll figure it out," I promised lightheartedly.

He frowned and his tone darkened. "Yes, I'm sure you will. Some day."

"Would that be bad?"

The frown quickly disappeared, as if he hadn't realized it was there until I said that. He peered down at me as we walked a few steps in silence. "I don't know yet."

Honesty and seriousness filled his tone . . . and a bit of sadness. I sighed in frustration. He raised more questions than he answered.

"Something wrong?" he asked.

I wanted to tell him how annoyingly cryptic he was. But I didn't. Because he could always turn that back at me.

"No, I guess not."

"We better turn around," he said.

I looked behind us and saw we had walked much farther than I realized. We played in the water on the way back, kicking it up at each other and running away from the splashes, then he took my hand and pulled me to dry sand, where we sat to watch the sunset. We gazed in silence, both in the same position— knees pulled up, arms wrapped around our legs. I rested my chin on my knees.

God displayed His divine artistic ability, painting the sky with brushstrokes of dark violet, lavender, magenta and soft pink against a light blue canvas, with a bright splash of gold at the horizon reflecting on the water. Waves gently lapped at the sand and seagulls cawed at each other. I inhaled deeply, trying to pull it all into my body and embed it in my memory as one of those perfect moments to be cherished forever. The brackishness of salt water and the sweet-tanginess of Tristan's scent nearly intoxicated me.

I turned and Tristan cocked his head to look at me, his

beautiful eyes sparkling, immediately calming me. In fact, I'd never felt so content. His conversation with my mom seemed vague and nonsensical now. He was right. She needed to let go. Because I wanted to be nowhere else than right here with him.

"Ready?" he finally asked.

I frowned. *Ready to go back to my empty house and spend the evening alone? No, not really.*

"I can hang out with you, if you want," he said, as if reading my mind.

"That sounds . . ." *Wonderful. Fabulous. Perfect.* ". . . good."

As soon as we entered the cottage, I panicked. I hadn't been truly alone with anyone besides my mother in years. I suddenly realized just how inexperienced I was—not just in the whole man-woman thing, but in any kind of relationship. I stopped abruptly in the small foyer, not knowing what to do in my own house.

"I'll be right back." I dashed into the bathroom and couldn't close the door fast enough. I leaned against the back of the door and took deep, calming breaths. My stomach twisted itself into knots, untwisted and twisted again. *What do we do? Eat? Watch TV? What if he's bored? Oh! What if he's expecting something? How much would I give?!* I jumped at the knock on the door.

"Alexis?" Concern filled Tristan's voice. I could only imagine how terrified my face looked before I fled to the bathroom. "I was thinking . . . I'm actually kind of hungry. You want to go get a pizza at Mario's?"

I took a deep breath, picturing it. *Public place. Lots of people.* He seemed to know exactly what I needed. After another deep, cleansing breath, I opened the door and said, more calmly than I thought possible, "That'd be great."

Mario's was a pizza-parlor-slash-bar. When we arrived at nearly nine o'clock, it took on more of a bar atmosphere. The lights were dimmed and neon beer signs glowed colorfully on the walls. The jukebox played oldies music and people talked and laughed loudly over it. We shared a sausage-and-mushroom pizza and, after eating, Tristan somehow convinced me to play darts.

He was excellent at it. I sucked. He seemed to be able to easily zero in on his target—several times I swore he aimed away from the bulls-eye to prove he could "miss." Most of the time I couldn't hit the board, let alone any specific place on it.

Tristan's close eye on me didn't help. He leaned against a table about halfway to the dart board and to my right, watching me with an amused expression. He made me nervous. I held the dart in my hand, up near my face, eyeing the board—no particular place, just the board in general. *It's a big enough area. Surely I can hit it at least once.* Just before I let the dart go, my eyes slipped to Tristan.

And the dart flew. And missed the board. By a long shot.

"Oh, oh, *oh*!" Both hands flew to my mouth. *Holy crap! I stabbed Mr. Beautiful!*

I stared at the dart lodged in his bicep. He raised his eyebrows with an I-can't-believe-you-just-did-that look as I hurried over to him. "I'm so *sorry*! Are you okay?"

He grimaced. "I don't know."

I lifted my hand gingerly to pull the dart out. He flinched and I jumped back.

"Don't touch it! Aren't you supposed to leave these things for the doctor to remove?"

I fretfully bounced on the balls of my feet. "Then what do I *do*?"

The grimace disappeared and a huge grin spread across Tristan's face as he easily plucked the dart out of his arm. He leaned forward and whispered, "You can kiss it and make it better."

I narrowed my eyes and scowled at him. He burst into laughter.

"I'm . . . sorry . . . but . . . you . . . should've . . . seen . . . .your face!" He nearly fell over from his belly laughs.

I crossed my arms against my chest and glowered at him. I couldn't hold it for long, though. He was laughing so hard and he was so dang irresistible. I couldn't help it. I started laughing, too.

"I am seriously sorry," I said again once we regained our composure. "I can't believe I did that. Are you really okay?"

He lifted his sleeve. The only evidence of my assault was a miniscule hole, though I was sure the steel-tipped dart had pierced at least half an inch, maybe more, through his skin. I exhaled with relief, expecting it to be worse.

"I think I'll live," he said, grinning. "But you *are* rather dangerous. Let me show you how it's done before you really hurt someone."

He stood close behind me and tried to teach me the proper way to hold the dart and when to let it go, but the electricity from every touch distracted me. We laughed at my absurd technique. I had more fun than I'd had in a long time—maybe ever.

When he slid the bike into the driveway a little after midnight, though, the panic started to set in again. Not like earlier, but enough to make my stomach flutter.

"Did you have fun?" Tristan asked as he walked me to the door.

"Yeah, I did. Thank you." I watched the ground.

"My pleasure. Maybe we can do it again sometime?"

I took a breath to steady my nerves and looked up at him as we stood on the front porch. "Hmm . . . you're brave."

He chuckled. "I'll just be sure to stand behind you next time."

"You saw my throws. That doesn't guarantee anything."

"Yeah, you're right." He smiled. "But I'll take my chances."

My heart raced as I looked into his sparkling eyes and wondered if he was thinking about kissing me.

"I better let you get some rest," he murmured.

"Mmm, yeah. I do have to open the store in the morning."

He held my gaze for a moment and then cupped his hand gently around the side of my face. My skin tingled. Then he leaned over and ever so lightly brushed his lips across my cheek, then whispered in my ear, "Good night, *ma lykita.*"

I closed my eyes as the sensations washed over me—his smell, the warm breath on my ear, the electric touch on my face.

"'Night," I breathed. He let go of me and when I opened my eyes, he was already half-way down the walk. Electricity still pulsed on my skin and throughout my body. Part of me wanted to call him back, but, with a heavy sigh, I turned and went inside instead. And I realized I didn't get to ask what he called me. It couldn't be bad, but it was annoying not to know. It had sounded like something in French. I made a mental note to research it.

The two-bedroom cottage was quiet and usually comforting. It was one of the few places we lived that actually felt like home. Usually, our moves required leaving everything behind except the bare necessities, but since we actually brought our belongings this time, they were at least familiar, if not nostalgic. Mom decorated in browns and beiges, but with leather and wood furniture and chenille and silk throw pillows, the variety of textures kept it from being boring. Rather, it was cozy and calming, like "Mom's place" should be.

I was scared to death to be here alone.

I paced the cottage several times, mentally going through self-defense motions. Being alone at night for the first time ever—Mom had never left me before—brought renewed fear. Not fear of those *others*, who couldn't possibly exist. Time and distance had caused that memory to fade to the point where I doubted any of it actually happened. I felt foolish now for being so afraid of a dream. But the wife-beater, on the other hand . . . what if he sought revenge?

I whirled on a whispered sound, my heart hammering. It stopped when I did. Then I realized it was only my own feet sliding across the tile floor.

Feeling the emotional tolls of the day, I finally talked myself into going to bed. But while lying in my bedroom, my eyes wouldn't shut and my ears strained, my mind imagining various monstrosities lurking in the rest of the house. Eventually I curled up on the couch with all the lights on, and, somehow, sleep overcame me. I awoke several times, thinking I heard something outside, but when I listened, all was quiet and I fell back to sleep.

Chapter 7

The store felt empty and ominous when I first arrived, but I came early to have a little extra time before opening. Mom kept a small office in the back room and I thought she might be more likely to hide something there than at home, where I might find it. I tugged on all the drawers of her desk and filing cabinet, but, of course, they didn't budge, locked against intruders . . . and snoopers like me. There were no loose papers on her desk and only one large, flat envelope in her inbox. She was annoyingly organized.

I glanced at the single piece of mail and my eye caught on the corner where the return address should be. Instead of an address, though, there was a strange, yet vaguely familiar symbol and the word "Amadis" embossed into the paper. I picked the envelope up and studied it closer, holding it to the light, but I couldn't read anything inside. I briefly debated whether I could get away with opening it and resealing it, but eventually just dropped it back into the tray. It was probably from a publisher and I had seen the symbol on a book's spine. Or, for all I knew, it was just junk mail, not worth the risk.

Curiosity gripped me all morning. I impatiently waited for Owen to relieve me of my duties, only taking the time to answer his questions of how I was after yesterday to confirm he hadn't seen me punch Phil. Then I hurried home to search Mom's room. I didn't expect to find anything I hadn't already discovered while unpacking, but there was something right on her nightstand. A lone piece of paper with that strange word "Amadis" printed at the top. The paper contained a list of names with numbers next to them. Some were obviously phone numbers; others had the wrong number of digits and I didn't know what they meant.

Two names stood out: Katerina and Stefan. Katerina because it was my middle name. *Does the name on this paper mean anything?* The number next to it wasn't a phone number. I wasn't sure why Stefan struck me. The name felt familiar, but I couldn't place it.

A sticky note with Mom's handwriting clung to the bottom corner of the page:

> Alexis,
> This is for emergency use only. If Owen can't help, call these people until you reach one. They will know what to do. If this is not an emergency, though, you put us at risk. SO STOP SNOOPING!
> Love, Mom

I chuckled. She knew I'd be prying. I put the paper back and lay on her bed, thinking. What did Amadis mean? Who were the people on the list? Did she actually go to see one of them this weekend? And how would I be putting us at risk? That last question made me anxious. I knew Mom well enough to know she wouldn't joke about this. *Is just calling them risky? Or is all of my research?* I sighed. Regardless of the answers, my research and snooping only led to more unanswered questions.

I tried to study, but my mind drifted in various directions, eventually toward Tristan. I didn't know when I'd see him again and as the afternoon wore on and evening encroached, I really didn't want to be alone. As if in response to my thoughts, the sound of a motorcycle resonated right outside the cottage. I sprang to the window and my breath caught.

Tristan still sat on the metallic-blue crotch-rocket, looking like a dream. He ran his hand through his wind-blown, sandy-brown hair, slightly taming the wild look. His muscles strained against his just-tight-enough t-shirt, tucked into faded jeans cinched at the waist with a black belt. He slowly pulled the dark sunglasses off and studied the cottage, his eyes sparkling brightly. I almost expected to see cameras—he looked like a model in a photo shoot. *Is he really here for* me?

He swung his leg over the bike. I beat him to the door.

"Guess I can't sneak up on you," he said, smiling.

"I seem to be specially tuned to the sound of motorcycles."

He chuckled. I hoped he understood my innuendo.

"So, I have these exams to study for and I thought it wouldn't suck so bad if I was sitting on the beach," he said, then added with a smile, "and if you were there, too."

My stomach quivered. "Just give me a sec, okay?"

I hurried inside, threw my books into my bag and grabbed a beach blanket. Tristan took my bag from me and we walked again, but not in silence this time. We talked about how boring the day had been for each of us so far and how we'd both been procrastinating on studying.

Once on the beach, we spread the blanket out on the sand and then spread our women's studies books out on the blanket. We read in silence, stopping now and then to ask each other a question or make a comment. More than once we discussed the differences in how each gender thinks. He didn't act superior at all and seemed genuinely interested in learning the thought patterns of females . . . well, at least mine.

"Of course, I'm not exactly your typical girl, so take it for what it's worth," I said. I packed up my books and stretched out on my back, staring at the white wisps overhead. My brain couldn't take another minute of studying and the sun was low in the sky anyway, hovering just over the horizon, like a timid swimmer not quite ready to make the plunge.

Tristan packed his things, too, and tossed his backpack to a corner of the blanket. He lay on his side, facing me.

"I think it's worth a lot," he said. "And I'm glad you're not the typical girl."

He picked up my hand and turned it over, then traced the lines on my palm with his finger, having crossed that no-touch boundary last night. I continued staring at the sky, the cloud wisps turning a peachy-gold color against a deepening blue background. I tried to control my breathing as the electricity radiated up my arm, wondering what caused it. Was it just because his touch was new? *Or just so dang thrilling . . . ?*

I wondered what he would think when he eventually found out just how atypical I was. It was just a matter of time— one small cut on the finger was usually all it took. Of course, I reminded myself, he already knew more than he should, seemingly more than I even knew. Because I knew so little.

"What are you thinking?" he asked quietly. I turned my head to look at him. He watched his fingers on my hand, now moving them along my wrist and inner arm, light as a feather. I fought the natural urge to pull back from the tickle.

"About how you know more about me than I do about you," I said honestly.

"Ah. But you're wrong. I know so little about you. You don't share much. I can't even tell how you're feeling most of the time."

Good. I'm doing my job then. The wall's still holding. But I frowned because I really didn't want to push him away. "Tell me what you want to know and maybe I'll give you an answer."

"See what I mean?" He raised his eyes to mine and they looked hurt, making my heart squeeze with sadness. He must have seen it in my own eyes. "I'm sorry. I'll give you space and you can share when you feel comfortable. I won't push you."

"Thank you," I whispered.

He sat up and tugged on my hand, pulling me up, too. "Let's just watch the sun set."

He pulled me between his legs, my back against him. I drew my knees up and he curled his body around my back, his chin resting on my shoulder, his face right next to mine. His tangy-sweet breath made my head buzz pleasantly. He draped his arms around my shoulders and held my hands in each of his, entwining our fingers. That strange electric current flowed around and between us as we gazed out over the water, completely silent except for our hearts. I could feel both racing. I was grateful the beach had nearly emptied by then.

"Lovely," he breathed in my ear.

"Yes, it is," I whispered, afraid anything louder would blow the moment away.

"I didn't mean the sunset," he murmured, his lips close enough to my cheek to tickle.

He let go of my left hand and slid the back of his fingers along my jaw from my chin to my ear. I fought a shudder and turned toward him so I could look into his beautiful face. The emerald green of his eyes shone brightly and the gold flecks danced in the reflection of the setting sun. His lips pulled into a small but tantalizing smile. And I knew then what was coming. My heart flipped erratically.

His hand cupped around my face and he gently pulled it up to his. He hesitated, still gazing intently into my eyes, his face less than an inch from mine, our noses nearly touching. The rest of the world disappeared as his eyes held mine. The sounds of the waves and the seagulls faded out so all I heard was my heart pounding and his thumb lightly brushing against my cheek. He must have heard my heart whirring like a hummingbird's wings. He smiled and held his other hand to my chest as if to quiet it. The usual calming effect he had on me didn't work. It sped even faster.

He leaned in slightly and his lips barely touched mine.

A spark jumped between us and we both flinched.

Then we moved into each other and let the electricity fly. He pressed his lips against mine, soft and full, moving tenderly but longingly. I opened my mouth slightly and tasted his delicious scent and breath on my tongue. I moved my lips with his, the electricity charging through my body and warming places that had never been so warm before. My heart stopped and I forgot how to breathe. We both finally pulled back to catch our breaths.

"Can you tell what I'm feeling now?" I whispered breathlessly.

"I'm not sure." He smiled and his eyes sparkled brightly. "Let me try again."

He held the back of my head gently in his hand and I placed my hands on the sides of his face and closed my eyes as he kissed me a second time. The world faded out again. Nothing else mattered. Nothing else even existed but Tristan and me. My fingers slid into his hair and I pulled him into me, desire rising in my chest as the tip of his tongue lightly traced my bottom lip. I leaned into him, nearly giving in to the sudden and ridiculous urge to climb up and attack him. *Losing control!* I forgot to breathe again and finally had to pull away.

I looked into his eyes and froze.

The gold sparks in Tristan's eyes had turned to flames and for just an instant—not even a second—he actually looked more than just dangerous but . . . *murderous*. Then the flames disappeared and his eyes filled with pain. In one swift motion, he closed them and turned his head away from me. There was something wrong—I hadn't imagined it—something going on in his head. But the frightening look in his eyes was gone so quickly, I didn't know exactly what I saw, except for the sadness that followed.

I dropped my hands into my lap and leaned against him. I could hear his heart pounding hard against his ribs and I wished I could do something for him. I tried to slow my own heart and breathing, tried to regain control, and his breathing told me he was doing the same. His arms held me tightly, as if he was afraid to let go. We sat completely still until most of the sky turned dark blue. We lay back down on the blanket, his arms still around me, and we stared silently at the stars as they blinked to life one at a time.

Then both of our stomachs growled, ruining everything. We laughed, sat up and started gathering our things. He seemed to have recovered from whatever thought or memory had hurt him so much. I wondered if he'd ever tell me about it, but I didn't dare ask now. I wasn't sure I wanted to know.

We cooked dinner together at the cottage. I taught myself to cook, with the help of Emeril and Martha, and quite enjoyed it, but it had never been so much fun as it was with Tristan. I had to stop to admire his perfectly sliced peppers and onions. Every piece was exactly the same size and he had done it so quickly. I was impressed—and intimidated. He cut the prep time in half and it wasn't long before we sat down to chicken fajitas.

After cleaning up, we watched a movie. He laughed at the choices I offered, my favorites—*Interview with the Vampire, Lost Boys, Willow* and *The Princess Bride.*

"You seem to have a thing for vampires and magic."

"Yeah, actually I do," I admitted with a small smile.

"Really? You like that fantasy stuff?" He seemed surprised.

"The lore fascinates me. You know . . . how it got started, if it was ever based on any kind of truth. I like to believe there's magic in this world. And that it can be used for good."

"Hmm . . . interesting," he muttered. Not in a sarcastic way, but as though he found my fascination unexpected. His brows furrowed for an instant and then his face relaxed. "Let's go with *Willow.* It won't give me nightmares."

I laughed. I had a hard time believing scary movies bothered him. "If you're that much of a wuss, then let's watch . . ." I scanned the other movies on the shelf. ". . . *Legends of the Fall.*"

"Oh, no. That would be the worst nightmare of all."

I gave him a questioning look as I slid the movie into the player. I used to have a crush on Tristan Ludlow, Brad Pitt's character, but hated how he left his loved ones. It wasn't exactly nightmare material, though.

"I might dream of you with that other Tristan." He pulled me onto the couch next to him and put his arms around me. "And that would be horrifying."

He nestled his face into my hair at my neck. I smiled.

"I prefer this one."

"This one prefers you, too," he whispered.

He leaned back on the couch, pulling me with him. I felt so comfortable, so relaxed in his arms, I couldn't understand now why I had panicked at the idea of being alone with him. Nothing felt more natural.

"Lexi," Tristan murmured as he stirred on the couch. "Wake up, Lexi."

"Huh?" I sat up, a little disoriented. "Is the movie over?"

"I think it was over a while ago. We both fell asleep."

The TV's menu screen silently glowed bright blue.

"Oh." I snuggled back against him. "Can we just stay here?"

"I think I better go," he said quietly.

He stood up and pulled me up, too. I held his hand as we walked to the door, and then he pulled me to him. Sparks flew through me again as he leaned over and kissed me. I wrapped my arms around his neck, dug my fingers into his hair and pulled tightly as I kissed him back. Passion rose as his mouth traveled along my neck and jaw line and his hands slid down my back, pressing me against him when his lips returned to mine. A tiny sound might have escaped from me. I don't know. His touch and scent and taste all together at once overwhelmed me. *Losing control again . . . .*

He abruptly pulled back. Those flames sparked in his eyes again, glowing brighter than before. I stepped back, surprised (*frightened*).

"Yes, I better go," he muttered. He was out the door before I could react.

I stood there breathless, not able to say anything because I didn't know what would come out. *Yes, go. No, stay!*

"I'll see you in the morning. We have more studying to do," he called over his shoulder. I shut the door and slid to the floor—my legs weak, my insides still throbbing and my heart racing. I stayed there while I listened to the motorcycle's engine fade into the night.

A knock at the door startled me back to alertness. I stood up and peeked through the window.

"Owen?" I said with shock, pulling the door open. "It's two in the morning. What are you doing here?"

"Hey, Alexis." He seemed to be giving me a once-over. "I was just in the neighborhood and wanted to make sure you were okay. I know you're home alone and I saw the lights on . . . ."

What the . . . ?

"Uh, I'm fine." I stared at him with bewilderment.

"Yeah, I'm sure you are," he mumbled as he turned to leave. "Sorry to bother you."

He started down the walkway. *Oh, no. Oh, no, she didn't!*

"Hey, Owen?" I called after him.

He stopped and turned. "Yeah?"

"Did Sophia put you up to this?"

He started walking again and called back, "Just doing my job, Alexis."

Son of a witch! She had Owen checking up on me. And he'd conveniently shown up right after Tristan left, as if he'd been watching. *A babysitter?! Seriously?!*

But then I wondered if it had been Owen whom I heard outside last night, checking on me. That would be a good thing. He gave good vibes and Mom trusted him, so I should, too. Right?

෪

Tristan showed up at the door at ten the next morning with coffee, croissants and his backpack in hand and we spent the morning studying. By one o'clock, he'd had enough. He strode over to the backdoor and gazed out the window.

"It's a beautiful day for a ride," he hinted. When I didn't answer, he came over to my chair, dropped on his knees, clasped his hands together and stuck his lower lip out deliciously. He lowered his voice. "Please?"

Like I could resist that. Or the offer.

"Why not? My brain's fried, too."

He grinned. "You'll want to put on jeans and real shoes. No flip-flops for this ride."

We cruised the streets of Cape Heron, and then headed for I-75. The interstate, where everyone drove eighty miles an hour. *Holy crap! What am I thinking?* I had absolutely no control! I put my life into his hands! I squeezed my eyes shut and held onto Tristan tightly, my muscles tense as the wind rushed against my face and the sounds of cars and trucks seemed way too close. Exhaust fumes and the smell of hot rubber filled my nose. My body was welded to Tristan's back by the time we left the highway only a couple exits later. I breathed a sigh of relief that we survived.

At the slower speed, the ride was spectacular. The sun shone brightly in the clear October sky and the smell of oily warmth rose off the pavement. After a while, we crossed the causeway to Gasparilla Island. I rested my chin on Tristan's shoulder as we cruised along the tree-lined boulevard, catching an occasional glimpse of the Gulf of Mexico on one side and the bay on the other, between the large houses. We rode through the quaint little town of Boca Grande, which reminded me a lot of Cape Heron. He stopped the bike in a parking lot at the end of the island and we gazed over the sugary sand and steel-blue water as pelicans dive-bombed for their dinner. Two dolphins jumped and twisted in the air, playing with each other.

"Nice, huh?" Tristan asked.

"Perfect," I breathed. I was still close against him, my arms wrapped around his waist. He held my hands in front of him.

"Let's take a walk and stretch our legs, then I'll take you to this great little seafood place I found."

As we rode down my street later, sadness grew within me, knowing our perfect day was coming to a close. Night had fallen and the street was quiet except for the Harley's engine. As we pulled in front of the cottage and I saw Mom's car in the driveway and a light on inside, I was sadder still that our perfect weekend was over. We both took a deep breath and sighed heavily after he cut the engine, knowing the next few minutes, at least, wouldn't be pleasant. I leaned against the backrest, not wanting to get off yet.

"Do you know why she doesn't like me?" Tristan asked.

"No, not really."

He was quiet for a moment, then said, "I'm sure she's worried about you because she loves you. And she has valid reasons for feeling the way she does, so you should probably listen to her."

That sounded like a warning. Of what, I wasn't sure and I didn't want to know. Not now.

I leaned my forehead against his back and whispered, "Please don't."

"Don't what? Don't be honest?" His voice was low and heavy.

I sighed. *Why should we start now?* But that's not what I'd meant.

"Tristan, I don't know what will happen as soon as we walk in there. I've never seen her like this. But I had an amazing weekend with you and that's how I want to leave it. Let her be the one to ruin it. Not you. Please?"

He didn't respond right away.

"Understood," he finally said. I reached my arms around him and he took my hands in each of his and gave them a squeeze. "Just one thing, though. Just remember it's your life, Alexis. Do what you need to do for you. Not for me, not for her. Okay?"

"Yeah, of course," I answered simply. I'd already decided

that Friday but guilt still filled my heart. So did anxiety. If she reacted as badly as she had before, I could be living on my own in a day or two. But I didn't regret my decision. Not yet anyway.

"You had an amazing weekend with me, huh?" Tristan asked, his voice light and lovely again as we walked up to the cottage hand-in-hand.

"Very amazing." I smiled at him. "No matter what happens, it was worth it."

"I agree." He squeezed my hand, smiling back. "And thank you for telling me how you feel."

The door flew open before we reached the front porch. Mom stood in the doorframe, crossing her arms and glaring at us.

"Alexis," she said curtly. "Tristan."

"Hi, Sophia, how was your . . . uh . . . convention?" I asked, trying in vain to sound relaxed and nonchalant.

She glared at Tristan and I saw him shake his head out of the corner of my eye, answering her silent question.

"Not what I hoped it would be," she answered coldly, still staring at Tristan. Her eyes softened just a bit, though, as if his keeping her secrets meant something to her.

We all stood there awkwardly in deafening silence.

"I think I better go . . ." Tristan broke it first. It was almost a question, though.

"That's a good idea." Mom leaned inside the door, picked something up, and held his backpack out to him.

He took the bag and squeezed my hand. "See you in class tomorrow."

Mom closed the door and followed me to the kitchen table, where my books were still spread out, waiting for my return.

"Alexis, I need to talk to you."

"I really need to study. Mid-terms tomorrow."

"Please. Just listen for a minute."

I plopped onto a chair and looked at her expectantly, waiting for the lecture or tirade or whatever was coming. But she surprised me.

"Listen . . . there are apparently things I just need to work out with myself. There's obviously nothing I can do about this." She threw her hands in my direction, but I knew she meant "this" to mean Tristan and me together, as a couple. "Did you spend a lot of time with him this weekend?"

I hesitated before answering, but I couldn't lie. "Yes."

"And you obviously still like him?"

"Yes."

"Anything more?"

"I don't know. Maybe." I sighed. "I think so."

She pursed her lips together and stared at me for a long moment. "Just don't rush into anything too serious, okay?"

I didn't answer and she blew out a heavy breath.

"Never mind. I shouldn't have said that. You do what you feel is right and I'll just have to accept it. I knew it was coming. It was just a matter of when."

She lost me. "Is this specifically about Tristan or just about me getting serious with anyone in general?"

She pondered this question. "Both. But, in the end, it doesn't matter. You're going to do what you want and so is he. I know everything will go the way it's supposed to. It will be good."

She said those last two sentences as if trying them on, feeling for their meaning, deciding if she truly believed them. Her face showed she didn't, but wanted to, kind of doubtful and hopeful at the same time. I debated whether to force an explanation and decided to let it go, for now, anyway.

"Thanks, Mom." I threw myself at her in a grateful hug— grateful for her blessing and her return. She didn't let go and I knew she missed me, too. "There's just one other thing."

She stepped back and studied my face, her own expression leery.

"I feel really good with Tristan so—" I hesitated, bracing myself. "There might come a time when he needs to know about things . . . things I don't know yet."

"Alexis—"

"If he understands, maybe he won't get mean or run." My voice cracked on the last word.

Mom put her hands on my shoulders. "You *do* really like him, don't you?"

I nodded. She sighed.

"Let's just see how it goes, okay? Maybe we can talk about this again later . . . or maybe it won't be necessary." With a kiss to my forehead and a turn on her heel, she clearly stated the discussion was over. I didn't know if I'd won just a little or not.

She went to bed and I reviewed my notes one more time. Just as I finished, there was a tap on the kitchen door. I nearly fell out of my seat at the seemingly loud sound in the dead silence. I sat there, frozen, trying to figure out what to do. My heart had jumped at the sound and now it raced. *Should I run?* I glanced over at the knife block on the counter. *Fight?*

Another tap on the door's window.

Would Phil really knock first?

"Alexis, it's me." Low, sexy voice muffled through the glass pane.

I laughed internally at myself and hurried over to open the door.

"What are you *doing?*" I whispered. "You scared the hell out of me."

"Sorry." He grinned, like he really wasn't. "I just had to make sure she hadn't killed you or planned to take you away or anything."

I smiled giddily. "No, actually, I think it's all good."

"Okay, good." It came out as sort of a whoosh of relief.

"Is that it?" I asked when he just stood there.

"Well . . . I didn't get to say a proper good-bye and I couldn't sleep without this." He bent over and brushed his lips across mine. Then he smiled and winked. I stared at him, dazed. "Okay, better. I can sleep now. Good night."

"'Night," I murmured. He disappeared into the darkness.

Chapter 8

Tristan sat on his motorcycle waiting for me when I came out of the cottage Monday morning, greeting me with his most stunning smile. "I thought we could save gas and ride together today."

I accepted the ride. And I accepted his hand when he took mine as we walked across campus and his offer to take me out to lunch. And I definitely accepted him as more than just a study buddy or whatever it was that we had been. I discovered the feeling of being so completely aware of someone that you can't help but touch their hand or arm or, in Tristan's case, just lean over and plant a quick, good-luck kiss right on my lips outside my calculus classroom. Every touch was electrical and I didn't exactly get used to it, but I at least learned to expect it. I floated through exams, hoping I gave them the attention they needed but not remembering much about them when I was done.

We did our own thing Tuesday—I tried to write but my mind wandered in pleasant places most of the day—until he showed up at my door just as the sun was getting low. After sitting on the beach for the sunset again, we made dinner for Mom. She watched us carefully at first but by the time Tristan left later that night, she seemed much more relaxed.

We had planned to take a motorcycle ride to a different beach Wednesday, but I woke up late to a gray, wet day. So I worked on my book and could actually concentrate enough to write a whole chapter. Tristan did whatever Tristan does, but arrived again in the late afternoon, although the sun was blanketed in clouds and there was no sunset to watch. It was the perfect kind of evening to spend snuggling with your sweetie at home. And I actually had a sweetie to snuggle with. So, although we were on fall break, we lay on the couch together and read some articles for our women's studies class. We had a paper due Monday when classes resumed.

"Huh." Tristan suddenly looked up from the article he was reading.

It had been so quiet that the small sound startled me. "What?"

Mom was reading a mystery in the leather recliner and she looked up from her book, curious about the break in the precious silence.

"Just something I read in this article. Have you read it?" He held it up for me to see.

"Oh, yeah, that one, the one about arranged marriages. Creepy, huh?"

Mom went back to her reading, seemingly disinterested.

"I find it . . . interesting." He didn't elaborate and lay there thoughtfully for a moment. "What are your thoughts on arranged marriage?"

Mom's head snapped up. She narrowed her eyes at Tristan for just a brief second. Then she shook her head and went back to reading.

"Hmm . . . I don't know," I said. I sat up for the conversation and Tristan did, too. "Personally, I wouldn't want to be told who I was going to spend the rest of my life with. I think that should be left to fate. And love."

I noticed Mom looking at me through her eyelashes, her head still down, but listening intently.

"Yeah, that thing called love," Tristan agreed. "But maybe the marriage *is* their fate. It was meant to be, but it was just planned by people, too."

I thought about that idea and shrugged. "Yeah, I guess you could look at it that way. I still don't know that I'd like it, though. It seems strange to grow up knowing you have no options."

"What if it's a family obligation, like your family was depending on it?" Mom asked, deciding to join the conversation.

"I don't know," I admitted. "I guess it would be hard to turn your back on that."

"That's usually the reason for those arrangements," she pointed out. "Often the family's survival is at risk and the arrangement holds the key to their continued existence . . . or, at least, their way of life."

"Yeah, this article debates that point. I just don't understand how they work, though. I mean, they're matched together when they're very young, especially the girls. What if he's a horrible person . . . or she's a . . . a *wretch*? What if the man doesn't want to be with her anymore, when she's grown up and he sees what she's really like? Or he turns out to be a wife beater?"

"What if they're not? What if they're perfect for each other . . . meant to be together?" Tristan challenged.

"That would be pure luck," I scoffed.

"Or fate," he added, "you know, destiny."

Mom peered at us and then bent her head back over her book, her point made.

I chuckled with skepticism. "Yeah, I guess you could call it that. But do you believe in destiny?"

"Actually, I do." He looked at me and his eyes were intense. "So, what if they were given the chance to get to know each other, fell passionately in love and then found out the whole thing had been arranged?"

I pulled my eyes from his to consider this. "Well, I guess that *would* be their destiny. If they love each other all on their own, then I guess it wouldn't make a difference if it was arranged or not, right? But they'd both have to be in the dark, I think. After all, if one knew about the arrangement and didn't tell the other . . . that's not a relationship built on trust."

Tristan's brows furrowed. "Good point."

"On the other hand, whether people are involved in the arrangement or not, if they're really meant for each other, if they're true soul mates, then it *was* planned all along . . . by God."

I saw Mom's head tilt as I said this. She was still listening but seemed to have nothing more to add. I couldn't tell if she was really interested or annoyed that she couldn't read in peace.

"So . . . if you believe in true love and you were truly soul mates, then it wouldn't matter," Tristan summarized and added with doubt in his tone, "But you have to believe in the idea of soul mates first."

"And you don't?" I peered at him.

"I don't know. I didn't used to . . . ," he said quietly, his eyes focused on the coffee table. He glanced at me from the corner of his eye. "What about you?"

He had essentially voiced exactly what I was thinking. *I wanted to believe but never could. Until . . .* I felt another click of my heart settling.

"I don't know, either," I answered instead. "I'd like to believe in it. The thought of two souls being made for each other and then actually finding each other in this big world . . . it's a nice idea." *Shut up! Sharing too much, too soon.* Contrary to my feelings, I added, "Just seems a little unrealistic, though."

He studied my face for a minute and then grinned. "And I thought all girls were sappy romantics, waiting for their soul mate."

"Sappy romantics, huh? Have you met Sophia?" I laughed. Mom aimed a throw pillow at me and, of course, hit me right in the head.

"I think you two need to get back to studying, so I can read," she said.

"We are," I protested. "We have to write a paper on this crap."

"Thanks to both of you for your points of view," Tristan said. "Knowing what women think about this helps ensure I keep my A."

We quieted again and went back to reading about women's roles in different cultures. I was the next one to break the silence. We were done with our articles, anyway, and I started gathering and straightening the papers.

"So, based on what we read . . . all these different cultures and the woman's role in them . . . which one would you most like to live in? As a man, I mean."

Tristan lifted an eyebrow. "Hmm . . . good question. Are you, perhaps, trying to find out what kind of woman I like?"

I grinned. "You got me."

"I see . . . well, I think I might quite enjoy the Amazon culture. Big, strong, independent women . . . I could handle being a boy toy." He laughed.

"Hmph. I guess I don't match up then," I said. "I'm not big or strong. And I definitely don't need a boy toy!"

Tristan laughed again. "Yeah, you *are* little, but you're also independent. And I'm pretty sure Sophia could take me on anytime, so if you're anything like her . . . ."

If he only knew! Then again, if he were related to Lenny, he probably did know.

"Don't ever forget it," she said to Tristan. She was teasing, but a warning colored her tone. Or maybe it was just my imagination. She *did* seem to be warming to him. She folded the corner of the page over in her paperback and rose out of her chair. "I think it's time for this little Amazon to go to bed."

"'Night, Sophia." I stuffed my notebook into my bag and dropped it on the floor. I plopped back onto the couch and cuddled against Tristan's side. He wrapped his arms around me. "Sure you don't want your big Amazon woman?"

"Sure you don't need a boy toy?"

"I wouldn't know what to do with him," I said.

"Mmm . . . I could show you." He nestled his face in my hair and kissed my ear. I giggled and pulled away, lifting my shoulder as a barrier. "Ah, seems I found a ticklish spot."

"I think that could make me crazy," I admitted, rubbing the goose bumps on my arm.

"Nice." He squeezed me. "Three points for me."

I tilted my head to see his face. "Points? For what?"

He grinned proudly. "I get a point for learning something new about you, a point because you actually told me and a bonus because it makes you crazy in a way that I *like*."

He's giving himself points? It took less than a minute for me to realize he wasn't making a game out of us. The points—whether they were real or he just now made them up—marked the accomplishment of learning something about me. I shifted my position. He had to drop his arms, but I wanted to look at him. He turned, too, so we both sat sideways on the couch, facing each other.

"So what makes *you* crazy?" I asked.

"Lots of things." He lifted his eyebrows twice and chuckled.

But then he became serious, looking at me intensely. "What makes me craziest is not knowing what you're thinking or feeling and, even more than that, why you don't tell me."

I looked back into those beautiful hazel eyes, the gold sparkling but not as bright as usual. It made me sad.

"Do I get points for that?" I asked, trying to reroute the conversation and keep it light. "You just told me something about you."

"Doesn't count. I've told you that before." He smiled but the gold in his eyes didn't sparkle any brighter.

"So what's the score?" I desperately tried to prolong the superficial talk, avoiding the dive he apparently wanted to take into my head and heart.

"Don't worry. You're winning."

"Ha! Then you're a terrible scorekeeper."

"I'll admit to that when it comes to you, but why do you say so?"

I thought about it for a minute. It seemed we both felt that we knew very little about each other. *So how can we have such a strong connection like we do?* It felt like more than lust but . . . was it?

"Let me ask you a question," I finally said. "If you had to introduce me to someone, how would you do it?"

"What do you mean?"

"I mean, what would you say, exactly?"

"This is my sexy Lexi . . . ?" He grinned.

I rolled my eyes.

"*Ma lykita?* Is that better?"

"I don't even know what it means."

"Right."

"And?"

He shook his head, the smile still on his lips. "Nope. My secret."

I groaned. "Fine. Then be serious. I'm going somewhere with this . . . and I promise you'll get something out of it, too."

"Okay . . . I'd say, 'This is Alexis, my girlfriend.' Is that what you mean?"

"Yeah," I mumbled. I got hung up for a moment on the word "girlfriend." I'd never been anyone's girlfriend. *Isn't that what I want?* I smiled. "Okay, now what if you were telling someone about me? What would you say?"

"Ah, that would be easy." He ran his hand through my hair and brushed it along the side of my face. "Long, coppery hair that shines in the sun; soft, smooth skin that feels like silk; big, beautiful, brown eyes that pull you into their gaze; and a hot little body that I'd like to get to know."

His eyes glinted with mischief. I picked up the throw pillow and tossed it at him.

"Really? If someone asked you what I was like, that's what you would say?"

"Oh, no. Sorry. That's what I think every day about you. But I wouldn't want anyone else to be thinking about you like that."

I shook my head. "If you won't take me seriously, I won't tell you what I was thinking."

"Okay, I'm sorry. I mean it." He took a moment to think. "I would tell them that you're a beautiful, smart, kind, independent young woman with a good sense of humor and a laugh that makes my heart soft; who likes to go to the beach, cook, read and watch vampire movies but is self-protective. And I wouldn't say this to anyone else, but I think there is a reason for that shell you have around you, that you have experienced betrayal and have a difficult time trusting people."

Bam! Hit the nail on the head! So, although I was good at hiding my feelings and thoughts, I was, at the same time, transparent. I looked away from him, sure he could see everything in my eyes. I stared down at the couch cushion instead, studying the lines and wrinkles in the brown leather.

That last statement sounded as though it made him sad or worried . . . like he truly cared.

My heart balanced on a fulcrum, teetering one way and then the other. Which was better? Not sharing the real, whole me with him and enjoying this charade of a relationship, which would eventually end anyway because it was based on lies—his, mine and my mom's? Or giving my whole self to him and taking the chance he'd run from the freak show? And what if he did stay? Is that what I really wanted?

"Ah, I think I'm on to something," he said, again sounding sad. "You've been hurt. And I will accept that as part of you."

I blinked back the tears pooling in my eyes, refusing to let them fall. I continued staring at the couch cushion and whispered, "You don't have to."

He took my hands in his. "But I want to, Alexis. I want to be with you, shell and all. I hope one day I'll be the chink that cracks your shell and I'll know all of you. I won't push you, though. It's up to you. But it pains me to think of someone else getting in there."

"And if you don't like what's in here?" I could hear the edge in my tone.

"Is that what you're afraid of? That I won't like you?"

I didn't answer, didn't even acknowledge the question.

"Ah, I see." He leaned his head down, his lips against my ear, and whispered, "It's a little too late for that."

I finally looked up at him and he shrugged.

"I already know the kind of person you are and that's all that matters to me. I have my own issues and yours can't be any worse. Trust me. Unless . . ." He pulled back and lifted an eyebrow. "You're not really a guy in there, are you?"

I smiled. "Not the last time I checked."

"Because that would cross my line. Anything else . . ." He shrugged again. "I can handle."

He must have seen the doubt in my eyes.

"The last thing I want to do is hurt you, Lex. Please trust me."

His eyes delved into mine, searching deep for something buried under layers of betrayal and pain. As I looked back into his beautiful eyes, I knew I didn't want to push him away. But what he asked for . . . I didn't know if I had it to give.

"The problem with trust," I said slowly, deliberately, "is that you don't know that it's broken until it is, when it's too late."

"But you can't know that you can trust me until you try," he countered.

"Everyone I've ever trusted has betrayed me in a very big way, except Sophia."

"And when will you realize that I'm not everyone else?"

I already knew, at least to some extent. But just because he was different than most people didn't mean he could accept *my* differences.

I shrugged. "I don't know. I guess I need more proof?"

"Ah. Okay. So, my goal will be to build your trust in me, one little piece at a time." He lifted my chin with his thumb so we were looking eye-to-eye again. "Will you let me do that?"

As I looked into his eyes, my heart stopped teetering and tumbled over. I hadn't realized it before, but I knew now. He'd already cracked my shell and eventually he'd make the whole thing crumble, leaving every bit of me exposed for his scrutiny. And I would let him and just have to deal with the consequences. I wanted to take the risk that came with trusting him, even knowing if he turned out to be like all the others, it would be the worst pain I'd ever experienced. He'd already settled too deeply into my heart. He'd snapped himself into place with each of those little clicks I'd felt over the past two months.

It went against everything I knew was for my own good, but I could feel a tugging deep down that I needed to do this. That it was right. We needed to dispose of the lies. If he was willing to do one piece at a time, I could handle that.

"Baby steps?" I whispered.

"Baby steps," he agreed.

I took a deep breath and let it out slowly. "So I still owe you."

"You just gave me more than I thought I would get in months."

Months? Am I really that bad?

I shook my head. "No, there are rewards I promised and I'll deliver. Besides I don't want you to think I was fishing for compliments. I was just trying to understand exactly what you know about me—or what you *think* you know about me, anyway. So, I'm going to tell you now what I know about you."

"As if you're telling someone about me?"

"Yep. So . . . I would say you are a sweet, funny, considerate, fun, intelligent, multilingual gentleman who is good at math and likes to cook, ride motorcycles and watch sunsets on the beach—"

"Sounds like a personal ad." He chuckled. "Except for the math part. That's not very sexy."

I smiled—even that part was sexy about *him*—and held up my hand. "Wait, I'm not done. I know you, too, have a difficult past that you won't talk about. But, unfortunately, that's about all I know about you. And that's why you're winning."

He opened his mouth to protest, but I held my hand over it.

"But I do know other things," I said. "Things I wouldn't tell anyone else . . . things like how my heart dances when you just look at me a certain way or, God forbid, wink . . . or how it feels like an exciting current flows under my skin when you touch me anywhere—" I picked up our clasped hands—my right, his left—and brushed the inside of my other wrist with his fingers and said, "But especially here." I brought his hand to my neck. "And here." To my ear. "And here. And—" I slid the tips of his fingers along my lower lip. "Here." I took a breath and smiled. "Now, for all the bonus points you get for learning what I like, I think you just racked up another fifty or so."

He held the back of my hand to his lips as he considered this, the gold flecks shimmering in his eyes. "You're right. I owe you. Ask me anything and I will tell you."

A hundred-and-one questions flew through my mind. The most guarded answers, I was sure, had to do with the conversation between him and my mom, what he knew, how he knew, who he really was. Answering those honestly will be the ones that would truly gain my trust. But those weren't baby steps and if I expected baby steps, I would give them, too.

"What do you do? I mean, when you're not with me or at school. Do you have a job?"

"Hmm . . . not really a *job*, but I have plenty to do. I do some, uh . . . consulting . . . and use that money to play the stock market. I've built up a decent portfolio. It allows me to buy toys." He grinned. "And I do some computer programming for a couple of software companies. It's all stuff I do at home, mostly. And I indulge in Aikido."

"Eye—what?"

"Aikido. It's a form of martial arts. I use it to practice self-control."

"Really?" I thought of the wife-beater. "You have control issues? Never would have thought . . ."

"Ha ha," he replied with matching sarcasm. Then he frowned. "Actually, I had quite a bit of control the other day. I was angry, but I was fully aware of what I was doing. Otherwise, I might have just killed the lowlife."

A chill ran up my spine and I fought back the shudder. I knew he wouldn't have—*couldn't* have—killed the creep . . . but, with his football-player build, he was fully capable of doing some serious damage.

"Your Aikido must be working, then. That's the only time I've seen you come close to being anything other than calm and cool."

"Hmm. Ironic. Because when I'm around you is when I need more control than ever . . . because I really want to *lose* it with you." The tone was serious but a smile played on his lips. I didn't know what to make of it. Then I remembered the fire in his eyes and the controlled breathing every time we kissed. I had a hint of understanding.

"But if it's practicing self-control, how is that an indulgence?"

"Because I spar and that's *fun*." He grinned.

"Spar, as in fighting?" I asked, my stomach clenching.

"You want to come watch sometime?"

"Ugh. No, thanks, I'll pass on that one."

"So . . ." He lowered his voice to its most irresistible. "Do I get to ask a question?"

I narrowed my eyes, wanting to tease him about how much I'd given him tonight. But he said baby steps and I had to trust that's what he had in mind—so, it couldn't be too bad. I nodded.

"What do *you* do when I'm not around? I know you don't work at the store all that often. So either you're mooching off Sophia or you're doing something else."

Okay, maybe kind of bad. But of all the things he could have asked, this was probably the safest—not about my past, my mom or any big secrets—but it was still uncomfortable. It was one thing for him to know I wanted to be an author. It was a whole different thing to admit I was actually doing it when it would likely be an epic failure. *No, not bad, just personal . . . but that's okay.*

"Actually, both. I'm writing a novel. Sophia thinks it'll get published and she's paying my way so I can write and still go to college."

"Wow. A novel, huh? That's impressive."

"Yeah, well, don't get too impressed. It's not even done yet."

"Can I read it?" he asked eagerly.

I thought of the childhood game, Mother May I, and felt like he asked to take one giant leap forward when he was only allowed baby steps. If I gave him my writing, I may as well give him my whole soul. I didn't let anyone read most of my writing, not even my mom. Her assertion of my talent was based on essays and short stories I'd written for school. Sharing the outline with her had been difficult. Letting go of the actual book would be a huge leap. I knew I'd have to take it eventually, but not yet.

"Hmm . . . baby steps, okay?" I answered.

"Okay," he agreed.

Baby Steps was the game we played every day for weeks. He got a question and I got a question. They often led to more questions, but they were generally superficial topics. We discovered that we had similar tastes in music—a preference for alternative and classic rock, but could enjoy anything but rap and country was just bearable. I learned he wanted to be an engineer or an architect. He'd lived in many places throughout Europe, as well as several cities in the U.S., had spent time in Japan to study Aikido and had traveled to every continent except Antarctica.

He learned I'd never been out of the United States but had

a passport because Sophia thought it practical and that I took four years of Spanish in high school and could say maybe five full sentences and count to one-hundred. I told him I could name every Edgar Allan Poe story and recite by heart nine Emily Dickinson poems. I even admitted that I had tried my own hand at poetry.

I learned he didn't like Halloween, saying it wasn't right that little kids wanted to be witches, vampires and other monsters. I admitted I'd always been a witch or a vampire, but always a good one—as a vampire, I carried around a cup of donor "blood." He guessed correctly it was Mom's idea. She preferred fairies, princesses and humorous costumes to the gory and scary ones. He asked Mom if my interest in monsters and fantastical creatures was healthy. She just laughed. I talked him into taking me to a couple haunted houses and he growled fiercely at the monster-actors, making *them* jump and shriek. I laughed so hard I almost peed my pants. He admitted it was the most fun he'd had on Halloween.

By Thanksgiving, we knew all of each other's favorite everything . . . colors, bands, authors, actors and actresses, food, ice cream flavors, books . . . . All the top-layer stuff that really had little to do with who we were and why . . . the stuff that made us real. Little hints and nuggets could be gleaned from these surface subjects, but they didn't touch the deep, inner-workings of our hearts or souls and definitely had nothing to do with the secrets we kept and pain we hid. I knew, though, it was only a matter of time before those things came out.

And when they did . . . well, it certainly didn't happen in a way I could have ever expected.

Chapter 9

"Owen and I could have done that," Tristan said as Mom and I climbed step-ladders in the bookstore's expansive front window, a string of Christmas lights stretched between us.

It was the night before Thanksgiving and Tristan and I had spent the day helping Mom and Owen prepare for the holiday rush. Mom didn't believe in selling Christmas before Halloween or even Thanksgiving, so here we were, nine o'clock at night, still decorating. Nearly finished, Mom had just sent Owen home. Not two minutes ago we had two perfectly able—and perfectly tall—men to hang the lights. But this was Mom's way of making sure everyone (well, Tristan specifically) knew we depended on no one.

"Alexis and I are quite capable of doing this," Mom replied. "In fact, you can go home, too, Tristan."

"Nah, I'll stay. Although, we could be done a lot faster if you didn't do it the hard way," he said as he picked up empty boxes that had held the decorations.

Mom mumbled something under her breath, but all I caught was "normal" and "mainstream." Tristan chuckled as if he heard her clearly, though he was at least twenty feet farther away from her than I was.

I opened my mouth to ask what that was all about when a pair of headlights racing down the street distracted me. The shops on Fifth Street closed hours ago. I could see lights of restaurants and bars down another block, but our block was deserted, except for this one car. So I didn't understand when the headlights suddenly swerved, arcing right into the store's window. Then I realized the car barreled straight for us.

"*Mom!*" I shrieked without thinking.

The car continued racing right at us, way too fast to stop in time.

"Alexis! *Jump!*" Mom yelled.

Before we even had a chance to jump, though, we both flew off the ladders and into Tristan's arms. I stared wide-eyed like a deer caught in headlights—literally—my mind somehow registering several things at once. When the car was about twenty yards away, still going way too fast, a light flashed on something directly to the right of it—the driver's door, swinging open. Then Owen, who had just left through the back door, stood in the street, but out of the car's path, and he thrust his hands out toward the car as if willing it to stop. The driver must have finally slammed on the brakes—the tires squealed as it nearly stopped just before crashing into the store.

And then it hit. Sliding into the window. Glass imploding.

Mom and I tucked our faces into Tristan's shoulders. He bent over to shield us. Glass chinked and shattered as it rained to the floor around us.

When it was finally quiet, I lifted my face and immediately smelled the night air, mixed with lingering exhaust fumes. The orange car sat quietly only a couple of feet inside the shop—right where Mom and I had been only seconds earlier. The ladders lay on their sides, part of one under the car, along with the Christmas tree and fake presents we'd just set up.

"That was . . . intense," Tristan muttered as he straightened up. "You two okay?"

Mom shook her head, not to answer but to shake her hair out. A couple of small pieces of glass hit the floor. "I'm fine."

She twisted in Tristan's arm and he let her go. I noticed pink lines on her arms—minor scratches already healed. She healed much faster than I did. I hoped Tristan didn't catch that.

"Uh, yeah, I think I am," I breathed. "Are you?"

I started to look up at him, to make sure he wasn't cut anywhere, when Mom sucked her breath, distracting me.

"Alexis, honey, don't move," she instructed, her words slow and deliberate, as she moved to my right between me and the car. Tristan cupped his hand against the side of my face and tilted it up toward his before I could see what had her enraptured. He pulled me tighter into him.

"Just look at me," he said quietly.

"What's going on?" I whispered, afraid to know. Tristan held my eyes with his and I could tell by his expression it wasn't good.

I immediately thought of the driver and the car door swinging open just before impact. *Did he fly out of the car? Is he under the car?* My stomach lurched at the thought.

"It's all right. It's not in an artery or anything," Mom said and then a sharp pain tore through my thigh.

"Ouch! Son of a *witch*!" I screamed, trying to twist myself free, but not able to in Tristan's tight clutch.

I looked over my shoulder and Mom held a shard of glass at least five inches long and two inches wide, half of it covered in blood. My blood.

In a strange, delayed reaction, the pain suddenly screamed up and down my leg. Then more stabs and throbs in my arms and one on my head. A tickling sensation ran down the back of my head and I lifted my hand to it. When I pulled it away, blood coated the tips of my fingers. I glanced up at Tristan while squeezing my hand into a fist to hide the blood. I could tell he'd already seen it, though. *This is so not good.*

"Police," he said.

"Huh?"

"*Police*, Alexis, you need to get out of here," Mom said.

It finally registered when I heard the sirens a few seconds later, still several blocks away. *Oh, crap! Witnesses!* I felt the cuts on my arms already starting to heal.

"Everyone okay?" Owen called from outside. *Not Owen, too!*

"We're fine, Owen. Check on the driver and anyone else in the car," Mom called back. She lowered her voice. "Tristan, can you take care of Alexis?"

"Yes, I'll take her home."

"*Sophia!*"

She ignored me. "Are you sure, Tristan? There's a lot of blood—"

"I'm fine, Sophia. I love her. She'll be fine with me."

I heard the confidence in his voice, but hardly paid attention to the meaning of the words. Except for that one phrase. *He loves me?!* He'd never said that before. While I rolled that over in my mind, wondering why he felt the need to say it *now*, they stared at each other for what seemed like several minutes, but it had to have been only a second or two. Then Mom nodded.

"Get her home, then," she said. I panicked.

"Sophia, please, *no!*" I begged her as Tristan bent down to cradle me in his arms.

What the hell is she thinking? How could she let me go with him? She knew this was my biggest issue.

"Honey, I have to stay here and take care of this mess. Tristan will take care of you. Don't worry. He'll be fine with it all."

I didn't have a chance to argue. She already hopped onto the car's hood to pass through the window and help Owen with the driver, and Tristan already walked swiftly toward the back of the store, easily carrying me like I was nothing but a sack of feathers. There was no real argument, anyway. Mom obviously had to stay and I couldn't exactly walk home. Not yet, anyway, and there was no time to wait—the sirens wailed just a block or two away now.

My head and leg throbbed with each step Tristan took. I bit my lip, fighting the tears and trying to keep a straight face as we exited through the back door. I knew from previous experience to pretend like nothing was as bad as it looked, so it wouldn't seem quite so bizarre when it healed freakishly fast.

Tristan set me down on my feet at the bike and I realized quickly I couldn't put any weight on my right leg. He pulled off his t-shirt and tore a sleeve off, bunching it up and giving it to me. "For your head."

I held the wadded cloth against the cut on my head while he carefully tied the rest of the shirt around my lower thigh, padding as much as he could against the cut, about two inches above my knee, on the outside of my thigh. I couldn't help the winces of pain.

"Are you okay to ride?"

"Yeah," I mumbled, "it's not far."

I couldn't even enjoy the fact that I leaned against his bare back, my arms around his bare waist, as panic and pain fought with each other on the short ride home. The smaller cuts on my arms were already closing. The bigger gash in my thigh hurt like hell, so I knew it would take longer—I could feel the shard had cut through deep, severing tendons and muscles. I squeezed my eyes shut to keep the tears at bay and tried to focus on a plan. The four-block ride wasn't long enough, though. Too soon, Tristan lifted me off the bike and carried me inside.

"Um . . ." My voice came out in a rough whisper. "Bathroom."

He carefully set me down on the tub's edge and I rearranged his sleeve to find a clean section and pressed it against my head. He opened the cabinet under the sink and while his back was to me, I pulled the sleeve off my head again and quickly glanced at it. It came away clean. I sighed. *Why do I have to be such a freak?*

"Should we use these towels?" he asked, holding up Mom's pretty guest towels. Why we had them, I didn't know—we never had guests. But I saw the opportunity and seized it.

"Get the old ones in the kitchen, in the broom closet. Sophia'd kill me if I ruined her good ones."

As soon as he was in the hallway, I lunged forward to shut the bathroom door, quickly locking it before he realized what I'd done. I grabbed a towel—an everyday one, just in case Mom really would mind—and crawled to the bathtub. Tristan pounded on the door.

"Alexis! What are you doing?"

"Um . . . going to the bathroom?" I hated that it sounded like a question.

He didn't respond at first. I turned the tub faucet on just enough to dampen the towel and started cleaning my arms to see the damage. Almost all the cuts were completely gone, no evidence at all they ever existed. A few that must have been deeper were just red jags. They'd disappear, too, within ten minutes or so.

"Can I come in now?" Tristan called through the door.

"You know what . . . I'm fine," I said, trying hard to make my voice sound right. "You can go now. I can take care of this.

It's really not that bad."

Guilt stabbed at me. I hated lying to him. I didn't want to hide things anymore, even this. I had the urge to just let him watch . . . see the healing process with his own eyes. He must have heard the lie in my voice.

"You are not fine. Let me in!" He pounded on the door again.

Damn it! I was precisely at the moment I'd been dreading and desiring at the same time. I wanted Tristan to know everything about me, but I was actually *scared* of his reaction—more scared than anything that already happened tonight. *Will he call me a freak, too? Will he* leave *me?* The tears finally welled in my eyes, not just from the physical pain, but also from knowing the emotional pain that would cut even deeper.

Ignoring his pleas, I took the wrap off my thigh, needing to see how bad it was before I decided what to do. The pain screamed as I twisted my body and bent my leg at an odd angle to see. *Ugh.* A wave of nausea rolled over me.

The shard must have gone in at an angle, because the gash was at least three inches long and jagged. I dabbed it with Tristan's shirt and saw dark red meat. I was afraid if I looked too closely, I might see the bone, but blood flooded back to the surface, hiding the worst of it.

"Alexis, I'll break this door down if you don't let me in *now!*"

I sighed. No question he could do it, surely on his first try, even. I couldn't fight the tears any longer and they fell down my cheek, one by one. I crawled over to the door, holding his blood-soaked shirt back against my thigh.

"Tristan?" I said through the door, just loud enough to be heard without straining. I heard him slide down the door to my level.

"What, Alexis? Are you okay?"

"Um . . . no . . . I don't . . . think so," I admitted, breathing through the pain.

"*Please* let me in." Desperate concern filled his voice and another pang of guilt stabbed at me. But I couldn't let him. Yet.

"I will, but I need to know something first."

"Anything. I'll tell you anything. Just let me help you."

I took a deep breath and exhaled slowly.

"Do you really love me?" I finally asked.

"What?"

I pressed my cheek against the door. It felt comfortingly cool against my warm skin.

"You told Sophia you love me. Were you serious?" It came out so quietly, I was surprised he even heard me.

"Yes, Alexis, I really, truly love you with all my heart," he said almost as quietly, and I could hear in his voice he really meant it.

I didn't understand how either of us could feel it. We'd only known each other barely more than three months. But I knew it was true, at least for me. Until now, I'd only known love between a mother and a daughter. When I was little, Mom had a boyfriend who I loved and I thought he loved me, but then he disappeared out of our lives. I'd been painfully mistaken then. I hoped I wasn't about to make the same mistake again.

I gathered everything I had and pushed back the thought that I may regret what I was about to do. If he reacted like everyone else, it would be the worst pain ever. But I had to say it, knowing it may be my one and only chance.

"I love you, too, Tristan."

He exhaled loudly. "Good. Now, can I come in before you bleed out?"

I wiped away my tears, reached up and unlocked the door, cracking it open. He sat on the floor right in front of the door. "Close your eyes, please."

"*What?* What is wrong with you?" He obediently closed his eyes, though. I opened the door, crawled into his lap and kissed him, hoping and praying it wasn't the last one ever.

"I needed that first," I whispered. I watched him as he opened his eyes. "I hope you really love me . . . because things are about to get weird."

"What's going on?" he asked, his beautiful hazel eyes filled with concern.

I reluctantly held my arms straight out in front of him. He studied them, running his fingers over the last of the pink marks. I watched his face with trepidation and braced myself for the worst.

"They're perfect," he said matter-of-factly. He tilted my head, gently separating my hair to examine the head wound. "Nothing. It's gone. So what's wrong?"

I narrowed my eyes at him, suspicious at his reaction or, rather, non-reaction. "You don't see anything wrong?"

He smiled slightly. "No. They're all healed. I *think* that's a good thing."

I held my breath, watching him and waiting . . . and waiting . . . and still no reaction. *I know he's not stupid. . . .* He'd seen the blood on my hand when I touched my head at the store. He knew there had been some kind of wound there not ten minutes ago. And now *nothing.* He said so himself.

"Ah, must be your leg," he said, his hand moving toward my thigh. I instinctively shifted away, tumbling off his lap, onto the bathroom floor. "Lexi, I won't hurt you."

"That's not the problem!"

"Then what is?" Both concern and bemusement filled his face.

"Tristan . . . you saw how much my head was bleeding."

He shrugged. "Head wounds bleed a lot. It must not have been bad and it's gone now."

"Exactly! It's gone. So are the cuts on my arms. Don't you find that . . . I don't know . . . a little *weird*?"

"Not at all. Should I?"

"Uh, yeah, you should. It's not normal. I'm a freak!"

He laughed and I glared at him. *Here it comes.* He abruptly stopped and put his arms around me. "What ever gave you the idea I thought you were *normal*?"

"Are you mocking me?" I pulled away and stared into his eyes. The gold sparkled beautifully. He wasn't freaked out. He wasn't being mean. He wasn't counting the seconds to get out of here and never return. He was just concerned.

"Alexis, you are really making a big deal out of nothing. I don't care that you heal fast. Remember what I told you? I can handle anything. You could grow a second head and I would love it."

"You expect me to believe that?"

"Okay, a second head may be a little weird," he admitted. "But healing yourself, well, that's just not a deal breaker for me. Okay?"

I stared at him, not able to think of a single thing to say. *He's not running. He's not laughing. What's* wrong *with him?*

"Now, please let me look."

He turned me so he could better see the injury and pulled my hand with the now red, wadded t-shirt away. I was too dumbfounded to fight him off anymore. Besides, I knew this one was *not* healing so fast . . . if at all. It actually scared me now. The pain continued to shoot up to my hip and down to my ankle and it still hadn't stopped bleeding. Mom and I didn't know the extent of my body's ability to heal and this was the worst injury I'd ever had. It could be my body's first real test. If it didn't heal on its own, Mom had a professional grade first-aid kit with needle and thread. But Mom wasn't here.

"Alexis, have you taken a good look at me since that car came through the window?" Tristan asked as he studied the injury.

Huh? Is he trying to distract me? That would be a good way to do it. I was taking a good look at him right now, actually—he still had no shirt on. His body was perfect. He glanced up at me when I didn't answer and his face was perfect, as usual, too.

"Of course. You're beautiful, as always," I mumbled.

He rolled his eyes. "I mean, no cuts, no blood."

I thought back over the last ten or fifteen minutes, since the accident. *Yeah . . . no cuts or blood on him.* And he had shielded Mom and me. He should have been the worst off.

"How come you're not hurt?" I gasped as he poked at the raw flesh. "Ouch!"

"Sorry. This is pretty serious."

"And you know because . . . ?" I asked, momentarily forgetting my first question.

"Because I have medical training. The glass cut through rather deeply. There's so much blood still." He grabbed the towel I'd been using and soaked it under the tub's faucet. "I can't even see if it's healing on its own."

He dabbed at the wound and I winced.

"So how come *you're* not hurt?" I asked again through clenched teeth, now trying to distract myself. "That's hardly fair. *Ow!*"

He'd gone in deeper.

"Here." He put my hand on his leg. "Squeeze as hard as you need to, if it helps."

I squeezed. Hard.

"I heal, too," he said, "and much faster than you."

Chapter 10

"*What?*"

Tristan definitely had me distracted now.

"Any surface cuts from the flying glass would've healed before they even bled," he said. "It'd take a shard like what did this to even pierce my skin. Or a dart . . . ." He glanced at me with a slight smile, then went back to work.

I ignored the dart comment as my breaths became shallow. I didn't know if it was from the pain or a reaction to what he said. Or perhaps I was going into complete shock, overwhelmed with everything happening on this insane night.

"You . . . *heal?*" The towel jabbed deep, hitting a raw nerve and making me jump. "Holy crap, *ouch!*"

"This isn't working," he said with a sigh. He glanced down at my hand on his leg. My fingernails dug into his thigh.

"Sorry," I whispered, loosening my grip.

"You're not hurting *me*, but *you* are hurting and I don't like that." I could see my pain reflected in his eyes. He lay the wet towel over the wound, apparently giving up. "Yes, I heal, among other things. And you, *ma lykita*, are not. At least, not quickly enough."

I groaned. "Call Sophia. She can sew it . . . I think."

He shook his head. "There's no way she's done already. The police can't know you were there and injured or they'll make you go to the hospital. And that's out of the question."

I frowned. "Right. So what do we do?"

He stared at my leg for a long moment, seeming to think about our options. Then he placed one of his knees on each side of my legs and leaned over, placing a hand on the floor on each side of me so he knelt on all fours, his face very close to mine.

"You really love me?" he asked.

His delicious breath wafted over me when he spoke. He gazed intensely into my eyes. My mind started to fog.

"I . . . think so," I whispered.

"You *think?*" He rocked back onto his heels and stared at me.

"Well . . . you just . . . you can . . . you *heal*," I stammered.

"So . . . that *is* a deal breaker for you?"

Is it? I couldn't think straight. My thigh throbbed even harder now after he'd been poking around in it. And here he was, all perfect and beautiful and half-naked, straddled over me with that breathtaking smile, his delicious scent enveloping me. I tried to focus. *How could I mind him being able to heal?* But, I knew, that wasn't the real issue. The real issue was our whole relationship was built on secrets and lies . . . more than I ever realized.

"Not that you can heal," I finally said. "But you didn't *tell* me."

He raised an eyebrow. "You've been holding back, too. We've both known that about each other."

"I know," I admitted. "It's just, well, it seems you've known all my secrets. At least the two biggest ones. You're not surprised at all by my ability to heal. And I know you know Sophia is really my mom."

There. That's out now. He narrowed his eyes for a second, then nodded. "You're right. But a secret is a secret. A lie is a lie. *You* didn't tell *me* either."

I lay back on the floor with a groan and stared at the ceiling, tears stinging my eyes again. *He's right. Now what?* His face came into my vision as he leaned over me again. He smiled and the gold sparkled in his eyes.

"I don't care, though," he whispered. "I've known Sophia for a long time and I know these things about you and I don't care. Even the secrets and the lies. I know it comes with who we are."

My brows knit together.

"I don't even know who we are, though," I admitted. "I don't know who I am and I really don't know who you are. I know I have these stupid, freaky things about me and I'm glad you don't care. But you apparently have quirks, too. I love the person I've known for the last several months, but . . ." My voice trailed off.

"But you want to know the rest of me," he finished.

"*Yes.* I want to stop the lies and the secrets. I want a *real* relationship with you, Tristan. But I need to *know.*"

His eyes darkened. "You'll change your mind."

I shook my head, rocking it on the tile floor. "I'm not changing my mind. I need to know. For *us.*"

"I meant about loving me," he muttered, his eyes dropping so I couldn't see them.

Is it really that bad? I couldn't imagine it being too horrible—he was just too *good.* Good like Mom good. And I knew he wasn't just good *to* me, but good *for* me. Whatever secrets he kept, I thought I could get over them. And regardless, our relationship just couldn't go on any longer like it had been.

"Just tell me," I whispered. "Tell me who you are. Tell me *everything.*"

He raised his eyes and held mine so I knew he was serious,

then simply said, "Okay."

"*Okay?* For real?"

"Yes. Okay. You deserve to know . . . and I'll deal with whatever happens." He smiled, but it was sad. "But . . ."

"Of course there's a 'but'," I moaned.

"*But*," he continued, "I can't do it alone. You have to get Sophia to agree, too."

"*Why?* What does *she* have to do with it?"

"Well . . . to understand me, you need to know more about yourself. And only she can tell you that."

I groaned with frustration. Of course, it had to be the ultimatum I knew would not be met.

"Trust me, she'll do it," he said.

"I doubt it," I muttered.

"She knows it's time. She'll do it." He sounded more confident than he should. I wondered how he could know, but he distracted me with his intense gaze again. "Right now, though, I really need to know if you love me."

As I looked into his eyes, I knew what I felt, at least for now. And I didn't know if anything could change my mind.

"Yes, Tristan, I love you."

He leaned down and kissed me. "Good. Because I'm going to make you better . . . but now things are going to get *really* weird."

Tristan removed the towel from my thigh and I propped myself on my elbows to watch. He lowered his head and placed his mouth over the wound.

The pain immediately subsided, replaced by those strange but pleasurable jolts shooting up and down my leg. His hands gently held my upper thigh and calf, spreading electric tingles along my skin, as his mouth moved around the edges of the gash like passionate kisses. It was the most sensual thing we'd done so far—this was so unlike him. He looked up at me, sparks in his eyes.

"There's so much blood," he groaned quietly.

He lowered his mouth again and I felt a stimulating, tugging sensation as he sucked. A distant voice way back in a far corner of my mind tried to tell me something, but I ignored it. I *wanted* his mouth on me, doing whatever he was doing because it felt so *good*. Warmth spread through my lower body, his hands caressing my leg. I'd never had an orgasm before, so I didn't know what it felt like. But I thought this might be close.

"Tristan!" Mom gasped, suddenly behind him in the hallway, yanking me out of the oblivion.

"Oh! What the hell are you doing?" I shrieked, lurching my whole body away from him.

I stared at him, my eyes bugged as I realized *exactly* what he'd been doing. My stomach tilted. He stared back at me, an unreadable expression on his face, the sparks in his eyes dimming to just gold flecks.

"Tristan, what *were* you doing?" Mom asked.

"He was sucking my blood like a freakin' *vampire*!" I answered for him.

Tristan actually laughed. *Laughed.*

"I thought you like vampires," he said.

"Not for real! Is that what you thought? That I'd *like* it?! You're a bigger freak than I am!"

He shook his head as he rocked back on his heels at my feet, a smile still on his face.

"I didn't purposely suck your blood. It was just . . . in the way." The smile disappeared as he turned to look at Mom. "She's not healing, Sophia. At least not fast enough. I was trying to help."

"What? You think your saliva heals? Like a *dog*?" I snarled.

"Actually, yes . . . it does," Tristan said quietly. I stared at him, waiting for the humor to return. It didn't.

"He's right," Mom confirmed with a nod.

"*What?*" I shrieked. "How do *you* know?"

"Alexis, relax." Mom squeezed into the tiny bathroom, sat on the tub's edge behind me and smoothed my hair. "There's a lot to explain, but right now, I just need you to trust us."

"*Trust* you?"

"You trust me, right?" Mom asked.

"Yes," I said automatically. "But . . ."

Does she really expect me to believe all this? Does she really believe it?

"Alexis, does your leg still hurt?" Tristan asked.

I narrowed my eyes at him. I didn't *want* to tell him the truth. I was too stunned . . . and mad at him. I could feel something in my heart starting to crack, realizing he really was too good to be true. I'd known all along there had to be something wrong with him, for him to like (*love*) me. I'd just never imagined this. He turned my fascination with vampires against me in a bizarre, sick way to try to get me into the sack after all. Either that or . . . his secrets really were worse than I ever thought. *What have I gotten myself into?*

But I couldn't deny that the pain in my leg was gone. It wasn't that my leg was just numb, either.

"No," I admitted quietly. "Actually, it feels good."

Mom leaned over and peered at the injury. "It looks like it's trying to heal."

Tristan examined it, too, holding my leg gently but firmly when I tried to pull away from him. "It looks a lot better already. It finally stopped bleeding."

Mom scooted down between my back and the bathtub. "Finish, Tristan."

"*What?*" I tried to get up and away from them both. *Is she* crazy? But Mom wrapped her arms around me and held me tightly. She nodded at Tristan but he didn't move, except to shake his head.

"No. Not if she doesn't want me to."

"You are *not* doing that again!" I squirmed in Mom's arms. My thigh hit against her leg and the wound seared with pain again. "*Ouch!*"

"If you don't be still, it'll start bleeding again," Mom whispered calmly in my ear. "If there's no blood, he doesn't have to suck it out. He can just heal it. Or, you can sit here in pain for a few hours and hope it heals itself. If it doesn't, I'll have to sew it and you can be in pain for a few days. So . . . you can be miserable or you can trust us. The choice is yours."

Tears welled in my eyes again as the throbbing returned. I stared at Tristan through the tears and his face looked just as pained as I felt. His eyes were dark, the gold dim.

"Lexi, I can make it go away," he said quietly. "But only if you want me to."

I knew then he was honestly doing it for me. To help me, not to take advantage of me. I leaned back against Mom, squeezed my eyes shut against the tears and nodded. As soon as his mouth was against my thigh, the pain disappeared, replaced by the exciting tingles. My eyes still shut tightly, I tried hard not to envision what he did. I didn't feel any sucking. It just felt like warm, wet kisses, but not nearly as sensual as the first time. Perhaps because Mom was there. *Or because now I realize how freakin' weird it is!*

The kissing sensations stopped and all I could feel were the lingering tingles and the familiar sensation of my body healing. I slowly opened my eyes.

"Much better," Tristan said, studying the injury.

Mom leaned over me to check it out. "Yes. Much."

I couldn't look at Tristan, not sure exactly how I felt at the moment. Disgust, guilt, fear . . . Curiosity won and I eventually gave in and looked at the wound.

"Whoa," I breathed. I watched with fascination as the deep fibers knitted themselves back together, the wound closing from the inside outward. I could only watch for so long, though—it was pretty gross and nauseating.

After a few minutes, Tristan ran his hand up and down my leg, sending currents under my skin. "See. Your leg is nearly as sexy as it was this morning."

I looked again and, sure enough, the gash had completely disappeared. A long, dark bruise marked its place—bruises took longer to heal than cuts, something having to do with blood vessels in the deeper tissue. It'd be gone by Thanksgiving dinner tomorrow.

"Is *that* your medical training?" I demanded.

He laughed. "No. That comes naturally."

I narrowed my eyes and jabbed my finger at him. "*You* have a lot of explaining to do."

He grabbed my finger and kissed the tip of it before I yanked it away. He sighed and his eyes dimmed. "Yes, I do. Sophia?"

I dropped my head with defeat, knowing her answer.

"Yes, we both do."

My head twisted around as far as my neck allowed to see her face. "*Really?*"

She closed her eyes and exhaled sharply, as if she didn't like the idea. "Yes, really."

"You're really going to tell me all about me . . . us?"

She shook her head and opened her eyes. "No, not everything. I can't provide a lot of details. My soul's existence relies on keeping our secrets until you are *able* to understand. You'll just have to wait for most of it, but I will tell you what you need to know to understand what Tristan has to say."

Her soul's existence? She'd never put it like that before.

"First, though, we have some things to deal with at the store," she continued, squirming to stand up without success.

Crammed into the tiny bathroom, we had to stand one at a time, Tristan first. He held his hands out to help me up. I ignored him and stood on my own, gingerly putting weight on my right leg. It felt fine. Mom squeezed past me, already heading for the front door.

"I need to get back there. I told the police I was just going in the backroom to make some phone calls and right now Owen is handling everything."

"Oh! How's the driver?" I asked. "Is he okay?"

She frowned, shook her head and whispered, "No, I'm afraid he's . . . dead."

"*What?* How?"

"I don't know yet. Just wait about fifteen minutes after I leave, then come to the store, as if I'd called you. We can talk about everything while we clean up."

I couldn't believe all the bombshells dropped in the last ten minutes and now I had to wait . . . again.

"*Mom . . . ?*"

"I guess that one's out, huh?" She turned to look at me and Tristan, her hand on the doorknob. "Alexis . . . I've known Tristan a long time. Well, our family has. He's familiar with who I am and what that means for you."

"Our *families* know each other?" I didn't even know our family.

"I don't have any family," Tristan muttered bitterly from behind me.

"Actually, my relatives—*our* relatives—have known Tristan for a long time. I'll explain later. For now, well . . . you can trust Tristan. I wasn't sure at first, but I know now."

Before I could ask anything else, she was gone, the door shutting behind her. I stared at it for a long moment.

"I need to go," Tristan said quietly from right behind me.

I spun around and glared at him. "Oh, no, you're not! You're staying here and explaining yourself, just as you said. You're not running away from me now, Tristan! You will—"

His glorious smile stopped me.

"What?" I asked with bewilderment. *What is he smiling about now?* As far as I was concerned, there was absolutely no reason for it.

"You really don't want me to leave?" he asked.

"Of course not!" I blurted.

He placed a hand against the door on each side of me, leaning close. My back pressed against the door as his eyes penetrated into mine. "Why? Because you want to hear what a freak *I* am? Or because you really want me to stay?"

I hated how he looked at me so intensely. It disarmed me. I forgot to be mad. "Um . . . both?"

He sighed. "I really need to go."

"Please don't," I said quietly, "don't leave me."

"Why?" he demanded again, his eyes searching deeply into mine.

I swallowed hard.

"Because . . . because I'm afraid you won't come back," I finally whispered, dropping my head so he couldn't see my eyes. "Just like the others . . . ."

"Alexis," he murmured, lifting my chin with his thumb to look me in the eye. "Lexi . . . I'm not like the others, but I *do* have to go now."

The corners of his mouth twitched, like he wanted to smile, but his eyes were dark, serious. And when I felt that crack in my heart again, I knew it didn't hurt because I was scared of who he was. It hurt because I was afraid to lose him. I jerked my face away from his hand and ducked under his arm. I didn't want him to see the betrayal and sadness quickly rising to the surface.

"Fine, if that's what you want," I muttered, my back to him.

"Yes, it's what I want," he said and the crack grew larger, making my breath catch. "Because if we're going to the store, I think I should have a shirt on. I promise I'll be right back."

And, just like Mom, he was out the door, shutting it behind him before I could respond.

I spun around and slammed my fists against the door. *How does he do that to me?* I could imagine the huge, smug grin on his face.

"Who *are* you, Tristan Knight?" I asked the empty house as I slumped against the door.

Chapter 11

After a minute or so, I finally straightened up and locked the door. *If he comes back, he'll have to* beg *me to come inside!* Then I stomped to my bedroom to change out of my own blood-stained clothes. I never heard the motorcycle come or go, but Tristan was back by the time I'd washed the dried, matted blood out of my hair and dressed. He sat at the kitchen table, waiting for me, when I skidded to a stop in the doorway.

"How did you . . . ?" I asked with wonder, looking at the front door I knew I'd just locked and back at him.

"You should really lock the doors when you're home alone," he said.

"I did!"

He nodded at the back door, off the kitchen. "Are you sure?"

I groaned. "Don't do that to me! For a second there, I thought you could just magically appear out of nowhere, too!"

He chuckled. "Are you ready?"

"Absolutely. I need some explanations before I go insane."

The phone rang just as we reached the front door. I considered ignoring it, but thought it could be Mom, needing us to bring something. Tristan followed me back to the kitchen.

"Alexis, honey, you can't come here," Mom said when I picked up. "You and Tristan both need to stay away."

"Why?"

"The media is here," she said, as if that were enough explanation.

"And . . . so?" Since we supposedly hadn't been there, they wouldn't have anything to ask us.

"Honey, you both just need to stay out of it. Owen and I will finish up and I'll be home as soon as I can." Her voice was firm and I knew there was something more she couldn't tell me. "We'll talk about everything when I get home, okay?"

"Promise?"

"I promise, honey. You deserve to know. Can you please start a pot of coffee? We'll need it."

"Yeah, sure." I hung up and headed for the coffee pot, telling Tristan about the media.

"Hmm . . . yeah, wouldn't be a good idea," he said, leaning against the counter. "We need to stay under the radar."

"Why?"

"You and I, well, we don't need to be broadcasting we're together. Certain . . . *people* . . . don't need to know," he said cryptically. I stared at him, waiting for an explanation. "You'll find out soon. Tonight. Just wait for Sophia."

I groaned with frustration and impatience. Coffee grounds spilled everywhere as I sloppily scooped them out of the can and practically threw them into the filter basket. I took a deep breath to calm myself and thought of a question I could ask and not have to wait for the answer.

"So, what kind of medical training do you have, anyway?"

"Well, um, to be completely honest . . . pre-med and some med school."

I looked at him, confused. "How did you do all that already? You're only twenty, right?"

He grimaced. "Yeah, about that . . ."

"What?" I asked with trepidation, quickly realizing this wasn't such a safe topic after all.

"Well, uh . . . you know how Sophia doesn't age?"

"Yeah." I waited for him to finish, but he just looked at me with his eyebrows raised. "You . . . ? *No way!*"

He smiled weakly and shrugged.

"*Really?* So how old *are* you?"

"Well, um . . ." I'd never heard so many "well, um's" come from Tristan, never seen him so uncomfortable. He really didn't want to tell me. "I was, uh, born in 1743, but I don't like to think of it that way. I prefer to be somewhere between nineteen and twenty-four."

My mouth dropped as I held the coffee pot in mid-air. *What the . . . ?* Then several things flew through my mind . . . his quick reflexes and uncanny physical abilities on the basketball court . . . his travels all over the world . . . he could heal . . . his strength . . . how he appeared in my kitchen when there was no reason the back door would be *un*locked . . . the fire in his eyes . . . Mom at the store, stressing how much blood there was . . . . I inhaled sharply. *He sucked my blood!*

"Oh! Oh, oh, *oh!*" The coffee pot shook in my hand and then began sliding through my fingers, but I was in too much shock to do anything but watch it fall. Just before it hit the floor, Tristan's hand darted down and caught it. I jumped back several feet. "Oh, holy *crap!* You *are* a vampire!"

He looked at me and something flickered in his eyes.

"Alexis," he said as he set the pot on the counter, "don't be absurd."

"*Absurd?*" I shrieked, backing away from him. "I *know* vampires. I read and watch and research and write about them all the time. And you have all the characteristics! Well, except the pale skin. And you can go out in the sun. And you don't have fangs or anything. But maybe those are just myths . . . ."

"Alexis, are you *listening* to yourself?"

I stopped and stared at him. And then I realized what I said and knew he was right. It was quite absurd. But the whole night was completely absurd.

"Are you listening to *your*self?" I shot back. "All night long . . . all these things about you . . . . Or are you making them up, still thinking I have some fantasy to be *with* a vampire?"

He chuckled. "I promise you, that's not what I'm doing. Please stop thinking such nonsense."

"Well . . ." Frustration overwhelmed me. "I'm sorry! But this night is completely crazy! What with almost being killed and *you* and everything else . . . I mean, I'm totally freaked out! At this point, I'm not sure what to believe!"

"Do you know how you *weren't* killed?" he asked calmly.

"Yeah, I know . . . you yanked us off the ladders. That doesn't mean anything. If vampires really exist . . . well, if you *are* one, then I know you'd be a *good* one."

"I didn't *yank* you off the ladders. Not the way you're thinking, anyway. Last I checked, vampires couldn't do this." He flicked his hand and somehow I flew the eight or so feet between us and was suddenly in Tristan's arms. My breath caught and my heart stopped beating. "*That's* how you and Sophia didn't end up under the car."

"How . . . did you . . . *do* that?" I croaked.

"It's a special . . . ability," he said quietly.

"Don't let go of me," I whispered, "or I might pass out."

"Don't worry," he murmured, his lips right against my ear. "I like you right where you are."

"You're really not a vampire?" I asked.

"Absolutely not. I'm *much* more dangerous." He lowered his mouth against my neck and sucked lightly. "But I can pretend to be one, if you ever want me to."

"Tristan . . ."

"Sorry. But you do taste quite delicious." He sucked again.

"*Tristan.*" I squirmed out of his arms. "You're distracting me."

"Good." He grinned. I rolled my eyes. "Then what would *you* like to do while we wait for Sophia?"

I returned to making the coffee, filling the pot with water.

"Tell me more, what you *can* tell me. Are you really that . . . *old?*"

The smile disappeared and he didn't answer for several moments. "Yes, I am. But, like I said, I prefer not to think about it like that. You'll understand—I hope, anyway—by the time the night is over."

I could tell there was something ominous coming later. I hated having to wait for it, but I wanted complete answers, which I wouldn't get without Mom.

"Okay, then . . ." I poured the water into the coffee maker and turned it on while trying to think of a different subject. "So, uh . . . if you went to med school, how come you're not a doctor? Oh, wait. You probably are, aren't you?"

He shook his head. "No, I could never complete the program, since I didn't age through it."

I could actually understand that. "Oh, yeah, right. Mom's had similar . . . problems."

He looked at me for a long moment and then took my hands into his and gently pulled me closer to him. "Alexis, you're going to find out some things about me . . . about my past . . . that you won't like. It may be enough to make you detest me and never want to see me again."

I shook my head. "I highly doubt that."

"Don't decide yet. Hear it all out. But I need to tell you something, in case this is my last chance." He cupped his hands on each side of my face, holding me there so he could gaze directly into my eyes. "Alexis . . . you are my soul mate. I've loved you since the day you first sat next to me in that women's studies class. I didn't know it then, but I can't deny it now. Now that you're going to find out who I really am, you'll understand how incredibly amazing, but so unexpected this is. I didn't even know I *could* love anyone. But . . . I love *you, ma lykita.*"

I stared back into his eyes and, although I knew he wasn't who I thought he was—not *normal*, in other words—I still felt what I felt. So when he pressed his mouth against mine, I happily kissed him back. As he continued to kiss me, his hands slowly slid down my neck, over my shoulders and down my arms. I cringed as sharp pains shot through my forearms at his touch.

He abruptly pulled back and lifted my wrists in each of his hands, studying my arms.

"Ah, shit," he muttered.

I looked down to see what caught his attention. Two bumps on my left forearm and three more on my right, bigger than large mosquito bites, swelled under my skin. "What are they?"

"Glass. You healed with pieces of glass still in the wounds."

"What?" I knew he spoke real words, but I couldn't grasp the meaning. It just wasn't registering.

"Alexis . . . your skin grew around them."

I stared at my arms. *That's a new one.* I'd never thought of it being an issue before and now that I did—imagining the glass embedded under my skin—my stomach clenched.

"*Ew,*" I breathed, totally incapable of saying anything else, not able to take my eyes off the lumps in my skin.

"Where does Sophia keep her medical kit?" Tristan asked. He started throwing open and banging closed the kitchen cabinet doors.

"Um . . . in her bathroom, I think. Why?"

He took my hand and pulled me toward the hallway and Mom's bedroom.

"I need to see if she has a scalpel in there."

"*What?*" I stopped as if I'd run into an invisible brick wall, yanking him to a halt.

"We need to get the glass out, while it's still close to the surface."

I gulped.

"You have to *cut* it out?" I looked at the lumps on my arms, imagining the cutting and digging. My head became light and woozy as the blood drained to my feet.

"You're turning green," he said, wrapping his arm around my waist. "You okay?"

"Um . . . *no!*" Sweat beads popped out on my forehead.

Mom came through the front door just then, quickly shutting and locking it behind her. She gave us a strange look as we just stood there in the hallway.

"Honey, are you okay?" she asked, concern quickly filling her eyes. "You're green."

I lifted my arms for her to see. I could tell she knew immediately what was wrong—her whole body seemed to sink in defeat.

"Can this night get any worse?" she muttered.

"Tristan says we have to cut them out?" I made it a question, really hoping she had a better idea.

She quickly regained her composure and started barking orders. "Tristan, get some old towels from the broom closet. I'll get my kit. You, Alexis, just sit and put your head between your legs. You really don't look so good."

Within a few minutes, my desk lamp was set up on the kitchen table, the bright light glinting off a scalpel, tweezers, a needle and syringe and a small glass bottle. Mom sat down on my right side, taking my hand to stretch my arm across a folded towel for padding.

"Uh . . . maybe Tristan should do it," I said apprehensively. "I mean, he did go to medical school and all."

Mom glanced up at Tristan, who still stood beside me.

"Yeah, there's been a lot that's come out already," he admitted. "But I think you'd better do this. Your hands are smaller."

He gave her a quick run-down of what I already knew as he sat in the chair to my left and took my free hand into his.

"Don't worry, Alexis, I know what I'm doing, too," Mom said. She slid the needle into the rubber top of the bottle and filled the syringe with a clear liquid. "I used to be a nurse, after all."

"Seriously?" I asked. "I never knew that."

"Actually, that's how I first met Tristan. During the Second World War—"

"*The Second World War?*" I flinched more from surprise at what she said than from the needle she just stuck into my arm. "That was, what, the nineteen-forties? But . . . you're only forty-three. You weren't even born yet!"

"Yes, well, that was easier for you to understand, when you did the math. But I'm actually . . . a-hundred-and-sixteen."

"*What?*" I stared at her in shock and a hysteric laugh burst out. *They're both so old!* "But . . . *how?* Will I be like that, too?"

"I can't answer the first one and yes to the second." She stood up and poured us all a cup of coffee as I tried to absorb that, but I couldn't. *I'm going to live that long . . . or longer?* I looked at Tristan and he squeezed my hand.

"Think your mom's a vampire, too? Or you, for that matter?" he asked with a small smile.

"Vampires? Ha! If only it was so simple," Mom said, bringing our coffee cups over to the table. She sat back down and we sipped our coffee for a few moments, waiting for the anesthetic to take effect. She pressed her fingers in several places along my forearm.

"Can you feel that?"

"No." I really didn't know if it was from the anesthetic or if I numbed all over from renewed shock.

She picked up the scalpel and I must have turned green again.

"You probably shouldn't watch," she said.

I lay my head against the table, looking away, toward Tristan. He brushed my hair back and stroked my cheek. I felt pressure on my arm, but no pain. I concentrated on Tristan's face, trying hard not to visualize what I felt.

"So . . . to start at the beginning," Mom said as she worked, "we—me, you, our family—are a part of the *Amadis*. The best I can explain it for now is the Amadis is like a society or culture. Our family is the original Amadis, but others have joined us."

"Like a cult?" I asked, looking up in surprise.

Mom shook her head. "No, not a cult. It's the society or civilization for . . . people like us."

"There are other people like *us*?"

"Not exactly like us . . . but they're not like normal people either. That's all I can say for now." She picked up the tweezers, about to poke them into the hole in my arm. I lay my head back down.

"So our family started this uh-MOD-eez"—I sounded out the foreign word—"but others have joined it?"

"Right. Others who are sort of like us and want to live like us—for good, not evil. So, the Amadis, our family, and Tristan's . . ."

She hesitated, like she didn't know what to call Tristan's relatives.

"Creators," he filled in for her, his voice hard. "I'm telling everything about me, so let's just get it out there. I was technically born, but those were not anything I would call parents. It's more accurate to say I was created. Genetically designed . . . to be the ultimate warrior."

Chapter 12

Genetically designed? The ultimate warrior? I wanted to laugh—
it sounded ludicrous—but Tristan's face was completely serious.

"The ultimate warrior for the *Daemoni*," Mom said, disgust
filling that last word, and I knew this was no joke. "The Amadis
and the Daemoni are, well, we'll just say innate enemies. You'll
have to wait for the story behind it, but you can understand
I mean much more than rivals or feuding families. Our very
kinds are, by nature, opposites."

"Our *kinds?* What does *that* mean?"

The tugging sensation in my arm stopped as Mom sighed
in frustration. "Honey, you just have to accept some things as
just the way they are without further explanation. Yes, our *kinds,*
as in our kinds of species."

My head shot up again. "*Species?* We're not even *human?*
What the hell are we, aliens?"

To my complete bewilderment, both Mom and Tristan
chuckled.

"We're human . . . sort of," Mom said, "just different than everyone else, which you already knew. And that's all I can say. Besides, *you're* still very much human and you will be for a long time."

Of course. The Ang'dora. So the *Ang'dora* would make me less human . . . and more like Mom. She didn't seem like a different *species,* though.

"You can't say things like that and not explain."

She studied my face for a moment. "I'm sorry. I know it's not fair, but I'm not allowed to go into it. This is about Tristan, not us. I can only tell you what you need to know to understand him."

"But you're saying he's a different *kind* than us! How am I supposed to understand?"

"I'm not, really, a different kind, I mean," Tristan said. "Just be patient. You'll understand soon."

My eyes bounced between the two of them. Tristan looked apologetic—like he understood my frustration and wanted to tell me more. But Mom's face was set firmly. She wouldn't budge.

"Okay, fine," I sighed. "So our family—"

"My side of your family," Mom corrected. *Of course, there's another side.* I tended to forget that. The sperm-donor, as I referred to him when I had to, had never been a part of my life and Mom never spoke of him. Now there seemed to be a reason why she made that distinction . . . but she quickly jumped on my thought. "No, I can't tell you about the other side right now."

She bent her head over my arm again, squirting it with water to flush out the blood. Then she picked up the tweezers.

"Right. Of course not," I mumbled, laying my head back down. I didn't mind avoiding that topic as much as the others. "So, the Amadis . . . if we are natural enemies of the . . . ?"

I couldn't remember the word.

"Daemoni," Mom filled in.

"Right. Day-MAH-nee. And the Daemoni created Tristan, then he is . . . ?"

Tristan's face darkened and his eyes dropped from mine.

"Basically . . . designed to kill your kind," he said grimly, wincing at his own words, as if they physically hurt him. "Their main purpose in creating me was to lead them into victory over the Amadis . . . and, eventually, humankind. The instinctual desire to seek your kind out and kill without hesitation was *bred* into me."

I raised my head and tried to gulp down the boulder-sized lump in my throat. It remained stuck.

"*Kill* us?" I whispered around it.

He slowly lifted his eyes back to mine. They looked horribly pained.

"But . . . you're not a killer," I said quietly, finding this more difficult to believe than anything else they'd told me . . . or not told me. He dropped his eyes again and stared at our hands, mine in his, in his lap. I had sensed a bit of danger in him. *But murder?* It didn't make sense. I shook my head in denial.

"I *have* killed people, Alexis," he answered just as quietly, still keeping his eyes from mine. "Innocent people. Amadis. That was my way of life."

I gulped and blinked back the tears stinging my eyes.

"*Was* your way of life, but not anymore," Mom added. "Right, Tristan?"

"Absolutely right," he said fiercely. "I turned my back on that many, many years ago, before you were born, Alexis, thanks to Sophia. She persuaded me to see the Daemoni from a different perspective and I saw how evil they were . . . how evil *I* was. They are, in all respects of the word, demons. Evil spirits. Followers and soldiers of Satan himself."

His voice was cold, his face contorted in disgust. A chill traveled up my spine.

Looking at him and knowing him the way *I* did, I just couldn't believe it. Then I thought about the flames I'd seen in his eyes. And how, this very night, he'd said he was much more dangerous than a vampire. I'd thought he was joking at the time. I shivered. He frowned, his brows furrowing.

"A little over twenty years ago, Sophia somehow convinced me there was good inside me," he continued, his tone and expression softening from revulsion to appreciation with each word. "She took me to the Amadis and they taught me how to change inside, how to pull that good out and allow it to be the overpowering force within me."

"See, in their greedy desire to create the perfect warrior, the Daemoni underestimated the power of two types of blood they included in Tristan's," Mom explained. "There is enough Amadis and enough humanity in him that he was able to overcome the evil."

"So, you have Amadis in you? You *are* like us?" I asked, feeling hopeful after all the repulsive information they'd told me about the man I loved.

"If you trace it back several centuries, we have ancestors in common. I do have Amadis blood, but that doesn't make it easy to be like you."

"Tristan's been through a lot of pain and turmoil to strengthen this side of him," Mom added.

"It still takes solid concentration and self-control, but it's worth it. I'll *never* return to who—or *what*—I once was." The conviction was clear in his voice—as clear as the pain. "So . . . I came here to find you and Sophia, but I knew it had to be done in a certain way. It had to be in a place where you would be safe, just in case . . . . The Amadis told me you were taking classes at the college here, so I enrolled, too, hoping we would cross paths and I knew I could be around you without having an overwhelming urge to . . ."

His voice broke at the end and he was unable to finish.

"Kill me," I finished in a whisper.

He finally looked at me again and agony filled his eyes. He seemed to be pleading for me to understand. I tried to imagine what it would feel like to have an inherent desire to kill someone—as strong and natural as the need to drink when parched or eat when starving—and then to try to overcome that force when the object of desire was right there to be easily taken. The morsel of food or jug of water . . . or innate enemy . . . right there, taunting . . . The thought of harming someone repulsed me so much I couldn't complete the picture in my mind. I just knew it had to be nearly unbearable to fight that impulse . . . and the feeling of *not* conquering it could only be worse. Especially when the person you wanted to hurt—to kill—was the person you also loved.

I tempted this urge in him and didn't even know what he went through. My heart ached for Tristan and the struggle for control he had to fight every time he was with me. I squeezed his hand once to communicate I understood and then tried to pull my hand from his, thinking that just holding his hand made it even worse for him. He held tighter to mine, though, and shook his head.

"It's way too late for you to worry now," he whispered.

"Done with this arm," Mom said, standing up. "Trade places with me, Tristan."

Tristan took my hand as soon as he was seated again, now on my right.

"This is why I was so concerned when I first saw you with Tristan," Mom said as she rearranged everything in front of her. "I hadn't seen him in twenty years and I didn't know how he was. The Amadis told me over the years he was still *with* us, but he stayed away most of the time, so I didn't know for sure."

She filled the syringe again and I looked back at Tristan as she stuck the needle into my arm.

"I was too ashamed," Tristan muttered, dropping his eyes from mine, staring at his lap again. "I am supposed to be this strong, invincible, nearly perfect being, but it took immense effort to control my own nature. I didn't want the Amadis to see and know that about me. I would check in to let them know I hadn't gone back to the Daemoni and to absorb Amadis power when I needed it."

"Amadis power?" I asked. "What is that?"

"Sorry, hon," Mom said. "I can't give details. Just remember you and I—and Tristan—have unusual . . . abilities. Our powers must come from somewhere, right?"

Abilities? Powers? I'd never thought of them that way. They'd always been annoying quirks that made me weird. But after everything that happened tonight . . . and thinking about everything Mom and Tristan could do that just wasn't normal . . . I realized that's exactly what they were. I looked at Mom and opened my mouth to ask a question, but she shook her head.

"This is about Tristan, Alexis," she reminded me, seeing my frustration.

She pressed along my left arm and, not able to feel it, I shook my head. She picked up the scalpel and I immediately turned toward Tristan.

"Can I tell her what the Amadis power does for me?" he asked Mom. "So at least she can understand some of it and its importance to me?"

When Mom didn't answer—and I didn't feel any pressure on my arm yet—I looked at her. She seemed to be considering it, then finally nodded.

I lay my head against the table again and watched Tristan as he stared at the table and explained. "Amadis power allows me to conquer the . . . *monster* . . . within me. It strengthens the goodness, so it can overcome everything else bred into me."

"So it's good for you," I said.

"Yes," he answered quietly. "I *need* it."

"You would've been better off staying with them," Mom admonished. Tristan didn't answer. He looked at me again and returned to what he'd been saying.

"Once I realized that, with great effort, I could control myself with you, I wanted to learn more about you. You intrigued me . . . and you made me *happy*. In all my years, I had never experienced that emotion—happiness—and you gave it to me in a day." He smiled, but it didn't reach his eyes.

I hurt to hear he'd never once felt happiness in his two-hundred-odd years. *That's such a long time to live. And to be miserable the whole time?* But I never had either. In my very short life, I could not remember ever feeling real joy. Mom and I had some good memories, but not true happiness. Not like what I felt when I was with Tristan. He brought the best out of me. And now I couldn't imagine not being with him—going back to my old, dark, lonely life . . . I knew I just couldn't do it. Even knowing what I did now.

"So," he continued, "I started looking for more ways to spend time with you without scaring you off. I realized immediately when I'm with you, that monster inside . . . well, it doesn't exactly go away, but it's . . . quiet, repressed. *You* bring out the good in me."

"Like the Amadis power?" I asked, surprised.

He smiled again, less sorrow in it this time. "That's what I thought at first."

"It couldn't be," Mom said. "Until the *Ang'dora*, Alexis, your power is extremely weak. Not strong enough to do what you have for Tristan."

"And it's different," Tristan added. "It's just who you are naturally, what you do to me. Nothing special or extraordinary. Just you being you. You bring out the best in me."

Funny. I'd just been thinking the same about him. It dawned on me the connection we had—we each *needed* the other to truly thrive, to be the best we could be.

"So you *don't* want to kill me, right?" I asked.

Tristan grimaced. He stared at the table for a moment and then looked me directly in the eye. "I could not consciously harm a single hair on your head. I knew when I met you I *had* to maintain control—I could *never* hurt you—and it has become easier every day since. Even all that blood tonight . . . at one time that would have caused all hell to break loose. Literally. But not anymore."

"Why?" I asked. "I mean, why do you think it's easier to control now?"

"Because I love you," he said matter-of-factly, still holding my eyes. "The pain I would feel if I ever did anything to you far outweighs any desire or force within me. Sometimes that other force tries to fight it, but my love for you is overpowering every other urge."

"Love tends to do that," Mom said quietly. "What you need to understand, Alexis, is how amazing it is for Tristan to feel that . . . to know love. He was created for the exact opposite . . . hatred and evil—"

Tristan cringed.

"Sorry," she apologized. "But, unfortunately, it's true. I personally thought it was impossible for Tristan to love anyone. He's surprised us all, though me more than others. Many of the Amadis believed it could happen, that he could love. I didn't think he would go back to his old life—I wasn't positive, but I didn't *think* he would—but I never thought he could come so far as to *love*. And I have to admit it bothered me at first, that the person he loves is you, my own daughter. But I see you two together every day. I can't deny the truth . . . ."

We sat there quietly for a while, Mom continuing her mini-surgery on my arm. I closed my eyes and my mind whirled. A ticker tape of questions ran through my head. I hit information overload, unable to process it all.

"But now that you know the truth, Alexis, I'll understand if you can't love me," Tristan said quietly. "It's a lot to accept."

I chuckled. All this time I'd been worried about him not accepting me. He watched me as he waited for my answer, his eyes noticeably darkening with each beat of my heart. I knew he expected the worst. But all I could think about was what he overcame—his own natural desires, what he was *made* for—so he could be *good*. And I knew to my very core he was good. And he loved me. I squeezed his hand.

"I told you I wouldn't change my mind," I said.

He gazed into my eyes and he must have seen the truth because immediate relief washed over his face. He lifted my hand to his mouth and pressed his lips against the back of it.

"Okay, you're glass-free," Mom said, sitting back in her chair with a heavy sigh. "What a night."

"Oh, yeah, what happened at the store?" I asked. With such a surreal discussion, the accident now seemed like a different lifetime or dimension. "I mean, with the driver?"

"The police think he was drunk and tried to escape the car before it hit the store," Mom said. "The door was open as if he planned to jump, but apparently, he must have just fallen out and under the car, because it rolled over him, crushing his chest."

"Ugh." My own injuries from the night now felt miniscule. I could only hope it was quick for him. "Do they know who he was?"

"His name was Phillip Jones. He lived here in the Cape. Some people from the bar came down to the scene, said he'd been drinking since this morning because his wife left him."

Phillip . . . Phil . . . My mind flashed on the orange car sitting partially in the store . . . and then the orange Camaro the wife-beater at the park had jumped into when Tristan scared him off. *Oh!* I looked at Tristan, my eyes huge. He nodded with immediate understanding.

"Owen told me what happened at the park and this was the same guy," Mom said.

I bit my lip. "What did he tell you?"

"That you interrupted a domestic situation." Her voice trailed off and her eyes narrowed as the truth came to her. "Alexis! You *hit* him?"

Tristan spewed coffee out of his mouth. "I knew it!"

I jumped up for a paper towel, needing to escape their stares.

"He pissed me off," I mumbled, handing the towel to Tristan.

"Why didn't you say anything?" Mom asked.

"It wasn't like James, but—" I tugged at my hair and glanced at Tristan. "But I was afraid you'd make us move anyway."

Mom shook her head. "You and your temper. What am I going to do with you?"

I ignored the rhetorical question.

"Did Owen tell the police?" I asked. "They need to know, don't they? Tristan and I should probably give a report, too, right? Probably tell them everything."

"No," Mom said, to my surprise. "Right now the police think it was a drunk driver who lost control. Just an accident."

"But, Mom . . . that's obstruction of justice! He was purposely aiming for us!"

"Alexis, we don't know that for sure and we never will.

What more justice can there be, anyway? He's dead. What good can come of making it more than it seems?"

"Do you want that little girl to grow up thinking her dad attempted murder?" Tristan asked quietly.

I sighed heavily as I slumped back in my chair, thinking of that poor little girl. I didn't know whether to be relieved to know her dad would never hurt her or her mom again . . . or sad she would have to grow up without a dad at all. I decided to be relieved. From what I'd seen, he wasn't much more of a father to her than my sperm donor was to me.

"I'm exhausted and I think we better go to bed before this night gets any worse," Mom said, standing up and stretching. "It's late, Tristan. You're welcome to stay. Just remember . . . I'm right in the next room."

He nodded, the corners of his mouth twitching as he fought a smile at her comment, and then he turned to me. "Is that what *you* want?"

I thought about whether I wanted him nearby or if I needed time to think by myself. There was still so much I didn't know about him. I knew I wouldn't be able to sleep and if I needed to talk about anything, I would want him there. And I still wanted to be *with* him. I still loved him. Perhaps even more than I did just a few hours ago.

I placed my hand over his. "Yes, I want you to stay with me."

Chapter 13

I brushed my teeth and changed into a tank top and pajama shorts before Tristan joined me in my room. I sat on the bed nervously while he stood just inside the door.

"Are you okay with this?" he asked, hesitantly. "I mean, with me in general, first of all?"

I considered what he meant. My heart said I was okay with him, but my mind played devil's advocate. *He's killed people.* True, that was something I had to accept about him, but that was his past life. Not who he was now. Not *my* Tristan. *He wants to kill me.* No, he said he can't, I reminded myself. He said his love was stronger.

"Yes, I am more than okay with you."

"You're not scared of me now?"

"Should I be?"

He walked over to me and knelt on his knees so we were eye-to-eye, placing his hands on my thighs. "Do you still love me?"

"Definitely."

"As cliché as it sounds, I strongly believe our love will conquer anything else . . . at least, anything inside of me."

"I believe that, too. Besides, if you'd wanted to kill me, you've had plenty of opportunity."

He grimaced. "Let's not make light of it, okay?"

"Sorry. It's just that I . . . *trust* you."

He chuckled but there was no humor in it. "I tell you all this terrible stuff about me and *now* you trust me?"

"Yeah, ironic, huh?" I thought about that for a moment. "I guess it goes to show how powerful the truth is. Whatever you did in the past doesn't matter now. You've been forgiven. I love who you are *now*." I held my hands to his face, stroking his cheeks with my thumbs. "You are now more a part of me than ever."

"Yes, I have given you everything," he murmured. "Before I met you, I didn't even know I really had a heart. And now it is yours—all yours."

I pulled his face to mine and kissed him gently on his satiny lips. Then I kissed his forehead . . . and his eyelids . . . and his cheeks . . . and his chin . . . and the corners of his mouth. The built-up emotions of the night—fear, anxiety, shame, pain, sadness—crashed down on us and then were pushed away by the strongest of them all: love. Our lips moved together hungrily. I tasted the tangy-sweetness on his lips . . . his breath . . . his tongue.

Our kisses became more passionate as he leaned into me. My heart raced with excitement, my body pulsing with electrical charges he sent through it with every touch. I wrapped my legs around his waist and pressed my body into his while pulling him closer still with my arms. I wanted to just melt into him and let him feel that I did really love him.

He laced his fingers into my hair and pulled gently back, exposing my neck. He moved his lips along my jaw, down my throat. I let out a sigh as he kissed my collar bone and then pulled my head back further, lifting my chest. He nestled his face between my breasts. His rigid body trembled against mine. I squeezed him with my arms and legs.

And then he let go of my hair and his body slackened as he breathed heavily against my chest. My own breathing was ragged as I struggled to use my brain, to figure out why he'd stopped.

We both sat there for a minute, him on his knees, his head against my chest, me holding him tight, but starting to relax. When the fog cleared from my mind, I knew it was good he'd stopped. I wasn't ready for anything more.

"I don't think we should push it any further," he finally said.

"Right," I agreed, reluctantly letting him go.

"I should probably go home."

"Please don't," I reacted. Then I remembered what I did to him—his internal struggle between wanting to love me and wanting to kill me—and my heart hurt for him again. "I mean, I wish you would stay, but if you think you need to . . ."

He rocked back on his heels and his face was tight, as if concentrating hard on something. His eyes were closed and he took careful, controlled breaths. When he opened his eyes, the gold looked more like fire than sparkles, but not bright flames like I'd seen before. That's when I realized what the flames meant . . . he was about to lose control. Each time I'd seen them, we'd been in a moment of passion and passion led to loss of control, regardless of who—or what—you were. I knew that already just from the little bit I'd experienced. He stopped us not just because he was a gentleman, but also to protect me. I shuddered.

"I do scare you," he said quietly.

I shook my head.

"I trust you, Tristan," I whispered, my throat hot and dry. A cold glass of ice water suddenly seemed absolutely necessary. "You want a glass of water?"

He smiled. "That would be wonderful."

I stood up and found my legs to be slightly weak and wobbly. By the time I returned and we both drained our glasses, we felt cooled down enough to lie safely together. We lay on our sides in my small bed, my back against his chest, his arms around me, holding me close. But my mind continued to spin, not ready to shut down, questions still flying through it. I started with an easy one.

"So, when's your birthday?" I asked.

"Ah. Now the questions." He chuckled in my hair. "October 31."

"*Halloween*? Oh . . . I guess that shouldn't be surprising."

"It was just a coincidence, though, especially since I was premature," he said. "I was *born*. They didn't hook me up to a machine and turn a switch on."

"So you're not like Frankenstein?" I asked with a giggle.

"Definitely not. They just made sure the right genes . . . and other things . . . were a part of my creation. But I'm more like you than you realize."

"You keep saying that and I believe it . . . although I still really don't know who I am."

"I'm sorry I can't tell you, but it's not my place." He kissed the back of my head. "If you pay attention to your mom and to me—and really believe we're very much alike—you'll get an idea of who you'll become."

"Hmm . . . good idea. So, we missed your birthday. I'll have to make that up to you."

"No need. I prefer not to acknowledge it," he said sadly. I realized the real meaning of his dislike for Halloween.

"So are you twenty-one now?"

"My age is irrelevant. I can be whatever you'd like me to be."

"Well, I'm eighteen, almost nineteen . . ." I sucked in my

breath as a thought occurred to me. "You know, you are quite the dirty old man!"

He chuckled quietly in my ear. "I guess you could look at it that way. But I'd rather not. Let's say I'm twenty, okay?"

"Okay. That works for me. So, how'd you meet Mom? During the war, I mean."

"She was a nurse, I was a soldier."

"You were a soldier? You fought in the war? Wait . . . which side were you on?"

He sighed. "I've fought in many wars and most of the time not on the side you would prefer. But, in that one, I was on the Allied side. The Daemoni had an ulterior motive for me with some American soldiers."

"Oh." I didn't know how to respond.

"I never completed it, though."

"Why not?"

"One of my . . . targets . . . was severely wounded. Sophia took care of him. I knew who she was, but I couldn't bring myself to do what I'd been created for. She was so tender and caring. She didn't know this guy at all, but she showed so much . . . *love* for this complete stranger." He paused. "That's when I first started to comprehend the action of love—not the emotion, but at least what it looks like in action. I'd always hated the way I was, but I didn't know any other way. Not until then. So I left her alone, left him alone. He became an influential reverend and then U.S. senator—that's why I was supposed to take him out. So, I considered leaving the Daemoni then. I started thinking about whether I *could* be any different. It took nearly forty years, though, before I knew for sure I could change—the next time I met Sophia, when she took me to the Amadis."

Wow. Tears filled my eyes. "She saved you," I whispered.

"Yes, she did. That's how I knew I was okay with her—I

could be around her without any of those . . . urges—and I just had to worry about you. I knew she wanted me to stay away from you, but I couldn't, and it was difficult to defy her like I did. I owe everything to Sophia—more than just my life. So much more."

We lay there silently for a minute or so. I thought he was done, but then he continued. "When I joined the Amadis, I shed that old life permanently, Alexis. It was like a rebirth. I took the name Tristan Knight and started a whole new life, never looking back. I need you to understand that."

"I know already," I said quietly, squeezing his hand. "And, in that way, you *are* only around twenty."

"Yes, that's how I like to look at it." I could hear the smile in his voice. "Now, can we change the subject? Or go to sleep?"

Sleep? Yeah, right.

"If you wanted to sleep, you should've gone home."

He chuckled. "Then ask a different question. Preferably, something about the present. The past is gone and I'd rather you not think of me the way I was."

"To me, you'll always be my Tristan. I love the person you are now. We can leave the past where it belongs."

He hugged me tighter in appreciation. I kissed his hand while I thought about an easier topic.

"Do you really do all that stock market and consulting stuff? Or was that just a cover?" I finally asked.

"No, I do that. I tried to be as honest as I could with you. The consulting I do is for the Amadis. And one of my abilities is I can open my mind to see all the possibilities in a situation and identify the best solution or path to take, as long as I have the facts. So that stuff is easy to me."

"Wow. That must make school easy. But why do you even bother with school anyway?"

"Right now, as I said, to meet and get to know you. And it's an appropriate thing to do at my age."

"Isn't it boring? I mean, surely you've learned all this before, especially these lower level classes."

"If I'm actually going for a degree, yeah, some things can be repetitive. But many things have changed so much over the years that much of it is new to me, too."

"How many degrees do you *have*?"

He chuckled lightly in my ear. "Three bachelor's—finance, engineering and architecture—and an MBA. I've done the medical thing a couple of times, because medicine really has changed over my time."

"Wow," I breathed. "That's . . . *incredible*. You don't act or talk like you're so educated. I mean, not that you act stupid or anything, you just don't . . . talk down to me or the others, I guess."

"I adapt, remember? I become the person I need to be for the situation."

"Hmm . . ." This bothered me. I couldn't help but wonder how much he'd adapted himself to be the person he needed to be for me.

He seemed to read my mind. "Don't worry . . . I'm still me. Well, the me *I* want to be," he said. "I just meant the way I talk, the words I use . . . . The reason I said soul mate earlier—that I believe we are meant to be together—is because, first of all, you are the only one who has made me capable of loving, and secondly, because I can be the me *I* want to be and it works with you."

"It works very well," I agreed, comforted. "Tell me about this healing stuff. I mean, how you can heal other people. Mom and I can't do that. Well, I don't *think* Mom can."

"You won't know what you can do until after the *Ang'dora*. But, for me, every ability I have is more powerful than anyone else's. The healing ability is strong in my DNA, so, in my saliva, in my blood . . . ."

"Ah. So what are your other abilities? What does it mean to be the *ultimate* warrior?"

He sighed. "It means they designed me to be nearly perfect in mind and body to win any type of battle . . . mental or physical. They gave me the best offenses and the best defenses. But, I'm not completely infallible. I have my weakness . . . ." His voice trailed off.

"My kind?"

"You specifically . . . in so many ways."

"What do you mean?" I wanted to turn over, to see his face, but he held me tightly.

"You not only tempt my innate inhuman urges, but also my very basic, human desires. We are hazardous to each other. And I am weak to your happiness, so anything you ask of me, I will probably give. But the worst of it is if others—the Daemoni—see my love for you, they will know they can use it against me . . . which means hurting you."

"That's why they can't see us together. Why we had to stay away from the media tonight."

"Exactly. This is a dangerous love we share."

"So they'll come after us?" As soon as I asked I wondered if they already had come after me. I almost asked if he knew anything about that night in Arlington. Had they been Daemoni? *Impossible. They weren't even real.* I'd convinced myself it was just a dream. A tremble of fear shook me anyway.

"It's okay, *ma lykita*. You have me—*your* ultimate warrior. I'm kind of created to kick some serious ass." Although he lay behind me, in the dark, I knew he was grinning. I relaxed in his arms.

We lay in silence for a while. The green numbers on my clock glowed 3:14. I started to feel tired and my mind finally wound down. The electric currents had settled down, too.

"Tristan?" I asked, wondering if he was still awake.

"Hmm?"

I almost didn't ask . . . it would be embarrassing if he didn't feel it, too.

"Um, do you still feel that electric current between us? It seemed like you did before, when we first got together."

He chuckled. "Definitely."

"Do you know what it is? I mean, is that part of . . . you? Who you are?"

He didn't answer at first, seeming to be thinking about it. "I honestly am not sure. I *think* it's part of who *we* are . . . but I haven't figured that one out yet. But I like it."

"Yeah, me, too," I said with a grin. "Are you glad it's all out now? I mean all the secrets? Because I am. It's a relief to finally talk about it."

"Now that I know you love me, yes, I am. I knew it had to happen and part of me couldn't wait to tell you everything. Do you remember when you threw the dart at me?"

I snorted. "How could I forget? I was mortified!"

"I saw it coming as soon as you let go. I could have plucked the dart right out of the air before it got close." He snapped his fingers in the air as if grabbing an invisible dart.

"Why didn't you? I was so humiliated!"

He chuckled. "You were adorable. And that's why I didn't. I decided in that moment your reaction to super-human reflexes could be worse than to my ability to heal, since you can do that, too. So I made the safe choice. But you didn't even notice."

"I did notice the hole in your skin was pretty tiny, but I didn't know what would've been normal. I generally don't throw darts at people."

"Just me, huh?"

"Yeah, you're special." I giggled, giddy from exhaustion. "But you didn't say anything about healing then."

"No, I let it go. I decided it was too soon. And I haven't said anything since then because I've been afraid I'd lose you forever and I didn't know if I could handle that."

How ironic that I'd been feeling the same way and my secrets were nothing compared to his. I realized how difficult it must have been for him, not just tonight, but since the day we met.

"I love you, Tristan," I whispered.

"I love you, too, *ma lykita*," he murmured into my ear. He kissed my hair and I felt myself relax into him and let sleep take over.

Chapter 14

The next month blew through like a fast-moving hurricane, with school, helping Mom at the bookstore, finals, the holidays and Tristan swirling around me. I hardly had time to take care of necessities, like sleep, let alone write between Thanksgiving and Christmas. I didn't even feel the void in my life as the manuscript waited patiently on my computer. There was too much going on and my brain was too full to think about that whole other fictional world.

It felt like a strangely normal life, putting aside all the peculiar things. Sometimes, especially when I was alone in bed at night, I'd think about what Mom and Tristan had told me. Questions floated lazily in my head just before I'd crash from exhaustion. I usually forgot them by the time I had the chance to ask. Mom shut me down on the few I did ask her—they weren't relevant enough for her to give me answers. Tristan was more open, as long as they were about him, but not about his horrible past and definitely not about the Daemoni. Because of his willingness to tell me so much, I opened up to him, too. We started building a *real* relationship.

On the Sunday before Christmas, finals out of the way and only the holidays to worry about now, Tristan and I went for a ride on the Harley to Gasparilla Island. We hadn't been there since that one extraordinary weekend that now felt like a lifetime ago. It wasn't quite the same as I remembered—like anything you hold in your memory as a special treasure, built up over time and looked forward to with great anticipation, it's never quite as special as the first time. But it was still a favorite place. The air was cooler than it had been in October and the breeze stronger. We didn't dare kick off our shoes and walk on the cold, wet sand. So when we stopped to enjoy the view, we watched from our perch on the bike, my body leaned against the back rest and Tristan's against mine, my chin resting on his shoulder.

"So, I was thinking . . . ," he started to say as we gazed over the beach.

"Uh-oh," I teased. "That can be dangerous, you know."

"Hmm . . . I'll try not to hurt myself."

I smiled at the thought of this genius hurting himself because he was thinking too hard and skimmed my lips across his cheek.

"You're trying to distract me," he murmured.

"Maybe."

"Seriously . . . I've been thinking about what to get you for Christmas."

"Ah. It's less than a week away, you know. You should have started thinking a long time ago."

"I did, as soon as I realized you and Sophia celebrate Christmas. I think I have the perfect gift, but I want to know what you want, just to be sure."

"I have what I want right here." I ran my lips over his cheek again.

"Hmph. I'd like to give you something you can keep with you to remind you of me when I'm not around."

"Like I can ever forget you." I kissed his ear and he sighed. "Well, before you *do* hurt yourself over this, I need to tell you the house rules. We only give gifts to each other that have significant meaning. So they can only be something we, ourselves, love dearly and are willing to give to the other, or something we've created with thought and love. Does that make it easier?"

"Hmm . . . then, yes, it's perfect." He relaxed. "Any other rules I need to know about?"

I told him the traditions Mom started when I was young.

"Huh. That's interesting. I thought Christmas was about Santa Claus and presents and watching football on TV."

I chuckled. "Not the way we do it. So, you game?"

"Definitely. It sounds . . . fun."

I kissed his cheek again and then brushed my lips down along his jaw line and back up to his ear.

"Thank you for today," I whispered. "I needed it."

"It's not nearly over. I'm taking you someplace special for dinner."

"Oh," I said, stiffening. "I should get home to change then."

"No, not necessary. You're fine . . . well, maybe overdressed." He smiled.

I furrowed my brows. I wore a long-sleeve cotton shirt and jeans. *How special can this place be?* When we returned to the Cape, he didn't take me home. We traveled on unfamiliar streets lined with royal palms and obnoxiously huge houses with canals in their backyards. I hadn't been in this part of town, so I had no idea where we headed. We came to the end of one of these streets and, although the view was blocked, I knew the beach and the Gulf spread beyond the other side of the foliage lining the dead-end. He pulled into a wide, private driveway leading to a large, concrete-and-glass structure overlooking the water.

"This looks fancy. You said I was *over*dressed," I whispered when he cut the engine to the bike.

He chuckled. "This is my house, silly."

My mouth dropped. He'd never brought me to his house; we'd never had any reason to come here. I'd imagined he lived in a small, bachelor-pad type of place . . . like where a twenty-year-old college kid would sleep and shower because he was never home for anything else anyway.

The entire lower level appeared to be nothing but garage from the outside, with four full-size overhead doors. Tristan poked some buttons on a keypad by one of the doors. The door opened as he came back to the bike and started it up. We pulled into the garage and parked next to the crotch-rocket.

"Holy crap, Tristan." I giggled, nearly at a loss for words as I looked around. "This is . . . *outrageous*."

"I told you I like toys." He laughed and closed the garage door while I walked around, admiring the "toys."

One side of the garage housed a speed boat, a Waverunner and other water sports equipment. On the other side, besides the two motorcycles, were a big, metallic-blue pick-up truck, a shiny black Mercedes convertible and a hot red Ferrari Spider—which I only knew after caressing my hand over the shiny emblem.

"You don't even use these . . . do you?" I'd never seen them before.

"Not so much. I prefer feeling the freedom on the bikes. But when I want them, they're right here waiting. And they're nice to look at." He'd come up behind me and put his arms around me, pulling me close to him. He murmured in my ear, "Almost as nice as you."

Heat rose to my face . . . in both embarrassment and

excitement at his breath on my ear. He brushed his lips down my neck. Goosebumps rose on my arms. Then he took my hand and led me upstairs to the rest of the house.

From the stairs, we came into a large, open room with floor-to-ceiling windows on the opposite wall, overlooking the Gulf of Mexico. Low sunlight streamed through the windows. The décor was sparse, looking more like the lobby of a business than a home. There was a sitting area in the east half, at the top of the stairs, that included glass end tables, a boxy, black-leather couch and loveseat sitting on a white, shaggy rug. Various paintings hung on the walls and an easel with a half-finished image stood at the window-wall. Long tables displaying what looked like doll houses edged the western half of the room.

Tristan picked up an electronic gadget from one of the tables and when he touched the front of it, the screen glowed. He touched it several more times and some lights came on in the house and music started playing through speakers in the ceilings.

"Another toy?" I asked with a raised eyebrow. He just grinned.

"Come on, I'll show you around before I start dinner," he said, taking my hand again and leading me down a hallway off the living room.

The first room was an office with a large, chrome-and-glass desk, three computer screens and two walls lined with glass shelves full of books. Calendars and various charts hung on a third wall and the fourth wall was windows, facing the Gulf. An oversized, white suede chair with fat cushions and an ottoman squatted in front of the windows. I imagined curling up in the chair with a book, reading until I fell asleep.

"This is where I spend the majority of my time when I'm not with you," Tristan said and then he led me to another room, across the hall. "And this is where I am the rest of the time . . .

unless I'm at the big gym."

It was a home gym, complete with weight machines. A large, thin mat covered half the floor, where various sized punching bags hung from the ceiling along one edge of it. The walls were bare, except for one picture. I took a couple steps closer to it and realized it was a beautifully hand-drawn picture of me, framed and matted.

"Tristan?" I asked, not able to pull my eyes away to look at him.

"It's a reminder of why I need to improve my self control," he explained quietly.

"*You* drew it?" I looked at him with awe.

He smiled sheepishly. "I started with a sketch when we were studying . . . well, *you* were studying. It was shortly after we met."

"Wow . . . I never knew," I breathed, not realizing the extent of his talent. I'd seen the cartoons he'd drawn during class, of course, and still had one tacked to my bulletin board above my desk. But this was no cartoon. He'd captured my expression perfectly in the photo-like drawing. "You're so talented."

"It's easier when I have a beautiful subject," he said with a grin. I rolled my eyes.

Also off the hallway were a bathroom, a laundry room and a closet housing all kinds of baffling electronics. He explained it was the control room for the system that automated the lights, music and hurricane shutters. One of the tall, black cabinets held a CD-changer with *hundreds* of CDs in it. I just shook my head, at a loss of words for such . . . indulgence.

He then took me upstairs to the top level, which was nothing but a large master-suite loft looking over the living room. A huge—had to be bigger than a king size—platform bed faced the western wall of windows. I eyed the bed, with its black, satiny comforter and many pillows.

"You really need this big of a bed?" I teased.

"I actually hardly ever sleep in it anymore. It feels too big and empty. I prefer the chair in the office these days. But . . . I think it has potential." He raised his eyebrows and grinned mischievously. Butterflies fluttered in my stomach. "Maybe we'll find out . . . some time. Right now, I need to start dinner."

He quickly showed me the master bath and I imagined the potential in there, too, with the big Jacuzzi tub and a shower the size of my bedroom. Back downstairs, he led me into the most amazing, dream kitchen. The décor was a little cold for my style—mostly concrete, stainless steel and glass. There were tons of cabinets and immense counter space, though, including an island in the middle and a bar at the western end.

"Tristan, you've been holding out on me!" I slid my hands along the smooth countertops and gazed at the six-burner stove. "This looks like so much more fun than Mom's tiny kitchen. We wouldn't be bumping into each other all the time."

He grinned. "I thought you might like it."

We cooked together, while listening to music and drinking wine. He usually played the role of prep-chef and I did the main cooking. While his slices and dices were precise, I was good at mixing, stirring and adding ingredients to give it the right flavor. We traded roles tonight and the linguine with clam sauce and a side salad tasted delicious.

After cleaning up, he poured us some more wine and played with his little toy to change the music while I took a closer look at the houses—they were actually architectural models, complete with landscaping. Each was in a different style and in a different setting. I leaned over to study the intricate details he'd added to each one.

"I showed you mine. Will you show me yours?" Tristan said from behind me. I whirled in shock. He laughed at my expression. "You've seen my creations, now. When do I get to see yours?"

Oh, my book. I circumvented the question by taking my glass from him, draining the wine and rerouting the conversation to the models.

"These are truly incredible. They must have taken you forever."

He shrugged. "I've done these since I moved here last summer. I'm still trying to figure out my dream home, I guess. I can't decide which one I like best."

"Why don't you just build all three, then you don't have to choose?" I giggled, thinking it may not be so unrealistic for him.

He laughed. "I've seriously thought about that. But . . . well, I'm waiting to get some input from the person I'll be sharing them with some day."

He smiled seductively. Butterflies fluttered again and my head went fuzzy. I never drank more than one glass of wine with Mom, so it didn't take much. And, of course, Tristan had that effect on me all by himself, especially like now, when he walked up to me, put his hands on my shoulders and gazed into my eyes, the gold in his sparkling brightly. He leaned over and kissed my jaw, his hands gliding down my back.

"So what do you think?" he murmured.

I couldn't answer immediately, his touch electrically stimulating my body, then finally, I giggled. Again. "I think I'm in no frame of mind to be thinking."

I put my arms around his neck and had to concentrate to keep his face in focus. I smiled, closed my eyes (*that feels better*) and tilted my face up for a kiss. He didn't deliver. I opened my eyes reluctantly and he stared at me with a funny expression. I thought it was concern, but didn't know why.

"What's the matter?" I asked, but it came out more like, "Wass da madder."

"Alexis, are you drunk?"

I giggled. "No, I don't think so. I have a really good buzz, though."

I sagged against him, still holding onto his neck. I kissed his chest through his shirt.

"Yeah . . . I think you're drunk. I better take you home."

"No! I don' wunna go home." I pulled myself up against him and kissed his neck and then put effort into speaking correctly. "I want to stay here with you. Be with you . . . maybe in that nice big bed upstairs?"

"Yeah, uh, I don't think so. I'm taking you home."

"Tristan, please?" I breathed. I pressed my body against his, pulling his head down closer and nuzzling my face against his neck. Then I stood on my toes and slid my lips along his jaw and, just as I reached his mouth, I lost my balance and would have fallen over if he hadn't been holding me.

"Nope. Let's go," he said firmly, extricating himself from my arms, while still holding me upright.

"Please?" I pouted, trying to look at him through my eyelashes. I probably looked like a fool. He shook his head. "Why?"

"Because I won't take advantage of you like this."

"You wouldn't be taking advantage of me. I promise." I smiled, trying to be seductive.

"As tempting as that sounds, *ma lykita*, I will not do anything with you that I may regret."

The smile fell off my face and unexpected tears pooled in my eyes. *Okay, self, wine makes me emotional . . . and stupid.* "You would regret it? You'd regret being with me?"

He rolled his eyes. "Yeah, you must be drunk if you think I'd regret being with you."

"But that's what you just said."

He sighed, but his expression looked amused. "What I

meant is I'm not going to do something that I'd always have to wonder if you really wanted it or if it was the wine. Okay?"

I sighed. "No, it's not okay."

"I think you'll get over it. Come on, I'm taking you home." He took my hand and pulled gently.

I reluctantly followed him downstairs and naturally headed to the motorcycle.

"Oh, no. I don't think you're in any shape for that," he said, pulling me over to the cars.

"Oooh, can we take the Ferrari? Let's be obnoxious!"

He laughed. "No, that's for going fast . . . *very* fast. You're not in any condition for that either and I'm not about to take the chance you'll puke all over it."

"I'm not that drunk, silly." I giggled again as he held the Mercedes door open for me. "Can we put the top down? I love driving topless."

He raised an eyebrow and that brought me to tears with laughter as he lowered the car's roof and pulled out of the garage. The cool December air blew on my face and sobered me quite a bit by the time we drove the two miles to my house. I shivered as we pulled in front of the cottage.

"Sorry," I said, as we headed inside. "I don't think I should mix you and wine. It's too much for my system."

He gave me a squeeze. "I thought it was just *you* who intoxicates *me*."

❧

The following week flew by as we managed the Christmas rush at the bookstore. Owen had gone home for the holidays, so Mom needed the extra help. Because we'd kept the store open until six on Christmas Eve, Mom and I didn't have much time to bake birthday cakes—the first part of our tradition. So we went over to Tristan's house to take advantage of his kitchen and all three of us made one at the same time.

While the cakes baked in the oven, we exchanged gifts, leaving Christmas Day for a birthday celebration. My stomach tightened with apprehension. Mom was easy and I knew she would love the CD I compiled for her. It was something she'd be able to play in the store and she was excited when she opened it. She gave me an emerald green blouse I'd seen her wear once and had told her how gorgeous it was on her. I didn't fill it out like she did, but I loved it . . . and so did Tristan when I modeled it.

It was his present I worried about. He wanted to read my unfinished book, but I wasn't nearly ready for anyone to read it, especially him. So I wrote him a poem about my love for him and had it framed with a small picture of me. The poem came directly from my heart, so it was, admittedly, pretty sappy. I didn't know if he'd like it or laugh at it. I sat on the couch next to him with my knees to my chest, tugging and twisting my hair as he opened and then read it. I held my breath the entire time.

He looked up at me and his eyes sparkled and . . . glistened. He bent over and kissed me on the cheek, murmuring, "It's perfect. Thank you."

I sighed hugely with relief and let myself relax.

"Your turn." He handed me a flat box. My hands trembled as I opened it.

I sucked in my breath. "Tristan, it's exquisite," I breathed. I couldn't take my eyes off it. "But I can't accept this. You cheated!"

Inside the box lay a silver chain with a beautiful pendant— two spaghetti-thick strands of silver entwined around each other and shaped into a circle with a triangular ruby dangling in the center. I'd never seen anything like it. When I looked up at him, his expression was pained and guilt stabbed my heart.

"Oh, I'm so *sorry!*" I said sincerely. I threw myself into his lap, put my arms around his neck and looked directly into his eyes. "I absolutely love it! And, even though you broke the rules, I'll keep it forever."

He swallowed. "But I didn't break the rules. The chain is new, but I designed and made the pendant myself."

I looked at the pendant and back at him. "You *designed* this?"

"Just for you. It's symbolic." He lowered his voice. "Two lives intertwined around one love."

"Oh. *My.*" I studied the pendant and happy tears filled my eyes. I treasured it more than anything I'd ever owned. I lifted my hair. "Put it on me. I'm *never* taking it off."

He clasped the chain and kissed my neck before I dropped my hair.

"Tristan . . . ?" Mom asked, her voice mixed with concern and wonder as she eyed the pendant against my chest. "Is that what I think it is?"

"Yes."

I looked at him questioningly.

"The stone is unique and very precious," he explained.

"Does it mean anything?" I asked. "I mean, besides the symbolism?"

"It's the closest I can come to giving you a piece of my heart." He shrugged it off, but his eyes told me it meant a lot.

"Thank you," I whispered, fingering the ruby. It felt strangely warm to the touch. "I'll wear it forever."

"Thank you for your love," he said, indicating the poem. "I'll keep it forever."

"I *might* let you have it that long," I teased.

He pulled me against his chest. "You don't have a choice because I'll never let it go. And I'm much stronger than you."

∾

Christmas Day was the best Mom and I ever had. After delivering the cakes to a homeless shelter and nursing homes, we drove around, scoping out opportunities for random acts of kindness. The first one came when we saw a lady and four small children clambering out of a car. She tried to unload gifts from her old station wagon, while keeping the kids out of the street. Tristan and I carried the gifts to the house for her while Mom helped her with the kids. Tristan slipped her something as we left and she stared after us, her mouth hanging open with shock. He did the same thing each time we helped someone. I didn't ask about it because that was the point of the day, but I knew when we stopped at a convenience store.

We'd just bought drinks and the man behind us argued with the clerk about why his credit card didn't work at the pump. He carried on about how he needed to get to Miami to see his kids for Christmas. Tristan tucked something into my hand, nodded at the man and strode out of the store. I looked at the folded one-hundred-dollar bill in my hand, smiled and stepped over to the man at the counter.

"Here, go see your kids," I whispered. I placed the bill in his hand and hurried out the door before he could stop me. We took off as soon as I was in the car. When I looked back, both the man and the clerk stood outside, watching after us.

Chapter 15

As December slipped into January and January disappeared into February, I spent as much time as I could on the book . . . when I wasn't in class or with Tristan. I was surprised at how easily most of it came to me, almost like it wrote itself and I was just a tool. The book would be better than I expected and I nearly finished the first draft by the middle of February. Then I got sick.

Valentine's Day and my birthday five days later were both miserable. I caught a horrible cold that fell into my chest and became bronchitis. I felt even worse because Tristan had planned a weekend in Orlando for my birthday that included seeing one of our favorite bands in concert. Instead, he made me homemade soup and we watched my favorite movies.

"You probably shouldn't be here," I said to him my first miserable night. My voice was hoarse and nasally.

"It's Valentines. Of course I want to be with my love." He sat on the end of the couch, my head in his lap, and stroked my hair.

"You really don't want to catch this, though." A fit of coughing emphasized my point.

"I don't get sick," he said. "I didn't think you could, either."

I started to answer, but coughing took over again. My head and shoulders and chest—oh, hell, my whole body—ached from it.

"Her body's not that strong," Mom answered for me. "Her skin can heal, but her internal organs aren't as powerful. She'll get over it quicker than most, but she still gets sick."

"I'm still somewhat normal, in other words," I croaked.

"That explains how the wine made you drunk," he said.

"You guys don't get drunk?" I asked with mild wonder. Tristan and Mom both shook their heads.

Then Tristan looked at me thoughtfully. "What about your bones?"

"We don't know. That cut last fall was the worst I've ever been hurt. I've never broken a bone, so we don't know if they'll heal on their own or not."

"Hmm . . . you're more fragile than I realized," Tristan said. I looked at his face, trying to understand the grim tone. "I must be extra careful with you from now on."

❧

I was disappointed but also relieved that Tristan had to cancel the plans for Orlando. I knew there'd be more opportunities, but I thought a weekend away, just the two of us, may take us to the next level . . . we'd have sex, in other words. I'd been thinking about sex a lot. I knew our relationship was serious enough for this to become a hot topic anytime now. I'd never really planned my first time . . . though many times I wondered, when I was younger, if I'd ever *have* a first time . . . so I had not specifically decided to keep my virginity until I was married. In fact, I wasn't sure if I thought that was fair to either party. Mom had repeatedly lectured me about how it was the most important gift I could ever give and I could only give it once, "So you make it count." I thought I'd know when the right person and right time came along, whether it was before marriage or on my wedding day. Now I was torn.

I knew the right person had come along, but I hadn't yet figured out the right time. Every time we'd get passionate, my body would scream to continue. But my mind—and Tristan's self-control—always won and I always felt relieved it ended that way. I didn't want to regret it when it did happen. I wanted to know for sure it was right and not just hormones taking over. Tristan helped. He had his own issues to deal with—like trying not to kill me. We would go a little longer and get a little further each time before he had to stop.

Not until late March did it even become a discussion between the two of us. It was a memorable night—for more than one reason—at the end of Spring Break, which I had used to finally finish the book. It was just the first draft, but the story was finally out of my head. Tristan took me out on the boat and then to his place so he could make me a celebratory dinner. At least, that's the reason he'd given me.

After dinner, we went out to the beach to watch the sunset. Unlike the beach by Mom's cottage, this one was empty. Beaches were generally public property, but people assumed those in front of the big houses were private. Tristan spread a blanket out for us and I sat down facing the water. He usually sat behind me so he could hold me, but this time he kneeled in front of me, his back to the sunset.

"You're, uh, facing the wrong way," I pointed out the obvious.

"I prefer this view," he said with a stunning smile. It was cheesy, but I fell for it anyway and smiled sappily at him. His smile faded as he seemed to be thinking hard about something. "Can I ask you a question?"

"Sure . . . you can always *ask*."

He ignored my old answer. "How do you see the rest of your life?"

"Oh. Huh." He caught me off guard.

We hadn't really discussed this, at least seriously, since that night I learned there was more in store for my life than I ever realized. The night I learned I could possibly have true love, but nothing else about my future would go as planned. No settled family life in a comfortable home with normal kids who played sports or music or danced and had lots of friends who came to our house to play. Instead, I had a future that may or may not include writing, may or may not include love and may or may not include children . . . but would definitely encompass moving frequently, possibly running from danger and whatever else would happen after the *Ang'dora*. And my time stretched out long before me, possibly hundreds of years or more, if I was anything like Mom or Tristan.

"Well, that's a long time you're talking about. You mean my immediate future or later, after . . . ?"

"Both. The *rest* of your life."

"Hmm . . . well, I have no idea what it'll be like after, unless it's just more of the same, since that's how Mom's life is. I'd still like to write. And I definitely still want real, soul-mate love and a family . . . if that's possible."

"What if I can make it possible? Can you see me in the rest of your life?"

I took a moment to seriously consider it—not that I hadn't already. I'd thought about it many times, but now I had to answer him. And I still came to the same conclusion. Although I didn't even know what it was like to be with anyone else, I just couldn't imagine feeling stronger love for another man. I just didn't think it was possible. Our connection was too deep. Just *who* we were told me we were meant to be together.

"I definitely want you to be in it." I searched his face, trying to figure out why he brought this up now. His eyes sparkled brightly and a smile played on his luscious lips. "I said 'soul-mate love' and I believe you are my soul mate."

"And I know you are mine." He took a deep breath. "So, Alexis Katerina Ames . . . will you do me the honor of allowing me to spend the rest of my life with you? Will you marry me?"

He held his hand out and opened a small box to reveal a ring. The air caught in my throat and my heart stopped beating. I couldn't even see the ring clearly as tears filled my eyes. I looked at him instead, his eyes serious and pleading. So loving. So damn beautiful.

I froze. *He did not . . . ? Oh, yes, he did! Oh, my!!*

"Oh . . . " I finally breathed. *Speak, stupid, or he'll take it the wrong way.* "Um . . . yes . . . of course . . . Yes, Tristan Knight, I would love to spend the rest of my life with you."

"Thank you," he breathed with relief. *Did he expect any other answer?* He slid the ring on my finger and before I could get a good look at it, he took my face in his hands and kissed me passionately.

We fell back on the blanket and his hand slid down to my neck, around my shoulder and down my side as our kisses became more fervent. He held my waist and our lips and tongues continued their dance. His mouth traveled slowly down to my neck, kissing and sucking, his hand gliding up the front of my stomach, sliding over my breast. A small sound slipped through my throat. He gently cupped and caressed my breast, moving his lips slowly over my skin to the opening in my blouse, slipping his tongue under it. One of my hands clawed at his back while the other twisted in his hair.

With one hand, he undid my two top buttons, enough to expose my chest, and kissed around the tops of my bra on both breasts. He traced the birthmark—a strange design of slightly lighter pigment—over my left breast with his finger, then his lips, kissing and sucking. I tugged at the bottom of his shirt and he pulled it over his head as I undid the last buttons of my blouse, letting it fall open. He pressed his body down, so hot and hard against me. His lips found mine again, sucking and tugging, his hand between us on my breast, his fingers slipping under my bra. With so much skin-to-skin contact, the electricity stimulated every nerve. I couldn't control the moan or the spasm as my pelvis jerked against him.

And that was the breaking point.

He groaned and pounded his fist into the sand next to me. He sat up on his knees over me and I started to reach up and touch his bare chest and stomach. He was so beautiful, so perfect. Except his eyes. Fire burned within them. I dropped my hand. He stood up and strode away without a word. I lay there, drawing ragged breaths, staring at the darkening sky. My heart raced and the blood throbbed in delicate places. After several minutes, I finally buttoned my blouse with trembling fingers and sat up. The sky had darkened enough that I couldn't see him anywhere. I picked up the blanket and his shirt and headed inside.

Tristan wasn't in there, so I sat on a kitchen chair and waited. His house wasn't quite home to me, not like Mom's cozy cottage. The more time I spent with him and the more time we spent at his house, though, the more it grew on me. Or maybe I was growing into it. The cottage was small and warm and soft, like childhood. Tristan's house was large and new and angular—

modern and very adult-like. As the newly placed ring on my finger indicated, I had grown up and would soon be starting a new life with Tristan. This house would become my home.

I studied the stunning ring he'd slid on my finger. The main diamond was square and large but not gaudy and it was set with marquis diamonds and blue sapphires on each side. The band was either silver or platinum—knowing Tristan, it had to be platinum—with an unusual design around the large diamond. I twisted my hand, letting the light hit the diamonds and create tiny rainbows dancing around me, when he finally walked in.

"I'm sorry," he said quietly, dropping to his knees in front of me. His face looked pained, his eyes sad. I raised my hand to his face and stroked his cheek with my fingertips.

"You can't help it."

He hung his head. "I should be able to. What kind of boyfriend or *husband* can I be for you?"

I put my hands on his shoulders, leaned over and whispered in his ear. "I'm not ready yet anyway. You'll be fine when the time is right. And that's when we'll get married."

He looked at me appreciatively. "I don't deserve you. And you certainly don't deserve me."

I frowned. "Tristan, don't talk like that. It's just an obstacle we'll eventually get over."

Disbelief overcame his face and he was suddenly on his feet, striding around the room. "*Just an obstacle?* Do you realize what I can *do* to you?"

With hardly any force, just a twitch of his wrist, his fist hit the wall and pieces of concrete fell to the floor, leaving a divot with cracks spreading from it. I froze in my chair. He glared at me.

"I'm under control right now, Alexis, and that's what I do without meaning to. You wanted to know some of my abilities, I'll show you."

He flicked his hand and the table next to me—ten feet from him—rose off the floor then crashed to the ground. The wooden legs broke into pieces under the weight of the marble top. He twitched his finger. The chair next to me slid across the concrete floor to him. He picked it up and a leg splintered into pieces with a squeeze of his hand. He threw the splinters at the window. They pierced through the concrete in a neat row across the window's encasement.

"That's not much, but should give you an idea. And you . . . you are so *breakable*. Imagine what I could to do to you if I lost control!" His voice filled with anger, but his eyes held no fire.

"But you wouldn't! You *couldn't*!" I nearly screamed.

In a flash, he stood in front of me, looking down at me. Power emanated in waves from his body, but I didn't shrink away. He growled, "Don't underestimate the force that lies beneath."

"And you don't underestimate the power of our love!" I stood up on the chair and glared into his eyes. "You *love* me! You know our love is more powerful than anything else."

His face twisted and his voice rose. "Don't you *get* it? It's not something I would do *intentionally*! But if I *ever* lost control and hurt you, I would not be able to *live* with myself."

"I can heal!"

"You don't know that! What if I crush your bones? Crack your skull?"

"Don't talk like that! I will be fine. And so will you!"

"And if I *kill* you?" he snarled.

"Tristan, stop it! *You will* not *kill me! I won't let you do that to yourself!*" I pounded my fists on his chest. It was hard as rock.

His hand twitched and the marble top of the kitchen table he'd just broken lifted from the floor. It hovered threateningly in the air near me. I knew he wouldn't do anything to me, but it aggravated me how he held it there.

"And what are *you* going to do about it?" he snarled.

"WHATEVER I NEED TO DO TO PROTECT US!" I grabbed the marble slab with both hands and hurled it across the room. It hit the concrete wall with a deafening crack and crashed loudly to the floor. The noise echoed off the walls, sounding like gun shots.

Followed by silence.

We both stared at it for at least a minute, too shocked to remember our anger.

"Did you just . . . ?" He looked from the wall to me and back to the wall in amazement.

I tilted my head, still staring at the marble slab. "Um . . . yeah . . . I just did."

"You know that slab weighs at least three-hundred pounds?" I felt him staring at me.

"Really? Huh." I looked at him. "Well, what you did was a lot weirder—all that levitation crap and those splinters in the concrete. I've heard of tornadoes doing similar things, but . . ."

"I'm sorry. I wanted you to know, but I didn't mean to scare you."

"You didn't scare me, you idiot, you just really pissed me off. My whole point is I'm not afraid of you because I trust that *we* will win together. But . . ." I narrowed my eyes and tilted my head, a smile teasing my lips. ". . . since I just agreed to marry you, I think I should know if you're always going to act like a broody teenager and throw an angsty fit every time you get mad at yourself."

He lifted an eyebrow, the gold dancing in his eyes as his lips pressed into a guilty smile.

"You're right. I'm sorry."

He grabbed me in a hug, pulling me off the chair, and buried his face in my hair. I kissed his cheek and he turned his head to meet my lips with his. We started to get into it again when he had to pull back in frustration. There was no fire in his eyes; he wasn't losing control. But we both knew we couldn't carry on. *No make-up sex tonight.*

"One of these days, we *will* make love," he promised.

"I know." I smiled. "Hey, we get to go a little more each time, you know. We'll get there. I have faith in you. Maybe by our wedding night . . ."

"We're not getting married until I *can* be a real husband to you."

"That sounds like a good deal for us both. Because I know by our wedding night, I will be ready. And it will be our wedding present to each other." I smiled at the thought.

"Then it's a deal." He grinned, too.

I looked at the ring on my finger, giddy at its meaning. "I love my ring."

"I designed it."

"I thought so. It's perfect." I hugged him and he held me in silence for a while.

"Shall I take you home?" he finally asked.

"You want help cleaning up first?"

We looked around at the destruction.

"I don't think there's much you can help with, unless you can pick up that marble top again." He chuckled.

"Only if you make me mad again." I made a stupid face and growled, "You won't like me when I'm angry."

He laughed, but then sobered quickly. "You know, you do scare me."

I lifted an eyebrow.

"I think I may have finally met my match."

"What are you talking about?" I asked with bewilderment.

"You have no idea, but you're going to be very powerful.

I don't know if I'll be able to handle you, after the *Ang'dora*."
Then he smiled. "But you will make a kick-ass Amadis. And you
are definitely *ma lykita*."

"Are you *ever* going to tell me what that means?"

He thought for a long moment and I was sure he still
wouldn't tell me.

"It's short for *my little Lykora*," he finally said.

"Little . . . what?"

"*Lykora*. Sophia never told you the legend of the *lykora*?"

I wracked my brain for all the fantastical and supernatural
creatures I knew about. I shook my head.

"Supposedly it's a mythical creature, it's so rare, but I've seen
one myself. It's one of the most beautiful creatures I've ever seen.
It looks like a snow-white wolf, but with black stripes like a tiger.
And it has wings—they're supposed to be like angel wings."

I cocked an eyebrow with skepticism. "And *why* would you
call me that?"

He grinned, his eyes sparkling, and held out his hand.
"Because a *lykora* is small enough to fit in my hand. But it is
fiercely protective and very loyal, so when it feels a loved one is
in danger, it grows as large as it needs to be and protects."

I laughed. "You're making it up."

"You don't have to believe me," he said with a shrug, "but
it's still what you are."

A few minutes later we pulled into Mom's driveway and I
suddenly felt apprehensive. I wasn't sure how she'd react. After
everything came out in the open and then Tristan spent so
much time with us, she had finally accepted him as a key part
of my life. I thought she might almost love him like a son. But
I wasn't sure and I didn't know if she'd be happy with my being
engaged already, especially at nineteen. I sat on the motorcycle
and stared at the lit-up cottage.

"Relax, my love," Tristan said. "She already knows."

"She *does?*"

He shrugged. "I had to discuss it with her first. There's all that other stuff that can get in the way."

"Oh, yeah. We're kind of like a really twisted Romeo and Juliet, huh?"

"I've thought about that. But there's a big difference. *Your* family supports us."

Mom waited expectantly, already in the foyer when we opened the door.

"So . . . can I see?" she asked, skipping any preliminaries. I held my left hand out for her. She inhaled sharply. "Nice job, Tristan. I'm impressed."

He grinned.

She looked at me. "You *will* finish this book first. And you *will* finish college."

"I'll definitely finish the book first. And I'll finish college, but probably not before we get married." I glanced at Tristan and I knew he was also thinking about our deal because he winked at me.

❦

I'd never imagined it possible to be so happy. It lasted about a month. Then the subjects of sex and trust came up again and it was a devastating turning point. We both seemed to have a blockage with Tristan seeing me naked. I lay on his boxy leather couch in just my bra and panties, while he paced the semi-dark room. He wasn't trying to regain control—the fire was already gone. Something else was wrong. I pushed him off this time as he started to unhook my bra. *I* felt a loss of control and something deep inside hit the panic button. I sat up and pulled my shirt and shorts on.

He finally came over and knelt in front of me, looking into my eyes.

"I was getting close, but I think that was you this time," he said quietly.

"I know," I admitted, hanging my head. "I'm sorry."

"You don't trust me nearly as much as you think you do," he said flatly, as if it was fact.

I looked up at him. "No, Tristan, that's not it. I *know* you won't hurt me."

"That's not what I mean. You still have a shell, even for me."

"What do you mean?" I thought we'd overcome that. I'd opened myself up and let him in. He knew more about me than anyone, even my own mother . . . and, apparently, more than I knew myself . . . .

"You let me in to a certain point, but you're still protecting your most vulnerable areas."

I knew the confusion showed in my eyes as I stared into his.

"You won't let me read your book," he pointed out.

"If it gets published, I don't have a choice. You can just go buy it." I tried to smile. He remained serious and my smile disappeared.

"Don't you love me?"

"Of course! More than anything."

"But not enough to share something so important to you."

I sighed. *How'd we get on the subject of my book?* "You wouldn't even like it."

"And you're making that decision for me?"

"Tristan, it's about a witch and a werewolf and their unlikely romance and magic and myths—the stuff you laugh at me about."

"I don't laugh *at* you." He scowled. "I just don't understand your fascination with them."

"And I don't understand your fascination with numbers and angles and the lines of a building."

"But you like the finished product." He waved his hand toward the house models. "I would like to see your finished product."

I sighed again. He had a point. "It's not even a finished product. It's just a draft. It needs revisions, holes in the plot need filling . . ."

"I don't *care*. It's important to you, so it's important to me. Why can't you share it?" He studied my face, his eyes filled with sadness. "Why can't you share yourself? Even if I'm not there yet, I thought *you* would want to be with me by now. But you don't."

The pain and rejection in his voice felt like daggers in my heart.

"Tristan, we both need more time. We'll get there."

"But *why*, Alexis? Why do *you* need more time?"

"I don't know," I whispered honestly.

"I *do* know. You're still protecting yourself, protecting those most personal, intimate parts. You won't let me read your book. You stop me from enjoying your body, even when *I* can go further. Why can't you give yourself fully to me yet?"

I sighed sadly, leaned over and pressed my forehead to my knees.

"You still don't trust me," he answered himself.

The words burned my ears and tears stung my eyes as I realized he was right. I was willing to give him the rest of my life, but I couldn't give him all of *me*.

"Tristan . . . ," I mumbled into my thighs.

He sighed heavily, sadly. "You don't need to say anything, Alexis. I get it. You love me . . . just not completely."

I sat up and saw the pain written all over his face. Tears streamed down my cheeks.

"Tristan, please . . . ," I whispered. "I do love you, more than . . ."

"Just stop, Alexis. I know you love me. But stop lying to us both about how much. Don't even say it until you can *completely* trust me with *everything*. Otherwise, it's not the same love I have for you."

He stood up and strode over to the wall of windows, staring out at the darkness spanning to the horizon. I leaned back over my thighs and cried into them for several minutes.

"Do you want your ring back?" I asked, choking on the words.

He was on his knees in front of me in a flash.

"Is that what you *want?*" His voice cracked with pain on the last word.

"*No!*" I cried.

He cupped the side of my face in his hand. "Then it is yours always, just as my heart is. I just hope, one day, I will have yours . . . all of it."

Chapter 16

After that critical night, our relationship felt fragile and brittle, as if it would shatter from the least bit of pressure. We spent time with each other every day, but not as much and conversation felt superficial, sometimes even forced. Sex wasn't even an issue because we didn't even try. I missed the emotional and physical closeness and berated myself for not letting him completely in, but I didn't know what to do to knock that wall down. I questioned just how much I did love him and if it would ever be enough to completely trust him. If I was even capable of loving that much.

I thought maybe it was just my self-image and fantasized about the *Ang'dora*, hoping I'd become as gorgeous as Mom. And a better match for Tristan.

"Mom, when will I change . . . become like you?" I asked one night when we were alone, putting my textbook to the side. We had more of those alone nights lately. I could feel Tristan pulling away out of pain and I couldn't seem to pull him back.

She shrugged and put her own book down. "It's been different for all of us. It seems we must experience a certain amount of real humanity. We haven't been able to pinpoint a specific cause-effect relationship, so it's difficult to say when or what will do it."

"When did it happen for you?"

"I was thirty-four, but I was the youngest ever. I was also the only one to have a baby after the *Ang'dora*. Besides me, the ages have ranged from thirty-eight to fifty-something. Most were somewhere in their forties."

"I'll get that *old* first?" I hadn't been prepared for that. Mom had never given me details before and I just assumed she stopped aging in her mid-twenties. Tristan said he just stopped aging at twenty-one, so I thought it was the same for us. "Wait…I have to wait that long to know anything?"

Mom's lips pursed together. "I'm sorry, honey."

I groaned. "How could you stand it?"

Her shoulder lifted in a shrug. "I didn't have to. I didn't even know anything was different about me until the *Ang'dora* started. None of us did, except you. We just lived normal lives until then."

I opened my mouth to protest how unfair it was for me, but then I thought about living that many years as a somewhat normal human, which meant there was a good chance I could still have the settled life I sought, at least for a while. Except I would get old and Tristan would not. I knew there would be some difference—Mom looked older than Tristan—but I'd never expected I would be near *forty* . . . or *older*.

I sighed sadly. "I hoped it would be sooner."

"I wish I could help, but we really don't know, honey. All I really know is we have each experienced true love first. Real love, like what you and Tristan have. So who knows with you? You're quite different than the rest of us, anyway."

"Will I be as beautiful as you and Tristan?"

She smiled brightly. "You will be *splendid*. Ours is an inner beauty that radiates outward. It is part of who we are. And you have so much love, hope and faith within you already—you will outshine all of us."

I figured that's what all Amadis moms told their daughters, because I surely didn't feel much love, hope and faith. In fact, they seemed to be buried under despair and distrust . . . mostly distrust of myself.

"As for Tristan," Mom continued, "he was made to be exceedingly attractive, another tool in his toolbox—or bait in his tackle box would be more accurate. I do have to say, though, his outer beauty has improved since the first time I met him and, I admit, even more over the last several months."

I thought I was the only one who noticed. *Great. He's getting even more attractive and I'm still plain me.*

❦

The night following my last final exam, Tristan and I met some of my classmates at Mario's to celebrate surviving the semester. Carlie from communications had been in one of my spring classes, too, and, since they were coming to the Cape, she'd invited us to join her, her roommate, another friend and a couple of guys from our class. Neither Tristan nor I really wanted to be there, but it was something to do to avoid being alone.

Not particularly enjoying the conversation, I slipped into observation mode. Carlie's roommate and friend were a lot like her—pretty in an all-American, girl-next-door kind of way. I noticed they were quite flirtatious with Tristan and, for someone who didn't want to be there, he was exceptionally warm toward them.

After seeing the engagement ring on my finger, Carlie had mentioned once that maybe she'd been wrong about Tristan. I wondered now if she'd noticed what Mom and I had and decided he wasn't so scary after all. She'd been right in the beginning that there was a dangerous side to him, but . . . she missed the part of how exceptionally loving and generous he was, too. He was an unbelievably rare and beautiful creature, inside and out, and I was doing a pretty good job of completely blowing it with him. I sighed.

His head snapped up and he looked at me with an odd expression, then his eyes darted to something behind me. I couldn't tell if anger or interest flickered in his eyes as they narrowed. He pursed his lips, then went back to the conversation with the girls. I was so used to being the center of his attention, I even noticed how he hadn't looked back at me, but focused immediately and directly on Carlie and her friends.

Trying not to be too obvious, I snuck a peak over my shoulder to see what caught his attention. Mostly men lined the bar—except for one leather-clad, long-legged female who took a seat at the end closest to the door. Her long hair was almost as white as the silk, low-cut blouse she wore. Her skin was nearly as pale, smooth as a porcelain doll. The black leather mini-skirt and knee-high boots contrasted starkly with the rest of her. She was absolutely gorgeous. All the men at the bar agreed—they stared at her with their mouths hanging open.

I sighed again. *Yep, I'm really blowing it.*

My self-esteem plummeted right through my feet and into the floor. I bit my lip and stared at my lap, my right hand turning the engagement ring on my finger round and round. *How can he love me when he can have that? Why would he want to be with me? I definitely don't deserve him.*

Disgusted with myself, I mumbled something about needing to get home for something stupid, nearly knocked my chair over as I hurriedly stood up and made a beeline for the door. I didn't even wait to see if Tristan followed. I was close enough to walk home and almost welcomed the idea. As I passed the bar, though, a rough-looking man stepped away from it, directly in my path.

Evil! Stay away! Bad! Danger! Evil!

"They're cute," he said, nodding at Carlie and her friends, "but you, lassie, you're a pistol. There's fire in your eyes."

My alarms sounded loudly but I stood frozen in place, staring at the man in astonishment. He might have been attractive at some point in his life, but his face was rough, weathered, threatening. He looked like an ugly, overgrown leprechaun.

What are you doing?! Run now! Evil!

I inhaled sharply—the smells of booze, cigarettes, rotten meat and, strangely, sweet citrus poured off him—and eyed the path to the door. As soon as I shifted toward an opening, he shifted that way, too, grinning maliciously, exposing crooked, yellow teeth. *Not a leprechaun . . . an ogre.*

"Where ya goin', lassie?" he asked with an Irish accent. "I just got here. Don't leave already. Lemme buy ya—"

Someone grabbed my left hand from behind me and pulled me back. My heart jumped as the thought he had an accomplice flashed through my mind, but Tristan stepped in front of me, holding my hand at the small of his back. He stared angrily at the vulgar man, stopping him in midsentence. I was pretty sure Tristan couldn't kill with just a look, but if he could, this man would have dropped to the floor dead.

"Ah, Seth," the man said. They glared at each other and then the ogre nodded at me. "This one yours, huh? 'Bout time ya took advantage of what ya got. Nice catch."

I looked at Tristan, confused. The ogre acted like he knew him.

"Back off," Tristan growled.

"Ah, come now, I was just having a little fun. Got your name on her, huh?"

"I don't even know her. Just leave her alone." He squeezed my hand, I thought to send me a message. I took it to mean to go along with it or keep my mouth shut. I did both.

"Ah, just a play toy, then?" The fiend sneered. "Why don't ya share?"

"I said to back off!" Tristan took a half-step forward.

The ogre laughed throatily. "I think we need to have a little visit. It's been a while."

"Not here. My place."

"Ha! Ya think I'm stupid? Nah. We stay in public, where there's witnesses. O'Shea's, by the beach." The ogre tossed back the amber-colored booze the bartender had just set down, threw money on the bar and started for the door before we even moved. He glanced over his shoulder. "And don't even think about letting her go. Bring the lass."

"Tristan, who *is* that?" I asked once the ogre left.

"Shh . . . he can still hear us," he whispered.

"Hey, Alexis, Tristan, you still leaving or did you change your minds?" Carlie asked from behind us.

Tristan swore under his breath, then said, "We have to go."

He pulled me toward the door, not letting go of my hand. I followed him to the car in silence, nearly jogging through the rain to keep up, narrowly avoiding big puddles from the day's downpours.

"Now?" I asked once we were in the car. He nodded. "So, who is he? He's wretched!"

"Yes, that he is." He stared forward out the windshield, his jaw muscle twitching as his teeth clenched. "Give me your ring."

I instinctively hid my hand far away from him and stared at him wide-eyed. *He changed his mind? I already blew it?*

He looked at me and his face softened, as did his voice. "Just for now, my love. He can't see it. They can't know, remember?"

"Who?"

"Who do you think?"

As I realized what he meant, terror overcame me. My voice

trembled. "Why can't you just take me home?"

"Because he'll follow me and I'll lead them right to you and Sophia." The anger had returned, but he stroked my face gently. "Don't worry. I won't let anything happen to you. Don't forget who I am. There's a reason he doesn't want to be alone with me."

He grinned, but not with humor. In fact, it was spine-chilling.

I pulled my ring off and reluctantly handed it to him, my hand shaking. He stuffed it in his jeans pocket, then reached over and tucked my necklace under my shirt, then he drove us to O'Shea's, an Irish pub by the beach. He took out his cell phone and dialed a number as he drove.

"Ian's in town . . . Headed to O'Shea's . . . Yeah, she's with me . . . I know, but I don't have a choice. I can't take her home with him on my tail . . . . It's not necessary . . . I'll bring her home as soon as it's safe." He clapped the phone shut.

"Who was that?"

"Sophia. She needed to be warned."

I panicked. "She's not coming, is she?"

"I don't know. She really needs to stay away for both of you."

"He's a . . . a *Daemoni*?" I asked, nearly choking on the word.

He nodded. "He is now. Wasn't always. Just as Sophia brought me to the Amadis, the Daemoni are sometimes successful in bringing your people to their side."

"Oh," I breathed. "Why did he call you 'Seth'?"

His face twisted in the light from the dash. "That was my Daemoni name. They refuse to use the name Tristan."

I reached out for his hand, needing to hold him, at least some part of him.

"Listen . . . He'll probably figure it out—your looks give it away anyway—but we need to try to not let him know who you are. And he definitely can't know about . . . *us*." He glanced at me. "Remember what I told you about my weakness?"

I nodded. *Me.*

"I'll probably have to say things I don't want to . . . just remember, it's just as hard for me to say as it is for you to hear. Remember, too, deception is his most powerful weapon. Don't believe any of it, okay?"

I swallowed hard and nodded. We turned into O'Shea's parking lot.

His voice softened to nearly a whisper. "I love you more than life, Alexis. Always remember that."

"I love you, too, Tristan. Please believe that," I whispered. He squeezed my hand and nodded.

"He can hear us now." We pulled into a parking space and a motorcycle parked next to us. The rain apparently didn't bother the ogre.

Keeping his own body between mine and Ian's, Tristan gently pushed me in front of him, as Ian followed us into the pub. I'd never been inside before and when we walked in, I was sure I wasn't legally allowed to be there. I was underage and this was no restaurant. It was dark and kind of dingy, the odor of beer and harder liquor strong in the air.

I smelled a familiar scent and noticed Owen sitting at the bar. *Oh, no!* I looked away before I caught his eye, afraid he'd see the fear in my face. I definitely didn't want to drag him into this mess. I briefly wondered what he was doing in a place like this; it didn't seem his kind of hang-out.

Tristan directed me to a table, where we sat next to each other and Ian took a chair across from us. I started to reach for my pendant until I saw Tristan just barely shake his head, knowing that fidgeting with it had become a nervous habit. There had been a reason he'd tucked it under my shirt. Needing something to do with my hands, I yanked and twisted my hair instead, trying not to rip it out from fear.

As a waitress took our drink orders, the gorgeous blonde from Mario's entered the bar. That surprised me even more than Owen being there—it definitely didn't seem like her kind of place. Owen moved around the bar to sit next to her. She didn't look happy at all about it, but let him pull her into a conversation—from what I could tell, a strained conversation. I hoped they could keep each other company, or, at least, busy. I didn't exactly want her attention on Tristan. And I definitely didn't want Owen's attention on any of us.

Ian kept his pale blue eyes on us as he sat back in his chair, scrubbing his hand through his untidy, dull red hair, then folding his arms across his chest. He lifted his chin in my direction.

"Another toy for your collection?" His voice was calm, cool, but I could hear the menace in the tone.

"I told you, I don't know her. She's just a girl at the restaurant." Tristan was a smooth liar . . . except his actions spoke too loudly.

Ian smirked. "Yeah, see, I don't quite believe that. You're too protective of her."

"Only because she's an innocent girl, in the wrong place at the wrong time. Just let her go and you and I can . . . visit."

Ian chuckled, a disgusting rattle, and leaned forward in his chair. "Protecting the innocent these days, huh? Well, if she means nothing to ya . . . then why don't ya lemme play?"

Tristan leaned forward, too, and his muscles tightened against his shirt.

"*No!*" he growled.

"Hmph . . . yeah, what I thought." Ian looked smug, still peering at me.

"What do you want, Ian? What are you doing here?" Tristan tried to distract the ogre, but Ian stared at me harder.

"Well, I heard ya were around and I was in the neighborhood, so thought I'd drop in to say hullo, catch up, you know. But looks like I found an interesting situation." Ian leaned almost all the way across the table, his fumes nauseating me. He studied me closely in the dim light. "Ah-ha. Yeah . . . I thought I heard blondie call ya Alexis. Wouldn't happen to be Sophia's Alexis, would ya, lassie?"

"Don't be ridiculous," Tristan said.

"The looks are right. The name is right." He reached his hand out to touch my face and I jerked my head back in revulsion. In a flash, Tristan was on his feet and lifting Ian by the collar. Several people turned to look in our direction. Ian laughed quietly. "Just a girl, heh?"

"Don't touch her," Tristan snarled.

Ian held his hands up in surrender. "All right, all right. I get it."

Tristan let him go and they both picked up their fallen chairs and sat back down. The staring bar patrons finally looked away. I understood why Ian wanted witnesses—Tristan couldn't do anything . . . *unusual* . . . here.

The ogre grinned wretchedly and his voice returned to its coolness. "Ya know, Seth, ya play with fire, you'll get burned. Even you."

"What are you talking about?"

"Amadis *royalty*? The worst of all evils. Not even you, the *ultimate warrior*, can handle that. They'll take ya down."

A moment of silence hung around us as the waitress set our drinks on the table then scurried away.

"You've never been the clever one, have you, Ian?" Tristan said. "You never could tell your ass from your head."

"Oh, right." Ian nodded. "I almost forgot. You think the Amadis are good, *perfect*. I spent two centuries with 'em, lived with all their damn rules, under their control. And *I'm* the one who's ignorant?"

"Your lustful advances were rejected. You were out of line."

"Don't matter. I found my *true* family. *Your* real family, *Seth*. Ya think the Amadis are going to like this?" He waved his hand toward me. "Ya think you're just one of them now? You're the one who's mistaken. They'll stomp all over ya and throw ya out with the bleedin' rubbish . . . if they don' kill ya first. I'm surprised they haven't done it yet . . . ."

Ian's voice trailed off as his eyes widened. He nodded slowly, as if a realization had just dawned on him. He smirked again, his pale eyes moving back and forth between Tristan and me.

"Ahhh. That's right. They're still using ya, aren't they? Have a little assignment for ya to do?" Ian's voice was mocking. Tristan stiffened.

The question dinged in my head like an alarm or a reminder, but I couldn't grasp at the thought trying to come forward from the back of my mind.

"You're wrong," Tristan said.

"Oh, I don't *think* so. They let ya have a little taste of royalty arse here—" Ian flicked his hand toward me again "— they get what they want and ya get to walk free. Nice little assignment, ya lucky bastard."

"Lies, Alexis, remember what I told you," Tristan warned me. Instead, I remembered that thought I had tried to grasp . . . Tristan saying something about an assignment he had when we first met. *Is that what Ian's talking about?*

"Ha!" the ogre barked. "I was there, there when all the plans were made. Remember? Lil' Alexis, just a babe then, and they had it all planned for ya."

"Remember, Alexis, he's a deceiver." Tristan's voice had that steely undertone to it.

"No, this is the truth, lassie." Ian looked at me with glee in his eyes. "You were just a tiny bundle when the Amadis planned everything. You and *Tristan* here . . ."

"Shut the hell up, Ian!" Tristan nearly jumped out of his seat. Several people glanced over at us again.

My throat closed in and my stomach knotted as I realized what Ian said. *Is it true?* I tried to believe what Tristan had told me, repeating it to myself. *Deception is his most powerful weapon.* Ian carried on in a mocking tone and it was too hard to block out.

"Oh, yes . . . Princess Alexis and King Tristan, the perfect combination, making the most powerful Amadis baby ever." Ian bounced in his seat with excitement as he watched my reaction.

"*What?*" I choked.

"*Don't listen,*" Tristan whispered. "He's just trying to take advantage of the situation, turning things around."

He stood up and leaned threateningly over the table toward Ian. His voice was low, but no longer a whisper. "If you don't shut the fuck up, I will make it so you can never talk again. Witnesses or not."

"You two got a problem, take it outta here," the bartender called over in our direction.

Tristan held his hand out to me. "Come on, Alexis, we're done here."

I started to move.

"Ah, so ya don't know yet," Ian said to me, stopping me, somehow mesmerizing me with his voice. Or maybe it was those pale blue eyes, like shallow pools of water, just deep enough to pull me under. "Looks like Seth's the one who's been doing the deceiving. What'd he do? *Pretend* to fall in love with you? He's the best liar, I'm sure ya believed every last word . . . every kiss. Did he feed ya the Amadis *lie*? Did he tell ya that you're *meant* to be together when *he* don't even believe it?"

The air caught in my throat as I tried to breathe. My chest squeezed and my pulse throbbed in my ears. I looked up at Tristan, my eyes wide and burning. With no air, my voice was small. "Tristan?"

He turned stiffly to look at me. Muscles in his neck bulged and his fists clenched, veins popping out.

"I'm sorry you had to find out this way," he said flatly. Then he turned back to Ian, his eyes hard as marbles, his voice cold as ice. "She means *nothing* to me. Leave her alone and deal with *me*."

The air I'd been holding in my lungs came out in a whoosh. I shook my head, tears stinging my eyes.

"So you *did* lie to her. Back to your old ways, huh?"

Too fast to even see, Tristan had Ian pinned face down on the table, his arm twisted sickly behind him. "GET THE FUCK OUT OF HERE. *NOW!*"

I trembled on the rickety wooden chair as everything inside me plummeted to the darkness of hell. *It* is *true. Tristan's been lying.* I heard a choking sound and thought it was Ian but realized it was me, my chest heaving, my throat squeezing. *He doesn't really love me. Tristan. Doesn't. Love. Me.*

Ian rolled his eyes up to me, drinking in my reaction.

"Looks like my work is done here anyway," he said with a smirk. "Ya know you'll be welcomed back where ya belong, Seth . . . if the Amadis don't kill ya."

Several people surrounded our table by then, including Owen and the blonde. I couldn't focus on everything going on as I tried to simply *breathe.*

"Vanessa, I swear to God, if you touch her, I'll come after you myself," I heard Tristan say from what seemed like far away.

"So now you're swearing to *God*, huh?" a musical voice responded, sounding just as distant.

There was a lot of commotion and then I heard Ian's cackling and a chiming laugh fade toward the door. I vaguely heard Tristan say we were leaving, too, but I couldn't move. I was frozen, lost within myself.

Tristan doesn't love me. He never did. It was all just a lie. His words echoed in my head. *She means* nothing *to me.* I wrapped my arms around myself, clutching at my abdomen, my chest still heaving. My heart felt like it had been squeezed until it ruptured and now just sat in my chest, limp and lifeless, a burst balloon. *I'm just an assignment to him. Nothing else.*

Tristan came over to me and I shrank away from him.

"Alexis, we need to go." He reached out for my hand and I jumped off the chair, knocking it over. "Let me take you home and explain."

"*Don't you touch me!*" I screamed, not caring who surrounded us.

He grabbed my wrists with one hand and pulled me close to him, holding my chin firmly with his other hand to make me look up at him. He was too strong for me to break loose. "You have to listen to me because you can*not* believe him."

"But you even said . . . ," I choked out.

"I told you I'd have to say things I didn't mean. You have to believe me that I really love you, Alexis. *Please* believe that. Please *trust* me."

No, he said he would have to say things he didn't want *to say.* There was a difference. He even lied to me now. The tears disappeared as anger enveloped me. I broke away from him, yanking my hands out of his. My voice rose in volume and octaves so I didn't even sound like myself.

"*Trust* you? After all this, you expect me to *trust* you? This whole thing has been nothing but a lie! *You* are a liar! *You* are the deceiver! And you are so good at it because that is what you are *made* to do!"

I glared at him as if he were a monster. I didn't even know who he was. His eyes—his whole face—filled with pain. And I was glad. I wanted him to hurt. I wanted him to hurt like hell. Because he had done the ultimate pain job on me.

"Go back to wherever you came from, Tristan, because you don't belong with *me!*" I ran through the pub, out the door and across the street to the beach.

Although the sand made it difficult, following the beach was the quickest way home. I ran for a while, not noticing the rain, not caring how dark it was, with only the light of the moon reflecting on the water. Someone came out of the darkness and grabbed me by the waist. I kicked and screamed.

"It's not *safe* for you out here," Tristan growled.

"I don't care!" I yelled, still kicking and thrashing my arms. "I'd rather be dead!"

"Alexis, please don't say that," he murmured in my ear.

"You've already ripped me into pieces. I'm as good as dead, anyway!"

"Lexi, *please* . . ."

"Let me take her, Tristan." Mom's voice came from the darkness. Her small frame stepped out of the black trees and shrubs lining the top of the beach. "I've got her now."

I squirmed and Tristan let me go. I ran into Mom's arms and fell against her, my body racking with sobs.

She held me and stroked my hair while I cried, the rain pouring on us almost as fast as my tears. "Let's go home, now."

We left Tristan on the beach, standing alone in the rain. The last image burned on my eyes was his beautiful face contorted with agony.

Chapter 17

As soon as we were home, I stripped my wet clothes off, put on sweats and a t-shirt, crawled under the covers of my bed and sobbed. *He doesn't love me. He never did. I mean nothing to him.* The phrases chanted in my head like a sick mantra. When my stomach and chest hurt too much to sob anymore, I just lay there, tears streaming silently. I don't know when I fell asleep or for how long, but when I woke up, it was still dark and I was still crying.

As the new day dawned, I realized it was the first day of the rest of my life without Tristan. Without love. Without hope. When the tears didn't come, anger did. Anger at Tristan, anger at my mother, anger at myself.

"How could he do this to me?! Why would she let him?! *How did I fall for it?!*" I screamed at the walls and the ceiling. I beat on my pillows and bed, letting them take the wrath, and finally broke down into sobs again . . . then silent tears . . . then exhaustion.

Sometime in the late morning there was a knock on my door.

"Go away!"

"Alexis, I need to talk to you," Mom said through the door.

"I said to go away!" I turned over on my side, facing the wall, my back to the door in case she came in anyway, but she didn't knock again or say anything else.

Later that afternoon, I quietly slipped to the bathroom, relieved Mom didn't catch me. When I came out, though, she was waiting, a look of deep concern on her face. I glanced past her, into the living room, and saw the familiar sandy-brown hair over the top of the couch. Fresh tears sprang into my eyes.

"Leave me alone," I muttered and rushed back to my room. I swung the door closed, but she caught it. I crawled back into bed, my back to her.

"Alexis, please let me explain," she said.

I turned over and glared at her. "Why? It's all just bullshit lies."

"That's why. So you can understand the truth."

I sat up and hardened my eyes. "You mean the half-truth—no, not even half, the *partial*-truth. You two never tell me the whole truth. The only two people in this world who I thought I could trust. Why should I believe anything now? It's all *lies*!"

"You have to believe he really loves you, Alexis."

I glared at her. "And *that* is the biggest, bald-faced, bullshit lie of them *all*!"

I heard heavy footsteps, then the front door open. Mom looked over her shoulder toward the door and then back at me. "You're killing him, you know."

"Good! He's already all but killed me. In fact, I would have been better off if he *had* killed me when he wanted to."

The front door slammed shut. He'd heard that. I was glad. *Not really.* No, not really, but I *wanted* to be glad.

Mom came over and sat at the end of my bed. I scooted myself away until my back pressed against the broken headboard, a casualty of my anger fits.

"You know what really gets me, *Sophia?*" I fumed. "You knew all along. You let all this happen. You're supposed to be my *mother*."

Her eyes narrowed. "That's *exactly* why you need to listen to me, Alexis. I *am* your mother. I would not let anything or anyone intentionally hurt you. Do you really think I would have let this go on with him if I didn't believe he truly loved you?"

"Wasn't that the *plan?*" I spewed.

"You don't even know the plan. You're all worked up about something you don't understand."

I crossed my arms over my chest. "So educate me. Tell me what I'm missing here that makes the lies okay."

Mom studied my face, took a deep breath and blew it out. "Over eighty years ago, when I went through the *Ang'dora*, we thought our bloodline would die out and the Amadis would collapse. Remember, the Amadis is a society. Our family started it and continues to rule it. It'll fall apart without us. I was the last in our bloodline and I'd had no children. Since no one had ever reproduced after the *Ang'dora*, your conception and birth seemed like miracles to us. Realizing there was hope for us to continue, it was decided it'd be in our best interest of survival—possibly our *only* chances of survival—if you joined with the strongest, most powerful male with original Amadis blood . . . ."

"Tristan," I spat.

"Yes, Tristan. A child from the two of you would guarantee our survival for many centuries. I can't tell you what it means for the Amadis to survive, but perhaps you can understand if you remember the Daemoni are our enemies and, well, let's just say it's not good for them to be left without us."

I nodded reluctantly. I knew where this was going.

"So where does this farce of a relationship and love come in?" I demanded. "Haven't the Amadis heard of in vitro fertilization?"

Mom shook her head. "Just back up a bit here. When you were born, I took you to the Amadis and that's when the council made its final decision . . . the plans for you and Tristan. I adamantly opposed it, believing it would not turn out well. Tristan opposed it, too. He thought it wasn't fair to you. But the council was settled.

"The council, in general, believed the two of you were meant for each other and you would be true soul mates. They tried to convince Tristan and me, but neither of us believed it possible. We both eventually agreed to the decision, though. For the next eighteen years, he went his way and I took you my way. I figured at some point, when you were much older than you are now, the two of you would find a way to make it happen and then go your separate ways.

"After waiting and brooding over this for so long, though, Tristan became curious. As soon as you turned eighteen, he came looking for you. He's told you the rest from there."

I stared at Mom. I still didn't get how the last nine months had anything to do with it. "So it was all just a set-up. Why did he have to lie about *loving* me, though? How can you *justify* that?"

"I don't believe it's a lie, Alexis," she answered quietly. "I *feel* it's the truth. I've felt it since the day I came back from that trip and saw how happy you two were together. I just didn't want to feel it then. But not wanting it doesn't make it go away. I believe the council was right and you two were meant to be together. You *belong* together."

My eyes hardened with my heart. "I don't buy it. He came here to complete his little assignment so he could get on with his long, miserable life. I was just a responsibility and he wanted to get it done and out of the way."

"You're being ridiculous, Alexis, and you know it deep down in your heart."

I shrugged. I didn't want to know what hid deep down in my heart because it meant pain (*love*).

"Whatever," I finally muttered. I punched my pillow and lay back down on my side, facing the wall again.

"Alexis, you love him, don't you?"

I ignored her. She eventually got the message and left.

She was right. I *did* love him, to my core. If I wasn't sure before, the intense pain I felt now proved it. But he didn't really love me. He had to play through the whole thing so he could get used to being around me without wanting to kill me. After all, we couldn't create a kid if he murdered me in the process. He just needed to make it seem real to keep me around long enough. Even went so far as to propose . . .

I broke down in tears and then full-body sobs again. When the anger followed, I mostly directed it at myself for being so damn stupid. A part of me knew it all along . . . the part still protecting my most vulnerable, intimate areas . . . the part that knew he really was too good to be true, that it never was real. That I had good reason not to trust him. I cried through another night.

The next few days consisted of crying, anger, staring at the walls and restless sleep. I didn't eat and had to force myself to even take a shower. No school, no Tristan . . . no reason to care. My future, my whole *life* was over. Not over, as in I wanted to kill myself. Just over as in that chapter ended and I couldn't find the beginning of the next one. So many unknowns loomed in my future, and the one thing I'd finally become so sure about—my anchor—was gone. I didn't know what to do with myself anymore.

I lost all track of time. He came by the cottage several times, but I stayed in my room and refused to acknowledge him. He could only be there for one reason—to explain himself and end it in person. I couldn't deal with the rejection all over again. It was easier to just be mad, because I was afraid of what my heart would do if I even heard his lovely voice or saw his . . . *Nope, not even going to think about it.* When I'd hear him leave, I had to fight the urge to run after him. So I cried instead.

❧

"Good to see you out of your room," Mom said one morning when I slouched into the kitchen. She was about to leave for the store. "It's only been nearly a week. You look like hell."

"A *week?*" I couldn't believe I'd wasted so much time being miserable.

She looked at me with concern. "Maybe you could at least go to the beach or something. I bet you'd like that. It would make you feel better."

"Yeah, maybe," I mumbled. I doubted it would make me feel better. I loved the beach, but it happened to be where I had a lot of memories I didn't want to stir up.

Mom left as I sipped a cup of coffee, staring at the cream-colored kitchen walls and trying not to think. I eventually poured a bowl of cereal I really didn't want. I took a couple bites and watched the rest turn to mush when there was a knock at the door. I stiffened in my chair. It could only be one person. I panicked. I couldn't slip to my room without him seeing me through the door glass. I didn't want to answer it, but he'd become familiar enough to usually enter on his own. I leaned over in my chair to peer around the corner at the door. *Whew.*

"Hey, Owen," I muttered when I opened the door.

"Hey, Alexis. You, uh, look like hell."

I still wore pajama bottoms and a tank top, my hair pulled up in a sloppy pony. I could only imagine how red and swollen my face was.

"Nice to see you, too," I said. I peered at him and noticed

bruises all over his arms. "You look like hell, too. What happened to you?"

I reached my hand out to his arm, stopping just before touching the purplish marks. He cleared his throat. "That would be, uh, your boyfriend . . . or fiancé . . . or whatever he is."

"Ex," I mumbled under my breath. But then it hit me what he was saying. "Oh, my! *Tristan* did that to you? What on earth *for?*"

He chuckled. "We sparred at the gym. He's just been, um, a little aggressive lately. No one else will even spar with him anymore and I'm pretty sure he's holding back."

Well, yeah, or he would've killed you. I felt horrible for Owen—normal Owen who had no idea how bad it could've been and he couldn't even heal himself.

I sighed. "I'm really sorry, Owen. I think you're getting the brunt of . . . our break up."

"I can take it. Rather me than someone else," he mumbled.

I waved for him to come in and he followed me into the kitchen. "Mom left like an hour ago. Do you need something?"

"No, actually, I just stopped by to see how you're doing."

I spun around, surprised. "Well, I've had better weeks, but I'll be fine."

He smiled. I'd never really paid attention to how nice his smile was. In fact, looking at him now was like looking at him for the first time. I realized he was actually kind of attractive. I also knew he was a good, sweet guy. I thought maybe someday, when I put myself somewhat back together, we could at least be friends. Real friends who hung out and did things.

Then I remembered Tristan was the only person who hadn't fled when he learned the truth about me. I swallowed hard, fighting tears down, not wanting Owen to see me cry.

"No visitors?" he asked.

"Uh, no." *Why would he want to know that?*

"Okay." Awkward silence. "Would you, uh, want to go to the beach or something . . . maybe . . . sometime?"

He must have been asking if Tristan, specifically, had visited. I wondered if he was afraid of him, knowing what just a small bit of Tristan's wrath felt like.

"Um, I don't know right now, actually. I've been ignoring my book and . . ."

"Yeah, that's cool. I understand." He smiled weakly. We stood there awkwardly, then his head cocked and his eyes seemed distant for a brief moment. He headed for the door. "Well, uh, you're okay here?"

I smiled and thought my cheeks would crack from the falsity of it. "Yeah, I'll be fine."

"Okay." He didn't seem convinced, but didn't press it.

"Very weird," I muttered to myself after he left. Over time, we'd become a lot friendlier at the store, but nothing more. He came around sometimes to fix something around the house, but we never talked; I was always shut in my room, writing. I wondered what prompted him to stop by and just check up on me. He hadn't done that since Mom had left town that one weekend. I figured he was just trying to be a friend, worried after seeing the whole thing go down at the pub.

I headed to the kitchen to dump my soggy cereal. There was another knock and the door opened.

"What now, Owen?"

I took two steps into the hallway and ran into—electric pulses through my body—*Tristan.* My stomach rolled and fell to my thighs.

"Oh," I breathed. We both stopped dead. *Mmm . . . he smells so good.* I couldn't look at his face, though, so I stared at the floor. He put his thumb under my chin—more electric shocks—and lifted my face, forcing me to look at him.

"You look like hell," he said. I pulled my face away and headed back into the kitchen.

"Yeah, that's what I've been told." I turned and glared at him, then said harshly, "You can thank yourself for that."

He scowled. "I do blame myself," he muttered.

He didn't look too good either. Still beautiful, just . . . wrong.

"You look like hell, too," I said.

He looked down at the box he held. "I brought this over for you."

He held the brown box out to me. I didn't take it.

"I don't want anything from you," I said coldly. His face broke, sadness overcoming it. *Why am I acting like this?* I couldn't look at him so I grabbed my bowl of soggy cereal from the table and took it over to the sink.

"It's your stuff," he mumbled. He set it on the table. "I was going through things before I started packing."

I whirled on him, dirty milk sloshing everywhere.

"You're *packing?*" Panic squeezed my chest.

"Yes, I'm moving."

"You're *moving?*" The bowl fell out of my hands and clamored into the sink. I couldn't breathe. *Don't leave me!* I swallowed hard to push down the lump in my throat. I thought it was my heart. I fought back tears, refusing to let him see me cry again.

"I shouldn't be around here." He studied my face, tried to look into my eyes, but I looked away, afraid of what he might see. He added quietly, "And, I guess there's nothing to stay for."

Me! Stay here for me! You can't leave me! I took a deep breath. I hoped he didn't hear how ragged it was . . . or that he did. And then I hoped he'd see the tears fighting to break so he'd know how I felt without my having to say it. Then I was scared of his reaction . . . or non-reaction. That he wouldn't care.

"Oh," I finally said, not able to say anything else, because if I did, it would only result in more rejection and pain.

"Are you okay?" he asked.

"No," I said honestly. He scowled again. "But I'll be fine. No permanent damage done, I'm sure."

Liar! Pain flashed across his eyes and then he composed himself.

"Yeah, of course. Well, I guess I'll leave you alone." He lifted my chin with his thumb again and gazed into my eyes. I couldn't even see the specks of gold in his, they were so dim. No sparkle at all. I could feel the tears again. His eyes softened and he looked so sincere when he said it . . . "I *do* love you, *ma lykita*. Forever."

Before I could even blink, he was out the door. I stood there in shock for several beats. *Oh, God!* I bolted for the door, threw it open and ran outside.

"*Tristan!*" I yelled.

He was already gone.

Some kids across the street stared at me while I just stood there, still in my PJs, looking frantically up and down the street. It was as if he'd disappeared.

I trudged back inside and cried for several hours. I didn't know what to believe anymore. Part of me wanted to run to him, to believe he loved me. Another part screamed in protest, reminding me I couldn't trust him, he'd only hurt me again. And a very small third part said to stop crying and get over him already. The other parts yelled at that one to shut the hell up because I didn't want to get over him. Even if it meant being miserable.

I remembered the box, brought it into my room before I opened it and found only a couple of things inside. There was my blouse I'd been wearing one night when we made dinner at his house and the sauce splattered all over it, so he gave me one of his t-shirts to wear. His scent permeated my blouse. I buried my face in it and inhaled deeply. *Mmm . . . mangos and papayas, lime and sage, and a hint of man . . . .* I remembered I still had his shirt somewhere. I searched in the bottom of my closet for it and put it to my face before pulling it over my tank top. The only other items were the framed poem I'd given him for Christmas, my engagement ring and a note.

My Dearest, Beloved Alexis,

I love you. Te amo. Je t'aime. Σ' αγαπώ. Ti amo.

I love you. I love you. I love you.

I don't know how many times or how many ways I need to say it before you will believe me. I am sure you have lost all trust in me now and I understand. I hope you will understand one day it was not my place to tell you about the Amadis arrangement. All I could do was make it happen and that is what led me to fall completely, irreversibly, undeniably in love with you. You bring the very best out of me, especially the ability to love and allow myself to be loved. After all we have shared, I just don't know how else I can convince you that my love is irrefutably authentic. You <u>are</u> my soul mate.

I am returning the poem you wrote for me because I cannot keep it, knowing you do not feel that love for me anymore. I also want you to keep your ring. I designed it especially for you with the intent of you keeping it forever. Do with it what you want. It is yours and always will be—just like my heart.

I want to believe in you and me together forever, but if you do not come back to me, my forever is over. Without you, my world is bleak again. I beg that you will bring your light back into my life, but if not, I understand and will accept existing in darkness.

I love you more than any soul has ever loved another, my Lexi, ma lykita.

From the deepest, darkest corners of my heart,

ALL of my love,

Tristan

Tears streamed down my cheeks at the first line and I was bawling by the time I finished it. I read it over and over, tears staining it, causing the ink to run in places. I finally dropped it back into the box and held my blouse to my face as I curled up and sobbed.

Mom came in later, after darkness had consumed my room. She flipped the light on, blinding me.

"I thought this morning . . ." She stopped when I flicked my hand toward the box.

She sat on my bed and peered into it. She picked up the framed poem, read it and set it on my nightstand. I stared at it. I already had the poem memorized. I cried. She picked up my ring and the note and, after reading the note, she placed it in front of the poem and put my ring on top. I cried.

When she finally spoke, her voice was soft and quiet. "Alexis, I think you both want the same thing. Why don't you just . . ."

I interrupted her. "I just can't yet, Mom."

She stood up and picked up the now empty box. "Well, you're running out of time, honey."

"I know," I whispered.

I had another night of crying and restless sleep, my blouse and his shirt bunched around my face so I could smell him. By morning, though, I'd decided I'd cried enough. I told myself some fresh air and distraction was what I needed to clear my head and think things through. I went for a short walk on the beach. It wasn't a great idea; I felt so alone. So I went back home and escaped to my book, losing myself in an imaginary love story where everyone lives happily ever after.

"Do you know when he's moving?" I asked Mom that night.

"I don't think he's set a date yet. I think he's still waiting . . . ."

I just nodded and went back to my book. I spent the next day immersed in the fictional world I'd created.

"Has he set a date yet?" I asked Mom that night. She shook her head.

Chapter 18

I spent the next two days the same way. I worked on the book all day; I asked Mom the same question at night. She said no both times. I breathed a sigh of relief. By the end of the third day, I felt the novel was as good as I could make it without input from others. It was time to hand it over—let someone else delve into my fantasies and see what I think about, how weird and twisted and lovely my imagination could be. I practically danced around the printer as each page slowly slid out, feeling both nervous and excited for Mom to finally read it.

Needing something to do to pass the time before she came home, I took a long, hot shower and then painted my toenails purple. Finishing the book and then pampering myself cheered me up. *Maybe tomorrow I'll feel good enough to call him.* Maybe.

When I came out of the bathroom, I heard voices. I peeked into the kitchen to see who was with Mom. She leaned over the counter, her head in her hands, the phone in front of her. She had it set on speaker and when I heard Tristan's name, I stepped back to listen.

"I've tried to talk sense into him, but he's not listening," Mom said. "He insists there's nothing to keep him here, there's no reason to stick around."

"Stefan has been over there, too, with the same results," said a female voice through the phone's speaker. She had a foreign accent I couldn't place. "We cannot let him go, Sophia."

"I know."

"There is only one person who will get through to him. You know that."

"She's still unwilling. I think she wants to, but she's struggling to trust that he really loves her."

"Oh, of course he does! From what you and Stefan have told me, there is no doubt!"

"I know, but she doesn't. Or if she does, she won't admit it."

"You need to persuade her, Sophia. She needs to understand. Otherwise, we will lose him forever."

Mom sighed heavily. "Yes, I'm sure of that. I'm pretty sure he's going back to them."

"So am I."

My chest constricted, strangling my heart. *Oh, no! Oh, God, no!*

"Do you think they'll kill him?" Mom nearly whispered. My stomach lurched, filling my mouth with the taste of vomit.

"I am not sure. They have a terrible desire to control him again, but if they think they cannot, they will undoubtedly kill him. Either way, we lose him."

I rushed into the kitchen and skidded to a halt in front of Mom. Her eyes held mine. She had to see the terror on my face, but put her finger to her lips. I wanted to scream at her and the woman on the phone, but could barely pull air through my constricting throat. I felt like I was suffocating.

"You have to convince her, Sophia! She is the only one—"

"I think we have an answer. I'll call you back." Mom quickly pressed the end button. "Alexis . . ."

The world fuzzed around the edges, then started to go black. I thought I was about to pass out, but I'd never done that before, so I wasn't sure. Mom caught me and set me in a chair, pushing my head between my knees.

"Mom . . ." I gasped. "Tristan . . . ?"

"Alexis, did you hear?"

My head shot up and pinpricks of light flashed before my eyes. I looked past them at her face. Her expression was a mix of several different emotions, none of them good. Fear, worry, grief, anxiety . . . I'd never seen Mom so distressed.

"Yes! What do I *do*?" I cried.

"I think you know," she whispered.

"How much time do I have?"

"I don't know. Tonight. Maybe tomorrow."

"*NO!*"

I bolted for my room. *Yes, I know what to do.* I dressed quickly in what I knew he liked, just in case it made a difference—the green blouse Mom gave me for Christmas and a denim mini skirt. I threw my hair in a quick twist to get it out of my face and emptied my school bag on my bed, scattering papers and pens everywhere. I threw the framed poem and his note into the bag. I tucked my ring into my hip pocket. I stood in the door and glanced around, trying to think if there was anything else that might help. My eyes landed on the manuscript I'd just printed. I'd promised Mom first read. *She'll understand.* I grabbed it, slipped it into a folder and shoved it in the bag. I flew out of my room.

Mom waited at the door for me. "I drive faster," she said.

"I can't be there without a car, Mom, just in case . . ."

"I'll leave it."

She waved off the look I gave her.

~ 220 ~

"I'll get home fine. Don't worry," she said.

She raced along the surface streets. It didn't feel fast enough. I tried to think of what I'd say or do but nothing came to mind. We turned into his driveway in two minutes. I'd have to wing it.

"You can do this, honey," Mom said. She pecked me on the forehead and then she was gone.

"*Tristan!*" I cried from the driveway. I rushed up the stairs to the dining room door and banged on it. "*Tristan!*"

I pressed my face against the glass to look inside. It looked empty except for some boxes and furniture piled at the far end of the living room. *He hasn't left. Yet.* But he never came to the door and I wondered if he was even home. I could see a light from the hallway, either the office or the gym. I pressed my ear to the glass and heard blaring music. *He'll never hear me over that! Damn, damn, damn!*

I ran back down the stairs to the keypad by the garage door. I had no idea what the code was and knew it was hopeless. Unable to keep still, pacing the driveway, I tried to think how he would think. It wouldn't be his birth date. He ignored that date. *But maybe . . .* Without anything to lose, I tried my birth date. *Holy crap! It worked!* The door right next to me started lifting. As soon as I was able, I ducked underneath it and hit the button to close it. I ran up the stairs to the house.

"TRI—"

His name lodged in my throat. A steel vise grabbed me by the neck and pinned me to the wall two feet off the floor. I couldn't breathe, couldn't even struggle. The bag fell from my hand. I heard the glass frame break. My heart raced even harder.

"*Alexis?*" The lovely voice twisted in horror.

Just as my vision started to blur around the edges again, I saw Tristan step back, his hand dropping from my neck. Then I was free and fell to the floor. My lungs seized to pull in air.

"Tri . . . stan . . ." I gasped, kneeling on all fours.

"What are you doing here?" he growled. "I almost *killed* you."

"I'm . . . sorry . . . I . . . banged . . . on the . . . door." I inhaled as deeply as I could, the air tearing at my throat like razor-blades. "You couldn't hear me."

"What are you *doing* here?" he growled again. Fire blazed in his eyes.

I scrambled to my feet.

"I . . . I came to stop you." My voice sounded small and weak with fear.

"Stop me from what?" His tone was unfamiliar. I didn't like it at all. He folded his arms across his chest.

"From wherever you're going." My voice grew stronger. *He won't hurt me . . . not on purpose anyway.*

"It's too late," he growled angrily.

"But you're still here!"

"You've made your feelings clear, Alexis. I have nothing to stay for."

"But I'm here. I'm here for *you*."

He glared at me.

"Where are you going?" I could hear the edge in my voice, the anger rising. I'd need that anger if I had to protect myself.

"Exactly where you told me to. *Where I came from!*"

"*No!* You said you'd never go back." I lifted my chin and narrowed my eyes, daring him to defy his own words.

"I've been wrong all along. I failed with you. I failed at this life. It's where I belong."

"But you didn't fail with me. I'm here, Tristan. I'm here for you!"

He glowered at me. "*They* sent you, didn't they?"

"No! I'm here for *us*. I love you. And I know you love me, too. And that means you did not fail at this life. You belong

~ 222 ~

with *me*. Stay for *me*." I lost the edge as tears burned my eyes.

"How can you say that? You don't even *trust* me, Alexis. You *can't* love me!"

"But I *do*, Tristan. I love you. I trust you! You are *everything* to me." I stared at him as he glared back with those fiery eyes. *Oh, God, please help me. I can't lose him!* I knelt by my bag and pulled the broken frame out. I held it out to him. "Here! This comes from my heart. It still holds true. It always *will*."

He ignored it.

I put it on the floor and pulled the note out and waved it. "Your letter! I cried over it for days. You said you wanted me back. I'm here!"

No reaction. I pled my love to a boulder.

"*Please*, Tristan," I begged. "Please listen to me."

I wiped the tears out of my eyes with the heel of my palm. His eyes narrowed, but he didn't budge. I pulled the manuscript out of the bag and held the folder open.

"My novel. I want *you* to be the first to read it, Tristan."

I thought I saw a slight change in his eyes. The fire dimmed just a bit. I stood up and held the manuscript at him, but he didn't take it.

"*Please*. I've shared it with no one else. I *want* you to be the first."

He didn't budge. I tossed it on a side table standing next to the three remaining kitchen chairs, waiting to be hauled onto a moving truck. His eyes followed the folder, then flew back to me. I took a deep breath, trying to think of what to do next. I fished the ring out of my pocket and held it up.

"I *will* keep this forever, but only when *you* put it back on my finger."

He still didn't move, but his eyes softened.

"I want to marry you, Tristan. I want to spend the rest of

my life with you. Forever with you. You and me together. You *can't* leave me."

I put the ring on the manuscript and pulled a chair over in front of him. I stepped up on it so I could look directly into his eyes. The flames still flickered, still bright, but I'd seen worse. I touched his cheek and flinched from the powerful electric pulse, but I didn't let it stop me. I put my hands on each side of his face. He stood completely still. I looked deeply into his eyes, noticing the flames dimming more.

"I love you, Tristan Knight. You will not leave me!"

Still no reaction except that slight change in the eyes. *Give him everything. Show him your trust.* I knew it was risky, with that fire still burning, but I didn't know what else to do. I'd already offered him everything I had. The book had softened him and I knew there was one last way to prove I trusted him completely, with *all* of my vulnerabilities. I unbuttoned my blouse and let it fall to the floor. I scooted my skirt down my legs and stepped out of it. I unhooked my bra and let it fall, then slid my panties off. I stood naked on the chair right in front of him and held my arms out wide.

"You have all of me now. I trust you with everything. I am *all* yours!"

His eyes traveled up and down my body.

"You're being really stupid," he growled. His hand twitched. *Finally, a reaction.* "I could *kill* you right now."

I lifted my chin and firmly set my voice. "If you're going to leave, if you're going back to *them*, then I *want* you to kill me."

The fire dimmed, though, instead of brightening. I knew it was okay. I took his face in my hands again, ignoring the shock this time.

"But you're not going to. You love me and you won't hurt me," I whispered. I pressed my lips against his. He remained unresponsive but I continued to kiss him, looking into his eyes

~ 224 ~

the whole time. "Please, Tristan. I know you love me. Please show me you're still here with me."

I slipped my hands back into his hair, tugging at it, and moved my lips over his cheekbone, to his ear and down his neck, then back up around his jaw.

"Please, Tristan."

When my lips returned to his, he opened his mouth slightly and I tasted him. I traced my tongue over his lips and slipped it between. He started to respond, moving his lips slowly with mine, tasting me. I moved my mouth over his face and neck again, kissing and sucking. I undid the buttons I could reach and gave up and tore his shirt apart, pressing my naked breasts against his bare chest. I felt his hands on my back, sliding down over my butt and back up again. I shuddered. Our mouths crushed against each other and we hungrily kissed and bit and tugged.

He pressed his hand against the small of my back and pulled me up. I wrapped my legs around his waist and he turned and sat in the chair. I traced my hands over his chest, down his torso and back up and over his shoulders and then pressed myself against him, electricity jolting through my body. My lower abdomen and groin tightened with excitement and anticipation. He unclipped my twist and let my hair fall, then pulled back on it, forcing my neck and chest up. His hand slid over and around my breast, squeezing it gently and then holding it as he kissed and licked and sucked, pulling my nipple tight, making it erect. He did the same with its twin. I ground my pelvis against him and I felt him hard underneath me.

"Ah, Lexi," he groaned. He looked into my eyes and the fire burned in his. But I felt safe.

I started working frantically on his belt, getting it undone, then his jeans button, while I ran my mouth around his jaw. "Make love to me, Tristan," I breathed.

He slid his hands down my sides, over my hips and under me, his fingers so close to that one area throbbing the most for his touch.

"Argh! No!"

His hands suddenly grasped my waist and he lifted me up and tried to set me on my feet. But my knees buckled and I fell to the floor. Tears pooled again as I looked up at him.

"You really don't want me?" I whispered, a tear slipping down my cheek as that fear of rejection started to wrap itself around me like a black cloak.

He stared at me for a long, painful moment and then slid off the chair, down to his knees in front of me. I watched his eyes as the flames dimmed and the gold started to sparkle. He smiled as he put his hand under my chin and rubbed his thumb across my lower lip.

"Oh, I want you, my Lexi, *ma lykita*. I want you more than life itself."

I breathed a sigh of relief.

"I'm ready. I'm ready to give myself to you. I *trust* you. Completely."

"You don't know how happy that makes me." He bent over and kissed me, long and gentle. "But . . . I don't know that I'm ready and I'm not taking any chances with you."

I stared at him as my heart settled down. I knew he could control himself. After what just happened, when the monster had been closer to the surface than I'd ever seen before, I knew he'd be fine. It was our love and my trust in him that would bring him through. That's what he'd needed all along.

He looked into my eyes, his full of love. "We had a deal."

"What?" *Why did that matter now?*

"We're waiting until we're married."

I shook my head. "That wasn't our deal. Our deal is we'll get married when we're ready. But if we're ready, why wait?"

He smiled. "Because we're going to do this right."

"Then let's get married."

He sighed. "You have another deal . . . with Sophia."

"It's done. The novel's over there." I flicked my hand toward the table where the manuscript lay.

"You won't submit it without anyone reading it."

I searched his face. "Why are you making this difficult?"

"Because *I* need more time." He pulled me onto his lap, wrapped his arms around me and kissed me again.

"How can you just cut things off like that?" I asked, still feeling the warmth and pulsing throughout my body.

"Hundreds of years of practice. I've mastered control over *that* part. It's . . . the monster . . . I have to worry about."

A chill ran up my spine, cooling the heat that remained. We sat there for a few more minutes.

"Are you . . . okay?"

He nodded. "Yes, now that you're here."

More silence. Then he said, "I'm glad you're ready. That you trust me completely. Why did you change your mind?"

I swallowed. "I didn't exactly change my mind. I just realized the truth that was there all along. When I thought I would lose you forever . . . you are more important to me than any part of myself."

He frowned. "I don't deserve that."

"It's not a matter of what you deserve or what I deserve. It just is. I can't live without you. I *need* you."

He narrowed his eyes and cocked his head. "It is *I* who needs you. Without your love, without you in my life, I am nothing but darkness."

"We need each other, then." I caressed his face. "You and me together."

He leaned his forehead against mine. "Forever."

He reached over to the table, picked off my ring and slid it over my finger.

"Think you can stand yet?" He smiled.

I sighed and wrapped my arms around his neck. "If I have to. But I really like it here."

His fingers trailed lightly up and down my spine and I shuddered. He nibbled at my ear and murmured, "You really need to put your clothes on. Before I lose control."

"You won't, though. I'm sitting in your lap naked and you're fine."

"No, I'm not *fine*. You have no idea how hard it is for me," he said.

I lifted an eyebrow, knowing exactly *what* was hard. A small smile played on his delicious lips, but I could see in his eyes he fought something inside—and not, I knew, just normal human desire. I didn't want to do that to him. I reluctantly stood up, picked up my clothes and headed for the stairs.

"Where are you going?" he asked, bemused.

"To bed, if you still have one," I said over my shoulder.

He grabbed the manuscript and followed me. "You're putting some clothes on."

"Yes, sir, I am."

His mattress and box springs leaned against the wall in his bedroom. Everything was in boxes. I looked at him sadly, realizing how close I'd come to losing him.

"It's an easy fix, my love." He started putting the bed back together, lifting the pieces with ease, making me shudder again as his muscles rippled. I turned away before *I* lost control and found what I wanted—his suitcase. I dug around for one of his shirts, put it to my face and inhaled deeply. I slipped on my panties and pulled his shirt on. He raised an eyebrow and smiled. "I like it."

We found all the bedding and the big bed was quickly back together and quite inviting. I started to crawl in when I remembered Mom. I called to let her know everything was okay, he was staying, and everyone could relax. Then I finally crawled into bed and snuggled next to Tristan, who sat up against the headboard, already several pages into the manuscript. He put his arm around me. I stroked his chest and kissed his jaw.

"I'm trying to read this really good book here," he said, his eyes not leaving the page.

Not knowing whether he meant it or not—and not wanting to know yet—I ignored him. "Thank you for not leaving me."

He pulled his eyes away from the manuscript, looked into mine and smiled. "Thank you for coming back to me . . . and for saving me from myself."

He kissed me gently. After nearly two weeks of hardly any sleep, and now finally content again, I was out as soon as his lips left mine.

Chapter 19

Sweet breath, wet kisses and a gentle tug on my lower lip awoke me.

"Rise and shine, sweet love of mine," Tristan murmured in my ear.

I smiled and stretched and peeked through my eyelids. He'd opened the window shutters and light flooded the bedroom. I squeezed my eyes shut. "Mmm . . . do I have to?"

I felt him crawl onto the bed next to me and lay behind me. He snuggled tightly against my back. "I've been waiting too long for you to waste the day sleeping."

I slowly opened my eyes and let them adjust to the light. When I could finally focus, I saw blue sky and the Gulf of Mexico spread out forever before me. "Wow. I could wake up to this every morning."

"That could be arranged . . . ."

I turned onto my back and Tristan propped himself on his elbow, gazing down at me, the gold in his eyes sparkling brightly, the green shining like emeralds. I reached up and caressed his face.

"I missed you," I whispered.

"I missed you, too, *ma lykita*." He gave me a long, loving kiss, then he scooped his arm under me and the next thing I knew, I was on top of him. He pushed me up into a sitting position, straddling his waist. "That's why I'm tired of watching you sleep."

"What time is it anyway?"

"Almost noon. You've slept over fourteen hours."

"Yeah, well . . ." I decided not to mention the last two weeks of hell. "How long have you been up?"

"A couple hours. I slept in, too. It's been a while since I've slept at all and then I was up most of the night reading." He grinned and winked. I stared at him stupidly, not even realizing I traced random shapes on his bare stomach until I felt his muscles flex.

"*That* feels incredible . . . and distracting," he said, grabbing my hand and entwining his fingers with mine.

"I'll remember that," I said with a smile. "So, what's on the agenda?"

"Whatever you want."

That was easy. "Can we ride to Gasparilla?"

He frowned. "Except that. It's rainy season and the storms will come in before we get back. It won't be much fun."

"Well, if we need to stay indoors, then we should get you unpacked." I glanced around at the boxes.

"We should probably leave that for now. Could be a waste of time."

I stiffened. "*Why?*"

"Don't worry. I'm not going *anywhere* without you." He brushed my lips with his fingertips. I immediately relaxed and narrowed my eyes.

"Don't *do* that to me." I swung my leg off him and crawled to the side of the bed.

"Don't leave. I'm sorry!" He sounded nearly as panicked as I'd felt a moment ago. I smiled.

"I'm just going to the bathroom."

When I came out, the wall of windows had disappeared and the room opened to the outside. The air was already muggy, but a breeze blew off the water, cooling the dampness. Tristan stood at the balcony railing, still wearing nothing but tan cargo shorts, his bronzed, muscular back to me. Seeing him without a shirt on made me shudder, for more than one reason. Of course, his body was absolutely delightful to look at . . . and touch . . . and kiss . . . and . . . *Yeah, it's quite distracting.* But the muscular build also reminded me what he was made for. He might not have looked exactly like you'd imagine the ultimate soldier to look like—bulky and brawny beyond attraction—but the strength and power were obvious.

When I joined him, I saw a cup of coffee, my manuscript in its folder and a rose on the little table. He handed me the cup and the rose. I took a sip of coffee then stuck my nose into the flower.

"Nice," I said. "Thank you. But you do know you're spoiling me."

"I intend to. Every day. Forever."

We stood against the railing in silence, arm in arm. I sipped my coffee while watching the waves crash on the beach. *I could do this forever.*

"So," I finally said, "why would unpacking be a waste of time?"

"I don't know that it is yet. We'll find out tonight. We need to discuss some things, figure out some plans."

"Like getting married?" I asked excitedly. He smiled down at me.

"Yes, that may be part of it, but we have more pressing issues to worry about." His brows furrowed and he frowned. "Just because you and I are good—"

"Perfect," I corrected.

"—doesn't mean everything else is," he finished, ignoring my correction.

"What's going on?" His concern was contagious and he must have seen it on my face. He changed his expression, smiling again.

"We'll get there soon enough. Let's not ruin our time together right now, okay?" He picked up the folder with my manuscript in it and handed it to me. I flipped through it. Notes marked the margins on many of the pages. "You're very talented."

"So you liked it?" I asked. He nodded. "Really? Wait. You *finished* it already?"

He nodded again. The notes went through to the last page.

"Oh, no. No, no, no. That's not *good*," I cried.

His brows knitted with confusion. "I thought that meant it's a page-turner."

"A page-turner is good, but if you breeze right through it, it's usually because it's just crappy writing." My heart plummeted to my feet.

"Alexis, you're being absurd. How old is your target reader?"

"Teens, I guess. Young Adult."

"I think I have a few more years of reading experience than they do. It's just right for them." He looked at me earnestly. I let out a deep breath and nodded. "My only problem . . . a *witch* and a *werewolf*? Puh-lease."

I'd expected him to tease me about that, so I just laughed as I put the manuscript back on the table.

"There's no way a witch and a werewolf would fall in love . . . unless she put a spell on him or something."

I shrugged. "It could happen. It's *my* world. I'm making it up and that's their story."

"Hmph. Still . . ." He rolled his eyes mockingly. "I admit you did very well at making it believable. Your characters felt real, even with all the good qualities that don't quite go along with canon."

I grinned, ecstatic that even Tristan liked my characters. "Mom gave me some fantastic ideas for them in the beginning. It's almost like she knew them before I did."

He gave me a significant look, his eyebrows raised, that I couldn't understand. It cleared almost immediately. "So, what's next? A normal human story, I hope."

I braced myself for the teasing I knew was about to come. "Well . . . I've kind of been thinking of something a little different than this one . . . like a human falling in love with a vampire."

"A good vampire, I assume. One that drinks donated blood?"

I smiled slyly. "I don't know . . . maybe he or she is horrible. I haven't decided who's human and who's vampire yet, but I think one wants to kill the other or they both want to kill each other . . . at least at first."

He gave me a dark look and I shrugged.

"Well, they say to write about what you *know*." I bit my lip, waiting for his reaction. *Shouldn't have said that, stupid.*

He just shook his head, chuckled and wrapped his arms around me. "You know, only *you* could bring love into the most unlikely situations."

"Everybody has at least a little good in them, so it's possible."

My face pressed against his chest, so I couldn't see his expression, but I felt his muscles tense. His tone was dark and serious. "Not *every*body."

Even with his warm body around me and the sun beating on us, a chill ran up my spine. *He would know.* I decided to let the subject drop.

"So, what do we do with the rest of the day?" I asked.

Tristan suddenly jumped toward the table and slammed his hand on the folder containing the manuscript, then a big gust of wind blew around us. I looked up and saw the dark steel-gray clouds building up and pushing toward the beach from the other side of the house. The typical afternoon storm came in quickly.

"Thank you!" I gasped. "How'd you know?"

"Heard it coming."

We barely had everything inside when the wind picked up again. Tristan pushed a button to close the window-wall, then he took my hand and led me downstairs.

"Are you hungry? I picked up some croissants with the coffee. Chocolate, your favorite."

I hadn't realized it until then, but I was ravenous. "Sounds good. I hope you bought ten. I'm starving."

He chuckled. "There should be enough to hold you over. Then I'll shower and take you home so you can get cleaned up, too. Maybe by then the storm will have passed and we can go for a short ride before tonight."

"What's going on tonight?" I asked as I lifted myself to sit on the counter.

"Like I said . . . plans to make, things to figure out." He shrugged, downplaying it, but I knew by the look in his eyes it was serious.

"You're holding back on me," I said pointedly. He grimaced.

"You're right. And I'm not going to do that anymore." He took a deep breath and let it out slowly. "Ian's little visit has more far-reaching consequences than you realize. Your safety is more at risk now than it ever has been. We need to decide what to do about that."

"Oh," I breathed. An onslaught of thoughts rushed through my head, giving me no time to think about each one as the next pushed it out: *Are we moving again? What about school? What about my book? Can we still get married? Is Mom okay? Would they really challenge Tristan? Would he be okay?* Those last three terrified me.

Tristan misinterpreted the look of fear I felt spreading across my face. He wrapped his arms around me and kissed the top of my head. "Don't worry, you've been well protected. I won't let anything happen to you. Why do you think I was at your house day after day, even when you wouldn't talk to me? I couldn't leave you alone, so vulnerable . . . ."

While I was immersed in my own miserable world, there'd been much else going on I hadn't even realized. And Tristan had put his own heart aside to protect me, even when I behaved so cruelly. I pushed my croissant away, my stomach in knots with heartache and worry. I leaned my forehead against his chest.

"What does this mean?" I finally asked. "What will happen? Can't you see the best solution anyway?"

His body stiffened and he didn't answer at first. Then he said firmly, "It's no longer an option."

"Why not, if it's the best one? What is it?" I looked up into his face. His eyes darkened.

"I won't discuss it. It's just not happening." He walked away, his back to me. "We'll figure something else out, all of us, tonight."

I hopped down from the counter and went over to him. I wrapped my arms around his waist and pressed myself to his back.

"I trust you," I whispered. "As long as you'll be okay."

His muscles relaxed and he pulled my hands apart enough so he could turn around in the circle of my arms. He lifted my chin with his thumb.

"You do *not* need to worry about *me*," he said. "As long as *you're* safe, I'll be fine."

He bent over and brushed his lips against mine.

"Now, I'm going to take a shower and, as much as I'd rather you not, you need to get dressed." He headed for the stairs and

I followed behind him.

"I could join you," I offered, my insides warming at the thought.

"I'd love that . . . but, my love, I need your patience."

My head fell in dejection, though I knew deep inside that my whole heart wasn't into the idea. I wanted to wait, too.

"I promise you, though, it *will* be rewarded," he added and I smiled.

Something white lying by the baseboard caught my eye as we crossed the living room. I picked it up and realized it was a piece off one of the house models. I looked around the room and didn't see any boxes large enough to contain the architectural renderings. I wondered what he did with them. As I looked back at the piece, I noticed it hadn't just fallen off—it was broken.

"Tristan . . . ?" I looked up at him as he turned to me. "Where are your houses?"

His face darkened and then he shrugged.

"Gone," he said flatly.

"What do you mean . . . gone?" I searched his face as a pit formed in my stomach with the thought of what might have happened to them. I could tell he didn't want to tell me.

"I . . . destroyed them," he admitted quietly.

"Tristan! How could you? *Why?*"

"I was angry at myself and decided I didn't want them anymore. I wouldn't need a dream home . . . without you to share it with."

A long carving knife of shame pierced all the way through my heart and then twisted around inside my chest.

"I'm *sorry!*" I cried, throwing my arms around him. "I'm sorry I doubted you. I'm sorry I hurt you. I'm sorry . . ."

"You had every right—"

"No, I didn't! How could I doubt your love? I knew it all along and I was just mad, acting like a child. And I hurt you . . . ."

"You were hurt first. *I* hurt you. I should have been more upfront with you. I deserved it."

"But it wasn't you! I know that now. All you did was what was best for them . . . and you loved me. I'm just so sorry I was too proud and bullheaded to realize it sooner. I almost lost you," I whispered miserably.

"But you didn't," he whispered back. "And now you know you love me and trust me fully."

I nodded. He wiped the tears from my cheeks.

"So, we're good." He smiled warmly and I nodded again. "Then let's get past this and look forward, okay?"

I nodded a third time. He picked me up in a tight hug. I gave him a long kiss, hoping the depth of my love for him would flow through it. But I didn't know if that was even possible. My love was so much more.

"We'll do the next one together—*our* dream home," he promised as we continued up the stairs hand-in-hand.

℣ℤ

As we headed home from dinner that evening, Tristan drove the motorcycle right past the cottage to the dead-end at the beach.

"Come on. We have just enough time to watch the sun set," he said.

The sun already hovered half-way behind the water and we sat in silence as it finished its descent.

"Listen," Tristan finally said, "we'll need to go soon, but before we do, I need to tell you something."

Somberness and foreboding filled his tone. My stomach tightened automatically.

"Why do I have this feeling I won't like what happens tonight?" I asked.

"I think, in the end, you'll be fine. First, though, there will be some surprises."

"*More* surprises? How much more can there *be?*" I moaned and threw my head into his lap. I laid there curled up, my head resting on his legs. "I don't know that I can take any more."

"So you don't want to know all these big secrets you haven't been allowed to know before? You don't want to know who you are?"

I shot up and stared at him. "*Seriously?*"

He looked at me thoughtfully. "Yes, I think you'll be learning quite a bit tonight. I don't see how it can be kept from you any longer. There's too much at risk. So . . . I want you to know, no matter what you hear, regardless of how . . . shocking . . . it is, I absolutely, unconditionally, undeniably love you. No matter what. I've known it all since before you were born and knew what I was getting into, okay? And I would've told you already, but, like their plan for us, it wasn't my place. Do you understand?"

I narrowed my eyes. "Um, *no*. Was that supposed to make sense?"

He chuckled. "I guess it probably doesn't right now. Come here."

He pulled me sideways onto his lap and held me close, brushing his lips across my cheek. He murmured into my ear, "I love you, no matter what. You are everything to me and nothing will come between us as long as I can help it. We are together forever."

"I can understand that." I found his lips with mine. He suddenly stopped kissing me, though, and cocked his head, then closed his eyes and let out a sigh.

"They're ready for us."

"How do you know? And who's 'they'?" I asked as we headed back to the bike. "I thought it was just my mom."

"You'll see in about three minutes."

Three minutes later we walked into Mom's cottage. I stopped

in the archway between the foyer and the living room, surprised to see all the people there—Mom, a woman who looked just like her and two men. I sensed extreme goodness from all of them as they looked at Tristan and me and smiled approvingly.

The lady who looked nearly like Mom's twin, dressed for a ball in a white, shimmery gown, rose gracefully from Mom's usual chair. She had all the same features as Mom and looked to be in her late twenties, but, somehow, seemed much older. "Hello, Alexis, I am your grandmother."

I jumped at the "sound." Because she hadn't spoken. *Her lips didn't move!* I'd heard it *in* my head, not with my ears. Somebody snickered. Tristan squeezed my hand.

"Mother, she wasn't ready for that," Mom said.

"Sorry, dear," my grandmother said aloud. Her real voice, just like the one in my head, was smooth and luxurious, like velvet, with a foreign accent I couldn't place. It seemed familiar, though. I heard it in my head again. "*You are just as beautiful as they have told me. Just wait until the Ang'dora. You will be magnificent.*"

I stood there awkwardly, forcing a smile on the outside while internally freaking out. *My grandmother's a* telepath*!*

She held her hand out to me. I didn't move. Tristan gave me a little nudge and whispered, "It's okay."

Without letting go of his hand, I took the two steps over to her. She clasped my other hand in both of hers and closed her eyes. Silence filled the room as everyone watched. I had no idea what she did, but a warm, pleasurable sensation washed over me. She smiled and then opened her eyes.

"Yes, magnificent," she said aloud. She looked at Mom. "She is amazing, Sophia."

Mom beamed. "I told you. Probably the best in many, many centuries?"

"Yes, I think you are correct." My grandmother sat back

down. Her body moved with the majesty and grace of a lead ballerina. She belonged in a palace, not in our little cottage.

"Alexis, this is your grandmother, Katerina. You can call her Rina," Mom said. She held her hand first toward a tall, broad man with hair in cornrows standing perfectly erect behind Rina, then at the man sitting next to her on the couch. "That is Solomon and this is Stefan."

Stefan barely looked at me. Although he radiated goodness, the way he hid his eyes behind his dark, curly hair gave me the impression he felt guilty about something. I wondered what it was. He seemed vaguely familiar but I didn't know why. I couldn't remember ever meeting him, but I knew his name from just the day before. He'd spoken to Tristan recently, from what I heard on the speaker phone. I now placed Rina's voice—she'd been the woman on the phone.

"These are some of the Amadis council members," Mom continued. "Our family line has always led the Amadis, with advice and guidance from the council."

Owen popped his head in the door then and called, "All's clear."

"Thank you, Owen," Rina said. "Please continue your watch."

I threw Mom a look.

"Yes, Owen is part of the Amadis, but he's not on the council. He's a protector." She smiled. "He's *your* protector."

Chapter 20

My protector—*as in bodyguard? Why do I need a protector? And am I the only one in the dark here?* I must have stiffened because Tristan stepped behind me and circled his arm around my waist. "Relax, my love."

He pulled me over to the loveseat. We hardly ever used it—there were never more than three people in the room—and it sat in the corner, out of the way. Someone had pulled it slightly forward and now, as we sat down, it felt like the focal point of the room as everyone scrutinized us.

"My darling, Alexis," Rina said, "you are probably wondering what we are all doing here?"

I felt like a child in the principal's office, not because I'd misbehaved, but because something was wrong that the adults needed to explain. I took a deep breath and nodded. "That'd be a good start."

"Our primary concern is your immediate safety," she said, "but for you to understand our discussions, you must be better informed. At our direction, Sophia and Tristan have only told you what you needed to know. However, recent events have shown you deserve to know more now, rather than waiting for the *Ang'dora*.

"We are the Amadis. All of us, including Owen, are part of the Amadis society. Solomon and Stefan are members of the council. You, your mother, myself and Tristan, too, are direct descendents of the original Amadis family bloodline. Women in our direct bloodline have ruled the Amadis since its beginning over two millennia ago. I have been the matriarch for over a half-century. At some point in the future, Sophia will inherit it from me and then you from her. There was a time when we thought our existence was all but extinct, until you miraculously arrived. You are full of such promise and I am convinced the *Ang'dora* will bring you powers unseen since our earliest leaders."

I felt my eyes grow wider with every sentence Rina spoke. She paused now, not only so she could take a breath herself, but so I could have a moment to process it. It was already too much. *Royalty? Unseen powers? Me?!* Tristan squeezed my hand and I felt myself slightly relax. I hadn't realized I'd become so tense.

Mom excused herself to get us all a glass of wine. I didn't know if that was such a good idea for me, but I did know I could really use it.

"Can I ask a question?" I asked while we waited for Mom. Rina nodded. "Actually, two. What, exactly, are the Amadis? And why are the Daemoni our enemies?"

Rina nodded again. "We are the protectors of souls. The Daemoni try to destroy human souls; we fight to save them. They are full of hatred; we are full of love. They are ruled by Hell; we are ruled by Heaven. They would like us to cease existing so they can rule the Earth. It is our job to prevent that from occurring. You will learn the whole story and know our full purpose, and yours specifically, one day, but not now. Is that enough?"

I nodded reluctantly. It really wasn't enough—I'd hoped to get more—but I was too intimidated to push it.

Rina continued where she'd left off. "As soon as we realized your righteous qualities and your strength, we had hope. We also knew our chances would be strengthened if you had a child—a daughter, of course—fathered by the most powerful male with Amadis blood. Tristan had just come to us, but we knew, even when he was not sure himself, he would become one of us. Most of us knew when you were just an infant that your souls were meant for each other. The Heavenly Host created you specifically for each other, the strongest connection two souls can have."

She paused as Mom handed each of us a glass of wine.

"There is only one problem with this Heavenly match," Rina continued. "The Daemoni would like to prevent it. Firstly, they still desire to have Tristan back. They promise him a kingdom, but we all know he would be under their rule. They believe him to be a possession. They have time and again tried to bring him back, using an assortment of tactics, from promises of greatness to violent force. Tristan refuses."

I saw him nod out of the corner of my eye. *I had almost pushed him back to them.* I could never let that happen again. I squeezed his hand.

"So, secondly, they seek revenge. If they cannot have their ultimate warrior, then they certainly do not want us to have him. They seek revenge against Tristan for betraying them and against the Amadis in general for taking him.

"Thirdly, this match will result in our family's, and therefore our society's, continuance. The Daemoni would like to see us extinguished. Add to that, young Alexis, the fact that they have always targeted the youngest Amadis daughter and you can see we have a complex problem on our hands."

Tension filled the room like a dense fog as we sipped our

wine. Well, everyone else sipped. I drained mine, but didn't expect it to have much effect on me. Tristan put his arm around my shoulder and pulled me close to him. That calmed me more than the wine did.

"We need to consider this from both an immediate and a long-term perspective," Solomon said. His deep, seductive voice, with a foreign accent different than Rina's, matched his attractive, yet exotic face—nearly white skin but, somehow, with a dark undertone, and features that looked African or possibly Caribbean. "The Daemoni know about our plan for the two of you and that it is being executed. The question is what they will do about it."

Stefan spoke next. Even his voice—smooth, clear, authoritative—sounded familiar, but I still couldn't place him. "Through our recognizance, we have heard them discuss four options and they are not yet decided whether to pursue any in the immediate future."

"Explain the options so we can all understand," Rina said.

Stefan spoke matter-of-factly. "First, they could try to kill Tristan."

My heart jumped against my chest. I instinctively shifted my body in front of Tristan and put my arm across him in protection, shaking my head. *As if I can do anything.* Tristan pulled me back to him, his arms wrapped around me like a human straightjacket.

"Relax and listen," he murmured.

Stefan glanced at us briefly and continued. "They believe this could prevent another Amadis daughter and would give them their revenge for Tristan's betrayal. However, they are not fond of this idea. They still have hope in Tristan."

Solomon shook his head, the long cornrows, some pulled back into a pony tail, swinging slightly. "They do not have the means to kill him."

I relaxed with this statement and Tristan let go of me. He leaned forward, his elbows on his knees.

"It would have to be an ambush. Lucas is the only one who might have a chance single-handedly, but they would not risk that," he said. He and Mom exchanged looks I didn't understand. He shrugged. "They've tried to kill me before. It is not *my* life we need to worry about."

"Until there is a daughter, we need you," Solomon said harshly, but he followed with an exquisite smile of gleaming white teeth. I wasn't sure how to take him and, I thought, that's the impression he intended.

"There are other options for offspring besides me," Tristan muttered. I threw him a dirty look.

"Tristan, daughter or not, we *are* concerned for your life," Rina said. "But you are right. This is status quo. Go on, Stefan."

Stefan said their next option was to kill me. "This would definitely prevent the bloodline from continuing and would give them revenge on Tristan by killing his mate. In their twisted way, they believe this could bring him back in remorse."

For some reason, I didn't have nearly as strong a reaction to my murder as I did to Tristan's.

"They can only kill her if they are provoked. They must have justifiable reason," Rina said adamantly, lifting her chin.

"Yes, according to ancient law, that is, ultimately, the only right they have, but they could still try," Solomon said.

"They know it would mean a major battle," Stefan said. "They are mostly concerned about fighting Sophia and Tristan, though—two Amadis daughters and their own warrior could be a major victory or a terrible defeat for them."

I looked at Mom, sick at the thought of her fighting these monsters to protect me. She glanced at me, seemingly unconcerned until she saw my face.

She came over to me, squatted in front of me to look me directly in the eye and said firmly, "Don't you worry about us. We are just discussing how the Daemoni see it. They will *not* get to us. We have the best and highest protection."

I nodded, trying to look calm, but I shuddered anyway.

"Let us take a moment for a breath," Rina said and then she looked at Tristan. He stood up, grabbed my hands and pulled me up. I wondered if she'd communicated telepathically.

"Come on. Let's get some fresh air," he said, leading me through the kitchen and out the back door.

The evening air still felt muggy and heavy against my skin, but I felt a sense of freedom as I drew it in. I smelled the humidity, combined with freshly mown grass, jasmine and magnolias from the neighbor's yard behind us. I took several cleansing breaths, trying to focus on steadying my pounding heart.

"You okay?" Tristan asked after a few minutes. He leaned casually against the house as if we'd just been discussing what new toy to buy rather than our own demise.

"Yeah, freakin' wonderful." I gave him a weak smile and walked over to him. I lifted my hands to the back of his neck, stretched up on my toes and tilted my head back. "Make me okay, please."

He kissed me and a sense of calmness washed over me with his scent and taste and touch. I inhaled deeply for an extra dose.

"Okay," I said.

Mom handed me a glass of ice water as I returned to the loveseat. I emptied the glass, the icy liquid light and refreshing, washing away the thick, bitter coating the wine had left in my mouth and throat. I finally nodded at Rina, who'd been watching me expectantly.

"Okay, Stefan, please proceed with the other options," she said.

The third option, according to Stefan, was business as

usual—the Daemoni would mostly leave me alone until they had Provocation. The way they all said "Provocation," I could hear the capital P, as in it must be official.

"And that leads us to the fourth option," Stefan said. "They capture Alexis to bring Tristan to them, using her as bait. This appears to be the most dangerous option for us. They would not have Alexis's blood on their hands, so they do not see this as a violation. They also have a strong desire to have both Alexis and Tristan alive, but in their hands, seeing the same great potential we do, but working for them."

Everyone in the room reacted to this statement. Solomon hissed. Mom and Rina gasped. Tristan swore under his breath. I didn't understand.

"I thought their natural instinct is to kill me. How could they keep me alive?" I asked. "And why would they want to, once they had Tristan?"

They all exchanged meaningful looks I didn't understand. Rina nodded at Mom and Mom sighed, closing her eyes and pinching the bridge of her nose. Tristan put his arms around me. Mom eventually came over to us and knelt on the floor in front of me, while everyone else stared at the floor. Something horrible was coming.

"Honey, it's time you knew something about your . . . father," Mom said quietly.

"You mean sperm donor," I corrected. "I don't *have* a father."

Her eyes dropped to the floor and she spoke so quietly, it was barely more than a whisper. "The last time I met up with Tristan, he was with Lucas. After Tristan, Lucas was—is now—the Daemoni's most powerful warrior. They were on a mission to kill me, but not in their normal, direct manner. Tristan thought they should act like they wanted to leave the Daemoni, become close to me, build my trust and then go in for the kill. Tristan really did want to leave and I was able to help him and bring him to the Amadis. But . . ." Her voice wavered and a tear slid down her cheek. And then another. I couldn't remember if I'd ever seen Mom cry before. Her voice filled with grief and longing. ". . . But I couldn't help Lucas. I tried so hard, did everything I could. I thought loving him, giving myself completely to him would do it. No one could have ever guessed . . . I'd already changed over and no one had ever conceived . . ."

"*What?* What are you saying . . . ?" I shook my head, knowing already.

"Lucas is your . . ."

Whop! The breath flew out of me. I felt like I'd just been punched in the stomach.

"I . . . I . . . I'm *Daemoni?*" I choked on the words. A heavy weight pressed down on my chest, making my breaths shallow. Tristan's words from long ago echoed in my ears . . . *pure evil . . . real demons . . . soldiers and followers of Satan himself. It flows through my blood?* I jumped up and paced the living room, shaking my arms out, as if I could throw the hideousness off of me. "No! No, no, *no!*"

"*You are* Amadis, *through and through.* Do not forget that!" Rina's voice thundered in my head. I stopped and glared at her through the tears in my eyes. She spoke aloud with calm surety, "Alexis, you are *not* Daemoni. You have Lucas's blood, but you are completely Amadis. All of your powers, all of your qualities, everything that makes you one of our most powerful descendents yet, are all good and righteous."

"How do you *know* that? How do you know for *sure?*" I demanded, throwing my arms up in emphasis.

"We evaluated you as a baby. I felt it again when you first walked in . . . when I took your hand, I assessed you. The evil is fully suppressed; I can hardly feel anything."

I didn't feel any better. The questions flying through my head panicked me.

"And what about when I change over? Do you know for sure I'll be like *you*? That I'll be *good*? What if I *don't* change? Or what if the evil strengthens with the *Ang'dora*? Do you have those answers?" The thought of being anything different than myself or Mom . . . anything *evil* . . . terrified me. I choked on the idea as if it were a physical object lodged in my throat.

Rina shook her head and admitted, "No, we do not have those answers. You are unique. But your powers are so strong, we are confident you will be perfect . . . *magnificent*."

"*You might not be here otherwise*," she said in my head. I recoiled, startled.

They would have killed me.

"*Quite possibly*," she answered silently. I stared at her, not realizing she could *hear* my thoughts, and she nodded. That put things into perspective. If I was evil, I would've been a threat to them, but they didn't feel that. In fact, they expected me to lead them in some distant future.

I fell back into the loveseat and dropped my head into my hands. Tristan rubbed my back. *Why isn't he mortified?* Then I remembered he'd already known and still loved me, even came looking for me. I realized why he'd been so adamant earlier about telling me he loved me no matter what. *Of course, he* was *Daemoni.* I turned my head toward him.

"Ha!" I barked hysterically. "I guess we really are perfect for each other."

He rolled his eyes.

I tried to tell myself I was physically no different than I'd been twenty minutes ago, just more knowledgeable. I closed my eyes, focused on that thought and tried to control my breathing and pulse.

"*There you go,*" Rina's voice soothed in my head.

"Can we take another break?" I finally asked when I felt control.

I refilled my glass with ice water and chugged the entire glass, though the cold made my head hurt, then I escaped to the bathroom. I splashed cold water on my face and caught my reflection in the mirror. *Do I look any different?* I couldn't help but wonder. I stared into my brown eyes, looking so much like Mom's and Rina's, but wondering if they really were. As I studied myself in the mirror, looking for signs of Daemoni, my stomach heaved and I barely caught the toilet as I vomited. The water mixed with the red wine looked like blood swirling in the white porcelain bowl. I wished it was the Daemoni blood pouring out of me.

I sat on the floor, breathing deeply. I really wanted to take a hot shower, thinking soap, scalding water and a lot of scrubbing would remove any evil from my system. *I'm being irrational. I'm no different than I was. I just need to get over this.* Someone knocked on the door and before I could answer, it opened and closed as Mom squeezed into the bathroom with me. I scooted against the bathtub and she slid down to the floor next to me.

"Are you okay?" she asked quietly.

"I think so," I whispered, a half-truth.

She put her arms around me. "I would say I'm sorry, but I'm really not, because I have you."

I didn't know what to say, so I just hugged her back and we cried on each other's shoulders for several minutes, until there was another knock on the door. It opened slightly, catching against Mom's foot, and Rina slipped in. She closed the door behind her and leaned against it. She studied our tear-soaked faces.

"You two have a very close relationship. I am glad to see that," Rina said. She smiled sadly at Mom. "I am sorry we never had that."

"Me, too," Mom said, but she waved her hand in dismissal. "It was a different time then. We had different challenges to deal with."

"Well, we all face the same obstacles now." Rina eyed us appreciatively. "Together we can overcome them. *Nothing* can thwart the power of the three of us together."

She held her hands out to us and we each took one. She was surprisingly strong—it shouldn't have startled me but it did—and she lifted both of us to our feet. She put her arms around us. "We are *Amadis*! *All* of us."

An unusual, powerful sensation charged through her arm into me. I instinctively knew at once it was Amadis power. And my body reacted positively to it, absorbing the warm and potent feeling into every cell. *Yes, I AM Amadis.* Rina smiled at me with that thought.

We stood there, three generations arm-in-arm, until someone else knocked on the door.

"We still have a lot to discuss," Stefan said from the other side.

We all sighed, our moment over. Mom and Rina stepped out while I quickly rinsed my mouth with water and gargled with mouthwash. When I caught my reflection in the mirror again, I saw a new strength in my eyes. The same strength as in the eyes of my kin—Mom and Rina. Amadis power.

Chapter 21

Tristan caught me in the hallway when I came out of the bathroom. He took my face in his hands and searched my eyes. I smiled.

"You're okay." It wasn't a question.

"I'm perfect. You?"

"Perfect." He brushed his lips against mine. I hoped the mouthwash did its job.

Solomon studied my face and Stefan briefly looked at me as I sat down again. I smiled at them both and their expressions relaxed. Solomon, especially, intimidated me, but I knew he was good, and Stefan emanated power, a good power, nearly as appealing as Rina's. It still bugged me, though, how he felt familiar. And, even more, how he had a hard time bringing his eyes to mine.

He picked up where we left off . . . before I got punched in the stomach.

"As I was saying, the Daemoni believe it would be useful

to have both Alexis and Tristan under their power. With Lucas's blood and Amadis royalty, Alexis will be nearly—if not equally—as powerful as Tristan. They believe there is a chance Alexis could come to their side and Tristan would follow her."

"Which I would do," Tristan muttered.

"No, we will not let that happen," Rina said. "Tristan, what do you see as the best solution?"

He stiffened and his jaw clamped audibly. Repeating what he'd told me earlier, he said through gritted teeth, "It is *not* an option."

"If it is the best, then we must know it so we can all consider it," Solomon said.

Tristan glared at him. His voice held that steely undertone as he spoke. "The best solution for Alexis's safety and long-time survival of the Amadis is for me to go back to the Daemoni. They'll leave you all alone for a long time. Alexis will have to find another mate."

"*NO!*" I cried.

"Absolutely not!" Rina said.

"Not an option," Solomon agreed. "What is the next one?"

Tristan chuckled grimly. "Definitely not an option. Alexis and I both go to them. They leave the Amadis alone. There's a chance we can still be together, have a child and possibly escape."

Mom and Rina gasped.

"Not an option," Solomon repeated harshly. "Give us something we can actually *do*."

"You wanted to know." Tristan took a deep breath. "Besides those two, I really can't come up with anything except protect Alexis and fight if and when necessary. If they go with any of their options, I believe it'll be the last one. That one serves their purpose the most."

"I agree," Stefan said. "We need to ensure they cannot even get close to Alexis. It will be much easier to abduct her than to kill her."

"Then that is what we will do," Rina said decisively. "We have Tristan, Sophia and Owen here. Solomon, make arrangements for at least one more protector at all times. Stefan, continue your recognizance and stay on top of their plans. And keep watch on everything here."

"I do not think they will act immediately," Stefan said. "It will be a difficult maneuver, very risky for them. They may never follow through on it."

"There are always rogues," Tristan said.

"And Vanessa," Mom added. The name ringed in my head as if I should know it, but I couldn't place it.

"Vanessa could become a problem," Tristan said, "but the rogues are a bigger threat. It's their nature to disobey and do their own thing. And *they* may take one of the other options."

"You need more protection, too, Tristan, in case they do take another path," Rina responded. "You are planning on marrying Alexis, no?"

"Yes," Tristan answered.

"You should do it soon," Solomon said. "Marrying royalty will bind you closer to the Amadis. You will become a member of the royal family and they cannot attack royalty."

"That will be done on *our* terms," Tristan said firmly, squeezing my hand.

Solomon narrowed his eyes at Tristan. "The sooner the better."

"It just needs to be done under Amadis power," Rina said. "You can delay your legal wedding if you need time to prepare, but marriage vows should be exchanged before the Amadis sooner rather than later to strengthen that bond."

"Let's do it now. I'm ready," I said.

"Alexis!" Mom gasped.

Tristan glared at me. "We'll discuss this later."

"Yes, we'll discuss it first," Mom said.

"If it helps you . . . ," I said to Tristan.

"That is *not* the reason we'll be getting married," he growled. I knew that tone and decided we wouldn't argue this in front of everyone.

"We *will* discuss this," I promised and added, "sooner, not later."

"Alexis, you need to thoroughly understand this," Rina said. "A true Amadis marriage—one between two people with Amadis blood—unites the souls into one. We have not had such a marriage in centuries. You and Tristan will have a bond like no one currently on this Earth has experienced or can ever understand."

"Oh," I said as that sunk in and then I shrugged. "I'm still ready."

Solomon beamed and Tristan grimaced. *Is he not ready for that?* We definitely did need to discuss this.

Rina changed the subject. She didn't have to hear Tristan's thoughts to know he wouldn't budge at the moment—his body language made it clear.

"I know it will not be easy, but you must not ever be alone," she said. "You are their primary target and you are also our most vulnerable. Until the *Ang'dora*, you will not be able to defend yourself. Do not worry about Sophia or Tristan or any of the others. We can all protect ourselves *and* you. You focus on keeping yourself safe, which means staying with one of us at all times."

"I understand." I swallowed hard when I thought about the only activity I did alone—write. I mumbled it under my breath . . . I thought. "I guess my book is out of the question now."

"That's absurd!" Mom said. "You will finish that book and we *will* get it published."

"Yes, you need to move forward with that," Rina agreed. I

stared at her in disbelief. "Your writing and story-telling ability is one of your special gifts, Alexis, and we would never ask you not to use a gift. We know it will be used for good."

"She should use a nom-de-plume," Tristan said. "It probably wouldn't do any good, but it could divert attention from her."

"No, we want the Daemoni to know," Solomon said. "They will feel threatened by the boldness."

I felt uncomfortable with the way they spoke. I felt a layer of meaning that I wasn't grasping hovering under the surface. Tristan didn't help.

"I don't like it," he said. "It's too risky."

"It is necessary," Rina said with finality. She spoke in my head, "*Your purpose, for now, is to write your stories. They will help us. That is all you need to know right now.*"

I nodded. Although completely confused, I could easily accept that writing was my purpose. In fact, I'd always felt it in my heart. And I was glad I had a way to serve them, even if I didn't understand how—that I could do something besides sit around with a babysitter.

"She will continue with school, too," Mom said firmly.

"Whatever is a part of her normal life, yes," Rina agreed. "We cannot show any fear."

"So we can stay here?" I asked hopefully.

"Yes, you are safe here, at least for now," Stefan answered. "Tristan, keep your house. It is built for protection from the elements and it will be a safe place should we need it. We would prefer you kept Alexis there with you."

"We'll work that out," Tristan said. "We shouldn't push anything too soon. She'll be safe here with Sophia and protectors keeping watch."

"Nonetheless . . . the sooner, the better," Solomon said pointedly.

"If we act too quickly, they'll only assume we're pushing forward with the plan and they'll feel threatened by that," Tristan said. "The more natural we are about it, the more time we take, the more time they think they have."

"You should proceed in secrecy," Solomon said. "The sooner there is a child—"

"Solomon, she's too young!" Mom interrupted. "At least allow her to finish college."

Solomon grunted.

"It is only a couple of years, darling," Rina soothed, reaching back to pat his hand. "That is nothing to us."

I squirmed in discomfort as they discussed plans for *my* future—*my* marriage, *my* child—as if I weren't there. Though nearly everything about the Amadis was still as murky as the Everglades swamps, I saw a few things with perfect clarity. A future I didn't like flashed before me, showing me as a puppet. I decided I better speak up now or I would be handing them the strings forever.

"Tristan and I will know when it's time to take each next step. *We* will determine that," I said clearly and firmly. "On *our* terms."

Everyone stared at me in mild shock. Except Tristan. He grinned widely. A smile eventually spread across Rina's face, too.

"*Yes, you will be magnificent,*" she said in my head.

And that was it. We said our good-byes, then Solomon hooked Rina's arm in his and they disappeared into the night— early morning, actually—returning to wherever they came from. I wondered where that was and I wondered if they were mates. Despite how much I'd learned tonight, I still knew so little.

"Stay together tonight?" Tristan asked me when we had a moment alone. I nodded. "Here or my place?"

I felt physically and emotionally exhausted and didn't want to go anywhere, but I remembered my broken bed and frowned. "Your place, definitely."

As we pulled out of the driveway, I watched Stefan and Mom on the front porch as they turned to go inside, still discussing plans for my protection, I assumed. Stefan stroked his square jaw and chin thoughtfully. In a strangely familiar way. In a matter of two seconds, it all came back to me.

Sheffie!

Sheffie who took me to the park, to the zoo and out for ice cream. Sheffie who drank my invisible tea, sang lullabies at bedtime and made the best French toast in the world. Sheffie who took me for a carousel ride when it was closed and somehow made it go, playing lively carnival music, my horse sliding up and down as I squealed with delight and he stood next to me, making sure I didn't fall off. Sheffie who loved me. Loved me like a dad. Or so I'd thought.

And then I remembered I *had* seen Mom cry before. Once.

"Stop! Tristan, stop!" I smacked his shoulder. He looked back at me. "Stop! Now!"

He stopped and cut the engine at the bottom of the driveway. Somehow I managed to scramble off the bike and nearly run up the front walk to the house. Mom and Stefan stopped just inside the door and turned toward me.

"You son of a bitch!" I screamed. And before I knew what I was doing, my hand slapped Stefan's face with a loud *smack*! "That's for what you did to my mom. And this one's for me!"

I raised and swung my hand again, but it was caught in mid-air.

"Alexis, what the hell?" Tristan asked with bewilderment.

I stared at Stefan as my chest rose and fell with anger.

"You want to know why I had such *trust* issues?" I fumed through burning tears. "You want to know what started it all? Ask him!"

"Stefan?" Tristan still sounded confused.

"Yes! But he was Sheffie to me. And he was the first one to leave and break my heart."

And I knew it was true when Stefan lowered his head and sighed sadly. That's why he couldn't look me in the eye all night. That's why I could feel his guilty conscience.

"You *left* us! You left *me*! You were the closest thing I ever had to a dad and you left me!"

"Lexi, my love," Tristan pulled me into his arms and I cried against his chest. "I think you're confused . . . ."

"No. No, she's not," Stefan said, his voice full of quiet grief. "She remembers right."

I looked at him through my tears and remembered him clearly now, although I had only been four or five years old the last time I saw him.

"You were the only boyfriend who cared about me. Who really *cared*. Not just because I was around and fun to play with. Not just to impress Mom. Or so I thought. I thought you really *loved* me."

"Alexis, I did love you," Stefan said quietly. "I still do."

"But you *left*! And you never came back!"

"I am so sorry." And I could hear it in his voice. My anger broke and all I felt was the sadness renewed.

"Honey, Stefan was never really a boyfriend. He was our protector then," Mom said. "Eventually, he had to move on to a new assignment. He *had* to go."

"But, you cried when he left, too."

"I cried for you, honey," she said. "Your little heart broke and you just couldn't understand."

"I deeply regretted doing that to you," Stefan said. "As you got older, I hoped you had just forgotten."

I shook my head. "I didn't forget. I didn't remember your face, but I never forgot how much I loved you and how much I cried when you left. I thought I did something wrong."

"It was nothing you did. I didn't have a choice and when your mom told me how hurt you were, we decided it was best for me to just stay away. I couldn't be reliable enough for you." Stefan held his arms open. "Please forgive me?"

I could see sincerest remorse in his dark eyes. And I somehow knew he'd never meant to hurt me. Maybe it was the Amadis goodness emanating from him. I don't know how or why—perhaps the passage of time to heal the wounds or the fact I'd just survived the worst loss, if only for a couple weeks, I'd ever experienced—but I couldn't help but forgive him immediately. I left Tristan's arms and fell into Stefan's.

"Sheffie," I cried into his chest.

"Ali-oop," he murmured, stroking my hair. I'd forgotten his nickname for me and giggled through my tears. "I am so sorry."

I nodded against his chest. "I know now. I'm sorry I slapped you."

"I deserved it." He held me for another moment then gently pushed me back. "I think you need to get some rest now."

I wiped the tears on my cheeks, took a deep breath and stepped back to Tristan. He wrapped his arm around my waist and I sagged against him. I'd spent every bit of emotional energy I had and that last bit broke me. I was absolutely exhausted. I didn't even know how we made it back to Tristan's house without me falling off the back of the bike.

"You're amazing," Tristan said as he half-carried me up the stairs to his room. My head lolled against his side, my eyelids drooping.

"Huh?" I asked through my grogginess.

"You're so forgiving. I think I suffered more for what Stefan did to you than he did."

I cupped my hand around his face. "I'm sorry you had to deal with my issues. You did take the brunt of it all and I love you for that. But I believe Stefan did suffer. I could see it in his eyes. Life's too short to hold grudges against people you love."

Tristan chuckled and even through the exhaustion, I understood.

"Even for us, my sweet Tristan. Love is just too precious."

❦

"You are such a tease," Tristan admonished the next morning.

I widened my eyes and looked at him innocently as he pulled a pair of jeans out of a box and hung them up. "What? I'm just looking for some clothes."

"In *my* closet?"

I smiled impishly. I'd just stepped out of the shower and had a towel wrapped around me, water drops beaded on my skin and my hair still dripped. I had panties on already, but he didn't know that. I *was* being a tease.

"Maybe I like wearing *your* shirts." I found a plain white t-shirt and pulled it on with one arm while holding my towel with the other. As I walked out of the closet, I let the towel fall in the doorway as the t-shirt slid slowly down to my thighs. I could feel his eyes on me as I left and I grinned to myself.

I went back to the bathroom to brush my wet hair. It soaked through the front of the white shirt, making it transparent, and I debated how mean I wanted to be. But when I looked up into the mirror, I saw Tristan behind me in the doorway, watching me with his arms crossed.

"*Why* are you doing this to me?" he growled.

"What?" I played innocent again. He was behind me in an instant, his arms wrapped around me and his face buried in the crook of my neck.

"You're so damn irresistible."

"Oh. Well, you do that to me all the time. All *you* have to do is smile and wink. I'm just fighting fair."

"This is hardly fair," he murmured.

His hands slowly moved down my body as he kissed and sucked my neck. I leaned back into him, feeling his powerful, warm body tense against my back. I put my hands over his and pulled his left hand up, across my body to my right breast while his right hand traveled down my bare thigh and slowly up the inside of it. I grasped his hand and pulled it away just before he reached the top, my whole body tingling.

"Hardly fair," I breathed. He pulled back and groaned in frustration as I turned around and hoisted myself to sit on the counter. I hooked my fingers in his jeans waistband and pulled him closer, wrapping my legs around his waist. I trailed my hands slowly up his abs and chest, up to his face, where I held him. "We don't *have* to do this to ourselves, you know. We could probably be married tonight or tomorrow, at least under the Amadis."

He closed his eyes and sighed. "Why are you suddenly in such a rush?"

"Because I love you, I'm going to spend the rest of my life with you anyway and I want to be your *wife*."

He smiled at that last word, but didn't open his eyes. "Not just because you want my body?"

"Well, that, too," I admitted. I slid my hands across his chest again.

He opened his eyes, braced my face gently in his hands and said, "You are incorrigible!"

He stomped out of the bathroom and sat hard on the bed, his head falling into his hands. I hopped down and followed.

"What's wrong with me wanting to make love to you?" I asked.

"Three days ago you hated me," he muttered into his hands.

My mouth fell open. "I never *hated* you!"

I threw myself back on the bed and stared at the ceiling.

"You didn't want anything to do with me and now you're ready to rush off and commit yourself for life. 'A bond like no other.' Don't you get it?"

I shot off the bed and stood in front of him, lifting his face with my hands and holding his eyes with mine. "Yes, I get it! My soul's already yours anyway, so you're damn right I want to commit myself. I made up my mind and I'm ready now. I know you are, too. If there was ever a time you would've hurt me, it would've been the other night. You can handle it now. So what are *you* waiting for? Are you having commitment issues? Do you have a problem with this bond?"

Pain flickered in his eyes, as if I'd slapped him. "Of course not! I already knew about it. I just don't want you feeling like you have to rush into anything. You're only nineteen!"

I threw my hands in the air. "Is that your argument? My *age*? Does it matter how old I am if we already know we're together forever?"

"I'm just saying there's plenty of time. Don't feel rushed because of lust or because you think it'll be safer for me."

"We could have sex right now and I wouldn't change my mind. And, yes, I would feel better if I knew you had every protection possible. Even if you don't think you need it, it would make *me* feel better. You are my life and the thought of losing you . . ." My breath hitched with the thought. ". . . *horrifies* me!

I *need* you, Tristan. Whatever binds us closer together, I'll do. *Now.* Before it's too late."

He pulled me into his arms and brushed his lips against my cheek. He lowered his voice to the loveliest of tones. "Be patient, my love. We're not doing this out of fear or threats or others' demands. We'll know when the time is right. *Our* terms."

I sighed with frustration. "If *we're* making the decision, it *is* on our terms. But I've made my decision and now it's up to you. So I guess now it's on *your* terms."

I didn't like giving that to him, but I knew he wouldn't like it either.

"Alexis," he growled.

I ignored him. I picked up my bag and went into the bathroom, closing the door this time. I thought I heard something hit the wall.

Chapter 22

Over the next several weeks, I concentrated on summer classes and putting the finishing touches on my book. I felt the pressure of getting it done, a big obstacle in setting our wedding date. After a couple weeks of teasing Tristan, hoping he would come around, I realized I frustrated myself just as much. So I gave it up and decided holding off on nearly everything would make our wedding night that much better. I stopped spending the night with him and as soon as the loving kisses became passionate and hands started exploring—his or mine—I cut it off. It was, admittedly, quite maddening.

"You are infuriating, you know that?" Tristan teased one night as we snuggled on Mom's couch. "I liked it better when you threw yourself at me."

I laughed. "Shouldn't have complained then."

"Will you please do it again?" he murmured against the hollow behind my ear.

"Nope."

"But I miss your body." His hand slid along my side.

"Then you will enjoy it all the more on our wedding night." I picked his hand up as it started sliding under my shirt.

"Are you trying to manipulate me? Because it might be working . . . ." He kissed and nibbled my ear, driving me nearly over the edge.

I sighed. "Not much longer, right? September First?"

"Five weeks, four days, eighteen hours."

Feels like forever. I moaned internally. But I smiled anyway and said, "Not long."

We'd just decided the date that day when we mailed the first query letters for getting my book published. Mom was satisfied and it was far enough away that we could have a legal wedding and exchange Amadis vows at the same time. The Daemoni had been quiet, according to Stefan, who dropped in every now and then for coffee or dinner, so I had to trust Tristan would be okay in the meantime.

Less than a week later, though, Hell blew in.

Tropical Storm Edmund brewed in the Gulf of Mexico, projected to make landfall somewhere in our area as a category one or two hurricane. Long-time locals told us it wasn't much to worry about—"Board up and hunker down. You'll be fine." Mom and Tristan seemed overly tense, though, considering they'd faced much worse than a relatively small hurricane. The first heavy bands of wind and rain came in as we finished boarding the cottage, having spent most of the day preparing the store.

"Something's going on besides this storm," Tristan yelled over the wind at Mom.

"I feel it, too," Mom yelled back. "We're almost done here. Get Alexis to your house. We'll be there in a minute."

Tristan and I ran for the car, leaving Mom and Owen to finish hanging plywood on the last window. Rain blew in sheets, looking like it marched across the road. We arrived at Tristan's house within five minutes, but in that short amount of time, the storm's intensity had already increased. The wind whipped at the trees, bending the palms at forty-five-degree angles, but the worst of the storm was still hours away. We pulled into the garage and as I stepped out of the car, I thought I saw something rather large blow under the closing garage door. Tristan saw it, too.

"Aw, shit! *Alexis, back in the car NOW!*" Tristan roared.

But I couldn't move.

Evil! Daemoni! Evil!

Someone grabbed me from behind and held me in a chokehold with one arm against my neck and a powerful hand clawed around my head. I didn't know if I gagged from the pressure against my throat or from the stench of rotten meat, vomit and feces. Flames exploded in Tristan's eyes. He swam in my vision, but I thought I saw him take a step toward me.

"*Don't!* Just a little twist of my wrist and she's dead," said a sickening, scratchy, barely human voice that sounded far away though it was right in my ear. My pulse thundered in my head, nearly drowning everything else out. Whoever held me stiffened behind me.

"And one little twist of *my* wrist and *you're* dead." I had no idea how she got into the closed garage, but I recognized Mom's voice. It sounded like I'd never heard it before. Low and vicious.

I was shoved to the ground, cracking my head on the Mercedes' bumper on my way down. In an instant I was in Tristan's arms. Each breath tore through my burning throat. I buried my face in his chest, trying to flush the reek out with his scent. There was a stomach-turning cackle and I turned to stare with fascinated horror.

The sordid creature barely resembled a human. Its eyes glowed red fire in its round, lumpy head and twisted, pointed teeth filled its misshapen mouth. I thought it might have been grinning, but if that was a smile, it was the kind that gives you nightmares. Black blood trickled down its neck where Mom held a blade, the point pierced into its skin.

"What do we do with it?" Mom asked, ignoring the creature's cackle, except for a slight dig with the knife.

"Take it upstairs and we'll see what it thinks it's trying to do. I'll be right behind you." Tristan carried me up the stairs as we followed Mom, who held the knife at the creature's throat. My head throbbed with each step and I could feel a lump forming on my forehead.

A strange popping sound came from the living room and Mom froze at the top of the stairs. The creature skipped away from her, cackling again. Tristan stopped right behind her and stiffened. The creature was not alone.

"What an excellent gift you've delivered, Seth—two generations of Amadis royalty and your heart all at once." This voice was smooth and clear, possibly appealing if I hadn't felt the evil rolling off the man who stood in the middle of the dark living room. The creature crouched at his side. "I couldn't have imagined it being this good."

"Your imagination has run away from you if you think you can get away with this, Edmund," Tristan said calmly. He set me on my feet on the landing and both he and Mom took protective stances in front of me as the man took a step closer to us. Terror gripped my heart as I realized how weak and vulnerable I was, unable to do anything but watch. Moving only my eyes, I glanced down the stairs, wondering if any others lurked in the shadows.

"I admit it's risky, but the rewards will be worth it," the man replied.

Hurricane shutters blocked out almost all light from the

windows, but my eyes adjusted to the darkness. I still couldn't see the man's face, but I could see the outline of his hulking figure. He stood nearly as tall as Tristan and much bulkier. I had to remind myself of Tristan's power because, I thought, if it came down to brute strength, I didn't see how he could win. My heart raced as I realized the inevitability of the situation—Mom and Tristan would have to fight for our lives.

"You're an imbecile if you think you'll be rewarded for shedding their blood," Tristan said. "The Daemoni would not welcome the war that would ensue."

"Yes, I said it was risky. But after all is said and done, I would be personally responsible for ending the Amadis for good. *That* will be rewarded."

I shivered at the menace in the man's smug voice.

"If you live through it," Tristan said pointedly.

"Which you will not," Mom added. "God Himself would not allow it."

The man shrank back at Mom's words and didn't reply. We all stood in silence and I knew they each calculated how to proceed. The wind picked up intensity outside, shaking the shutters. The storm seemed to be coming faster than expected. It would be foolish to try to escape outside into it. The trapped feeling caused the panic to rise even higher, tightening my chest.

Edmund's eyes darted back and forth between Tristan and Mom as he moved a few steps to our right and his creature scurried next to him. Tristan moved, too, while Mom remained still. Edmund and his creature moved back to our left. This time both Mom and Tristan moved with him. They angled themselves to take him from both sides without leaving a wide enough gap for him to get to me.

"So why don't you just make this easy for all of us, Seth?" Edmund finally spoke as they continued their macabre dance.

"You come with me and I'll leave them alone."

"*Never!*" Tristan snarled.

Edmund nodded at me. "You can bring her along, if you'd like."

A deep, guttural growl rumbled in Tristan's chest. He and Mom both took a step forward, their only reply.

"Then you'd rather fight it out." Edmund made a tsking sound and the creature's shape transformed. It fell on all fours, became longer and taller in the darkness. It paced like a guard dog in front of Edmund, its eyes glowing red fire, a low growl in its throat. I shrank back while Tristan and Mom positioned themselves to fight. "Or maybe I just take her and let you chase me."

Edmund leaped into the air, seeming to fly over Tristan and Mom. He landed right next to me, as they spun around. Tristan swore profusely. The dog-thing stayed behind them. It crouched to attack. It continued to growl and even in the darkness I could see its lips pulled back, sharp fangs glinting in the little bit of natural light seeping in at the edges of the windows. Edmund grabbed the back of my neck tightly and pulled me to him. My mind and body numbed in terror.

"*NO!*" Tristan growled roughly.

He lunged at the bulky man, knocking Edmund hard against the wall, pulling me with him. My hip smacked painfully against the baluster at the top of the stairs. At the same time, the dog-thing jumped at Mom. She spun at it. Her arms whacked it in the side like a bat hitting an oversized, misshapen ball. It sailed across the room, landing with an inhuman cry. It was back on its feet in a second and charged at Mom. She crouched, ready for it. They simultaneously leaped toward each other. While still in mid-air, Mom grabbed its head and twisted it with a snap. The thing fell to the floor with a thud.

Mom landed lithely on the balls of her feet and whirled

around to Tristan, the hulk and me. Tristan and Edmund glowered at each other in a standoff. Tristan held his hand up, palm facing Edmund but nearly two feet from him. He held the hulk flat against the wall with his paralyzing power. Edmund's hand still clutched my neck.

"LET. HER. *GO!*" Tristan roared. His eyes blazed with bright flames.

"You are such a traitor." Edmund smirked, his own eyes glowing blood red.

He slowly raised his free hand just an inch from the wall, fighting Tristan's power with evident difficulty. Mom stepped forward. Edmund was just able to twitch his finger. She flew into the loveseat, held there by an unseen force. Anger blazed in her eyes as she struggled against the power holding her, her shoulders and neck straining.

It pissed me off.

My heart pounded in terror but the anger rose above it. Just enough to give me the force I needed. It all happened so quickly, but it felt like slow motion as my mind registered every move, every detail. I wrapped my hands around the baluster and yanked it from its anchor. I lifted it as high as I could and slammed it down on the arm holding me. It wasn't much compared to the hulk's strength, but enough to distract him. He turned to look at me, his eyes wide. His mouth formed a silent O. He apparently never expected *me* to fight back. Tristan seized the opportunity and pounced. I freed myself from the hand before it tried to close back on me. I stumbled sideways and caught myself on the opposite rail to avoid falling down the stairs.

Tristan came down on the Daemoni, jabbing his elbow into Edmund's upper back. His knee landed in the back of the hulk's thigh. The femur snapped loudly. Edmund fell into a heap on the floor, howling with both pain and rage. Tristan grabbed his dark hair. I turned away as he slammed Edmund's head against the concrete floor. The crack made my stomach lurch and echoed in my ears. I looked back as Tristan dragged him over to the creature's body.

He leaned over and snarled, "Don't fuck with me unless you can finish it."

Pop! Pop! The man and the creature disappeared.

I thought the world stopped. The pounding in my chest abruptly halted. My breath caught in my throat. I collapsed to the floor, unable to restart my heart or make my lungs work. Mom caught me before I rolled down the stairs. She sat on the top stair and pulled me into her lap, her power flowing through me. My lungs filled with air again. My heart started with a jolt, pounding against my ribs. She held me for a long time, or maybe for only seconds, rocking back and forth.

I'd nearly stopped trembling when Tristan lifted me into his arms. My tense muscles finally loosened and I fell against him. He carried me over to the couch and sat down with me in his lap. I curled against him and closed my eyes. The recent events started to replay like a horror movie against my eyelids. I couldn't keep them closed so I stared wide-eyed at nothing in the semi-darkness. The sound of footsteps rushing up the stairs yanked me out of my near-catatonic state.

My heart raced again with renewed fear. My body automatically prepared for fight or flight. Stefan and Owen flew into the living room, dripping wet. I slumped back against Tristan as they surveyed the scene.

"Oh, thank God," Stefan said breathlessly. "We thought . . ."

"Daemoni were outside," Owen said. "They started to fight but fled instead. We thought maybe they got to you."

There were *more*. I shuddered.

"I wondered what happened to you," Mom said casually.

She sat in the loveseat, her legs folded under her, looking, somehow, *relaxed*. Like what happened was just an everyday pain-in-the-butt, like having to deal with an annoying door-to-door salesperson.

Owen eyed the broken baluster on the floor.

"What happened to your stairs, Tristan? Is this what happens when there's no one to spar?" He chuckled.

"Alexis did it," Tristan answered with a that's-my-girl grin. *How can they be so carefree?* Owen's eyes grew wide.

They traded stories, talking as if they'd just won an exciting football game. Owen knew something was wrong when Mom disappeared from our cottage, so he hailed Stefan. They scoped the outside before coming in and found two Daemoni watching Tristan's house. They fought briefly before the Daemoni fled. Stefan and Owen ensured they stayed away before coming inside.

I stopped wondering *how* people . . . or whatever they were . . . could appear and disappear in Tristan's house and wondered instead what the point was of it being our safe place.

"They will come back," Stefan said, now solemn. I stiffened. "Owen, go out and shield the house."

Owen disappeared.

"They won't be back today," Tristan said, giving me a squeeze.

"You probably should've killed them," Mom said, her voice grim, with a tint of sadness. "There's no hope for them anyway."

"There's no way to burn the bodies with that storm raging out there," Tristan said. "If we did it inside, the fumes would've killed us. Besides . . . I wanted to send them a message."

"They'll take it as a challenge," Mom said.

"The Daemoni won't officially. These were rogues. Many rogues will take it as a warning. But, you're right. Some will take it as a challenge."

"So they will be back," Stefan repeated.

Tristan's jaw clenched and he nodded.

The bottom of my stomach fell out and a feeling of despair washed over me. The false sense of safety and security for the past couple months blew away with the raging wind. We were doomed.

"They'll never leave us alone, will they?" I whispered. "We'll never have any peace."

Tristan didn't answer except by wrapping his arms around me and holding me closer.

"Solomon made a good point that night at Sophia's house," Stefan said. "When you two are married by the Amadis, Tristan, you become a member of the royal family. That means we all become loyal to you—not just Alexis. Right now, our first priority is Alexis's safety. If we had to make a choice, we would have to leave you to protect her."

"That's how it should be," Tristan said.

"Yes, but when you are married, we are bound to both of you. We do not have to make a choice. Increased protection is automatic for you both."

"We've already discussed this," Tristan said flatly.

"You have to see the benefits, Tristan," Stefan pressed. "Once you become a member of the Amadis royal family, the Daemoni may decide to leave you alone. Coming after you would be hardly any different than going after Rina, Sophia or Alexis. It is not allowed."

"That doesn't seem to stop them," Tristan pointed out.

"I think they came for you, Tristan," Mom said. "He definitely didn't expect me."

"How come they don't just . . . *know?*" I interrupted. "I mean, you and Rina know things, Mom. If they're really Hell's demons, wouldn't they have some way to just know things, like you coming here—read minds, predict the future?"

"Some demons have the ability to plant thoughts in humans' heads, deceiving them that they are their own thoughts. Others can completely possess a human. But none of them can read anyone's minds—not humans' and definitely not ours," Mom explained.

"They have seers who try to predict the future, but their magic is unreliable and their abilities are limited. Only God is all-knowing," Stefan said, then he added with a small smile, "and He's more willing to share with us."

This slightly comforted me. Then I had an idea.

"Tristan, we need to get married immediately," I said firmly.

He looked down at me. "We've set our date. It's not that far away."

"And we keep that date, because they'll hear about it and you know they'll plan to attack before then. They'll try to stop us."

"Yes, they will," he agreed grimly.

"So we get married under the Amadis *now*, in secret. They won't know until it's too late."

I watched as he clenched and unclenched his jaw while he thought about it.

"She is right, Tristan," Stefan said. "It is a good plan."

Tristan looked at me, his eyes hard. "We're *not* getting married out of fear."

I groaned in frustration and left his side, pacing the room angrily. *Why is he being so damn obstinate?* We knew they'd do everything they could to stop our marriage. The Amadis and Tristan, apparently, had full confidence in their ability to stave them off. But I personally had a problem knowing we could be attacked any time. That tonight's real-life nightmare would repeat. *And what if it's worse next time? What if they succeed?*

I threw myself at Tristan's feet. "Tristan, *please*. You know it's the best solution. Do it out of love. Love for *me*. I *need* it . . . I need the hope that we may be able to live without a constant threat hanging over our heads. I need that sense of peace that they won't be able to take you from me. *Please.* Do it for me, because you *love* me."

I gazed into his dark eyes, pleading with my own while holding his hand against my lips.

"Please? For me?"

He studied my face as he brushed my hair back from my forehead. He eyed the small, shrinking lump. His eyes flickered with what looked like sorrow or remorse.

"Okay," he said quietly. "For you."

I threw myself back into his lap and kissed him. "Thank you."

He sighed. "You *are* my weakness."

I leaned my head against his shoulder just as something banged on the dining room door. I thought it was the wind at first—apparently everyone did because we all stared at it but no one moved. When it really started clanging in its frame, though, Stefan stood up. He stiffened.

"Somebody's out there!"

Tristan jumped up, dropping me to the floor. The bruise that should have been healing on my hip flared with renewed pain. He and Mom were both across the room before I could even think *ow*, their bodies tense. *Not again! Not already!*

"It's Owen! Open the door!" Mom ordered.

Tristan pushed a button to raise the automatic hurricane shutter. A dark gray light poured through the glass, Owen silhouetted against it. Rain flew sideways at him as he pressed himself against the wind. Stefan opened the door just enough for Owen to slip in and he had to push with force to close it again. The shutter lowered as I ran to the bathroom.

"The house is shielded. No one can get in or out," Owen said as I rushed back with towels for him. "Of course, that meant *I* couldn't get back in."

"Can someone please explain what that means?" I asked as I handed the towels to Owen. "How you just appear and disappear . . . get in and out when this house is already supposed to be locked down?"

"It's just part of who we are. You'll do it, too," Mom said lightly. I eyed her, not letting her blow it off. I didn't accept half-truths anymore. She shrugged. "It's just natural. We call it flashing."

"Owen has placed a shield over the house now, preventing any flashing," Stefan added. "We did not have it in place earlier in case any of us needed to flash inside . . . which, of course, we did."

"Yeah, okay," I said stupidly, like I understood. *Is this for real?* I only knew it was because I'd seen it with my own eyes. "So . . . no one can get in now?"

"Not until we lift the shield," Owen confirmed.

A heavy weight lifted off me. We were safe . . . for now anyway.

While the storm raged outside, Mom and I huddled in the living room, planning my weddings. They would obviously be small affairs. It wasn't like I had anyone to invite anyway, but the first one—the one that truly mattered to me—had to be entirely secretive and done quickly. The longer we waited, the more chances the Daemoni had to attack before the September wedding, but Solomon and Rina needed a couple of days to arrive. They'd be marrying us.

After Stefan and Tristan lit candles and double-checked security because of the power outage, we debated where to hold the wedding. Stefan said it would be too suspicious if we all gathered at one of our houses and I really wanted it on the beach but didn't think it'd be possible. After concentrating on the options, Tristan came up with the idea of a secluded area on Gasparilla Island. He said everyone (but me, of course) could flash there without being noticed, it provided the necessary privacy for the ceremony and it would be easy for Owen to shield.

I had no idea what that last part really meant, but I trusted Tristan. And, I supposed, I was learning to trust Owen. I had to. He was my personal protector. It was still odd to think of him like that. I knew now when he was around, it was because he was doing his job, which meant he would take a bullet for me. Or whatever the Daemoni use. I hated the idea of anyone risking their lives for mine. I now felt even more impatient for the *Ang'dora*, because it would make me strong and powerful, like them. Funny how a year ago I never wanted it to happen because I wanted to be normal. Now, normal meant vulnerable and I was too normal for everyone around me—everyone I cared about.

Mom and Stefan started talking about the legal wedding— the fake one, from my point of view. Their plans became elaborate. If I didn't know it was to throw the Daemoni off, I would have protested every idea. I didn't care about that wedding; it was just a formality.

My eyes grew heavy as we sat in the warm darkness, the voices becoming distant. I fought their desire to close, afraid of what I might see behind my eyelids, but sleep eventually won. I saw myself standing on the beach on a small island in a blood-red satin and chiffon dress, the wind whipping at it, shredding it into pieces. Four or five dog-thing creatures circled around me, baring their fangs and growling gutturally, while flying men swooped overhead, cackling and cawing. Two huge men came out of the trees, grinning nefariously. Tristan suddenly stood at my side, but as he moved forward to fight, the flying men swooped down and grabbed him, taking him away.

I choked on a scream as I sat bolt upright and gasped for air. I looked around wildly. *Tristan's living room.* Everyone had left the room except for Tristan, who still sat on the couch with me. I lay back down with my head in his lap and he smoothed my damp hair. I realized my clothes were nearly soaked with sweat.

"It's so hot," I complained quietly.

"No A/C. Turning on the generator will only confirm to the Daemoni that we're still here. It may not matter, but we're taking no chances."

I tried to spread out better on the leather couch, looking for cool spots against my skin.

"Why don't we let someone else have the couch?" Tristan pushed me up by the shoulders. He picked up a candle and I followed him upstairs. He stopped at his closet for something and handed me one of his t-shirts after ripping the sleeves off. I let my shorts drop to the floor as I headed into the bathroom. When I came out, Tristan was spread out on the bed, wearing only boxers. I wanted to run my hands across his bare chest . . . and kiss it . . . and . . . *Damn, it's been so long* . . . . Voices floated over the loft's balcony, reminding me we had very little privacy. It was just too dang hot to do anything anyway. I sighed. *Not much longer*. I lay on the cool sheets on the far side of the bed so only our hands touched. I let the steady sound of the rain against the shutters and Tristan's calming touch lull me to a dreamless sleep.

Chapter 23

Edmund the storm brought very little damage, barely reaching hurricane force. The long-term damage from Edmund the Daemoni, however, was yet to be determined. Stefan and his troops were unable to gather much information over the next two days. We didn't know if the Daemoni even knew about either wedding, let alone if they planned anything. We constantly talked about the legal wedding every chance we had, unnecessarily loud in case they listened. When the third day arrived, I woke up excited to finally be allowed to focus on my *real* wedding.

I padded into the kitchen that morning, poured a cup of coffee and stared at the calendar while I sipped. July Thirtieth. The day that would change my life forever.

"I have good news and bad news," Mom said, rushing into the kitchen. Like Tristan, she had completely reversed her opinion about our marriage after Edmund's visit. She wasn't only supportive, but actually thrilled. Her voice sounded too happy for "bad news" to mean anything devastating—like an attack.

"No bad news today," I said.

"Sorry," she said, "but Solomon couldn't make it. The timing was bad for him, but he sends his regrets and his love."

"We can still go on, right?" I asked. I thought he was part of the ceremony. He seemed to hold an important position on the council.

"Oh, of course. We only *have* to have Rina, and Stefan can represent the council."

I exhaled the breath I'd been holding. Since I didn't know Solomon well, I wasn't too disappointed.

"So, what's the good news?"

"The good news is . . . ," she grabbed my hand and pulled me down the hall to her bedroom, ". . . the Amadis dress arrived."

"*Really*? I want to see!"

We stopped in front of her bed. A white garment bag, seeming to have an otherworldly shine to it, lay like a pearl on Mom's chocolate-brown duvet. It looked as if it came from somewhere magical. It scared me.

"Go ahead, open it," she said, bouncing with excitement.

I hesitated with trepidation. I had no idea what a traditional Amadis dress was. Mom wouldn't even describe it for me, wanting it to be a surprise. I carefully unzipped the bag and pulled the dress out by the hanger. *Whoa!* I was definitely surprised.

"Seriously, Mom? I'm supposed to wear this in front of other *people*?"

"You'll look exquisite! Come on, try it on."

I raised an eyebrow at her. *She's got to be kidding.* She started taking it off the hanger, fluttering her hands at me to undress. I reluctantly obeyed and let her dress me. I certainly needed help with the top of the two-piece dress—a tight, white leather bodice, cut low, with three leather straps on each side, front and back, leading up to a diamond-studded collar at the neck. The scalloped bottom barely reached the top of the white silk, a-line skirt, also scalloped at the bottom, ending a couple inches above my knees. It looked like something out of a gladiator movie. Mom gathered my hair and held it up on my head as she walked me to the full-length mirror. My mouth fell open.

"Mom . . . you're kidding, right? This is *traditional*?"

"Traditional for us. Rina prefers silk and satin gowns, but a couple of centuries ago . . . this is similar to what the matriarch would wear. You look beautiful."

I shook my head. I just couldn't see myself wearing it in public . . . around other *people*.

"Tristan will love it," she sang.

"Tristan likes new, modern, contemporary. Nothing that reminds him of who he was."

"Don't worry, this won't. It's not like women ran around in these dresses in the seventeen-hundreds. Trust me, he'll love it. Especially on you."

It's not like I had any choice. We'd shopped for gowns for the fake wedding, but I'd been planning on this dress all along for the real one, so I hadn't yet bought anything. *Tristan* will *love it.* I sighed and nodded in resignation.

"It's like leather lingerie," I complained as Mom showed me the trick to getting out of it by myself.

She chuckled. "No, the lingerie is in a wrapped box for tonight."

"You didn't!"

"Who else would?" She smiled mischievously and then went back to being a mother. "There's also a box of condoms. No babies until you graduate."

"Yes, I know. We've discussed this a hundred times." My stomach tightened. I wasn't so concerned about babies yet . . . it was the actual activity that *created* babies I was worried about.

"Mom . . . I'm kind of scared. I don't know what to do."

"Oh, I'm sure Tristan will do it," she said casually as she hung the dress back on the hanger. I stared at her in confusion. "Surely he knows how to put a condom on."

That visual made my insides squirm with panic.

"I mean the whole thing! All of it!" I cried.

"Oh." She looked at me with surprise and then her expression dissolved into understanding. "Honey, it will all come naturally."

"How do I know what natural is, though? How do I know what's right? What if I do it all *wrong*?"

She smiled. "The thing about men, Alexis, is they generally don't find any of it *wrong*. In fact, usually the more wrong it is, the more they like it."

"*Mo-om . . . !*"

She shrugged. "I'm serious. There is very little you can do that would scare him away. Just don't belch, fart or call out anyone else's name and you'll be fine."

"Sophia!" I couldn't help the laugh that escaped, though. Just one. Before the panic set right back in. "I just want to do it right. I want to make him happy."

"Oh, you will, honey. Trust me—you'll make him *extremely* happy. When I say it'll come naturally, I mean it. This is something Amadis daughters instinctively do very well." She smiled coyly and winked at me. I didn't feel any better.

Butterflies grew and multiplied in my stomach as the day went on. It felt like it dragged on forever and, at the same time, evening raced toward us, as if someone played with the hands on the world's master clock. Mom and I spent the afternoon driving all over two counties, stopping at bridal stores and flower shops, trying to bore anyone who might be following. Finally, a little after six o'clock, Mom made sure no one pursued us and we headed out to Gasparilla. She followed Tristan's directions down a road covered in sand from lack of use.

I felt so nervous by then, I practically danced a seated jig in the car. Stefan said the Daemoni had learned about the September First wedding, but he had no indication they knew about this one. If we could get through this next hour or so, we'd be on our way to peace. Of course, then I would have more personal issues to worry about . . . .

"Looks like this is it." Mom pulled into a space of patchy grass and sand between palmetto bushes. "We'll have to walk the rest of the way."

I changed in the backseat of Mom's car. She checked me over and fixed my hair she'd piled onto my head, using her finger to curl the stray locks around my face. She straightened the dress, adjusting my boobs, which nearly flowed right over the top of the bodice. We hadn't walked five steps on the uneven terrain when I decided the heels were a bad idea.

"Love the shoes, Mom, but they have to go." I stopped to pull them off and she frowned, but couldn't argue. Bare feet on the rough ground didn't work well either. I had no idea how far we had to walk and I grew more frustrated with each slow, careful step. I stopped, exasperated. "This isn't working either! How am I supposed to get to my wedding?"

"Can I help?" Stefan had come to meet us. He gently picked me up in his arms and carried me. He had a smooth stride, not affected at all by my extra weight. His pure vanilla scent brought back memories of when he carried me when I was little. "You look quite lovely. I remember your great-grandmother in a similar dress."

Wow. I never knew how ancient he was.

"Thank you. But I feel like a helpless child playing dress-up in mommy's naughty clothes."

He laughed, the sound of a baritone saxophone skipping through various notes.

"Are we still safe?" I asked.

"Yes, I am positive."

"I feel quite good about it, too," Mom said.

"All you need to focus on is becoming Mrs. Tristan Knight," Stefan said.

My heart pitter-pattered with delight to hear him say it. The statement also re-energized the butterflies and I was shaking by the time we reached the small, crescent beach—a little cove where the island indented just enough to be nearly surrounded by wild brush and trees. We had full view of the water and the lowering sun. Rina, Owen and Tristan stood near the water, waiting for us.

"Your bride, sir," Stefan said to Tristan as he set me on the soft sand.

"Thank you, Sheffie," I whispered. Stefan smiled and pecked me on the cheek.

Tristan took my breath away as he strode over to us. Dressed simply in white slacks and a white silky t-shirt just tight enough to emphasize his physique, and the gold sparkles in his eyes shining, he was even more beautiful than I thought possible. He gave me a once-over and raised an eyebrow with appreciation, then took my hand and kissed it. I stopped trembling. He smiled and winked. I stared at him, completely loving him and totally forgetting why we were there.

"Are you sure you still want to be my wife?" he murmured.

"Uh . . . yeah," I stammered, trying to clear my head. When the fog finally lifted, I smiled and said confidently, "Of *course.*"

"Good," he whispered, "because I'd never let anyone else have the pleasure of taking my place."

He led me over to Rina. She nodded at Mom, Stefan and Owen, who all stood in silence behind us. Tristan gently squeezed my hand as Rina began by reciting 1 Corinthians 13. I knew it by heart. It was one of the passages Mom made me memorize when I was five. We'd never gone to church, but Mom had taught me the Bible, saying she knew more than any pastor this side of Heaven.

"'And now these three remain: faith, hope and love. But the greatest of these is love.' Tristan and Alexis, is this the love you both share?"

"Yes," we answered together.

"Do you promise to uphold this love throughout eternity?"

"Yes."

"Tristan, you may state your vows," Rina commanded.

He turned toward me, smiled warmly and looked into my eyes. I was sure he purposely set his voice to its loveliest tone.

"Alexis, my love, with a happiness I had never known possible before I met you, I receive you into my life that together we may be one. I promise you my unequivocal love, my unending devotion, my tenderest care. I will love you faithfully through the best and the worst, through the difficult and the easy. What may come, I will always be there. Entrust me not to leave you or to return from following after you. For where you go, I will go, and where you stay, I will stay. Your people will be my people and your God will be my God. I will take care of you, honor and protect you, for as long as I live, into eternity. I lay down my life for you, Alexis, my friend and my love. Today I give to you, me."

Rina smiled and turned to me. "Alexis?"

I took a deep breath to steady my voice and then recited my vows, blinking back tears.

"My sweet Tristan, with deepest love I did not know could exist, I come into my new life with you. I thank you for who you are to me—my one love, my true soul mate. God created me for you and you for me. I will ever strengthen, help, comfort and encourage you. I will trust you and honor you. I will love you today, tomorrow and forever. Throughout life, as long as it lasts, even into eternity, I pledge to you my life as a loving and faithful wife, no matter what lies ahead of us. My love will never be taken from you. Today I give you my life to keep."

Tristan flashed the most sublime smile that reached into the depths of my heart. We turned back to Rina.

"Tristan and Alexis, with these vows you pledge your lives to each other for eternity. Do you promise to fight for your love and for each other for as long as you both shall live?"

"I do," we said together.

"Tristan, to come into this union, you must also give your life to God and to the Amadis. Do you promise to protect us, to love us, to serve us, to lay down your life for us, at all costs, for as long as you live, even into eternity?"

The air suddenly felt still and heavy as we all tensed. If the Daemoni knew what was about to happen, this would be their last opportunity to stop it. Once Tristan took this vow, he became Amadis royalty, pledging his allegiance to us and severing all ties to his creators.

Please, Tristan, just say it!

"I do."

Just then, a powerful gust of wind blew through the cove. At the same time, a warm sun ray beamed directly on our little group. The sun itself seemed to shine a little more brightly as it hovered over the horizon. Directly overhead, though, a dark cloud formed out of nowhere, lightning shooting across it and thunder cracking, the wind whipping around us. It made me think that something very evil was very angry.

Rina glanced up at the threatening cloud and a small, mysterious smile appeared on her face. She didn't say anything, aloud or otherwise, but her eyes looked triumphant.

She took a step closer to Tristan and me, placed a hand over each of our hearts and closed her eyes. I felt a warm tingling on my skin, then an unusual energy flow from her into my heart and throughout my body. A moment later I felt it flow down my arm, through my hand and into Tristan's, while at the same time, a different kind of energy flowed from his hand into mine. The two energies combined in my chest then flowed throughout my body.

Rina spoke mightily, her voice clear and strong, almost otherworldly. If there was any doubt before that she ruled something extremely powerful, it was blown away then.

"I am Katerina Camilla Ames, matriarch of the Amadis, protectors of souls and servants to God and the Heavenly Host. Under my power, I join these two souls together as one, forever bound to each other with an eternal love and loyalty that cannot be severed by anyone or anything."

My skin under her hand burned and prickled and the warmth radiated, encircling my heart.

Rina then took each of our free hands and joined them together, then wrapped both of hers around ours. She bowed her head and we all followed.

"Our Heavenly Father, God of the Universe, Creator of all things, we thank You for this union and the blessings You will provide as its result. We each lay down our lives for You in our continued servitude. Show us Your way and we shall follow. In Jesus' name, Amen."

Rina smiled and gave us a slight nod. Tristan gently tilted my head up with his fingers under my chin, bent over and delivered the most amazing, most loving kiss he had ever given me.

"I do not know what is above us, exactly, but it would be in our best interests to vacate immediately," Stefan interrupted, eyeing the unusual storm cloud above us. It wasn't low enough to threaten rain, but the lightning, thunder and wind continued, seeming to grow in anger.

We received quick hugs of congratulations and Owen took a quick picture of Tristan and me with his new, high-tech cell phone, the only camera available. Then he, Rina and Stefan disappeared. Tristan scooped me up and ran to Mom's car, Mom not far behind. He sat in the back seat with me as Mom chauffeured us to a small parking lot where Tristan's Ferrari waited.

"Tristan, you have her bag?" Mom asked.

"In the car. Let's go, *ma lykita*." He opened the door and helped me out.

The air here was perfectly calm. Still, as Mom drove off, I had an eerie feeling about the next time I'd see her. *Just nerves. We'll be okay now.* Well, "we" as in all of us. Now, me, for tonight anyway . . . I wasn't so sure.

Chapter 24

"Where are we going?" I asked Tristan as he held the car door for me. "I thought we couldn't have a honeymoon yet."

"Do you really think I'd let tonight be like any other night?" He kissed me before shutting the door.

Like that could happen. We could have gone home and watched movies, but in the end it would definitely not be like any other night. Not in my life anyway.

"So, where are we going?" I asked again when he was in the car.

"Somewhere special for my special wife on this very special night." He kissed my hand and winked. "Topless?"

I stared at him blankly. I wondered if he'd still have that same effect on me in eighty years. Or a hundred-and-eighty years. I hoped so.

"Guess not," he muttered.

"Oh, yes, definitely," I finally answered. He pushed a button and the car's roof began to lower.

We drove south and stopped at an upscale restaurant in Naples, overlooking the water. It wasn't crowded, but the people there gawked unabashedly at us. I thought it was the car at first, but their stares, from both men and women, continued as we followed the maître D' to our table by the windows. The table could seat four, so Tristan sat to my right, rather than across from me.

"Are you okay?" he asked when we were alone.

"I really didn't want to be seen in this by other people," I whispered, tugging at the top of the bodice. He took my hand to stop me.

"Don't let their admiration bother you. I'm quite enjoying it." He kissed my fingers. "I couldn't wait for people to see you in that dress. Because you are with me. Forever." He leaned closer, his lips tickling my ear. "At least let me enjoy it now, because I will have you out of that dress soon enough."

The butterflies awoke in my stomach. They fluttered throughout dinner and I could hardly eat. They grew and multiplied again in the bathroom when I overheard a couple of young women while I was still in the stall.

"He's absolutely gorgeous. And did you see the car they got out of? I think he's the singer in that one band," one said.

"I thought he was that actor . . . the one in that new spy movie, I can't think of his name," said the other. I knew whom she talked about. There was a slight resemblance, but Tristan was much more attractive.

"Oh, maybe you're right. I don't know who that girl is. She's pretty, but, man, he could have *anyone*. I don't get it. But *love* that dress!"

I blushed, though no one even knew I was in there.

"Lucky girl, huh? Did you see how his muscles rippled under his shirt?" She sighed.

Ha! If she only knew the real power . . . .

"I think I'd come at first touch."

They giggled like school girls. I opened the stall door then and strode out to the sinks, where they both stood, staring at me with their mouths hanging open and their faces beet red.

"Only a certain kind of woman can handle a man like that," I said with full confidence.

No, that didn't really happen. But I imagined it and wished I'd had the chutzpah to actually do it. Instead, the butterflies transformed into fish flopping sickeningly in my stomach. I stood in the stall until they left, taking deep, calming breaths, grateful that freesia-infused freshener permeated the air.

The door opened again and I felt the extreme goodness flow into the bathroom.

"Alexis?" an unfamiliar female voice asked. An Amadis protector, sounding alarmed.

"I'm fine," I said from the stall. The door hissed closed.

I washed my hands while giving my reflection a silent pep-talk. It didn't work.

"You've been awfully quiet and you hardly ate a thing," Tristan said once we were in the car and headed for the highway.

"I know. I'm sorry. I ruined your special surprise."

He laughed. "That was *not* my surprise. I thought maybe we should eat while we had the chance. We have a long drive ahead of us."

"Where are we going?" I asked once again.

"You'll see." He put his hand on my thigh where the skirt had ridden up and squeezed gently. I fought back a shudder. He let his hand rest there, absent-mindedly rubbing his fingers back and forth as he drove. The electric currents shot through me like his touch was new again. The shudder won. He looked at me with concern. "You're not okay."

I thought about what he would want to hear, what I should

say to him as his new wife. So I gave him the partial truth. "Every time you touch me, it's like it's the first time."

He grinned my favorite, most stunning smile. *That was a good one.* He moved his hand to caress the inside of my wrist and forearm. "You mean like this?"

Goosebumps rose. He moved his hand to my neck and stroked around my jaw line, down my neck and along my collar bone. I shuddered again. He grinned again.

"You're making me crazy," I said giddily.

"Good. You've been driving me insane all evening." His foot pressed harder on the gas pedal. I didn't even want to know how fast we were going. "I'll get us there as fast as I can."

We drove in silence for a while, the road fairly dark and empty across Alligator Alley, the stretch of highway connecting southern Florida's east and west coasts. I wondered if we were going to Miami. It wasn't long—less than half the time it should have been—before we approached the lights of the city. He drove a little slower with the added traffic, until we hit US-1 and headed south. I realized we were going to the Keys.

"It's an awfully long drive for just one night," I said. I'd checked into going to Key West for after our fake wedding and knew it was nearly a six-hour drive. Of course, Miami was over two hours and it took him less than one.

"Not when I'm driving." He grinned in the lights of the dash. "And we can stay as long as we want. We did it, my love. And with no problems. The sooner they know that, the better. It may prevent them from attacking unnecessarily."

"That wasn't the plan."

"It's the best solution I see now. As long as they *don't* know, we're essentially sending an invitation." A moment passed and he changed his tone. "Listen, this isn't what I want to discuss on our wedding night. This is a happy time for us. Let's see how we feel, check in with the others and we'll play it by ear, okay? You're done with summer classes and the semester doesn't start for a few weeks."

"I'm pretty sure I'm not packed for more than a night or two."

"No, but that's okay. I really don't plan on you wearing many clothes anyway." He grinned again. And the butterflies, which had been subdued for a while, flew around excitedly.

We rode in silence again. I couldn't pull my mind away from the night ahead and almost regretted saving my first time for my wedding night. I felt too nervous to enjoy what should have been the best night of my life.

"Your silence concerns me," Tristan finally said.

"I'm sorry. I'm just . . ." I couldn't say it. ". . . ready to be wherever we're going."

He glanced at me. "Too much hesitation. That's not what you're really thinking."

I debated whether to just come out with it or push through it. I'd told him I trusted him. In fact, I'd just vowed tonight to trust him. I thought in silence for a while. What I ended up blurting out was not *exactly* what I'd been thinking.

"Tristan, when was the last time you were with a woman?"

He looked at me in shock and let off the gas. I thought at first he'd slowed down out of surprise, but then he made a turn off the highway. And he still hadn't answered me.

"You're not going to tell me," I muttered. "It's not like I ever thought I was the first. You've been around for . . . a long time."

"This is another subject we shouldn't be discussing tonight."

"I'm just curious."

"Why are you suddenly curious on our wedding night?" He sounded angry and his jaw muscle twitched.

He turned the car into a private driveway ending at a large house. The moon reflected on the water behind it and bounced off the house's metal roof. He parked. I didn't move. All I could see in the darkness was a two-story house with the front door on the second level and stairs and a deck in front of it. I stared out the window at the lattice that wrapped around the ground level.

Tristan turned to glare at me and I finally looked at him.

"I know you don't like talking about your past and I'm sorry I made you angry. It's just . . . I'm just . . . nervous," I finally admitted.

His face softened and he sighed heavily.

"Not for over twenty-something years and only when it was necessary. That was my old life, before . . . I hate that's how it is for us, but it is." He watched me for a reaction and I gave it.

"So, at least it's not the blind leading the blind," I blurted.

He laughed, apparently caught off guard. "You are so . . . different."

"That's what I've been told." I scowled.

He leaned over and kissed me, then murmured, "I have *never* made *love*."

"It makes me happy to know I'm your first in that way." The butterflies only strengthened, though, and I sighed. "But it's not helping with the nerves. I seriously don't know what to do."

He gave me a strange look. "Who *are* you and what have you done with my Lexi?"

"Huh?"

"How many times have you started something with me and wanted to finish it?" His eyes danced playfully as his hand caressed my face and neck.

I smiled sheepishly. "A lot."

"So why the nerves now?"

"Because I know it's actually going to happen and I've had way too much time to think about it."

"Ah. Maybe you need to stop thinking then." He leaned

over and kissed me again. "You know more than you think you do. You certainly know how to turn me on."

He brushed his lips against my neck and up to my ear. I shivered.

"That's you turning me on," I breathed.

"Good. That's how it starts, by the way." He kissed my lips before I could retort. "Stay here, I'll be right back."

He jumped out of the car and was up the stairs and at the front door so quickly, I was sure he flashed. He opened the door, pressed a code into the alarm system just inside, and flipped on a couple lights. I knew he flashed back down to me because he stood inside the doorway and then instantly he stood right next to me. I laughed as he bent over the car door and scooped me out, carrying me up the stairs and inside.

"The tradition is you carry me over our *own* threshold," I said as he set me on my feet in the small foyer. The smell of fresh paint and lumber told me the house was either new or recently remodeled.

"This is. Well, yours anyway." He took my hand and pulled me through a doorway into a fabulous kitchen open to a dining area and family room. He put his arms around me from behind and nuzzled his face against my ear. "My wedding gift to you."

He nodded at a small pile of papers on the counter with keys on top.

"*What?*" Then I came back to reality. "You mean while we're here. This little trip, right?"

"Well, that, too. But I mean the house. It's yours."

"Tristan," I gasped. "A *house?* Are you *crazy?*"

He grinned and kissed my temple. "Thank you for being my wife."

I shook my head. "This isn't right. I didn't even have time to get you anything yet and you got a *house?* You can't give this to me."

"Will you please stop being difficult on this night of all

nights? Just relax and enjoy it, okay?"

I turned around and stared at him in disbelief. He cupped his hands around my face.

"Think of it as an investment for our future. I just had to put it in your name for tax reasons . . . among others. Okay?"

I relaxed and smiled, knowing this was his area of expertise.

"*Ours*, then," I said.

"If you prefer . . ." He gave me a quick kiss. "Stay here while I get our bags and then I'll show you my favorite room."

It took him longer than I expected. I walked around the island kitchen with its smooth granite countertops and into the family room, admiring the perfection throughout. Everything was exactly the way I'd design and decorate it myself, if I had any talent at all. Sand-colored walls, sun-bleached wood floors and furniture, fabrics in cerulean blue, coral, aqua and shell-pink— the feeling of the beach brought indoors. A wall of sliding glass doors led out to a screened-in balcony. The darkness swallowed anything beyond except the water still reflecting the moon.

"Sorry," Tristan said, appearing in the kitchen. "I had to get an update."

I looked at him expectantly.

"We're fine. We can just enjoy ourselves. So, what do you think so far?"

I walked over to him and stood on my toes to kiss him. "It's perfect!"

He let out a sigh of relief and smiled. "Good. Come on."

He took my hand and led me across the family room and through a door leading into a large bedroom suite. A big bed faced a small sitting area with a chaise lounge and more sliding glass doors. Everything was white except for splashes of jewel-tone colors, primarily amethyst, my favorite. It felt like a tropical island.

"I call it the Caribbean room," he said.

"I love it!"

"I hoped you would." He beamed, reminding me of a little kid proudly showing off his artwork.

"Oh! Tristan . . . did you *design* this house?"

His grin widened.

I stared at him in disbelief. "You're *amazing*!"

"*You* are amazing, *ma lykita*," he said, taking me into his arms. "And for some reason I still don't understand, you are mine."

I placed my hands on the sides of his face, tilting it down toward me, and gazed into his sparkling eyes. "You don't need to understand. Just *know*."

I pulled his face down to me and pressed my lips to his. The passion, pent up for the last several weeks, rose quickly in both of us. Our lips moved together longingly, kissing and tugging. Our hands caressed each other's faces and necks. I pushed my fingers through his hair and pulled him closer, separating my lips and welcoming his tangy-sweet taste on my tongue. I slid my hands down his strong neck, over his broad shoulders and along his hard chest.

As we kissed more fervently, his hand moved down my back, sliding between the bodice and the skirt and resting against the small of my back. His other hand caressed my neck and slid down slowly along the plane of my chest and back up. His mouth traveled over my chin and down my throat. I arched my back, lifting my chest against his lips. His mouth was warm and wet on my skin. His hand felt along the straps, up and around the collar.

"How do I get this thing off you?" he murmured desperately.

I smiled. "It's complicated."

I unhooked the choker and pulled my arms through the straps and then brought his hand to the hidden zipper in the back. The bodice fell to the floor. He cupped my breasts in his hands and my nipples hardened as he kissed and licked, electricity surging everywhere he touched me, rippling across my skin. He rolled one tip with his thumb, while taking the other into his mouth, suckling and pulling it into a hard nub. My lower body squeezed as if there were a direct line from my breasts to my groin.

I frantically pulled his shirt off and my skirt fell next. He lifted me up and I pressed against him, running my lips and tongue along his smooth neck, tasting, kissing, sucking. He carried me over to the bed and gently lay me down.

"You are dangerously beautiful," he murmured, appraising me as he slid off his slacks.

Keeping my eyes from wandering, I looked into his eyes and saw no fire—just beautiful emerald green and sparkly gold.

"You're . . . okay," I said quietly.

"I am truly Amadis now. The monster is buried deeply . . . maybe gone forever." His smile faltered. "Of course, we do still need to be careful. You're still so very fragile."

My heart raced as he climbed onto the bed and lay next to me. He placed his hand lightly around my neck and kissed my mouth with renewed fervor. His hand glided down, over and between my bare breasts, along my stomach, around the curve of my hip and along my thigh, leaving shocks of electricity along the path. His hand encircled my calf and he hitched my leg over his hip, then slid his hand up the back of my thigh. My body warmed and quivered with both yearning and fright.

My hands ran along his bare chest for the first time in way too long, feeling its smooth planes and curves. They trembled as they moved lower, along his perfect lines, his muscles flexing under my touch. He hooked his thumb under the elastic of my panties and, with a slight jerk, tore them off.

We explored new places we'd never been and we both hesitated before reaching those parts that throbbed with frantic desire. He was hard and big in my hand, exciting and scaring me at the same time as I stroked him and he moaned. His tongue flicked at my nipple as his hand separated my legs, caressing my inner thighs and then between. A finger slid into me. A small cry of surprise and pleasure escaped my throat.

"You're warm and wet," he breathed against my breast.

I froze and looked at him, not knowing what to say, heat rising to my face. "Um, sorry?"

He smiled. "That's a *good* thing."

He rolled over on top of me, gently moving between my legs. He must have seen the panic in my eyes.

"You okay? You look . . . really scared." His voice was low, kind, gentle.

"You're just . . . um . . ." I blushed again. ". . . really *big*."

I had a hard time imagining all of *that* inside little *me*.

A smile played on his lips. "Sorry."

I giggled, despite everything. "No, you're not."

He pressed down against me and ran his mouth across my cheek.

"No, not really," he whispered against my ear. He shifted and I could feel his stiffness pressing against me. "Ready?"

I stared into his eyes and nodded.

"I'll be gentle," he said softly. And he barely moved his hips, sliding slightly inside me.

OW! I bit my lip. He must have felt me tense because he didn't move. We both remained perfectly still, but I could feel him throbbing inside me. I also felt . . . something. I didn't think my body could heal *that* . . . that wasn't supposed to heal. But the pain subsided and I relaxed.

"Okay?" he asked, his eyes holding mine.

I nodded again. He slid in further and I gasped, but not with pain. He knew, too, because he continued slowly, an inch at a time, until he filled me completely. Then he moved, back and forth, in and out, slow at first, then faster. And harder. And deeper. Each stroke electrified me, sending jolts of pleasure throughout my body. My back arched and I clawed at him. I climbed quickly to my first ever orgasm. But he kept going and I kept coming, again and again, each one building on the previous one, bigger, better, higher, until I thought I'd fly over some unseen edge and into oblivion to never return again. And then he thrust himself inside me harder and deeper than ever and there I went over that edge, losing *all* control. Every muscle in my body contracted. My back arched. My head went dizzy with euphoria. I shuddered violently with a moan, squeezing him as he convulsed inside me.

He collapsed against me and we lay still for several moments, panting, our hearts pounding against each other's chests.

He finally rolled off and lay on his side next to me, running his fingertips randomly over my breasts and stomach. My body quivered as if I'd truly been electrocuted. We grinned at each other and I'd never seen his eyes sparkle so brightly. I knew exactly how he felt and wondered why people bothered with drugs when making love had to be the ultimate high.

Physically spent, I eventually turned onto my side, facing him, and pressed the full length of my body against his, our legs intertwining. We fell asleep naked in each other's arms. But not for long. I awoke to the tingling of Tristan's fingers running along my ribs and down my side.

"I'm sorry, but I can't get enough of you," he murmured.

"Don't be sorry. I'm all yours." I kissed him with a new hunger.

Knowing what to expect this time . . . wanting it desperately . . . I let my inhibitions and self-consciousness fall away. My natural instincts took over and the animal inside came out to play.

Chapter 25

Light filled the Caribbean room when I awoke only a couple hours later. I was snuggled up to Tristan's back, his arm thrown over my hip. I kissed his shoulders and ran my fingertips along his spine, hoping to wake him if he wasn't already. The air caught in my throat when I saw the marks all over his back.

"Tristan! What *happened* to you?" I cried, sitting up.

He rolled onto his back and they were all over his chest, too: long, purplish-yellow streaks like scratches but they were fading bruises. Larger bruises discolored his shoulders, ribs and hips. He glanced down at his chest and grinned.

"You."

"*What?*"

He lifted my hand and placed my palm against one of the bruises on his ribs. It was the perfect size. The bruised streaks matched the width of my fingers. The blotches on his hips were as wide as my thighs. I stared at him in horror.

"Looks like I wasn't the only one we should've been worried

about." He laughed.

I threw my hands to my face to hide my shame. "Oh, I am so *sorry!*"

He wrapped his arms around me and pulled me close to him. I was afraid to touch him.

"They only look bad because we did it so many times, but they don't hurt," he promised. Then he lowered his voice. "Besides, I kind of liked it. Actually, I *really* liked it."

I pulled myself away to get a good look at his face. He grinned. *Mom was right.* I rolled my eyes. And that's when I noticed the cracked and chipped headboard and a dent in the wall above it. I eyed Tristan.

"I don't know who did what, but I don't think anger is the only emotion that brings out your strength." He laughed and squeezed my thigh. I cringed—I had my own bruises.

We lay in bed until our stomachs growled and decided to take a shower before we ate. That's when I first felt, and then saw, the mark on Tristan's chest, right over his heart. I didn't know how I missed it before, perhaps distracted by all the bruises. This wasn't a bruise or a scratch. It had a design, dark red and slightly raised. I traced my finger over it and looked into his eyes.

"I've never noticed that before," I said.

He didn't answer, but he traced the birthmark over my own heart. It had always been faint, just slightly different pigmentation from the skin around it. Now it was also raised and pink. They had the same strange design . . . and now I realized it was the same design embossed on that envelope I found in Mom's office several months ago.

"What does it mean?" I asked.

"Sophia never told you? It's the mark of the Amadis family."

I remembered the burning, tingling sensation under Rina's hand when she held it right there. Her other hand had been over Tristan's heart. My breath caught.

"Rina *branded* you?"

Tristan chuckled. "It's always been there, underneath. *You* brought it out."

"Huh." I felt mine with my fingers and then went back to his. I couldn't help but kiss it.

We made love in the shower, trying not to break the tiles— six didn't make it. It was better than I ever imagined, and I'd dreamt about the scene many, many times. The water rained down on us . . . Tristan held me securely, my legs wrapped around his waist . . . . *Mmm . . . much better than any dream.*

After the shower, as I rummaged through my bag for something to wear, I remembered the condoms. I placed the box on the counter.

"We should be more responsible," I muttered.

Tristan pulled a box out of his own bag. "Yes, we should."

I laughed. "Do you think we have enough?"

"We can always get more . . . ."

We eyed each other. I was instantly in his arms again.

"Maybe we should let this new round of bruises heal first," I said, placing my hands on his chest.

"Mmm . . . I guess you're right." He gave my butt a playful squeeze. "I need to feed you anyway, keep your energy up."

Mom had packed me two sets of clothes, a bathing suit and the box I knew contained lingerie. Not knowing our plans, I decided to just not get dressed yet and wrapped the soft, thick towel around me instead. I padded out to the kitchen, where Tristan poked around the refrigerator.

"There's food in there?" I asked, surprised. I sat on a barstool at the island.

"I had some brought in. Not a lot, but we can get more if we stay."

I watched him with awe—he wore only shorts and it wasn't just his muscles that held my eyes. His tanned skin seemed to *glow*. I tore my eyes away and glanced down at the house papers in front of me. Something caught my interest. The owner's name was not mine. Maybe I did misunderstand.

"Tristan, who's Katie Andrews and why does her trust own this house? I thought . . ."

He placed some green grapes and cheese on the counter and turned to the pantry. "If you did some real digging through several attorneys' offices, you might be able to find that Katie Andrews is an alias for Alexis Ames. Hopefully, though, you wouldn't."

"Why'd you do all that?" I asked, impressed. I got up and found glasses and filled them with ice and water.

"Because there are certain people who don't need to know you own this house. I had it built for you and no one can take it away from you." He gathered the food in his arms. "Let's sit outside."

"Our life is way too complicated. Already." I set the glasses on the patio table.

"Unfortunately, *ma lykita*, we may be meant for each other, but not everyone likes it." He pulled me onto his lap.

"In the normal world, I would just tell them to go to hell."

"Yes, but in our world, they are already there. And that still doesn't stop them."

We sat in silence, eating cheese and crackers and grapes, and watched the boats pass by far out on the water. I munched on a cracker and traced the mark on his chest—it fascinated me—when there was a knock on the front door. We stiffened and looked at each other.

"Hmm . . . Stefan," Tristan said.

I hurried into the bedroom to dress while Tristan answered the door. I felt like he minimized the danger besieging us, so I rushed, not wanting to miss anything. They were just sitting down outside when I came out and joined them.

"I was just telling Tristan what a superlative estate this is," Stefan said, as I took a seat at the back of the table, folding my legs underneath me. "Beautiful, private, easy to shield. A better safe house than Tristan's place because no one even knows you are here."

"That was the idea," Tristan said.

Stefan told us the Daemoni still didn't know about our marriage, but said they were unusually quiet, unlike their normal, boastful behavior. Tristan told him what he'd told me last night—the sooner they knew, the better. Stefan said he thought it fine for us to stay, but he'd discuss it with the council and let us know.

"I would highly recommend . . . well, *insist* . . . you stay out of Key West," Stefan said as he stood to leave. "You well know that is a prime hunting area for the Daemoni."

"Yes, it's a favorite stomping ground for them," Tristan said, making my spine tingle unpleasantly. "Don't worry. I'd rather they don't know we're even in the vicinity."

We walked Stefan outside and after saying good-bye, he walked off into a mess of trees and brush. I had no idea where he went from there. While we were outside, Tristan showed me around the three-acre property, complete with its own small, private beach. He said our property shared the tiny key with four other homes. Most people driving through wouldn't even know there were homes at all—it looked like a wild jumble of overgrown vegetation from the highway.

The house was a big square, raised on stilts, with the ground level intended for storage. It had a light gray metal roof and darker bluish-gray stucco siding with white trim. The screened balcony off the family room and Caribbean room stretched across the full west side of the house. I hadn't yet explored the two other bedrooms and bathroom on the east side.

"This wasn't one of your models," I pointed out.

"No, this is just a beach house. Those models were dream homes."

"I can't imagine anything better than this," I said. "When did you do it? I never even knew."

"Hmm . . . I did the drawings last August . . . when I met you." He smiled down at me. "They broke ground in March . . . after you said 'yes.' I had to push hard to get it done in time since we kept moving the date up, but they did it. The important stuff, anyway. There are a few things they need to finish up."

"Whoever *they* are, you'll have to thank them for me." I slid my arm around his waist and pressed against him as we walked up the stairs. "And you . . . well, I'll never be able to thank you enough."

"You already have, my love. More than you can ever know." He gave me a squeeze and kissed the top of my head.

"So what are we doing today?" I asked as we entered the cool house, a relief from the heat outside.

Tristan glanced at the clock. "In about two hours, we need to go sign some papers to make this house officially the property of Katie Andrews' trust."

"So . . . we have two hours?" I asked, smiling mischievously.

"Hmm . . . that's what I'm talking about." He returned the smile and I led him to the bedroom, leaving a trail of clothes.

We drove back to Islamorada to an attorney's office to sign papers, Tristan supplying an array of documentation giving us both different names, his as the seller, Katie Andrews as the buyer. Afterward, Tristan took me to a couple of boutiques to buy clothes. They were a little too showy for my style, so I let him pick them out as I tried them on. He seemed to enjoy himself as much as a guy could and selected several sundresses. He bought a few things for himself, too, and we stopped for groceries.

Time passed strangely—sometimes charging forward,

bringing us toward reality way too quickly, and other times seeming to stand still and it was just the two of us in our own world with no cares. We did what we wanted. We sat on our beach and swam, sometimes skinny dipping. Tristan disappeared for a few minutes one day and came back with snorkeling gear, so we snorkeled around our little beach. Well, I snorkeled; Tristan could hold his breath apparently for hours. We prepared new recipes every night, taking turns choosing what to make. We made love . . . I lost count how many times, but a lot. We stayed in bed as long as we wanted, just talking.

"When we do have children, how many do you want?" I asked him one morning as we snuggled in bed.

"If it were possible, I'd love to have twenty with you," he said. "Making them is a lot of fun."

"*Twenty*? I'd be barefoot and pregnant *forever* . . . or at least until the *Ang'dora*. I was thinking maybe three or four."

He chuckled. "Whatever would make you happy would make me happy. However, Amadis daughters usually only have one baby—a daughter. That is all that is needed."

"Really? Just one?" My heart sunk. "I want a boy . . . who is just like you."

Tristan's brows furrowed. "Wouldn't be a good idea."

"What do you mean? You're perfect!" I kissed his chin.

He smiled. "*You* are perfect, *ma lykita*. And I hope our daughter will be just like you. Although, there'll be problems when she gets older, since her old man *and* her mom seem to have anger issues."

"Yeah, we'll have to make Stefan or Owen her bodyguard to keep her out of trouble and to keep us from killing any poor, innocent boys."

"There's no such thing as an innocent boy and that's what I'd be worried about."

I laughed. "So . . . you said we *usually* have only one baby. Is there any chance I can have a boy?"

"There's a possibility. Boy-girl twins run in your family."

"Twins? Cool! I wonder what the chances are . . . ."

"I hope not much." His eyes darkened. "Trust me—we really don't want a boy."

"That's not fair. You get your little girl. I just want a little Tristan."

He grunted. "If it does happen, we will *not* name him Tristan Junior."

"No, we won't," I agreed. "*You* are my Tristan. I just know he'll be like you. But what would you name him?"

"Never thought about it."

"I've always liked Dorian."

"Then, if we have a boy, his name will be Dorian." He peered down at me. "But I'm serious, Alexis. Don't get your hopes up for a boy."

I didn't like his tone, but didn't want to argue, either. "So what about our daughter's name?"

"Hmm . . . we don't make that decision. Rina will likely name her. It must carry on the Amadis royalty's tradition."

I frowned. "That's not very fair either. We should get to name our own child."

"We can make suggestions. Alexis had been my idea for you."

I stared at him open-mouthed. "*Seriously?*"

He nodded, grinning.

"Okay, that's just weird. You named your future *wife?*"

He laughed. "We *are* weird, my love. Rina trusted me even then, had me sit in on council meetings. They asked me my opinion and I gave it to them. It fits you perfectly. It means protector or defender."

"Yeah, I looked it up once a long time ago and I thought

it was an oxymoron for me. At least until I punched that guy in the face. I'm not proud I broke his nose, but *no* one calls my mom a whore." I cringed with a thought. "Of course, that was just the first guy I punched."

Tristan chuckled and hugged me again. "*Ma lykita.* My fierce little protector."

"And you are *my* ultimate warrior."

"I'll fight for you until the end of my days."

"That would be forever."

"As long as you are by my side, I hope that is true."

෨෫

We had many similar discussions about our future plans, keeping them on a happy note, avoiding the dark parts threatening our strange lives. It was easy to forget about our dangerous situation, because it felt like we lived in our own personal paradise. Like Adam and Eve in the Garden of Eden . . . before Satan's visit.

By the end of the second week, though, my mood shifted. Classes started soon and the legal wedding approached, too. Unless something changed our plans, we'd have to go home. I cherished our peaceful time at the beach house and didn't want it to end. On the other hand, we both grew a bit antsy, feeling somewhat confined.

"I wish we could go to Key West," I said at the end of that second week as we ate breakfast. "It looks like fun."

"You're not really missing much," Tristan said. "And it would definitely *not* be a good idea for us."

"I know. I guess I'm just starting to feel a little cooped up here. I don't want to leave, but I'd like to get out for a while." I pushed the remainder of my pancakes around my plate, the blueberries leaving purple swirls in the syrup.

"I should've brought the boat." He watched me for a while, and then finally said, "I have an idea. Get your bathing suit on."

He packed up my snorkeling gear and took us to a nearby marina, where he rented a speed boat.

"Are you sure it's safe?" I asked as we headed out.

"We'll be out in the middle of a big ocean. The worst things out there are sharks and I can handle them." He grinned. "In fact, that would be fun!"

I raised an eyebrow. "You're not serious, are you?"

"About fighting with sharks? Absolutely. Especially when they try to get away. You just hang on and let them take you for a ride. Better than the Waverunner."

I laughed. "You've seriously ridden a shark?"

"Yep."

"I don't believe you."

"I can show you. We'll go find some."

My eyes widened. "Okay, I believe you! *Please* don't go looking for sharks."

He laughed. "I thought you were bored."

"Not *that* bored. Just find some pretty fish to look at."

"How about lobsters? They just came in season."

I nodded. "If you get the lobsters, I'll cook them."

"Deal."

He took us south until we could no longer see land and only saw another boat every now and then and cut the engine. We lay in the sun, swam and snorkeled. I was amazed at all the beautiful life under the water—yellow, blue, pink and silver, solid, striped and polka-dotted fish, among other creatures. Tristan told me what we saw, but I couldn't keep track of what was what. There was much more to see here than there was at our beach. As promised, he caught a couple lobsters for dinner that night.

Toward the end of the day, I stretched out on the bow,

letting the sun bake me dry. I lay on my stomach, about to doze off, when Tristan untied my top and started rubbing my back. The warm sun and his electric touches made my skin tingle.

"Tristan . . ." I protested when he rolled me onto my back.

"There's no one around for miles," he murmured, keeping me from rolling back over by kissing me. It wasn't long, though, before he cocked his head for a moment, and then turned me back over. "I'm sure they're just passing by."

I lay there and listened as the sound of another boat's engine grew louder as it came closer. It seemed to be approaching steadily, not fading out as it turned off.

"Or maybe not," Tristan said, tying my strings for me.

I sat up to see the boat pulling up to us. The driver was alone. He apparently had spent many years on the water in the sun, his face the color and texture of beef jerky and his man-boobs hanging like leather pouches over his browned beer gut. My sense told me he was bad.

"He feels wrong," I whispered to Tristan.

"It's okay. He's not *them*," he said under his breath. He pulled his shirt on and handed me my sundress as the man gave me a slow once-over, giving me the heebie-jeebies. I put the dress on, not that it covered much.

"Hey, man, just wonderin' if you saw any lobster down there," Leatherman called to us, his voice as rough as his face, but friendly.

"Yeah, we saw a few," Tristan answered, returning the genial tone. "Caught us a couple for dinner."

They exchanged small talk as I watched the man suspiciously. I was surprised when Tristan invited him over to our boat, but I figured when you're the "ultimate warrior" and it's not a Daemoni trying to abduct your wife, you could be as friendly as you wanted to be. It can still bite you in the butt, though.

"You two look pretty young to be out here alone," Leatherman said after a while.

"Looks can be deceiving," Tristan answered with a small smile.

Misunderstanding, the man looked around. "You're certainly alone for now."

He was right. We couldn't see land or another boat at all.

He suddenly jumped up and grabbed me with one hand. He held a knife in his other. "Just give me whatever money you got and everyone'll be okay."

Damn it! One day out and this son of a witch has to ruin it! Tristan looked at the man's hand roughly gripping my arm. He shook his head and smirked. We caught each other's eyes and mine narrowed in anger. He nodded his head once. I shoved my elbow into Leatherman's fat gut and spit flew out of his mouth as he doubled-over. Tristan grabbed and twisted his arm, the bone snapping audibly. He heaved the man back over to his boat. Rattling off every cuss word imaginable, Leatherman quickly took off.

"That was unpleasant," Tristan said after he was gone.

"I told you I didn't like him." I scowled.

He chuckled. "Nice job."

"You, too. But you didn't have to break his arm."

"Sorry, didn't mean to. Do you forgive me?"

I nodded. I'd rather Leatherman's arm be broken than my neck be slit. I hoped that didn't make me a bad person. "Maybe he'll learn his lesson. We make a good team, huh?"

"Yes, we do. I knew there was a good reason I married you." He winked. I gazed at him while he started the engine and we headed back to cook lobster.

Chapter 26

Tristan's cell phone woke us up a couple of mornings later.

"Hi, honey, sorry to bother you, I know you're having a great time," Mom babbled.

"It's okay." It was actually good to hear her voice. I realized how much I missed her.

"Well, I just couldn't wait to tell you. Someone from a publisher called today and she wants to read your first three chapters!"

"*Really*? Already?"

"Yeah, it helps when you know peop—" She cut herself off, as if she let something slip in her excitement.

I was too excited myself to ask what she meant. "You know where to find the file, right?"

"Yes, I'll take care of it. This is great news, honey! *Whoa*!"

"Mom? Are you still there?" She didn't answer. "Mom, what's going on?"

"I don't know," she finally said. "It almost felt like a small earthquake."

"You're in *Florida*, Mom."

"I know. There was something, though. Oh, Owen's here. I need to go. I'll call you back." She hung up before I could even say good-bye.

"A publisher might be interested," I told Tristan, nearly jumping up and down on the bed. "Can you *believe* it?"

He grinned and gave me a bear hug. "Of course I can. I told you, you're very talented."

Tristan's phone rang again a while later. After looking at the number, he handed it to me. I barely had a chance to say "hello."

"Put Tristan on the phone. *Hurry!*" Mom didn't sound right at all.

I handed the phone back to him. "I'm here."

A long pause. Then he sat bolt upright.

"*Shit!* Motherfuckers!" More silence as Mom spoke. "No, we'll stay here for now . . . I'll call them . . . I know . . . I will."

He snapped the phone shut. *Something's wrong. Terribly wrong.* I stared at him expectantly as he just sat there in silence. His jaw twitched.

"Tristan . . . ?" I said quietly. He didn't look at me, but stared at the wall.

"My house—our house—is gone," he said flatly, distantly. "It exploded. Owen said it's just burning rubble."

"*What?*" I gasped, not comprehending.

He paced the room with angry strides. My eyes followed him, back and forth, as my mind raced, trying to make sense of it. Is that what shook the ground all the way at Mom's house? It had to have been a major explosion to reach that far.

"*FUCK!*" He yelled, slamming his fists against his thighs and making me jump. My heart hammered against my chest as I continued to stare at him wide-eyed. "The fucking bastards!"

He was serious. *His house is gone. Everything . . . gone.*

"What happened?" I asked, my voice small, frightened. I knew the answer, but didn't want to say it.

"I'm not exactly sure, but I have a pretty damn good guess," he seethed. He also didn't want to say it.

After he calmed down about an hour later, he called the authorities. He held his head in his hands as he listened to them, barely saying anything on his end. He snapped the phone shut and jerked his hand as if to throw it against the wall, but he held onto it.

His voice was frighteningly calm when he explained. "Their initial assessment is something ignited fumes from the generator. They said it wasn't properly shut off after the storm."

I stared at him in disbelief and terror. "Tristan . . . we didn't use the generator."

"I *know*." He paced the room again.

The vision of his sleek house on the beach . . . the motorcycles and other toys . . . all he owned . . . everything exploding in flames filled my head.

"I can't believe . . . your *house* . . . *everything?*"

He stopped pacing in front of me and lifted me in a hug. "It's just stuff, my love. At least we weren't there."

"Do you think they knew we weren't there?"

He held me tighter and said grimly, "Yes. I think it was a message."

My stomach clenched. I thought I would be sick if I had anything in it. *They know.* We held each other in silence for several minutes. A pounding on the front door made us both jump.

"Stefan," Tristan said, letting me go.

"Tristan, you have to get out of here. Immediately," Stefan said, bursting through the door as soon as Tristan unlocked it.

"But, we can't—," Tristan started, but Stefan interrupted.

"I know what happened, but you cannot stay here. They know you are around here somewhere."

"Son of a bitch!" Tristan pounded the counter, cracking the granite countertop. "*How?*"

"From what I have gathered, a local was drunk in Key West, complaining loudly about how a couple tried to rob him and broke his arm. He described you two perfectly, down to the mark on Alexis's chest." Stefan glanced at me grimly. "They do not know exactly where you are, but they know you are in the Keys and they are looking."

"Alexis, get ready to go. *Now*," Tristan ordered.

I hurried into the bedroom and threw whatever clothes I could get my hands on into our bags as quickly as my shaking hands allowed. Tristan closed all the shutters and locked up the house. We were on the road in five minutes and in Mom's driveway in two hours.

"I need to see if there's anything left at all," Tristan said, not getting out of the car.

"But I want to—"

"No, it's not safe. You stay here with Sophia." He leaned over and kissed me. "I won't be long."

He nudged me and I grabbed our bags and hurried inside. Mom rushed to greet me with open arms. She squeezed me tightly and then pushed me back. Her face looked sick with worry.

"You need to pack just the bare necessities," she said, the words coming in a rush. "We have to get out of here. Just the basics. And be sure to back up your book and wipe out your hard drive."

I gave her a confused look.

"You heard me. We need to go. It's not safe here anymore."

I obeyed. I knew what "bare necessities" meant from previous departures—enough clothes for a couple days and important documents. That was all. I saved two copies of the book on CDs and erased the hard drive. I gave one CD to Mom and put the other in my own purse. We were ready to go by the time Tristan walked in the door. I flew into his arms. I hated being separated from him and he, apparently, hated it, too, because he held me tightly.

"Anything?" I asked.

"No, didn't look like it. I didn't get too close, though. I'm sure it's being watched."

"We need to go now," Mom said. "The Daemoni know about the marriage and your vows to the Amadis and claim it's Provocation. They've given free rein on all Amadis . . . *especially* on royalty."

Owen and Stefan burst through the door.

"Tristan, get her out of here!" Stefan barked.

Tristan pulled me out to the car and threw our bags into the tiny trunk space. My heart hammered for the first hundred miles we drove, headed north, as I stared out of the window in fear. I imagined demons surrounding us, flying over us, waiting for an opportunity to swoop down and attack. I wondered where we could go for safety. *Can we ever get away?*

Then deep sadness eclipsed the fear as I closed my eyes and visions of the past year played against my eyelids. It all seemed so innocent and safe. *Will we ever have peace again?* The tears fell silently as I absently played with the pendant on the chain. Tristan gently squeezed my hand.

"I rushed us right into this mess, didn't I?" I said quietly.

He looked at me. "Don't *ever* blame yourself for this, Alexis. This started before you were even born."

"I insisted we get married, though."

"It would've happened anyway, whether we married now or ten years from now. The marriage was inevitable . . . unless they killed us first. So, at least we *are* married." He squeezed my hand again. "I wouldn't have it any other way. I'd rather fight for us forever than not have an *us* to fight for."

I kissed his hand and held it against my face.

"I love you more than anything, *ma lykita*."

"Together forever, right?"

"Absolutely." He smiled and winked at me. I didn't fog over. And that made me sadder.

We drove for hours, stopping only for gas. Finally, a little after midnight and somewhere near the South Carolina-North Carolina line, Tristan turned off the main highway, crisscrossed several country roads and found a small town with a motel.

"We need to stop at the drugstore," I said before he turned into the parking lot. I pointed at the 24-hour store down the road. "I didn't have time to grab anything from the bathroom."

Tristan sighed. "Make it quick."

He stood at the door of the store, pacing back and forth, watching me and the door at the same time. I loaded up on sample-size toiletries and toothbrushes. I couldn't remember everything we needed, so I hurriedly glanced down each aisle to jog my memory. Feminine Hygiene. *Uh-oh.* I counted backwards in my head. Twice. Then a third time just to be sure. *Crap!* I looked for the box I needed, grabbed it and headed to the front. I threw in a bunch of snack food at the register.

When he pulled in front of the motel office, Mom, Stefan and Owen stepped out of a dark corner. Mom and Stefan stood by the car while Tristan paid for the adjoining rooms and Owen disappeared to place a shield over the entire motel. I still didn't know how he did it—I just took it for granted it was there.

"Anything new?" Tristan asked the others once we were locked inside the rooms. I sat on a bed and pulled my knees to my chest.

"Nothing from Rina," Mom answered.

"There have been a couple of attacks on my people, just because they can," Stefan said. "But the Daemoni are really focused on you two. Fortunately, they do not know where you are. We have been able to sidetrack them, at least for the time being."

"There's still a safe house in Washington?" Tristan asked.

"It's being cleared for us," Mom said.

"We will need to divert them, though," Stefan said. "Go on north, past the safe house, and double-back the long way."

They discussed a watch schedule so everyone could sleep, then Mom, Stefan and Owen went into the other room. Tristan sat on the bed next to me and rummaged through the food sack. *How can he eat?* He opened a bag of chips and tossed a package of cheese crackers at me. The thought made my stomach lurch. I made a face.

"You need to eat," he said.

"I don't think I can."

"You haven't eaten for over twenty-four hours." He opened the package. I took a couple crackers to make him happy and after eating one, I realized how hungry I actually felt. I devoured the entire package and then started on a candy bar. Just as I swallowed the second bite, my stomach lurched again and I had to run for the bathroom.

"You okay?" Tristan asked when I came back out.

"Just really scared," I admitted.

He held me close in the bed and I trembled in his arms. I woke up once after a nightmare and the room was dark. I was alone in the bed.

"Tristan?" I whispered.

"I'm here, my love," he answered from somewhere else in the room. It must have been his turn to keep watch.

I felt Mom climb into the bed next to me. She put her arms around me. I fell back to sleep.

"Lexi, *ma lykita*," Tristan murmured, nuzzling my neck. "You need to wake up."

He picked me up and carried me into the bathroom, shutting and locking the door behind us. He kissed me fully awake.

"What are you doing?" I asked between kisses.

"We only have thirty minutes and it's been nearly twenty-four hours since I made love to my wife," he said, starting to undress me.

"Now? Here?" Despite the verbal protests, I automatically responded to his touch.

"Just be very careful so we don't break anything. I've already paid in cash."

He turned the water on and we stepped into the shower together. The bathtub was tiny and we had to be careful, so it wasn't nearly as wonderful as it usually was in the shower. But it was *real*. And it was *for* us, when everything else was against us. I gave myself to Tristan, not knowing when the next time would be that we could just enjoy each other.

Thirty minutes later, we left the motel. Mom, Stefan and Owen disappeared while Tristan and I drove for hours. I stared out the window, barely noticing the changing landscapes as we sped north, past the Washington, D.C., area, up through northern Maryland and even briefly crossed into Pennsylvania. Every time we stopped for gas, Mom, Stefan and Owen waited for us, as if they'd somehow been following. Mom accompanied me to the bathroom and she didn't say anything, but gave me a knowing look when I vomited every time. My stomach stayed knotted with fear.

In the afternoon, we looped back, dropping down into Northern Virginia. As we had several times already, we exited off the highway to take the back roads, sometimes crossing and retracing our path.

"We're getting close," Tristan finally said at about five in the afternoon.

We were somewhere in Fairfax County, Virginia. Though it was only twenty miles from where we lived in Arlington, I didn't know the area. The busy suburbia tapered into a more rural area, with large colonial-style mini-mansions in estate-type subdivisions. Then the subdivisions disappeared and houses were scattered on large acreage lots, thick woods separating them. We turned down a narrow street, sunlight filtering through the trees encroaching both sides.

"Shit," Tristan swore under his breath. The street dead-ended about two hundred yards away.

"Are we lost?" I asked, my voice small with fear. This was the worst time to be lost.

"No." His jaw clenched. "We're surrounded."

My stomach rolled. Vomit shot up my throat and I clamped my hand over my mouth, but it couldn't make it past the huge lump stuck in the passageway. I trembled all over.

"Hang on, *ma lykita*. Things could get ugly." He slammed on the accelerator.

We tore down the narrow street. I wanted to squeeze my eyes closed before we flew into the wooded dead-end, but my eyelids peeled back, refusing to shut. Just before we reached the end, the trees surrounding us opened into a large meadow. A grand mansion stood toward the back of it. Tristan sped for the structure.

A man suddenly appeared in the meadow, to our left. He turned toward us. Someone else flew out of nowhere, knocking him to the ground. More people started appearing with faint pops. Voices yelled over the Ferrari's engine. They started fighting with each other. The car slid and fish-tailed as Tristan swerved to avoid them. I turned in my seat to watch as we passed.

Some shot unseen powers at their opponents, sending

them backwards several yards. They were instantly on their feet, shooting power back at their assailants. Others traded violent blows in hand-to-hand combat. A long object sailed across the window. My head whipped to where it came from. One of the people fighting just lost an arm. But he kept fighting, unfazed.

Holy hell! Who are *these people?!* I didn't even know who was Amadis and who was the enemy. They all fought viciously, like animals. *Is this what it means to be Amadis? Is this what I'm in for the rest of my life?* Rina said Amadis were good, full of love, ruled by Heaven. Not this . . . this repulsive brutality.

The Ferrari abruptly stopped. My hands flew to the dash to brace myself before I sailed head-first through the windshield. The car door flew open. My body left the car seat and air rushed by. Then I was suddenly set on my feet inside the mansion. Owen stood next to me and Tristan appeared right behind us. My stomach heaved.

"Bathroom!" I bellowed. Another rush of air and I stood in front of a porcelain toilet. I leaned over and puked. Then my knees buckled as I fell to the floor, my body shaking violently.

"It's okay, honey. You're safe now," Mom said, pressing a cool, wet washcloth against my forehead. I had no response.

Eventually the trembling stopped and I tentatively stood. Mom led me down the hall to a dark living room filled with antique furniture. The curtains were drawn tightly shut, but I could still hear fighting outside. Rina rose from a wing-backed chair to my right and opened her arms wide.

"Alexis, my poor dear," she said. Her power washed over me as she embraced me. "Ah, a baby . . . or two?"

I stepped back and stared at her. *A baby? Or two?* Mom frowned and nodded. I'd completely forgotten about the pregnancy test I'd picked up at the drugstore last night. Tristan appeared in the doorway behind Rina. His brows momentarily furrowed, then he smiled at me, his eyes sparkling. For two beats. Then the smile disappeared.

He took my hand and led me through the doorway, into a library. Books lined the shelves, floor-to-ceiling, wall-to-wall. At each corner of the room sat a pair of chairs with a small wooden table between them, a reading lamp on each table. They were all lit, the only light in the room as there were no windows. Tristan took me over to one of these sitting areas and pushed me down into a leather chair.

"I need to talk to you," he said, kneeling in front of me to look me in the eye.

An ominous feeling brushed my shoulders and slid down my spine. I narrowed my eyes. "I don't think I'm going to like this."

"No, you're not. I hate it myself." His eyes were dark, the gold sparkle from just a few minutes ago gone. He took a deep breath and let it out slowly. "I need to go out there."

"What?! No!"

"I can put an end to it, Lexi."

Of course he can. Nobody can beat him. But I shook my head.

"You can't go fight! What if you don't come . . . *back*?" I choked on the last word, my voice cracking as I spit it out.

"I may not have to fight. They just need to see proof I've given myself to you and the Amadis and that I am truly part of the royal family."

"Oh." My chest loosened from the grip of panic. "Well, that's not so bad. Let's give them proof. What do we do?"

I searched his face and he looked away from me for a moment, then back into my eyes. He pulled the collar of his shirt down to expose the Amadis mark.

"They have to see it for themselves," he said grimly. "They've set a meeting place for me to meet Lucas."

Chapter 27

Lucas—the sperm donor, now their most powerful warrior.

"Absolutely *not*!"

"Lexi, it's the only way."

"It's a trap, Tristan. You can't go to them!"

"I *know* it's a trap. But if I don't go, they'll continue to fight and attack. They'll continue to hunt us. I put everyone's lives in danger."

I shook my head. Tears spilled. "*No.* You can't do this!"

I threw my arms around him, thinking if I held him tight enough, he couldn't go.

"I have to," he said. "I've made a vow to you and the Amadis that I would lay my life down for you."

"You also vowed you would never *leave* me. They're going to t-t-take you or . . . k-k-*kill* you!"

He grabbed my upper arms and pushed me back so he could look into my eyes. I quivered in his hands.

"They can't take me down, Lex, remember that. They don't know *how* to kill me."

"Then they'll take you away."

"*Nothing* will keep me from you, my love. I *will* come back to you." He pulled me back into his arms. "And then we can be together in peace."

I pulled back and looked him in the eyes. "Then take me with you if you're that confident. If they stop fighting, then there's no danger, right? And if it's a trap, like we know it is, we can at least be together."

"Absolutely not!" he growled angrily.

I stood up and strode around the room. "See! You don't know for sure this will work. You don't know that you'll come back. They don't want us together, Tristan, unless we're with them. If they're going to get you, they're getting me, too!"

"Stop the nonsense!" He grabbed me by the arms again. "You have to stay here, no matter what happens. You have a purpose and you have to do it for the Amadis."

"But I need *you*," I cried. "I can't do it without you. I can't *live* without you!"

I fell against him and sobbed. He held me, stroking my hair.

"You won't have to live without me," he said softly. "I *will* come back to you. Nothing can stop me. But I have to do this. For the Amadis. For you. For *us*."

I cried in his arms. My gut told me this was it. Once I let him go, I had no idea if I'd ever see him again. I held his face in my hands and looked into his eyes.

"Promise me," I whispered. "Promise you'll come back."

"I promise," he said firmly. "I can't live in this world without you, Alexis. I'll be back, no matter what happens. I *will* come back to you."

He sealed the promise with a kiss, loving yet urgent . . . like it was one of our last.

Then he took my necklace off, stood up and fished something out of his jeans pocket. He thread a small key onto the chain and clasped the chain back around my neck.

"Guard this with your life," he said. "This is literally the key to our future."

I nodded as I held the key and the pendant in my hand. He pulled an envelope out of his back pocket and handed it to me.

"Keep this in a safe place, too. There are copies, but you should have this."

"But you're coming right back," I said firmly.

"Yes. I'm just taking precautions." He nuzzled his face against my neck as he rubbed his hand over my lower abdomen. "You stay safe. You're carrying precious cargo."

I nodded, more tears flowing. He leaned down and kissed my currently flat belly.

"You need to come back for all of us," I whispered. "We need you."

"I will. I swear to you." He crushed his lips to mine. I only hoped I could communicate just a small portion of the love I had for him, because there was too much to be held in just one kiss. Too much for all the kisses in the world.

He pulled me by the hand back into the other room, where Mom, Rina, Solomon, Owen and Stefan stood. They all turned toward us, their faces bleak.

"Ready, Tristan?" Stefan asked.

Tristan nodded stiffly. My resolve fell.

"*No!*" I cried. "Please, don't! *Please*, Tristan! Don't leave me!"

He hugged me again and I clung to him.

"Please, *don't* . . ." I sobbed. "I love you too much."

"I'll be back." He kissed me one last time and I looked at him, into those adoring hazel eyes, memorizing his beautiful face.

I inhaled deeply, taking in his scent—mangos and papayas, lime and sage, and a hint of man—capturing it to memory. He smiled sadly and I clung to his last words. "I love you, *ma lykita*."

"I love you, my sweet Tristan."

He took me by the shoulders and gently pushed me into Mom's arms. Then the men left the room, leaving us three women to do nothing but worry. When they opened the front door, fighting sounds filled the air. The window rattled loudly as something hit it.

"Down to the shelter," Rina said to Mom. I reluctantly followed them. As we passed through the foyer, I glanced through the still-open door and saw Tristan several steps ahead of the others, leading them out to battle.

"*No!*" I yelled. I ran for the front door. Tristan's hand flicked and the door slammed shut just as I reached it. I banged my fists against it. "No! I have to watch. I need to know what's going on."

My feet left the ground and the air rushed past me again. Rina carried me, speeding down a hallway, then down several flights of stairs. I struggled in her arms, but she was unbelievably strong. She finally stopped, setting me down in a small room with concrete walls, lit by a single lamp dangling from the center of the ceiling. Mom pushed the concrete door closed, securing it with a large, wooden beam across the center. Four maroon recliners, each with a blanket folded over its back, and a coffee table furnished the room. Shelves full of food and jugs of water lined one wall. A toilet sat in a corner and a sink was bolted to the wall next to it. The three of us could easily stay here for three days. I certainly hoped that wasn't the plan. I couldn't wait three *hours* to see Tristan again, to know he was safe.

"Alexis, close your eyes," Rina said. "I will show you what is happening."

I inhaled deeply as I stared at her, trying to comprehend. She tapped her finger against her forehead.

"I can see. I can share."

Mom sat in one of the leather recliners and closed her eyes. I dropped into another and closed mine. A vision appeared in my head, as if I stood in the clearing in front of the house. Tristan's mere appearance wasn't enough to stop the fighting. Through others' eyes, we watched the battle. The viewpoint changed several times as Rina tapped into different minds. Sometimes I heard her voice as she gave commands to the soldiers. Sometimes we heard the terrifying thoughts of the Daemoni, then Rina would warn the Amadis what they were about to do. Sometimes she cut my visions off.

"I am sorry, dear, but there are some things I cannot allow you to see," she said to me.

I nodded, grateful to see any of it and not have to rely on my unruly imagination. But, as the battle heated, I didn't know if even *my* imagination could be worse than this. I had to fight the urge to not watch because I had to know Tristan and the others were okay.

It felt like we stood in the middle of it all. A blue light shot across our current vision, blasting its target into bits. Another light zipped right past us. A tree split with a loud crack. A piece of the fallen tree flew through the air, taking someone down. Stefan and Owen ran around the scene, shooting unseen powers out of their hands, knocking Daemoni to the ground. Everything—powers or solid objects—sent at Owen bounced back before it hit him, as if he were protected in an invisible bubble.

Out of our peripheral vision, we could see Solomon. Then Rina changed minds to see him better. His expression was blank, though he held a severed hand in his right palm. I gasped as I realized, seeing the stump of his left arm, that it was his *own* hand. He held the wrist of the detached hand against the stump and a second later, his fingers waved, then closed into a fist and opened again. *Holy crap!* He reattached his hand! *Can we all do that?* But I immediately forgot the thought as a Daemoni jumped at him. He grabbed her by the shoulders. His head dove toward her throat. And that's when I noticed his teeth. Especially his eyeteeth. *Have they always been so long? So pointed?* Rina instantly changed views.

I recognized Ian, standing away from the mayhem, his dull red hair shaking around his face as he cackled at the scene. Then a round object suddenly flew at us. I flinched, expecting it to actually hit me. It landed at our feet. We looked down to see a human head rolling to a stop. My stomach jumped. Acid burnt the back of my throat.

From another view, we watched from farther back, at the house. I heard the Amadis fighter's thoughts as he told Rina he was injured, but he could be her eyes to see the full scene. He looked down. His leg ended in bloody shreds where the knee should be. He held it in his hands, but they looked more like . . . *claws.* Then there were several popping sounds and his head snapped up. He focused on Tristan. I forced myself to watch.

Tristan fought off several Daemoni as dog-like creatures appeared all around him. *Dogs or wolves?* I couldn't tell from this viewpoint. They were definitely larger than any canine I'd ever seen, a few nearly as tall as Tristan. He shot power at them. Some fell to the ground. Others soared back several yards. The creatures continuously sprang and lunged at him. At first, he could keep them off. He whacked at them with his arms. He kicked them across the meadow. He blasted them with his force. Owen shot his power at the creatures, too, trying to keep them back.

But more popped into existence. *Pop! Pop! Pop! Dozens* of them.

I gripped the chair's arms, suppressing the irrational urge to run out there and help. Not that I could do anything against these . . . these *beasts*. But I felt so useless just watching the horror.

Daemoni and their creatures continued appearing all over the estate's lawn. They swarmed onto Tristan. *Oh, no! Oh, God, no! There's too many!* I cried out as a creature lunged at Tristan and grabbed onto his arm with its mouth. Its teeth dug into his skin, not letting go. Then a second one attached to his other arm. Another Daemoni jumped on his back.

Then there was Edmund. He glanced briefly at Tristan, then strode toward us, toward the mansion. He waved his hand and several creatures followed him.

But not enough to relieve Tristan. He fought off creatures while eyeing Edmund. His eyes narrowed and his chest lifted. He heaved a breath of exasperation.

Then he looked right at us.

His eyes bored into our seer's, through Rina's mind and into mine, as if he knew I could see him. And our eyes locked. Rina switched to his thoughts. His lovely voice reverberated in my head.

"I love you, *ma lykita*."

We flew through the air and tackled Edmund.

And then we went blank.

Rina switched back to the mind of the soldier near the house. The meadow was nearly empty. A few stragglers disappeared with pops and now everyone was gone. Including Tristan. My eyes flew open.

"Where'd he *go*?" I screamed, jumping to my feet. I looked wildly around the concrete room, disoriented for a moment. Mom and Rina finally opened their eyes, too.

"They are all gone," Rina said quietly. "I cannot find any thoughts out there. Nowhere in my range."

"He's gone to meet Lucas, hasn't he?" I demanded.

Rina nodded.

"Will they make it back?"

Neither Rina nor Mom answered me this time. They stared at the floor. Tristan hadn't gone alone—every Amadis fighter out there went, too. Which meant there would be more fighting.

I fell back into the chair and dropped my head into my hands. I pressed the heels of my palms against my eyes, trying to push away the scene replaying on the backs of my eyelids. The heavy weight of it all . . . the bodies dropping, convulsing on the ground, some completely still, dead . . . pressed down on me, trying to crush me into the chair, into the floor.

"Is this who we are?" I asked quietly. "This is what we do? Fight deadly battles?"

This was what I waited so long to find out? That we were really no better than our enemies?

"When we need to, yes," Rina said, taking a seat. "We try to prevent these kinds of atrocities. We prefer not to fight. We are *good*, Alexis. But we are the Angels' army on Earth. We must do what they need us to do. For them. For God. Just like in biblical times, just like David and the others. We must fight for what is right."

The Angels' army . . . the phrase bounced around my skull. It should sound empowering, but all I could think about was the fighting. The blood and pain. The deaths. My hands pressed against my belly as I tried to draw hope from the tiny lives inside. But I only felt despair. *What kind of world am I bringing them into? What kind of lives would they lead?*

Mom and Rina had been right all along. I was not ready for this. The *Ang'dora* would make me more like them and better able to comprehend and accept. I hoped. Right now, my feeble human mind could not relate.

I had to focus on something that made more sense—that was more within my grasp of understanding.

"Is this why we moved all the time?" I finally asked Mom. "I always thought it was the men. Were we being hunted and I just didn't know it?"

Mom sighed. "No, honey. The Daemoni never bothered us until they discovered you and Tristan together."

"Oh. So, then, why did Owen come into the picture? He was around almost a year before the Daemoni knew anything."

Mom didn't answer at first. She pursed her lips and stared at the concrete wall for several moments. "Remember how I knew Tristan was close before you ever brought him to the store?"

It only took a moment to understand. "Owen didn't come to protect me from the Daemoni. He came to protect me from Tristan."

Mom nodded. "At the time, I thought you needed it."

I chuckled darkly. "And I thought you tried to set us up."

Mom chuckled, too. "Actually, I'll admit I thought he was a better choice for you. But I was obviously mistaken. That weekend I went away, I went to see Rina and she was still adamant the two of you belonged together. I guess I knew it all along somewhere in my heart. I didn't try as hard as I could have to convince you or Tristan to stay apart. Of course, my power wouldn't have worked anyway. It can't be used to change what's meant to be."

"I do not know why you tried so hard to prevent it, Sophia," Rina said. "But at least it brought you to me for a personal visit, after so many years of your absence."

"You know we stayed away for Alexis's good," Mom said. "But now it looks like we will stay close. Today will not be the end."

"No, it will not," Rina murmured.

Thick silence filled the small room.

"So why didn't the Daemoni bother us all those years?" I asked Mom to keep the conversation going. I needed a distraction.

She shrugged. "They don't fare well with me and they gave up coming near me."

"Why?"

"Tristan isn't the only one I brought over to the Amadis. In fact, Lucas is the only one I *didn't* convert, given the opportunity." Despair colored her tone. For some reason, she still grieved over him. I hadn't realized the extent of her power of persuasion—or why she had been given that gift.

"We moved so much for many reasons," she continued. "We wouldn't have been able to stay in one place for too long anyway—people would notice I don't age. But that never became an issue. Sometimes, it was just because of who we are—like when you fell off the slide when you were in kindergarten and the cuts that should've needed stitches healed on their own, or the fleabag who tried to molest you and I nearly killed him, or the boy you sent sailing across the yard. Other times, though, you're right, it was the men."

"I never understood that. How come you always left them?"

"Well . . . normal, *human* men can't handle our love. I think you've experienced the results of our passion?" She looked at me and raised an eyebrow. "Bruises, broken furniture . . . I'm surprised the whole house didn't fall down with you two."

I couldn't help the small smile tugging at the corners of my mouth, even in my distress.

"You don't even have your full power or strength—you don't have a small fraction of it. Imagine what could happen to a *normal* man with me."

"Oh," I said, considering the potential injuries.

"Add that to the extreme love I feel for everyone—the same love you'll feel after the *Ang'dora*," she continued. "We can't help who we are. Unfortunately, sometimes the ones we love just aren't capable of handling it. I had to leave before I hurt them, emotionally or physically. It was always after they became too persistent about sex or when they proposed."

"Wow, I had it wrong."

She reached over and patted my hand. "Of course you did. I could never tell you what was really going on. I'm just happy you have a relationship where you never have to worry about it."

That was the wrong thing to say. It reminded me my love was gone . . . and I didn't know when I would see him again. Tears streamed down my cheeks as we sat in silence for what felt like hours.

"Where *are* they?" I finally asked, jumping to my feet as irritation sprang every nerve. "When will they be back? What's taking so long?"

"Patience, darling," Rina said. "They will return when it is safe."

I paced the small room, gripping my pendant and sliding it back-and-forth on the chain, pushing the little key with it. What may have been more hours, or possibly just minutes, passed. Then Rina suddenly stood up.

"Owen is back. The shield is replaced."

I bounced on the balls of my feet as she and Mom unbarred and slid back the concrete door. They grabbed me and sped up the stairs. We stopped in the foyer as soon as Owen burst through the front door. He stumbled inside, his face stark white.

"Owen!" Mom cried with relief. He stood there stiffly, his eyes wild.

I flew into his arms, standing on my toes to look over his shoulder for the others. I knew immediately something was dreadfully wrong. This was not laid-back Owen. His back was rigid. His face twisted in pain or grief or . . . *horror.*

"Where's Tristan?" I asked, searching the empty space behind him, panic already rising. He didn't answer or even look at me, his arms stiff around my shoulders.

"Where are the others?" Rina asked.

"There were just too many," he finally said, his arms falling limply to his side. "They kept coming. Too many to fight at once. *Stefan . . .*" He couldn't finish, a mix of defeat and grief on his face.

"No!" Rina and Mom gasped. He nodded.

"Sheffie?" I whispered, tears springing to my eyes.

"He's . . . dead," Owen confirmed darkly. *Oh, no! God, no!*

"*Tristan?*" I cried. He didn't answer.

"We never made it to the meeting place. They mobbed us. Only three of us got away," Owen said bleakly. "Solomon, me and . . ."

I didn't hear the last person, already screaming the name I needed to hear. I grabbed his shirt and shook him. "*Where is he? Where is Tristan?*"

He just shook his head, not looking at me, not saying anything.

"*WHERE IS HE, DAMN IT?!*" I yelled, panic and hysteria gripping my heart.

"I-I d-don't know," he finally whispered. "There were *dozens* on him. I think he's . . ."

His voice trailed off.

And the earth stood still. It stopped spinning on its axis and just hung in dead space as I stared at Owen and tried to comprehend what he was saying. The meaning was right there, stuck in midair between Owen and me, but my mind wouldn't, couldn't, *refused* to grasp it. Then the realization crashed down on me like a semi-load of concrete blocks. And the world lurched into motion again, spinning way too fast, swirling around me in dizzying blurs.

"*NO!*" I cried. My chest caved in and my stomach heaved like it had been punched, sending my heart into my throat. I choked on it, sobbing. "*NO! NO! NO!*"

I beat Owen with my fists. Mom pulled me off, into her arms.

"*NO!*" I screamed again as loud as I could and it echoed around the two-story foyer. "Oh, God, *no*! Not my Tristan . . ."

I collapsed to the floor and cried, refusing to believe it. I pounded the stone floor until my fists bled. I felt like I could die. Like my heart had been crushed into pulp and twisted out of my chest. I *wanted* to die. Babies or no babies, I wanted to be with my Tristan. I could not do this without him.

Mom tried to comfort me. I pushed her off.

"He can't die!" I yelled at her. "He's supposed to be invincible. *Immortal!*"

"Honey," she said softly, "there is only one way to immortality and it is not here on Earth."

"What do you *feel*?" I cried. She didn't answer. "Rina?"

Rina shook her head, tears in her eyes.

"Oh, God, *noooo* . . ." I sobbed into the floor.

Tristan's beautiful face swam in front of my eyes, his sublime smile, his love-filled, hazel eyes looking into mine, the green shining and the gold flecks sparkling. I heard his lovely voice murmur, "I love you, *ma lykita*," as if his lips were right against my ear. And my heart shattered into pieces, knowing I couldn't reach out and touch him although he felt so close. *So close. Right here, with me.*

"He's not dead," I cried into the floor. "He'll come back."

And I had to believe that because there was just no other option. I had to hold onto it. *He promised.*

And when he didn't come, my life fell into a black pit of nothingness.

Epilogue

8 Months Later

"CHOO-CHOO-CHOO" I panted through clenched teeth, keeping a train's rhythm, just as Mom instructed.

"Okay, honey," she said from between my legs. "Get ready . . . almost . . . again! PUSH!"

She didn't have to tell me. I could feel the pressure on my lower belly, squeezing inside, and all I wanted to do was *push*. I heaved down, pushing with every bit of strength I had left.

"I see the head. Almost there."

Yeah, no kidding. I felt the head, like a basketball wedged halfway inside me, ripping me apart. I'd been in labor for nearly two days. I'd been pushing for what seemed like hours. But I now felt too weak to keep going. The edges of my vision faltered. Pinpricks of light popped in front of my eyes.

"You need to push harder than that, hon." Her voice faded with each word.

"Alexis?" Rina sounded so far away, she must have been in another world.

Mom said something. It sounded like something about my blood pressure. But I couldn't hear her anymore. I couldn't see anything but grays. And then blackness.

❦

When I came to, Mom was tucking a tiny bundle into the crook of my arm and turning it toward my breast.

"Your son, honey," she said, aligning his mouth with my nipple. His eyes fluttered and he briefly looked up at me, the steel-blue of a newborn. The few strands of his hair were still wet and plastered to the side of his head. He latched on, his lips moving slowly, awkwardly as he drank for the first time.

"Dorian Stefan," I whispered through a groggy daze, tears brimming over and sliding down my face. One dropped onto his cheek. I gently wiped my finger across it, feeling the downy softness of his face. I fell right to sleep as he suckled.

I awoke screaming. It was typical for me. The same nightmare every night ended my dreams with terror. But this time was different. Not the dreams. Just the panic gripping me.

"My babies! Where are my babies?" I shrieked.

"Rina's changing Dorian," Mom said from a chair beside my bed. She sounded tired and . . . something else.

I calmed with the realization I was in my own bedroom. Well, it'd been my bedroom here at the safe house for eight months. It wouldn't be much longer. We'd have to move, as soon as the babies and I were strong enough. Which meant I wouldn't be able to stare out the window at the last place I saw Tristan, as I'd been doing since that dreadful day, waiting for his return. The last time I saw him was, of course, a horrendous memory . . . but my last memory of him, nonetheless.

Now, he'd missed the birth of his babies. *How much more would he miss?* Nobody knew. As far as I knew, we'd heard nothing since his disappearance, though I lay in bed withdrawn into myself, just trying to stay healthy enough for the babies' survival while my world fell apart around me. But if anyone knew anything, they didn't tell me. Tears leaked from my eyes.

"What about my daughter?" I whispered. "I haven't even met her yet."

Mom moved from her chair to sit on the side of my bed. She took my hand in hers. Her expression was bleak.

"Honey," she said, her voice rough and thick. Something was wrong. "Honey . . . you don't have a daughter."

I stared at her, uncomprehending. "Of course, I do. We *have* to have a daughter."

All Amadis daughters had baby girls. We didn't even accept a male sperm unless a female embryo was already formed. This much I had learned. A girl was needed for the future of the Amadis. *How could I not have a daughter?* Mom and Rina had both sensed a girl in the womb.

Mom shook her head slowly. A tear trickled down her cheek. "I'm sorry, honey. We were wrong. For some reason we don't know right now . . . you just didn't have one."

I swallowed hard. "No daughter? What happens to the Amadis now?"

Mom shook her head slowly. Her words came out so quietly, I barely heard her. "We don't know."

"Is there any hope at all? Can I still have a girl? I mean, when Tristan comes back?"

"No Amadis daughter has been pregnant more than once." The corner of Mom's mouth lifted in a half-grimace-half-smile. "But that's what we hope for. After all, you *are* unique."

Obviously. Always different. Never normal, not even with the weird stuff.

"Right now, you have this beautiful little babe," Rina said, entering the room with Dorian cradled in her arms.

I hadn't really seen her since shortly after that fateful day. She had to return home to attend to business as matriarch of the Amadis. By the time she arrived for the birth, I was deep in labor and barely aware of her presence.

Rina looked at me now and smiled, but despite how hard she tried to hide it, I saw the sadness and disappointment in her eyes. She placed Dorian in my arms and left the room. Guilt overcame me. *I really screwed up. Why do I have to be so messed up?* Though I had no control of it, it was my fault the Amadis would collapse.

I looked down at the precious bundle in my arms. His hair was dry and fluffy now. He didn't have much of it, but what was there was a shocking light blond, almost white. I could see his dad in his features already. He opened his eyes and I was surprised they already changed colors. They were no longer newborn-blue. They had wide, emerald-green rings on the outside of the irises and brown around the pupils. And yes, tiny gold flecks that sparkled.

Tears streamed down my face, happy and sad tears mixed together. Dorian was the greatest gift I'd ever received from Tristan and from God. He was a little bit of his father I could finally hold again. I felt so blessed to have him, but the despair of no daughter weighed heavily. As did Tristan's absence.

Nearly two years ago, I thought I knew what I wanted: a career as a writer, a family, true love and an explanation of the quirks that made me weird. Now I was about to become a published author, my first book due out in six months. I didn't yet have a full explanation of who I really was, but I knew I would one day lead the Angels' army, fighting real-life demons, though I was half-Daemoni myself. But, without another daughter, the Amadis would end when I did.

Only two things mattered now: family and true love. I was a mother now, a single-mother in most ways, but I refused to believe I was a widow. Nobody knew if my true love was dead or alive, but I knew. I could still *feel* him. I knew he would return to me. He promised. I had to hold onto that promise and to Dorian. Otherwise, I could feel an abyss not far away—a darkness I could easily slip into, letting the evil blood within my veins consume me if I wasn't careful.

Dorian started crying and I held him against my chest, sobbing with him. His tiny hand flailed, then latched onto my pendant. He quieted immediately. I wrapped my own hand around his to keep him from yanking on it. Warmth radiated from the pendant, through Dorian's hand and into mine.

"That's our link to Daddy, Dorian," I whispered against his cheek. "He can't be here, but he'll be back soon. Right now, you be my light, okay? Keep me out of the darkness."

His little fingers released the pendant and grasped my finger. And I swore I felt a squeeze of affirmation. A second promise to hold onto . . . but not all promises can be kept.

About the Author

Photo by Michael Soule

Kristie Cook is a lifelong, award-winning writer in various genres, from marketing communications to fantasy fiction. Besides writing, she enjoys reading, cooking, traveling and riding on the back of a motorcycle. She has lived in ten states, but currently calls Southwest Florida home with her husband, three teenage sons, a beagle and a puggle. She can be found at www.KristieCook.com.

Connect With Kristie Online

Email: kristie@kristiecook.com
Author's Website & Blog: www.KristieCook.com
Series Website: www.SoulSaversSeries.com
Facebook: www.Facebook.com/AuthorKristieCook
Twitter: www.Twitter.com/#!/KristieCookAuth
Tumbler: www.Tumblr.com/tumblelog/KristieCook
Google+: Kristie Cook

An Excerpt from *Purpose*, Book 2 in the Soul Savers Series, Now Available

"Alexis."

It wasn't the same voice.

Evil! Daemoni! Evil!

The alarms of my sixth sense rang in my head. The stunning face disappeared as my heart nearly jumped out of my chest. I shot up and realized I sat on my bed again. I glanced around the darkness for the source of the gravelly voice.

"Who's there?" I asked, my voice thundering through the silence.

A shadow shifted in the corner. Two small, red lights glowed from about two-thirds up the wall. I realized they were eyes. *It can't really be Daemoni—can it?* We hadn't been bothered for over seven years. Not a single visit or even a threat. Nothing at all. They had what they wanted.

"Don't you know?"

The shadow moved forward, just enough for the light from my clock to slightly illuminate a face—pale, bluish-white in the clock's glare, glowing eyes and . . . *fangs*. The light reflected off his glimmering teeth, bared in an evil grin, if that's what you could call it, and I knew for sure those were fangs. And I knew immediately what he was. From what I could see, he favored some of my characters, as if he'd stepped out of the pages of the books I wrote.

Such a strange feeling—to feel as though I'd awakened in my usual way but know I was dreaming again. I had to be. Monsters were real, but vampires were not.

"C-Claudius?" My voice shook. I knew this dream was about to become a terrible nightmare. With his dark hair floating around the sides of his face, this visitor looked similar to my Claudius, leader of the evilest vampire nest in my make-believe world.

"Ha!" the shadow barked. "So you do see the resemblance."

I didn't respond. I stared wide-eyed at the barely visible face, wondering what would come next. My heart pounded in my ears and my lungs seemed unable to pull in any air. I wanted to scream myself awake. But I couldn't. I was frozen.

The vampire came closer, almost near enough to touch . . . if I dared to reach out.

"I am *not* your dim-witted Claudius," he growled, "but my world and my ways are very similar. In fact, *too* similar. You are bold—and foolish—to tell the humans."

In a strange way, the dream made him more *real*. More frightening than any of my characters, even Claudius. The timbre of his voice held promises of horror, the sound more terrifying than I ever imagined when I wrote.

But his words made no sense.

"I-I d-don't understand."

"I am not stupid, woman, and I know you are not *entirely* ignorant. I know who you are. You know what I am. You have crossed the line in revealing our truths. You must stop writing and exposing us, Alexis. Or we will stop you ourselves."

The flaming red eyes narrowed. The nostrils flared.

The vampire cocked his head and growled again. "No more, Alexis, or we *will* come for you!"

Pop! The overhead light suddenly flooded the bedroom with brightness. I was sitting bolt upright in my bed, my heart hammering again, wide awake with the sound and light. I blinked at Mom's figure standing at the foot of my bed.

"Are you okay?" she demanded.

My eyes adjusted and now I could see her looking anything but vulnerable, though she only wore a short, baby-doll nightgown. Petite, but tough. She stood with her body tense, coiled and ready to fight, as her narrowed eyes scanned the room. Then she rushed to my side and braced her hands against my face. She seemed to appraise every inch of me.

"I'm fine," I muttered, pulling my face from her grip.

"You don't sound or look fine."

"You scared the crap out of me." I lay back down and closed my eyes. "And I had a bad dream. That's all."

She stood there for a long moment and I could feel her eyes still on me. I never heard her footsteps, but the light switched off and the door clicked softly in the latch when she left. Mom was used to me having bad dreams. She had no need to question me.

❦

When I awoke again, sunlight streamed under the blinds, creating narrow lines of light on the boring beige carpet by my bed. I lay on my stomach and stared at the floor for a while, not wanting to be awake. Then I remembered the dream—not the usual memory-dream, but the new one. I turned over and looked around the room. Of course, no evidence of the vampire. He was just a dream, but it had felt so real and was just so uncharacteristic. Last night was the first time I'd dreamt of anything but those memories since the day my husband disappeared into enemy hands.

Then I remembered the other anomaly of the night. The whispered promise. But neither the lovely voice nor the memory-dream had returned the rest of the night. *Damn vampire.* I closed my eyes and tried to pull the face I wanted to see into my vision. A pointless effort. Only a vague image appeared. I was forgetting.

As time had passed on, as the conscious memories faded, the feeling Tristan was still alive weakened. For the first few years, I'd felt his presence and the grief of living without him nearly consumed me. Eventually, a fog drifted in and settled, dulling the pain . . . and the memories. Foggy Alexis arrived and I liked her. She kept me numb during the day, allowing memories only at night, when I slept. But now the dullness seemed to be permanently obscuring my conscious memories and dissolving our connection.

Forcing myself to let it go, I focused my mind on the only things I'd been able to focus on for the last seven years: my son and my writing. Dorian served as the bright spot in my otherwise bleak life. He lit my path, keeping me from straying away into the complete darkness of insanity. If his father hadn't already set precedence, it would be hard to believe I could love anyone as much as I loved Dorian.

I sighed heavily and made myself stand up. I already felt today was not a good day. I felt all wrong. Something inside ticked, like a time bomb.

I considered writing out the evil vampire Claudius, after that rendition of him interrupted my dreams last night. Maybe the time had come to kill him off. Of course, he was one of my primary villains in this last book of the series, so he was necessary until the end. But I was pissed at him now. *How dare the asshole harass me at night!* I eventually dismissed him for the time being after deciding he *would* die, a final death, by the end of the book.

Tired of thinking so much about the stupid vamp, I closed my eyes and tilted my face toward the sun, focusing on the heat of the rays on my skin, giving me paradoxical goose bumps. I felt the burn of someone watching me, but I ignored the feeling. It had to be Mom and I didn't want to deal with her yet. With the warm sun washing over me, I actually felt . . . well, not *good*, but at least no longer Psycho. Then a slight breeze came up, light against my skin and just a little cool. And with it, a familiar scent.

Mangos and papayas, lime and sage.

CPSIA information can be obtained at www.ICGtesting.com
Printed in the USA
BVOW041020300412

289024BV00001B/83/P

I had a warped sense of time, but I was sure it had been a while since I'd had a really bad day. It had to have been months, probably last July on our anniversary, since Psycho Alexis or anyone but Foggy had made an appearance. Our anniversaries were always tough. The middle of March, though, had no meaning—even the anniversary of our engagement was two weeks away—so I couldn't understand why I felt so . . . messed up this morning.

Suck it up for now. Need to say good-bye.

It was after eight and Mom was probably getting Dorian ready for school. I wanted to say good-bye to him. Then I could lose myself in my writing.

"Hi, Mom!" Dorian greeted as I trudged into the kitchen. His face lit up, his mouth stretched into that all-too-familiar, beautiful smile and his eyes sparkled. He pulled his jacket on, getting ready to leave. I almost missed him. If I had and with the mood I was in, Psycho might have taken over immediately. But since he was still here, brightening my morning, I could enjoy a few minutes of being Almost Alexis.

"Hey, little man." I ruffled his hair—the snow-white color had been unexpected, but I had a feeling a similar-looking towhead had been running around a couple hundred years ago—and gave him a big smile, too. Only Dorian could elicit a real smile from me. "You ready for school?"

He shrugged. "I guess. Just today and tomorrow and then it's Spring Break. And Uncle Owen's coming!"

"No fighting at school, okay?" I warned. "I really don't want to make another trip to the principal's office this week."

"I'll try." He gave me the same promise every day . . . and rarely followed through on it. When it came to protecting loved ones, he had control of his anger about as much as I did. Usually, he fought kids who teased him about me, his weird mother.

"You said the same thing yesterday," Mom reminded him.

"That stupid Joey! I hate him, Mimi! He said my dad's a no good shithead who didn't want me."

"Honey, that's a bad word. You are too young to be using such language," Mom said.

"I didn't say it! Joey did!"

I fought back a laugh, but the anger at the memory flashed in Dorian's eyes—tiny sparks in the gold flecks around his pupils—and I suddenly felt renewed irritation, too. Once I became "America's favorite young author," the media quickly discovered I'd been pregnant at the tender age of nineteen and the father was nowhere to be found. People made up their own stories from there. So when Dorian didn't feel a need to protect me, he defended his so-called deadbeat dad. Because he knew better.

"Good for you!" I said, giving Dorian a squeeze. I would have done the same thing—punched the kid in the face. In fact, the lunatic in me this morning wanted to hunt down the little brat right now. The not-so-crazy part of me at least wanted to find his parents.

Mom shook her head disapprovingly. I ignored her.

"Don't you *ever* let anyone talk about your daddy that way," I said. "He's a wonderful man and he loves you very much. It's not his fault he's not here. You know that, right?"

He nodded, his cupid-bow lips quivering with sadness. I held my arms out and he gave me a bear hug—as big of a hug as a six-year-old can. He knocked me to the floor and I gave an exaggerated cry. He laughed and showed me his guns, flexing his biceps. I ooh'ed and aah'ed over them. They were actually impressive. He had his dad's strength.

Then he crossed his arms over his chest and looked at Mom and then me, his eyes lit up with mischief. "I'll stop fighting if you get me a dog. Then I'll have a friend and I'll ignore everyone else."

I bit my lip, not knowing whether I would laugh or cry. I knew how Dorian felt to want a friend so badly. I also knew he would promise anything to have a dog, which he'd been begging us for since his last birthday. I had a hard time believing, though, that he would stop fighting. It was just part of his nature.

I'd wanted to put him in an Aikido class to teach him self-control, but Mom wouldn't allow it—his unusual strength would draw attention we didn't need. So I had Owen work with him whenever possible.

"I turn seven in twenty-eight days," Dorian said when we didn't respond. And then I did chuckle.

"We'll see," I finally said.

"How about no fighting between now and your birthday and then we'll discuss it?" Mom suggested.

I looked at her with surprise. She was the one usually against adopting a pet. A dog would be another responsibility to worry about if we ever had to go on the run again. Then I realized she must have figured Dorian wouldn't be able to hold up his end of the bargain.

"Deal," he said and I cringed. I agreed with Mom on this one.

I gave Dorian another hug, then Mom took him to school. Since my book sales could support us and probably the entire Amadis, Mom made it her job to tend to Dorian and the house so I could work. Even before my career took off, my writing had always remained high on her priority list.

As soon as I was alone, I poured a cup of coffee, went out the backdoor and slipped around the side of the house for a cigarette. When I heard Mom's car return nearly an hour later, I snuffed out my third one and drained my third cup of coffee, then hurried inside. I munched on chocolate-chip cookies when she came through the door and dumped an armful of grocery bags on the counter. She eyed me, her mahogany eyes filled with disdain.

"Those are healthy," she said as she placed the bags on the counter.

"Breakfast of champions."

"Alexis—"

I felt a lecture coming on and there were plenty of areas she could pick on. Normally, I wouldn't blame her, but right now, the ticking that had been in my head all morning grew louder. Then some kind of switch flipped. I couldn't control the need. I *wanted* to lash out.

Psycho Alexis reared her ugly head.

"I don't want to hear it, Mom," I snapped, marching out of the kitchen. "I fucked up by not having a girl, but I gave it my best shot. I'm writing the damn books. At least back off everything else, okay? I'm trying as hard as I fucking can."

"Alexis!" she admonished, following me into my office. She hated my language, which was exactly why I used it. "I just wanted to remind you Owen will be here later. You might want to clean yourself up."

I looked down at myself. I wore the same raggedy t-shirt and sweatpants I had slept in. Pretty much my normal attire. *What the hell do I care what Owen thinks?* I didn't. Mom seemed to, though. In fact, she seemed to care a lot about what Owen thought lately.

"I'm fine," I snarled.

I grabbed my laptop and headed outside. The early Spring morning in Atlanta, Georgia, had been a little crisp earlier, but the air quickly warmed. It would be a nice day to write outside and I hoped the fresh air would help my mood. I set up the laptop on the patio table, opened the document and then stared at the screen. For a long time. I just couldn't focus on stringing words into meaningful sentences. Giving up, I gazed absent-mindedly across the yard, thinking about last night.